W9-BNG-585

A Bride *in the* Bargain

Books by
Deeanne Gist

A Bride Most Begrudging

The Measure of a Lady

Courting Trouble

Deep in the Heart of Trouble

A Bride in the Bargain

A BRIDE *in the* BARGAIN

DEEANNE GIST

BETHANY HOUSE PUBLISHERS

Minneapolis, Minnesota

A Bride in the Bargain

Cover design by Jennifer Parker
Cover photography by Mike Habermann

Published by Bethany House Publishers
11400 Hampshire Avenue South
Bloomington, Minnesota 55438

Bethany House Publishers is a division of
Baker Publishing Group, Grand Rapids, Michigan.

Printed in the United States of America

Library of Congress Cataloging-in-Publication Data

Gist, Deeanne.
A bride in the bargain / Deeanne Gist.
p. cm. — (Brides series ; 5)
ISBN 978-0-7642-0694-8 (alk. paper) — ISBN 978-0-7642-0407-4 (pbk.)
1. Seattle (Wash.)—History—19th century—Fiction. I. Title.
PS3607.I55B74 2009
813'.6—dc22

2009005403

Wanna know something cool?
That's my daughter on the front cover!
So, sweet pea, this one's for you!
Love, Mom

DEEANNE GIST has a background in education and journalism. Her credits include *People, Parents, Parenting, Family Fun*, and the *Houston Chronicle*. She has a line of parenting products called I Did It!® Productions and a degree from Texas A&M. She and her husband have four children in college. They live in Houston, Texas, and Deeanne loves to hear from her readers at her Web site, *www.IWantHerBook.com.*

Acknowledgments

I don't know what I would have done without my sister, Gayle Evers, and my critique partner, Meg Moseley. When I was in a crunch, both went above and beyond the call of duty. They gave abundantly of their time, their expertise, and their wisdom. Thank you seems so paltry for all that they did, but here it is anyway: Thank you, girls, so, so much!

I wanted to give a very special thanks to Ted and Marietta Terry, who welcomed me into their home while I did my research in Seattle. They have such an incredible gift of hospitality and have carved out a very special place in my heart. I love you both.

Jim and Ruth Darling graciously allowed me to use their beautiful lake house as a getaway those last few critical weeks before deadline. I have never been so productive in my life. Thank you so much!

So many folks in Seattle bent over backward when I asked for help with my research—the Pioneer Square Community Association, the Pioneer Association of Washington, the Washington State Library, the University of Washington Library, the MOHAI (Museum of History and Industry) Historical Society, and so many, many more. Thank you so much for your patience and assistance.

God bless you!

Chapter One

Seattle, Washington Territory
April 1, 1865

> ATTENTION BACHELORS! Due to the efforts of Asa Mercer, you can now secure a bride of good moral character and reputation from the Atlantic States for the sum of $300. All eligible and sincerely desirous bachelors assemble in Delim & Shorey's building on Wednesday evening.

Joe Denton scoffed at the ad and scanned the rest of the page. The lopsided ratio of men to women once again filled the columns of the *Seattle Intelligencer.*

Glancing at the mantel clock, he shifted on the maroon-and-gold sofa, then read the next page. The troops at Hatchers Run now had a series of signal towers along their entire line and almost every movement of the rebels could be observed. If Lee were to fall back in an effort to overwhelm Sherman, he would find Grant thundering close upon his rear.

The door to the parlor opened and the head of a small,

brown-haired boy poked around its edge. "I thought that was you I saw coming up the walk. You here to see my pa?"

"I am."

Sprout Rountree stepped inside and hitched up his short pants, revealing scuffed knees. His stiff white shirt was untucked, grass-stained, and torn at the elbow.

"Looks like you've had a hard morning," Joe said.

Sprout puffed out his chest. "I've been practicing to be a lumberjack, just like you."

"You have?"

A grin split his freckled face. "I have. I chopped down Mama's tree out back all by myself."

Joe hesitated. "That sapling, you mean? The Chinese pistachio your mother ordered from the Sandwich Islands?"

"I dunno. Just a minute and I'll show you."

He darted out of the room and returned in another minute holding what was left of his mother's pride and joy.

Joe swiped a hand across his mouth. "When did you do that, son?"

"This morning. I used my pa's ax. It sure is heavy. But I got big muscles for a boy my age. Ever'body says so."

"They do?"

"Yep. You wanna see 'em?"

Without waiting for an answer he strode right up between Joe's knees and flexed his little arm. It wasn't much thicker than the sapling he held, but Joe assumed a serious air and scrutinized the boy's arm, squeezed his muscle, then whistled. "Very impressive."

The boy beamed. "Lemme see yours."

"I can't roll up my sleeve right now. I'm waiting to see your pa."

His little shoulders wilted. "Aw, please?"

"Not today, Sprout."

"Could you let me squeeze it, then? You wouldn't have to roll up your sleeves for that."

Joe glanced at the slightly cracked door, then flexed, making his arm bulge.

Sprout's hand couldn't begin to encompass the muscle, but he squeezed what he could, his eyes huge. "Mine are gonna be just like that someday."

Ruffling the boy's hair, Joe chuckled. "I imagine they will. Until then, though, you might not want to chop down any more of your mama's trees. They aren't ready for the lumberyard just yet, and I'm not sure how she'd feel about you handling an ax."

"Then how am I gonna learn lumberjacking?"

"Well, maybe your parents will let you come out to my place sometime and help me."

His face lit up. "Can I go home with you today?"

Joe chuckled again. "No, not today but—"

"Sprout Rountree! Come here this instant!"

Burdensome footsteps followed the strident voice until the door to the parlor swung open. A young woman large with child stood at its threshold, her face pinched with anger.

Sprout eased back into Joe. "What's the matter, Mama?"

"What happened to my . . ." Her eyes went from the boy to the sapling he held in his hand. "Oh, nooooo!"

Placing his hand on Sprout's shoulder, Joe stood. "Afternoon, Mrs. Rountree."

She glanced at him. "O.B.'s in his office, Mr. Denton. You can go on in." She turned her attention to Sprout. "What have you done to my pistachio tree?"

The boy shrunk at his mother's tone. "I har-visited it, but I'll put it back if you want."

Joe didn't wait for her response. Instead, he picked up his hat and slipped through a connecting door leading to the library and office of Judge Obadiah B. Rountree.

A cloud of tobacco mixed with traces of lemon oil filled the room. Hooking his hat on a hall tree, he clicked the door shut behind him, cutting off the drama unfolding in the parlor.

The judge, with his back to Joe, scribbled on a piece of parchment while sitting at an ornate mahogany secretary that had come clear around the Horn. His white shirt, entirely too big for his small frame, bunched beneath dark suspenders crisscrossing his back. Short black hair surrounded a perfectly circular bald spot.

Joe ran a hand over his thick, wavy hair, letting out a silent sigh. Blond hair like his wasn't as apt to fall out, or so he'd heard. Perhaps he was safe.

A handsome tan volume of Shakespeare lying on the marble-top table caught his eye. Was it there for ornamentation, or did the judge actually read it? Joe shifted his weight to the other foot.

No more voices came from the parlor. He assumed the missus had taken Sprout to a private place for whatever she had in mind.

A robin with a brick-red breast and white throat landed on the windowsill, warbling a greeting. Joe caught a whiff of fresh air coming from the window. Spring had a distinctive smell and one he always welcomed. No other spot on God's green earth held such mild and equitable climate as did Seattle from April to November.

The bird darted off as quickly as he'd come, and the judge placed his pen in its holder, then blotted his writings.

"You in town to purchase a bride?" he asked, still sitting at his desk.

"I hardly think so," Joe said. "A man would have to be pretty desperate to let Asa Mercer choose his bride for him."

Standing, the judge turned and clasped Joe's hand. "I think it's a grand scheme. I hear he's collected money from almost three hundred men and is hoping to find two hundred more."

"Well, I won't be one of them."

"Have a seat, then, and tell me what I can do for you."

Joe eased his large frame into a dainty armchair. "I have news about my wife's death certificate."

Rountree brightened, settling into the chair facing him.

"Excellent. Let me have a look at it and we'll wrap up this whole mess."

"That's just the thing. I wrote to my brother back in Maine asking him to send me the certificate. I received his answer today." Joe removed the letter from his pocket and handed it to the judge. "He says the Kennebec County courthouse burned down and all the records with it."

"What about the doctor? Can the doctor issue another one?"

"Lorraine died ten years ago. Back then, the only doctors they had were itinerant. I'm not even sure they remember his name."

Rountree scanned the piece of parchment. "This complicates things, Joe. Tillney isn't going to settle for a letter from your brother."

Joe stiffened. "Are you questioning my brother's word?"

"Of course not. But those Land Donation Grants were very specific. In order to get the full six hundred forty acres, you had to have a wife."

"I did have a wife."

"You've no proof of that."

"I have a marriage certificate."

"That might have been enough to secure the land temporarily, but in order to keep it she needed to have made an appearance."

"She was going to. It's not my fault she died before she ever made it out here."

"No one's saying it's your fault. What we're saying is the intent of those donations was to encourage settlement. We can't settle unless we multiply. We can't multiply without wives."

"I was married when I signed up for the land. She would have come, Judge. I'd sent for her and everything."

Rountree blew out a huff of air. "There's no question in my mind your intentions were genuine. But the fact remains, it's been ten years and she's never shown up. In the eyes of the law, that makes you a single man, and single men only qualified for three hundred twenty acres, not six hundred forty."

Tightening his hands on the arms of the chair, Joe reined in his exasperation. "She *died*. I can't do anything about that."

"And if you produce a death certificate, then I'm willing to rule in your favor. But even that is pushing things a bit. I certainly can't award you the land based on a letter written by your brother."

"What if someone from the courthouse writes it?"

"No, Joe. I'm sorry. The only thing the clerk would be able to attest to is that the courthouse burned down. That won't solve the problem of you needing a death certificate."

"The only reason I need one is because you say I need one. You can just as easily say my marriage license is enough."

Sighing, the judge removed the wire spectacles from his nose. "I can't."

"Why not?"

"Because so many men in the Territory—when their wives wouldn't come west—just divorced them. That constitutes a breach of contract."

"Well, I don't see any of *them* giving up their acreage."

"Maybe not around here, but rest assured, many a man has been required to produce a bride or risk losing his land. Still, I'm willing to let you keep the land if you present proof of your wife's death. But if you can't do that, then Tillney wins the suit and your three hundred twenty acres."

Joe jumped to his feet. "I've spent the last ten years developing that land. My entire lumber operation depends on it. I need it. Every acre of it."

"I can appreciate that."

"Tillney knows how valuable it is." Joe raked a hand through his curls. "He knows that if he can win it, he'll not only get three hundred twenty acres of land, but he'll get skid roads, log chutes, water access, and enough lumber to last him for years."

The judge made no response.

"Are you making this difficult because Tillney's your wife's cousin?"

Rountree narrowed his eyes. "I'm going to ignore that remark, but our meeting is over." He stood. "Either you produce a death certificate or a wife, or Tillney wins."

"There is no death certificate!"

"Then I suggest you find yourself a wife."

"And how am I supposed to do that?"

"Mercer's holding a meeting tonight. Buy one from him."

Taking a step back, Joe gaped at the judge. "You cannot be serious."

"I don't care what you do. All I care about is upholding the intent of the grant." He shrugged. "Death certificate or wife. Makes no difference to me."

"Well, it makes a difference to me. Besides, it'll take Mercer months to go back east, convince five hundred Civil War widows and orphans to be brides to a bunch of lumberjacks, and then bring them all the way back here."

Rounding the chair, the judge removed Joe's hat from the rack. "He said it'll take him six months, so that's what I'll allot you."

"Six months might be enough for an average fellow, but you know Mercer. It'll take him twice that amount of time. I'll need a year, at least. Probably more."

Rountree pursed his lips, then gave a nod. "One year from today, then. If you don't have a bride or a death certificate by April 1, 1866, then Tillney gets the land." He opened the door. "Good day, Denton."

It was standing room only at Delim & Shorey's new building, which was dried-in but not yet finished. Men of all shapes, sizes, and occupations crowded the half-finished wagon shop. Most were lumberjacks, but Joe recognized several prominent businessmen from as far away as Olympia.

And right in the center was Asa Mercer, the president of the town's esteemed university, balanced atop a soapbox, lantern light bouncing off his red hair and pale skin. Raising his hands above his head, he shushed the crowd.

Joe leaned against the wall. Several of the men with their backs to him sported an *XXX Flour* legend on the seat of their pants, having used the empty sacks to repair their worn-out clothing. What were those eastern women going to think when they got a look at this bunch?

"Over three hundred sixty thousand men have lost their lives so far in the conflict between the North and South," Mercer boomed.

The room quieted.

"And though we mourn our lost brothers, the surplus of widows and orphans is becoming an economic problem for our eastern shores."

Joe shifted his position against the wall.

"Yet here in the West, we are lacking the very commodity that they have in overabundance. As a service to both shores, I am volunteering to go east, collect five hundred ladies, and bring them back to you, the fine, upstanding men of the Washington Territory."

A great cheer rose.

"As with any venture, however, there are costs involved. I intend to solicit most of this support from our government, which feels responsible toward these misplaced women. My plan is to appeal to President Lincoln himself, who bounced me on his knee when I was but a lad. There is no question in my mind he will supply us with a discarded warship to transport the brides."

The men murmured to one another.

"To ascertain which of you will have the privilege of receiving these women as their matrimonial prize, however, a deposit of three hundred dollars will be required to defray the cost of your bride's passage."

"Three hundred dollars is an awful lot of money," one of the men hollered.

"In exchange for your deposit, I will give you a signed contract which will clearly state that upon my return, you will receive one eastern bride."

"Who picks the bride? You or me?"

"I will," Mercer answered. "But your contract will include what particulars you are looking for, and I pledge to thoroughly interview each lady and choose only those of sterling character."

Pursing his lips, Joe considered what qualities he'd need in a wife.

Honesty. Practicality. Nothing flighty or fragile like Lorraine. And she'd need to be able to handle cooking for his lumber crew.

His men could put in a full day's work in the wet, cold, and mud so long as they ended at night with a lighted abode fragrant with food. And if that food was prepared by a woman, well, he'd have the happiest crew this side of the Cascade Mountains.

"That's good enough fer me," another shouted. "I got nothin' else to spend my chicken change on. Might as well be a missus. Sign me up!"

The men converged on Mercer, all speaking at once, all anxious to plunk down their money.

Joe slipped a hand in his pocket and clutched the heavy bag weighing down his jacket.

Three hundred dollars. It was a fraction of what his land was worth, but he still hated to part with the coin. If he had time, he'd go east himself. But he couldn't leave. Not now. The weather was warming and in another couple of weeks, he'd be driving logs down Skid Road as fast as his crew could cut them.

"Why, Joe. I thought you'd be staying away from here on principle." J.J. McGilvra, a pioneer lawyer, offered his hand. "Change your mind, or have you come to stare down your nose at the rest of us?"

With a sigh, he pushed himself off the wall and shook with

McGilvra. "To be honest with you, J.J., I don't know what I'm doing here."

The lawyer gave him a curious look; then the two of them took their places in the line that wrapped around the room three times.

Chapter Two

Granby, Massachusetts
December 13, 1865

> ATTENTION WIDOWS & ORPHANS! The S.S. *Continental* is nearly ready for sea and as my party is not yet entirely complete, I offer the following terms to those wishing to make the voyage through the Straits of Magellan to the Washington Territory. Passage at the very low rate of $200; poor girls, $50. Positions as domestics, teachers, or nannies guaranteed. Apply to A.S. Mercer, Emigrant Agent, W.T., No. 91 West Street, New York.

Fifty dollars. Anna Ivey had that exact amount sewn into the hem of her shift. But it wouldn't be enough. She would need to pay for travel to New York, plus a room while she waited to embark.

Escaping to the West sounded so appealing, though. The scars of the war would be here for many years—both in industry and the minds of the people. But on the Pacific, she felt sure the handclasp would be a little stronger.

She reread the ad. She'd always assumed the Washington Territory was a land of wild beasts and gold hunters. At least until she'd read Mr. Mercer's pamphlet on the topic.

According to him, the Territory was a promised land where all of nature breathed purity and healthfulness. A land that possessed all the qualities and characteristics necessary to produce happy homes.

She hooked a tendril of hair behind her ear. She'd almost forgotten what a happy home was like. Almost.

She skimmed the *New York Tribune* article concerning Mr. Mercer's mass exodus of women.

> This is the grandest female excursion ever inaugurated and will no doubt be very beneficial in its results. Mr. Mercer seems like a whole-souled, honest man, and has no object in view than the good of the community of which he is an honored member.

The gurgling of a pot trying to throw off its lid penetrated Anna's consciousness. Jumping from her stool, she gathered a corner of her apron and hurriedly lifted the lid off a batch of brilla soup.

The steam gave a great belch that smelled of turnips, thyme, and onion. Leaning back until the worst of it escaped, she stirred tonight's first course for the occupants of Pitchawam House.

"Looks to be a hungry crowd," Helen said, rushing through the door with a tray of empty mugs, her circular braids pinned against her round face and ears.

"Well, the brilla is ready," Anna said. "So you can serve it while I finish up the mutton and potatoes."

The girls worked in silence, the pings and clatters of their culinary operations a duet of soothing sounds. Finally, Helen lifted a tray of full soup bowls, then whisked back out the door.

Bending over a clear fire, Anna turned the cutlets. The door opened behind her.

"That was fast," she said. "Is something wrong?"

When Helen didn't respond, Anna glanced over her shoulder, then quickly straightened.

"Mr. Dantzler. We didn't expect to see you until later this evening."

Tugging on his jacket with one hand and smoothing his glossy brown hair with the other, he gave her a lazy smile. There was no question he was handsome. There wasn't a prettier face or more striking physique in all of Granby. But he'd changed since returning home from the war. And Anna had no regard for the man he'd become.

"You can call me Hoke when we're alone, Anna."

She swallowed back her retort. It wouldn't do any good and she didn't want to burn the mutton. Still, she tried not to bend over quite so far when she returned her attention to the cutlets.

She finished flipping the meat, then hastened to a bowl of steaming potatoes and began to mash them.

"You're looking rather flushed, my dear." He strolled to her side and placed a heavy hand on her neck. "Perhaps you'd like to step out of this heat for a few minutes? Take in some fresh air?"

"I'm fine, thank you." She strained against his hand.

Tightening his hold, he leaned in. "Don't pull away from me when I touch you." The stench of ale laced his breath.

She forced herself to remain calm. "I can't mash the potatoes when you're so close. I need more room."

He pulled the bowl from her grasp and turned her toward him. "The potatoes can wait."

"Perhaps, but what about your guests?" She lifted her gaze. "Will they be able to wait?"

His aqua-violet eyes fell to half-mast. "Mrs. Hamm can handle them."

She banked the panic that began to crawl up her spine. Usually all she had to do was mention his patrons and he'd leave her alone.

"Just the same," she said. "I'd best finish up."

"I believe I'll decide what is best. And I think that removing you from the heat of the kitchen would be best." His attention strayed from her face to the frayed neckline of her bodice.

She took a step back, but he encircled her waist with his arm.

"Stop it!" she hissed, squirming and pushing against him.

"Marry me, Anna." He buried his face in her neck, his hands groping.

"No!" Tucking her head, she dodged his lips but could not escape his foul breath or his hands. "I've told you. I've no intention of marrying you or anyone else. Not ever."

"Fine!" he exploded, shoving her back against the table only to pin her there with his arms. "In fact, that's even better. We'll dispense with the formalities altogether." He edged closer, sealing the distance between them. "Let's go upstairs."

"No!" She struggled and kicked but could not break his iron grip. "Move! Let me go!"

"I don't think so, my dear." Grabbing her waist, he pitched her over his shoulder, opened the door to the stairwell, and headed up the back stairs. The smell of burning meat was cut off at the slamming of the door behind them.

She pounded her fists against his back. "Put me down! I mean it, Hoke. Put me down this instant!"

He took the steps two at a time.

She screamed, but he threw her down on the halfway landing, cutting off her cry and knocking the breath from her.

"You want a fight, little girl, then that's what you'll get. You can scream all you want, but nobody can hear you while we're in this stairwell, and even if they could, they wouldn't do anything."

She sucked in a great gulp of air, but before she could release another scream, he slammed a hand against her mouth.

"I'm through with these cat-and-mouse games. You need a husband. You have no family, no home, and when I'm through with you, you'll have no options. You're going to be my wife, so you might as well stop struggling." He stretched out, pinning her beneath him. "You'll enjoy it, pet. I'll make sure of it."

His sweaty hand smothered her. She managed to pull in some air through her nose, but it smelled of his alcohol-riddled breath. In an effort to calm him, she stilled, her heart thundering in her breast.

"That's better. Now. I'm going to take my hand from your mouth. If you let out so much as a peep, I'll have to hit you."

Her eyes widened.

"Don't think I won't. You've lovely features and I'd hate to mar them, but I'll not tolerate any insubordination." He searched her face in the dim light. "Do you understand?"

She nodded.

He slowly peeled his hand away. "There. That's a good girl. Now, we're going to stand and walk up the rest of these stairs, then down the hall and to my chambers."

"Don't do this."

Brushing some loose hair from her face, he smiled with tenderness. "Don't worry, Anna. We'll marry. But first, we're going upstairs." He paused. "Are you ready?"

Gathering her wits, she prayed for courage. "There's something you should know before we proceed."

He cocked an eyebrow.

"There is no question that you can hit me and force me to your will. You are bigger and stronger. But if you do, then you'd better never go to sleep."

He frowned. "I beg your pardon?"

"I mean it, Hoke. If you do this, you'd better never, ever, not even once, close your eyes for a bit of rest. Because the moment you do, I'm going to slip down into the kitchen, get the meat hammer, come back to your chamber, and break your arm. Your right arm. The one you swing with."

He blinked.

The door at the bottom of the stairs opened. "Anna? Where the devil are you? It's time for the main course and the cutlets are burnt."

"Let me up," Anna whispered.

"Anna?" Helen placed a foot on the bottom step. "Are you up there?"

After a slight hesitation, Hoke rolled off her.

Scrambling to her feet, Anna rushed down the stairs, past Helen's astonished face and straight out into the alley. Ignoring the icy slap of winter, she continued to run until she reached the tiny attic room she let at the Hadley House.

Anna yanked her carpetbag from underneath her bed, unbuckled the latch, and widened its mouth. It wouldn't take long to pack. She'd sold everything of value she owned except her mother's watch pin. All she had left was a spare dress, a second set of underclothes, her seashell collection, and her father's letters.

She lifted the false bottom of the bag. The bound stack of correspondence she'd hidden was still in place. Slamming the divider down, she effectively shut the contents from her view, but not from her mind.

Every letter her father had sent was written on her heart. She laid her spare dress on the bed, placed several pouches of seashells in its center, then quickly rolled them up inside it. All the while, the closing line of her father's final letter repeated itself in her mind like a mantra.

"Don't you realize that when you and Leon argue and misbehave, the rebel bullets come closer to me? But if you and Leon are good, then God will take care of me and bring me home safely."

Her behavior had been particularly reprehensible the day that letter had arrived. The horror she'd felt at its contents still ricocheted through her. She'd immediately promised God that she would change and had begged Him to bring Papa home.

He'd brought him home all right, in a big pine box. And no one but she and God knew her actions that day had killed him, just as surely as they had eventually killed her mother and little brother.

Cramming the dress into the bag, she gave no regard to its condition, then swiped up her underclothes. She may think Hoke despicable and without honor, but she didn't wish him dead. And that's exactly what would happen to him or anyone else if they got too close.

So she'd leave. She'd go to the Washington Territory and secure a position as a domestic, a schoolteacher, or a nanny. But she'd never marry and she'd never have children. The risk was simply too great.

Latching the bag, she touched her chest to be sure her watch pin was in place, then grabbed her cape. The stagecoach office was just up the road. She'd secure a ticket to Amherst. From there, she'd catch the Boston & Maine to New York City.

A corner of Anna's cape whipped back, allowing the frigid New York wind to beat against her tattered woolen gown. Clenching the edges of her cape with one hand and her carpetbag with the other, she stopped in front of a modest brick building on West Street.

The markings on a square plaque next to the entrance were worn and difficult to read. The first numeral was either an eight or a nine. She squinted but couldn't make out the second.

A mule-drawn dump cart full of coal crunched past on the snow and ice, pulling Anna's attention to a sign across the street where the American Express Company's deliverymen came and went.

When Ladies Or Children Are About To Cross The Street, As They Are Frequently Uncertain And Confused In Their Movements, TEAMS SHOULD BE BROUGHT TO A FULL STOP UNTIL ALL UNCERTAINTY IS REMOVED.

Anna looked up and down the walkway but saw no evidence of any women, and she certainly couldn't imagine children in this part of town. Gone were the street vendors along with the carriages and sulkies carrying gaily dressed patrons about town. Instead, commercial vehicles, dray carts, and delivery sleds populated the streets, their drivers yelling out curses to both their animals and each other.

She turned her attention to the plaque once again, but with no more luck deciphering it than before. Still, building number 93 was next door. So this should be it. Placing her hand on the oversized doorknob, she pushed.

A gust of wind jerked the door from her hand and crashed it against the inside wall. Hurrying across the threshold, she dropped her bag and used both hands to close the door. Leaning against it, she pressed a hand against her frozen nose and tried to wiggle her toes.

The dim entryway led to a series of doors and a narrow staircase. The building wasn't much warmer than the outdoors, but at least there was no wind. She blew onto her gloved hands, then rubbed them together.

"Hello?" Her breath produced a puff of condensation while her voice bounced off the silent walls. "Is anyone here?"

A muffled shuffling from down the hall was followed by the creaking of a poorly oiled door. A swath of light cut across the hall, illuminating the tall, thin man who stepped into it.

"May I help you?" he said.

She straightened, shaking the snow from her skirts and retrieving her bag. "Yes, please. I'm looking for Mr. A.S. Mercer."

"I'm Asa Mercer." He moved toward her.

She didn't know what she'd been expecting, but this lanky young man with a shock of red hair wasn't it.

"Good afternoon, sir. I'm Miss Anna Ivey. I saw your ad in the *Tribune* and am here to inquire about passage to the Northwest."

He quickly took in her shabby clothing but gave no visible reaction. "Excellent." He took her bag. "If you would join me in my office?"

His "office" was no larger than the cook's closet at Pitchawam House. After hooking her bag on a peg, he hurriedly gathered numerous papers from a stool.

He looked to the right and left, but there was no clear surface to set them on. His half desk was completely covered, and rolls of paper had been crammed into every pigeonhole above it. Even the floor was covered with his papers.

Giving her an apologetic grin, he set the stack on the floor next to the stool and held out a hand. Taking it, she picked her way across the room and settled on the stool.

"Now," he said. "Tell me where you are from."

"Granby, Massachusetts. I've only just arrived, so please forgive my appearance."

His long legs filled the space beneath his desk. "No need for apologies, Miss Ivey, is it?"

"Yes. Ivey with an *E-Y*."

Picking up a pen, he wrote her name in lovely script across the top of a fresh piece of parchment. "Tell me, Miss Ivey, why do you wish to emigrate to the Washington Territory?"

"I read your pamphlet, *The Great North-West*, and found myself caught up with the idea of going to this Eden you've described."

Pleasure touched his rust-colored eyes. "You read my booklet?"

"I did, sir. I have it with me now, though it is quite dog-eared, I'm afraid."

He smiled. "Can you write as well as read?"

"Proficiently."

He made a note on the paper, dipped his pen in an inkwell, then held it poised. "And your family?"

"My ancestors are Scots, though my parents grew up in England. They came to America in fifty-one. I was four at the time."

"Your father's occupation?"

"He stained and embossed wallpaper." She rubbed her arms beneath her cape. "Actually, he invented a machine that made his handiwork unnecessary. His employer claimed and utilized the invention. So the very thing my father placed all his dreams upon proved to be the rock which destroyed his livelihood."

"I see." Mr. Mercer shook his head in sympathy as he continued to write. "What did he do then?"

"He joined the war."

"Ah. He's home, then?"

"No, he was killed at Antietam."

Mercer continued to write. "I'm sorry."

"Thank you."

"How is your family faring without him?"

She lowered her gaze. "Shortly after he died, my brother joined up as a drummer. He didn't last even a year. But it was disease that killed him, not the rebels. My mother . . ." Anna swallowed. "She never recovered."

"You are orphaned, then?"

"Quite. And destitute as well, I'm afraid."

He paused in his scribblings. "You have money for the passage, though?"

She moistened her lips. "I do not." She had spent a fair portion of her funds for the train ticket and needed more still for lodging.

He laid down his pen.

"I could pay you once I arrived and secured employment, though."

Mercer began to shake his head, so she rushed on.

"I saw in your ad that work as a domestic, teacher, or nanny was guaranteed. I'm not a trained teacher, though I am very well-read and believe I could teach. But I'd be better suited as a domestic or nanny. You see, I took charge of our home almost from the moment my father enlisted. After he was gone, I held many jobs, the latest as a cook for a popular inn in Granby."

He'd placed his pen back in its holder and had moved his notes to the side, when her last comment stalled him. "A cook, you say?"

"Yes. I prepared the menu and all courses for the morning, noon, and evening meals, having only Sundays off."

"You can cook for large crowds?"

"I can. And I'm most accomplished at it."

Mercer leaned back in his chair. "Well. We aren't taking any passengers on credit, but there is one man who wanted a br—, a woman who could feed the men who work for him."

She straightened. "Well, I daresay he'd be very pleased with me."

Mercer gave her a quick appraisal. "I daresay he would."

"How many men does he employ?"

"He's a lumberjack. I'm not sure how many men are involved in his operation. No more than a dozen, I'd say, if that."

A lumberjack. The word conjured up visions of pine forests, fresh air, and wilderness—something far removed from the bustling city, the aftermath of the war, and Hoke Dantzler.

"Goodness," she said, a flicker of anticipation whisking through her. "I could feed a dozen men with one hand tied behind my back."

He rubbed his hands against his legs. "Well, he was very specific with his request. So, if I allowed you passage, it would be on the condition that he paid your fare upon arrival and you would then have to work off your debt for him."

"I'm agreeable to those terms, if he is."

Mercer said nothing. Just stared into space. She could see his inner struggle. Was he worried she wouldn't measure up to her new employer?

Sitting a little straighter, she forced herself not to squirm.

Finally, he turned again to his desk and retrieved his pen. "Very well, Miss Ivey. I will draw up your papers and award you passage to the Washington Territory on the S.S. *Continental.*"

Chapter Three

THE LACROSSE DEMOCRAT

At 3 P.M. the noble S.S. *Continental* left her berth at pier 2 N.R. carrying off a petticoat brigade for the benefit of the long-haired miners and miserable old bachelors of the Pacific North-West. The cargo of Bay State Virgins sailed off in black stockings, candlewick garters, shirt-waists, spit curls, green specs, false teeth and a thirst for chewing gum.

First Night at Sea
January 18, 1866

The more the ship rolled, the more Anna's concern grew. A chopping wind howled against the side of the vessel. Loose hairpins and toothbrushes tumbled to the floor, clattering across it. The greatest noise by far, however, came from the women sharing her cabin. Moans overlaid with anguish filled its narrow confines.

Rising from her bunk, Anna decided if she was going home to meet Jesus, she didn't want to be in her nightdress. Stumbling about, she located her clothes, pulled them on, and stepped from the stateroom.

A jet of icy water impaled her, stealing her breath and soaking her from head to toe.

Pressing a hand against the wall, she gasped for air, salt stinging her eyes. Then panic shot a rush of energy through her.

Good heavens. Had the ship been hit? Sprung a leak? She looked up and down the passageway. Should she alert the crew or the women?

The sound of retching across the hall decided it for her. Corralling the women above deck without help would be an exercise in futility. She flew down the saloon, up the stairs, and flung open a door of a cabin on the portside.

The ship gave a roll starboard, throwing her into the arms of Mr. Conant, a reporter for the *New York Times* she had seen earlier on deck.

Grasping her around the waist, he pulled her into his cabin and slammed the door shut. The shock of their positions held them both speechless for a second or two.

Mr. Conant recovered first, a look of amusement touching his eyes. "This is what may be called the free and easy style of introductions, but if you have no objection, miss, perhaps I should assist you to your berth."

Anna sprang from his arms. "Water is pouring in belowdecks."

"Stay here." He disappeared, but she couldn't sit still and do nothing. From the sounds of it, the entire shipload of passengers was seasick. Why she hadn't been afflicted with the same calamity, she didn't know. But she knew the crew would have their hands full with the storm. The least she could do was help with the women.

And help she did. The water that had doused her turned out

to be no more than a porthole that hadn't been properly secured. And after the captain changed the ship's course, the rolling became easier, but the sea was by no means smooth.

They'd been out for three days, and the majority of passengers still suffered ill effects. Even though it was only noon, Anna settled a pale young widow into her berth, then soundlessly closed the door behind her and headed to the upper deck for some air.

Walking along the portside, she took deep breaths. Gray clouds bunched and dipped, spraying the deck with mist. Surely the entire voyage wouldn't be this unpleasant.

A small, fragile-looking woman who had to be at least sixty staggered into Anna's path. Placing both hands across her stomach, the woman crouched over.

Anna seized her by the armpits and hurried her to the railing, holding her while she cast her bread upon the waters. After several forceful episodes, the woman finally straightened.

Pulling a handkerchief from her pocket, Anna handed it to her, only then realizing her bread wasn't the only thing the woman had cast overboard. For her teeth had completely disappeared.

Anna scanned the water several hundred yards below. It frothed and churned, slamming itself against the side of the ship. No false teeth in sight.

"Tank you," the woman breathed, before slapping a hand over her mouth, her eyes wide.

Anna swallowed. "Don't be alarmed. I'm sure there are dentists in the Northwest."

The woman searched the greedy water below. "Wat am I to do? How will I eat?"

Slipping her arm about the woman, Anna helped her to a chair nearby. "I will speak with the cook right away and make arrangements for you."

"Oh no, no, no. How will I eber find a husband now?"

Anna choked back her surprise. *A husband?* Even with teeth, this woman would be hard-pressed to find a spouse at her age.

Tiny brown eyes the size of coffee beans looked at Anna from beneath heavily creased eyelids. "Mr. Mercer promised me a husband."

"Well," Anna said, scrambling for an appropriate response, "I cannot imagine why he would promise such a thing. Perhaps you misunderstood. The passengers are guaranteed positions as teachers, domestics, or nannies. Not wives."

The woman waved away Anna's words. "How can we teach children when dere are none? Only men. Men who want wibes." Having never considered that bit of logic, Anna didn't know quite what to say. Relief rushed through her, though, at the realization that her position as a cook was not dependent on children being present. No room for confusion there.

She patted the woman's hand. "Well, no need to rush into anything. The time it takes for new teeth to be made will be just the time you need to consider your matrimonial possibilities."

The old woman's eyes filled. "You don't understand. My dear husband, Clement, neber came home from the war. I have nutting left. I need a husband right away."

Anna squatted down in front of her. "Oh, I'm so sorry. My brother and father both died in the war, too, and my mother died not long after."

"You're all alone?"

Anna nodded. "I will never forget the day their names appeared on the casualty list in the newspaper. But we aren't all alone, you and I. We have God, and now we have each other."

Tears began to stream from the woman's eyes, branching off into numerous tributaries as they traversed her wrinkled face. "Tank you, my dear."

"There, there."

She blew her nose into the handkerchief. "What is your name?"

"Miss Anna Ivey of Granby, Massachusetts."

"It is so nice to meet you, Miss Ibey. I'm Mrs. Bert-a Wrenne of Lowell, Massa-chew-its."

"A pleasure, Mrs. Wrenne, I'm sure."

THE WALLA WALLA STATESMAN

Mercer and his bevy of Massachusetts damsels are now anchored off the coast of Rio de Janeiro. It won't be long before they, armed with green reticules, blank marriage certificates and photographs of Ben Butler—to hang on the andirons to keep their babies out of the fire—will be rounding the Horn and bounding over the watery reflections in search of a market for their kisses.

Seattle, Washington Territory
March 1, 1866

"They haven't even made it to the Straits of Magellan yet," Joe said, tossing a newspaper on Judge Rountree's desk. "It will take them two months at least to reach Seattle, maybe more. I need an extension."

"Tillney's not going to be happy about this."

"I couldn't care less what Tillney says. I paid Mercer for a bride almost a year ago. He said he'd be back in six months. It's not my fault he ran into such difficulties securing a vessel."

"No, it's never your fault, is it, Denton?"

Joe narrowed his eyes. "As a matter of fact, it isn't."

Rountree handed him back the newspaper. "Well, you'd better marry that gal the minute her slippered feet hit this shore. You understand?"

"I understand."

THE ALTA CALIFORNIA

The only thing Mr. Mercer has to fear, so far as I can see, is that in case the girls are young and pretty, they may be snapped up by some of your wifeless young men in the ports of call....

Lota, Chile
April 13, 1866

Anna tapped lightly on Mrs. Wrenne's door. "Mr. Mercer has called a meeting for nine o'clock. We mustn't be late."

The elderly woman stepped out, her eyes alive with excitement. "Hab you been on deck yet?"

"I have. And you must come and see." Anna took the lady's arm, assisting her up the steps. "Lota is a lovely little valley situated between two high bluffs."

"Oh, I can hardly wait to get off dis boat."

"Me too. But we shall have to wait in line, I'm afraid. I've been made to understand that it is a great market day in Lota. So everyone is determined to go ashore."

Smiling faces and bursts of laughter greeted them on the hurricane deck. After so many long and weary days of unbroken sea, the sight of land was arousing and invigorating.

Mercer clapped his hands, signaling a start of their meeting. "As you ladies know, I am deeply interested in your welfare. So much so, I cannot bear to have you out of my sight for even a single moment."

Anna lifted a questioning brow. He'd claimed more than once that no man living was so near Mount Zion as he himself, but she'd had her doubts ever since he'd called the ladies into his stateroom one by one for the purpose of extracting more money.

"I cannot sign a note for two hundred and fifty, sir," she'd told him when it was her turn. "You promised passage to me for fifty dollars, payable by my employer upon my arrival in Seattle."

"I'm afraid I miscalculated and have borne great expense on your behalf."

"I find that extremely hard to believe. In any case, we have a signed contract and I will agree to no more."

Crossing his hands atop his desk, he offered her a placating smile. "Now, Miss Ivey, I am only asking to be recompensed for actual costs incurred. I cannot see what possible objection you have when in all probability you will get a husband as soon as we arrive at our destination, and he would, I'm sure, be more than happy to cover any incidentals."

She shook her head. "Two hundred fifty dollars is not incidental. Furthermore, I have no intention of marrying."

His eyes widened with alarm. "You have no intention of marrying?"

"Certainly not. Nor do I intend to place a more significant financial burden on my employer."

"But your employer can afford it."

"I don't care if his pockets are lined with gold. According to our contract, the cost of my passage is fifty dollars, and fifty dollars it will remain." Turning, she'd swept out of the stateroom.

Unfortunately, Mrs. Wrenne had not fared so well. Mercer had assured her that he had a nice farmer lined up for her who had promised to take whomever he brought—teeth or no teeth. Mrs. Wrenne happily signed the two-hundred-fifty-dollar note. Just thinking about it rekindled Anna's anger—and her distrust of the man.

"I have learned," he was now saying on deck, "that cholera and smallpox are raging in Lota. It would be most unsafe for any of you to go on shore."

Murmurs of distress rippled through the crowd.

He held up his hands for silence. "Now, as much as I hate to place any severe restrictions upon you, I want you to distinctly understand that you are not to go on shore in the company of any gentleman other than myself."

Anna frowned. If the conditions in Lota were unhealthy, then having Mr. Mercer with them wouldn't make an iota of difference.

By afternoon, when a boatload of dashing Chilean officers and gentlemen rowed next to the steamship, Anna realized Mr. Mercer's objections. The Chilean men would in all likelihood woo his passengers away.

She felt a touch of sympathy for him as he tried to keep the men off the boat. He had, after all, worked very hard on this emigration scheme of his.

"These officers have designs on you," he frantically told the women. "If you give them any chance at all, it is certain to prove your ruin."

His warnings did not, however, keep the girls from welcoming the men on board. By the time they were ready to pull up anchor a week later, several had bowed at Cupid's knee.

THE MORNING CALL

The surplus sweetness of Massachusetts spinsterhood is soon to be wasted on the desert air of W.T. for the relief of territorial bachelors who now darn their buckskin breeches and d—n their hours of solitude. . . .

San Francisco, California
June 4, 1866

Anna rushed to the upper deck with the rest of the ladies for her first glimpse of the promised land. Hanging on to the rail, the wind whipped against her face, bringing the taste of salt with it.

They passed through the Golden Gate and all powers of speech failed her. Not because she was taken by California's beauty, but because she was horrified.

Nothing but brown in every direction. The hills were brown. The islands were brown. Even the town was brown. It was nothing like the pine forests and rich wilderness she'd imagined.

She scanned the entire coastline but couldn't spot a single tree.

"I hab neber seen any-ting so ugly in my life," Mrs. Wrenne said.

Anna glanced at the wharves rapidly filling with scruffy-looking miners whooping and waving. "The men or the landscape?"

"Bof."

Even as they spoke, the men piled into rowboats and began to make their way toward the steamer.

THE IDAHO WORLD

The ship is drawing near Seattle's port. Notice has been sent to the long-haired miners and rich bachelors of that auriferous section. The girls have been bathed by squads, platoons and brigades; their best raiment has been put on.

Washington Territory
July 8, 1866

Joe took one last glance around the home he'd built for Lorraine. She'd argued strongly against their coming out west, but he'd felt sure it was a once-in-a-lifetime opportunity for them, the likes of which they'd never see in Maine. As a compromise, he came over first to see if it was all he'd expected it to be. It was that and more.

So he'd sent for her, then worked hard to prepare a place, building what was still one of the finest houses in the Territory. He'd even planted a chestnut tree like the one in her parents' yard in Maine. The only thing he hadn't done was add the feminine particulars, like wallpaper, curtains, and such. He'd thought to save that for her.

But she'd delayed her arrival, making excuse after excuse for not joining him. And the longer she'd stayed away, the more betrayed he'd felt. And the more betrayed he'd felt, the more the land had seeped into his heart, his soul, until it had eventually replaced the spot that had once been hers.

It offered him company when he was lonely, solace when he was sad. It was steady, reliable, faithful, and beautiful. It became all he needed, all he ever wanted, to the point that even if Lorraine had actually arrived, she wouldn't have been able to reclaim that part of him that had once been hers.

And neither would some ready-made bride he'd paid three hundred dollars for. He'd marry whomever Mercer brought him, but only to save his land. In exchange for that, he'd give her a roof over her head, food for her belly, and all the pretty dresses she wanted. But he wouldn't trust her with his heart. That belonged to his land.

Still, he didn't want her to feel unwelcome. So he'd scrubbed his bachelor quarters from top to bottom, repaired the shingles, fixed the drafts, and piped spring water into the milk room to act as a natural cooling system. The merchant's wife at Fort Nisqually had ordered wallpaper, rugs, furniture, and even lace curtains for him.

He hadn't adjusted very well to the resulting transformation. All the niceties made him feel big and clumsy. He liked it better when things were simple. But nothing would be simple after tomorrow.

His gaze moved to the cup of wild flowers on the table. He'd placed them all over the house. It was the only welcoming gesture he could think of. If the boys ever discovered he'd succumbed to such sentimentality, he'd never hear the end of it.

But he had to do something. His bride would most likely feel frightened and out of place. He'd been here for eleven years. He knew all the folks in town. He was accustomed to the rain. He was used to the quiet.

Not so her. The move out west would be difficult. So he'd fixed up the house and stuck a few wild flowers here and there. He was only doing what he'd do for anybody.

He couldn't help but think it should have been Lorraine, though. If he had to have a bride, it could have at least been the one of his choosing.

Settling his hat on his head, he shook off the thought. They'd married only weeks after meeting, and he'd come to Seattle shortly after. He'd not really known her all that long, and because he'd felt so betrayed, he hadn't spent a great deal of time mourning her death. No need to dredge it up now.

Turning, he let himself out and headed to the barn. If he was bringing a woman home, he'd need to hitch up the wagon.

Chapter Four

Seattle, Washington Territory
July 9, 1866

Situated in a small clearing a quarter of a mile wide and a mile long, Seattle beckoned to Anna's travel-weary soul. She, Mrs. Wrenne, and two other women from the *Continental* caught their first view of the quaint little hamlet from the side of a plunger, christened *Maria*.

Anna swallowed, anticipation and trepidation warring within her. The thick pine forests she'd dreamed of had been in evidence all along the banks of the Puget Sound and now sheltered the perimeter of her new home.

What she hadn't expected, though, was to be able to see the Cascade Mountains far in the distance, accentuated by Mount Rainier reigning tall and proud to the south. She had read about the grand mountain in Mercer's pamphlet, and briefly wondered if snow frosted its majestic peak all year round.

Glancing at the sun that warmed her back, she judged the time to be about five in the evening. Townsfolk began to emerge from clapboard buildings and cottage-style homes, making their way down the hill and toward the wharf.

Did they know Mr. Mercer had arrived in San Francisco with only three dollars in his pocket and no funds to pay for the women's passages to Seattle?

Did they know a vast majority of women had defected in San Francisco, deciding to make California their place of residence?

Did they know that of all the women they started with, only twenty-five remained? And those had been split up and shipped north in lumber vessels, barks, and plungers?

She scanned the crowd at the dock. A great many men stood still and solemn, watching *Maria's* approach. Some were as rough-looking as the Californians, some wore the costumes of lumberjacks, and yet others looked as dignified as those from home.

Which one was her employer? Anna removed a slip of paper from her pocket, opening it again to read the name Mr. Mercer had scrawled across it.

Mr. Joseph Denton.

She lifted her gaze. On the dock, a woman with a child at her skirts smiled and waved. Would she become a friend? Anna waved back and received an enthusiastic response from the men as they whistled and shouted.

Mrs. Wrenne slid her hand into Anna's. Anna glanced at her and then back at the cheering crowd. Was there really a farmer out there who'd asked Mr. Mercer to bring him a bride? And if there was, what would be his reaction to this sweet elderly woman the girls on the boat had dubbed "Toothless"?

And what would be the reaction of Anna's employer when he was told he owed Mr. Mercer fifty dollars on her behalf? Because after spending the last seven months in the company of Asa Mercer, she feared he hadn't consulted Mr. Denton about paying for her passage.

She gripped the railing, her legs suddenly weak.

I want to go back, she thought. What had she been thinking to leave the only home she'd ever known?

But the *Maria* continued to chug forward, and all too quickly they arrived. The crew cast ropes to the men on the docks. A large, callused hand helped her from the boat, separating her from Mrs. Wrenne.

Trunks and valises were shouldered. Her own bag disappeared into the hands of a portly man walking away with a group of locals who escorted another shipmate, Miss Ida Barlow.

A man with a mouthful of rotted teeth took Anna's elbow, guiding her along a road filled with packed dirt and sawdust. Men crowded around them, pushing them toward some unknown destination. At least she was going in the same direction as her bag.

"Howdy, miss," the man escorting her said.

Stiffening, she missed a step.

He squeezed her elbow. "Easy there, darlin'," he drawled. "You all ri-ight?"

A rebel. What was a rebel doing clear up here?

She gave a gentle tug, trying to pull away, but he held tight. He was dressed a bit more flamboyantly than the other men—a red shirt with a yellow scarf holding up his denim britches and an eye-popping purple jacket resting on his shoulders. A mixture of peacock and lumberjack.

She hadn't realized southerners knew how to lumberjack. Her lips parted. What if Joseph Denton was from the South? What if the man she'd blindly agreed to work off her debt for was a rebel?

The blood from her head plunged to her feet. Not once in all this time had the thought occurred to her. The man at her side drawled on, completely unaware of her distress. She placed her free hand against her chest, her gaze darting from one man to the other.

"Here, Whiskey Jim, you're scaring her to death," said a clean-shaven man in a black suit. "Quit your blathering and give her a little room."

"I ain't frightenin' her," Whiskey Jim growled, pulling her closer to his side. "Am I, darlin'?"

She looked into his unkempt face, seeing only a rebel and not a man. "I . . . I . . ."

"For the love of Peter." The gentleman who'd come to her rescue tried to shoo Whiskey Jim back, but he kept hold of her arm.

"Now lookee here!" the rebel shouted.

"Please," she breathed. "I just need a moment."

Whiskey Jim released her, and when he did, the entire entourage stopped, forming a circle around her. Staring—no, gawking.

But they backed up and gave her some room. Too much room. Like the sun encircled by all the stars and planets in the universe.

Where was Mrs. Wrenne, she wondered. And the rest of their party?

But she couldn't see anything beyond the shoulders of all these men.

"Pretty little thing, ain't she?"

Murmurs of agreement flitted throughout the group.

Removing a handkerchief from her pocket, she dabbed her hairline and neck. Fifty pairs of eyes tracked every pat. She tucked the handkerchief into her sleeve.

"Who's yer man?" Whiskey Jim asked. Turning his chin to the side, he spit on the ground.

Frowning, she forced herself to take slow, deep breaths. "I'm sorry?"

"Yer man? Did Mercer give ya a feller's name?"

"Oh." She nodded. "Yes." She pulled the piece of paper from her pocket and opened it. "A Mr. Denton. Mr. Joseph Denton."

Groans of disappointment tumbled through the throng like falling dominoes.

"Joe?" someone shouted.

"Anybody seen Denton?"

"Here he is."

"This one's yourns, you lucky old tar."

Men turned. Shoulders jostled. And like a ball shot from a cannon, a man was shoved from the pack and into the hub of the circle with her.

With his flannel shirt and denim trousers, there was no mistaking him for anything other than what he was. A lumberjack. A tall, hulking giant of a lumberjack.

Golden curls brushed his collar. A face colored by many hours in the sun possessed the requisite eyes, nose, and mouth—but there was nothing ordinary about them. Every feature had been put together by a master craftsman.

Thick blond eyebrows framed clear hazel eyes that changed from blue to green and back to blue as readily as the ocean. High, sculpted cheekbones peaked above smooth valleys and a mouth with deep smile lines on either side of it.

His Adam's apple bobbed, drawing her attention to a neck as thick as a tree trunk.

Her heart constricted. He was beautiful. Even more beautiful than Hoke. The thought terrified her.

"Where are you from?" she asked.

His chin came up a fraction. "America."

She wasn't able to catch whether he had an accent or not. And his answer confused her. There was no America. Only the North, the South, and the West. And everybody in the West came from either the North or the South.

"He's from Georgia," someone to her right said, loosening the tongues of those surrounding them.

"No, he's from Maine."

"He's from both."

"Lived in the South as a kid, then moved north."

The crowd was so dense and the men's commentary so fast she hadn't time to identify one speaker before the next one interrupted.

"His family's still in Maine," yet another person said.

"He's got brothers, sisters. Supposedly even had a—"

Mr. Denton lifted his gaze from her face to a man just behind her shoulder, cutting him off midsentence with a single glare and dousing the plethora of information.

So long as he didn't have rebel sympathies, they'd get along fine. But those formative years in Georgia were a concern. "I'm from the North, Mr. Denton. From Granby, Massachusetts."

He offered no visible reaction. "And your name?"

"Miss Anna Ivey."

He removed his hat and gave a formal bow. "The pleasure is mine, Miss Ivey."

Joe thought she looked ready to jump out of her skin and, like any cornered animal, snarled at those who came too close. And no wonder, with everyone staring at her like she was a miracle straight from heaven instead of Massachusetts.

She'd certainly not wasted any time in clarifying her loyalties. Not all that surprising, though, for an orphan of the war.

"There's a welcome reception at the Occidental Hotel, where you'll be staying the night." Joe extended his arm. "It's just up the hill in the center of town."

She nodded, settling her hand against his sleeve like the whisper of a falling leaf.

Thank the Good Lord she'd made it. He'd wired Mercer some money for his bride's passage once he found out Asa didn't have the means to get her here. But rumors had been rampant when Joe arrived in town yesterday.

From what he'd heard, Mercer was being held in San Francisco by a man who'd paid him eight thousand dollars to bring over wedding suits for the grooms-to-be.

Yet Mercer arrived without a single wedding suit. Nor did he have anywhere near the number of brides contracted for. Some newspapers reported Mercer was bringing seven hundred ladies. Others three hundred. But never had anyone expected only two dozen.

Thank you for letting me have one of them, Lord.

He glanced surreptitiously at the girl beside him. She wasn't short, but he still dwarfed her. Her large brown eyes took in the avenue they traversed—a maze of logs and drift from Yesler's Mill.

Her excursion up the Sound had loosened her hair. The tendrils that escaped were not quite blond, but a very light brown.

He'd not been close enough to see much more than the top of her head until the boys had thrust him out in front of her. And it had taken every bit of control he had not to gape like the rest of them.

The woman had curves. Up top. Down below. And a tiny little waist in between. He'd prepared himself for the worst. Never did he imagine she'd be so comely.

What made a girl like her, who could have any man she wanted, come way out west for a husband? A husband she'd never so much as corresponded with?

He couldn't think of one good reason. Even poor, she'd have no trouble finding a man.

He wondered how old she was. To get married in the Territory, you had to be eighteen.

Please, Lord. Let her be eighteen.

He looked again at her smooth cheeks and wide eyes. He'd have to teach her how to cook. She was way too young and innocent to be able to handle herself around his crew. But he wasn't about to complain. By this time tomorrow, he'd be a married man and have his land sealed up tight.

Thank you, Lord.

Mrs. Wrenne's farmer rebuffed her. A Mr. D. Boynton, the name Mercer had written on her piece of paper, had shown up, then begged off.

Mrs. Wrenne was crushed. Anna was furious. She watched helplessly while Mrs. Wrenne withdrew to her hotel room and refused to come out until she could acquire some teeth. Anna tried to change her mind, but the woman was too humiliated.

Not knowing what else to do, Anna helped her into bed, then joined the reception in the parlor. The women of Seattle were thrilled at the prospect of shoring up their numbers and eager for news of the East.

Miss Lawrence, a full-bodied woman who had traveled up on the *Maria* with Anna, Mrs. Wrenne, and Miss Barlow, held the townsfolk's attention.

"I'll never forget where I was when news of our beloved President Lincoln reached me." Holding a handkerchief to her mouth, she shook her head.

"Is it true there were commemorative pieces made to memorialize him?" asked a woman who had a little boy leaning on her knee and a baby against her shoulder.

"Oh my, yes," Miss Barlow interjected. "I have in my bag colored prints of his assassination, death, and funeral."

"Oh, we should love to see them."

The longer they talked, the more caught up the ladies became. Folding her hands in her lap, Anna left the talking to them. The war had changed everything, and on her first night in town, the last thing she wanted to do was dwell on the very thing she'd come here to escape.

After a while, she excused herself and slipped out onto the veranda of the large, modern hotel. Seattle had been a surprise. A pleasant surprise.

She'd expected a wilderness. Not a village of two-story buildings complete with boardwalks. On the short trek from the dock, she'd noted a sawmill, a drugstore, a livery, and two residences. And that was just on one street.

On a hill above the city stood the town's university—a white cupolaed building with great round pillars. She'd read about it, of course, in Mercer's booklet. After having met him, though, she'd begun to doubt everything he said.

Yet not only was there a university, but apparently, he was indeed its president.

Shaking her head in wonder, she rubbed her arms against the evening's chill.

"A penny for your thoughts."

She whirled around. "Mr. Denton."

"Did I startle you?"

"Just a little. It's so quiet here, compared to San Francisco."

"Disappointed?"

"Relieved."

He shrugged off his jacket, offering it to her. She slipped it over her shoulders, the scent of cedar enveloping her.

"Are you all right?" he asked.

She hesitated. "Actually, I'm a bit concerned for my friend, Mrs. Wrenne."

"Is she ill?"

"No, not exactly, it's just that, well," she moistened her lips, "Mr. Mercer promised her a husband, of all things, but the man welshed on his deal."

He lifted his brows. "Why would he do that?"

The anger she'd managed to curb earlier surged to the surface. "Because she doesn't have any teeth."

Surprise flashed across his face. "What happened to her teeth?"

Anna felt her cheeks grow warm. "She lost them."

He studied her, then dragged a hand over his mouth. "We have a fine dentist here. I'm sure he can, um, see to her malady."

"I'm sure he can, for a handsome fee."

"He'll give her a fair price."

"Mrs. Wrenne doesn't have the funds it would require, Mr. Denton. She's destitute, just like the rest of us."

He slipped his hands into his pockets. "I see."

Anna spun around and faced the street. The lantern by the door threw a pool of light onto the porch, but beyond its arc, her view was limited. "The worst thing about it, though, is that now that I've had a chance to see for myself how many men there are here, I feel certain that if she had her teeth, she'd have no shortage of marriage proposals."

"This Mrs. Wrenne, she's a friend of yours, you say?"

Anna lowered her chin. "Yes. We became very close on the voyage over."

"Where is she now?"

"Trying to sleep."

He stepped beside her, then leaned a hip on the railing. "Well, you tell Mrs. Wrenne to go see Dr. Barnard on Main and not to worry about any of the incidentals. I'll be glad to see to them."

Anna lifted her gaze. The size of him made her want to take a step back, but his words stayed her.

"In exchange for what?"

He blinked. "For a set of teeth, I believe."

"That's it?" It was a brash question, but she'd been poor long enough to learn that nothing was free.

"Do you have some objection?"

"Only if strings are attached."

He frowned. "There are no strings, Miss Ivey. Mrs. Wrenne is new to town. She's alone. We take care of our own here in Seattle."

"Mr. Boynton doesn't."

"Boynton? Don Boynton? Was he the one Mercer assigned to Mrs. Wrenne?"

"I'm not certain of his Christian name, but it did start with a *D*."

He sighed. "Well, please accept my apology on his behalf."

She tried to read his expression but could find no artifice. "What about her hotel room?"

"I imagine the Occidental will give her credit until she finds a husband. If not, then let me know and I'll see to that as well."

"In exchange for nothing."

"That's right."

"Because Seattle takes care of their own."

"Correct."

His reasons may or may not be genuine, but she could tell his offer was. And, at the moment, that's all that mattered. She allowed herself a slow smile. "Thank you. She'll be so relieved."

"It's my pleasure." He pulled away from the railing. "Now that that's settled, I was wondering if you'd mind getting an early start tomorrow?"

"Not at all."

He nodded. "I appreciate it. My home's a half-day's ride away, so it wouldn't be wise to dally."

"You don't live in town?"

"No. I run a lumber company several miles north of here. Didn't Mercer tell you?"

"He mentioned you were in lumber. I guess I just, well, I didn't think. It makes sense, though. Of course you live out in the lumber camps."

If it was a half-day's ride away, she'd have to board at the camp as well. She schooled her features, hoping to hide her disappointment.

"It's not a big lumber camp," he said. "Not like the kind they have back east. It's a small operation right now. Though it's growing."

"I see."

A burst of laughter from the crowd inside filtered out through the window. She adjusted the jacket on her shoulders, releasing another whiff of cedar. With its warmth, the crisp outside air felt good against her cheeks.

He shifted his feet. "Is seven in the morning too early?"

"Not at all." She wondered if she should mention the fifty dollars, then decided against it. Tomorrow would be soon enough.

"Good. I'll pick you up then. Be sure to have all your belongings ready to go. We'll have breakfast and then, then . . ."

"I understand. I'll be ready."

He blew out a puff of air. "Thank you. And, I just wanted

to say, well, you've been a pleasant surprise." He sucked in his breath. "I mean . . . What I was trying to say was . . . I don't want you to think—"

"It's quite all right, Mr. Denton. I've been pleasantly surprised as well."

"You have? Oh." He cleared his throat. "Yes. Well." He tugged at his collar. "I, um, I guess I'll see you in the morning, then." Touching the brim of his hat, he stepped off the veranda and hurried down the boardwalk.

The darkness had swallowed him and the sound of his footsteps when she realized he'd forgotten to take his jacket.

Chapter Five

Most of the boys took their breakfast at Yesler's Cookhouse. Not this morning. It was standing room only at the Occidental's dining hall.

Joe hesitated at its threshold.

Alvin Sprygley gave a slow whistle. "Well, would you look at who's all slicked up and raring to go this morning?"

"When you making the jump, Denton?"

"The preacher says Joe and his sewing machine are saying their words this morning."

Doc Maynard whacked him on the back. "You sure aren't wasting any time, are you?"

Somebody from across the room answered for him. "I wouldn't be either if I had a petticoat like Miss Ivey wanting to hogtie me with matrimonial ropes."

"Yeah. I bet she'll put some flavor in his grub."

The ribbing continued, each taunt a little cruder than the last, until Joe was afraid Miss Ivey might overhear when she came down the stairs.

The thought had barely formed when she appeared in the doorway and a hush fell over the room.

She was wearing the same brown, travel-worn dress she'd had on yesterday. And from the looks of it, she'd done some hard living in it. Still, he noted she'd brushed it clean, pinned a piece of jewelry to her chest, and had taken special care with her hair.

No loose tendrils this morning. Everything was all tucked up, secure and tidy. Color filled her cheeks as she hovered at the entrance, scanning the room.

He jumped forward.

Her big brown eyes honed in on him, the full force of them making him miss a step.

"Good morning, Miss Ivey," he said.

"Mr. Denton."

He extended an elbow. "You sleep well?"

"For the most part, thank you."

Between the time he met her at the entrance and then turned back to escort her into the dining hall, a single vacant table had materialized—dead center of the room.

They wove their way through the crowd, every man along the way tipping his hat and murmuring a greeting.

Before Joe had a chance, Niles Embry pulled out Miss Ivey's chair and scooted her into her spot. Joe gave him and everybody else a hard look.

Like a gun at the start of a race, all the men returned their attention to their now-cold food and started conversing amongst themselves—a little too loudly and with a little too much enthusiasm.

But Miss Ivey's shoulders relaxed, so Joe took his chair. Then could think of absolutely nothing to say.

He wanted desperately to study the little piece of frippery she had pinned to her chest. Was it a watch? A family keepsake? Or just a bit of fluff? He was sure she hadn't worn it last night.

He didn't dare lower his gaze, though, for fear she might misinterpret what he was examining.

Unfolding her napkin, she slipped it into her lap. The conversations around them dipped with her movements, then swelled back up. Joe tucked his into the neck of his collar.

Owen Nausley, leading with his massive stomach, made his way to their table, his apron smudged with flour and grease, his brown hair sticking out in short tufts. He set two china cups of steaming coffee, complete with saucers, onto their table.

Joe looked askance at the tiny little cups. Where were the mugs?

Standing tall and proud, Nausley pressed his stomach against the side of the table and waited for Miss Ivey's reaction to his coffee. Silence again fell across the room.

Miss Ivey darted a quick look at Joe, then Nausley, then her cup. Picking it up, she brought it to her mouth and blew, her little finger sticking out for balance.

Placing her lips on the edge of the cup, her eyes captured Joe's across the rim as she took a delicate swallow.

He swallowed with her.

Setting the cup down, she pulled the napkin from her lap and touched each side of her mouth. "Delicious."

The noise in the hall rose to new heights. Nausley beamed, showing a set of teeth that looked like piano keys—one white, one black hole, one white, one black hole.

Joe emptied his cup in one swallow and shoved it into Nausley's beefy hand. "I'll have about twelve of those."

But his sarcasm didn't faze Nausley, as the cook took the cup and practically floated back to the kitchen—if that were possible for a man his size—the men slapping him on the shoulders as he passed.

Again, Joe scrambled for something to say but could think of nothing.

"So." Miss Ivey cleared her throat. "Perhaps we should discuss exactly what my duties will entail?"

The conversation around them came to a screeching halt. The boys didn't even try to pretend they weren't listening.

Was she asking what Joe thought she was asking? Heat crept up his neck. He wasn't about to discuss such a thing in front of the entire town—wasn't even sure he could discuss it in private—but he had to say something.

Purposely misinterpreting her question, he offered what he hoped was a reasonable response. "The boys who work for me only go to town on Saturday nights, then return to my place after dark on Sundays. So during the rest of the week I was hoping you'd be willing to cook them two meals a day along with packed lunches."

"How many men are on your crew?"

"Fourteen."

She smiled. "I should be glad to do that for you."

He nodded, pleased. "You know how to cook, then?"

"Quite well."

"Mercer had said you did, but, well . . ."

She gave a soft chuckle. "I understand your reluctance to take his words at face value, but in this instance, he was being forthright."

She took another sip of coffee, her extended pinky again capturing his attention, along with everyone else's.

"Do you have a cookhouse or a cook tent?" she asked.

"Neither. You'll be using the kitchen in my home."

She hesitated. "I see."

He realized he should have said *our* home, but before he could correct his mistake, Nausley appeared with plates of cold ham, poached eggs, new potatoes, hot cakes, fish chowder, hominy, bacon, fried biscuits, butter, and orange marmalade.

Joe spent the next few minutes assuaging his initial hunger pains. Halfway into his meal, he noticed Miss Ivey had stopped eating completely.

"Is something wrong?" he asked.

"No, no. I'm just not used to so much."

He cut a piece of ham, jabbed it with his knife, and stuck it in his mouth. She might claim she could cook, but if she wasn't used to eating decent meals, maybe that meant she wasn't used to preparing them, either.

"Mercer said you did the cooking for an establishment in your hometown?"

She sat up a little straighter. "Yes, that's correct."

"Weren't those meals similar to this one?"

She gave the fare on their table another look. "The portions weren't this large, but we served about fifty people at a time. So the quantity of food we cooked was rather significant."

"We?"

"Yes. One other girl worked with me."

He nodded.

"I was wondering . . ." She looked down, smoothing the napkin in her lap.

He took the opportunity to examine the piece of jewelry resting above her right breast. A watch. It was a spherical little thing hanging upside down from a delicate bow of gold. From her vantage point of looking down, though, he realized the face would be right-side up. The quality of the ornament contrasted sharply with her threadbare gown.

"Yes?" he said, drawing his eyes back up to her face.

"I suppose I'll find out soon enough, but," she lifted her gaze to his, "I was wondering where exactly I'll be staying?"

Exactly? She wanted to know exactly? As in . . . which room?

He tried to stop the blush but could not. Inwardly cursing himself for choosing such a public place to have their first intimate conversation, he took a bite of hot cakes, trying to formulate an answer. Again, the men around them quieted.

"I mean," her tongue shot out to moisten her lower lip, "where do the men who work with you sleep?"

Privacy. Of course. Being the only woman out there in the midst of all those men, she was worried about privacy. He released his breath.

"The men sleep in a bunkhouse a mile or so from the house you and I will be staying in."

Her eyes widened. "You and I will be staying in a house?"

"Well, yes."

"Alone?" she whispered, though everyone around them heard it and didn't miss the rush of color touching her cheeks.

Clapping his hands together, he indicated the untouched portions of her breakfast. "Well. Are you going to eat that?"

She jumped. "What? Oh. No. Thank you."

"Would you mind?"

She opened, then closed her mouth. "Well, Mr. Denton. I, well, actually, I do admit to being a bit concerned. I mean, do you think it proper?"

He lifted his brows. "To finish a meal I paid for?" He smiled. "I doubt the boys will be offended. That is, unless you would be?"

"Oh!" She fiddled with her watch pin. "Oh. My meal. No, no. Of course not. Please. Help yourself."

She quieted and he concentrated on eating, hoping she'd hold any more questions for later. But the longer they sat there, the more she squirmed.

He ate faster.

"Mr. Denton?"

Hesitating, he swallowed the new potatoes in his mouth. "Yes?"

She touched each corner of her lips with her cloth. "Did Mr. Mercer mention a contract I signed with him?"

He reached for his coffee, only to find Nausley had never returned with another cup. "Well, I didn't realize Mercer wrote one for you, but it makes sense, I suppose."

"You know, then, about the cost of my passage?"

He nodded. "Yes."

"And you don't mind?"

"I've already taken care of it."

A quiet rush of air left her. "Oh. Thank you. You'll not be disappointed with me. I promise."

He yanked the napkin from his neck and jumped to his feet. "Time to go."

He pulled out her chair, tucked her hand into the crook of his elbow, and whisked her from the room.

Anna scurried to keep up with him, taking three steps for every one of his. Men drew their legs from the aisle to let her pass but made no effort to disguise their fascination with her. She decided she'd never watch a fish inside a bowl again.

"Where are your things?" Mr. Denton asked as soon as they cleared the dining hall and entered the lobby.

"The front desk has my bag."

He steered her toward the counter. The clerk standing behind it reminded her of an old hound dog—saggy skin, slow movements, and big ears.

"Morning, Joe," he said. "Miss."

"Do you have Miss Ivey's things?"

"Sure do." He lumbered to the end of the counter and picked up her carpetbag. The jacket she'd borrowed from Mr. Denton lay across it, looking fresh from the brushing she'd given it. "Here you are."

"Thank you."

Her seashell collection clinked inside her bag.

Mr. Denton looked around. "Where's her trunk?"

"Trunk?"

"I don't have a trunk," she interjected.

Mr. Denton frowned. "You don't have a trunk?"

"No."

He looked down at the bag in his hand. "This is it?"

"Yes."

"You came all the way from Massachusetts and this is all you brought?"

She lifted her chin. "It is."

After a slight hesitation, he pulled some coins out of his pocket and pressed them against the counter. "Is that enough for breakfast and Miss Ivey's room?"

With slow movements, Mr. Collins unfolded a pair of wire spectacles, hooked them on his ears, then counted out each coin. Anna stared at the floor, embarrassed to witness the exchange of funds on her behalf.

Mr. Denton's large booted feet looked out of place on the beautiful burgundy and navy rug. He shifted his weight from one foot to the other.

"This will cover it nicely, Joe."

Nodding, Mr. Denton grasped her hand and pulled her out the front door, down the steps, and to a light spring wagon with a canopy on top.

She wasn't about to get in it with him. Not without knowing what was what. She jerked back.

Releasing her, he stopped. "Did you forget something?"

"Where are we going?"

"To the church."

She blinked. "The church? But it's only Tuesday."

He rubbed his forehead. "Listen, I've been away from my work since yesterday and I really need to get back. I know you must feel rushed, and I'm really sorry about that, but would you mind if we went ahead and stopped by the church, then headed out?"

She studied him, tempted to say no just to see what his reaction would be. She could sense he was anxious. Testing his temper now would be better than testing it on some isolated homestead where no one could come to her rescue.

"Please?" The curls he'd slicked down with water had begun to bounce free now that they'd dried.

In the end, she couldn't work up the nerve to rebuff him. "I have no outright objection to stopping by the church, Mr. Denton, but I do think we need to clarify some things between us before we leave town."

Men from inside the dining hall began to filter out onto the porch. Some settled into the rockers it offered, others hooked a hip on its railing. All were silent.

Mr. Denton lowered his voice. "I'll answer any questions you have. I just don't want to do it while every ear's turned our way."

A man wearing denim trousers and no jacket stepped up to his horse at the nearby hitching rail. Instead of mounting, he flipped up the stirrup, unbuckled the cinch, and began to adjust it.

She made herself take a calming breath. She didn't care for their audience either, but she had one question she wanted to ask while she still had two feet on the ground and a place to run to if her employer turned violent.

The only man as big as he that she knew was Hoke. And though Hoke had never actually hit her, he'd hit Helen. If Mr. Denton was of that same bent, she wanted to know it before she climbed into that wagon.

She kept her voice to a bare minimum. "Very well, sir. But before we go any farther, I have a question about my sleeping arrangements."

His face turned bright scarlet. "You will have your own room and complete privacy," he whispered.

"Then it will be just the two of us in your house?"

"I've no other relations living with me, if that's what you mean."

"And my reputation? What will people think with just the two of us living there and no one else?"

He frowned. "They'll not think a thing. Why would they?"

She tugged on her cuffs. "Why would they, indeed."

He cupped her elbow. "Perhaps we could discuss this on the way?"

She hesitated. "We're going to the church?"

"Yes. It's a few streets over. Normally I'd walk, but the wagon will allow us to talk without being interrupted or overheard."

She toyed with her watch pin. The fact that he wanted to visit the House of the Lord before he left town boded well. And it would also give her an opportunity to seek the preacher's counsel.

She placed a foot on the foothold. He took a step closer, his enormous frame blocking out the sun. Suppressing the urge to jerk away from him, she prayed for God's protection, then held her breath while he assisted her into the wagon.

Chapter Six

Anna hadn't been in a wagon since she'd left New York. The rocking of the vehicle combined with the rumbling of hooves, the jiggling of harnesses, and the creaking of wheels all blended together in a soothing lullaby.

An Indian woman swaddled in what looked like a blanket of woven bark moved down the boardwalk. Looking up, she waved at Mr. Denton, the brass rings on her fingers catching the sunlight, while the ones in her ears swayed.

Tugging on his hat, Mr. Denton smiled, his entire face transformed with the gesture. His eyes turned sky blue while a double set of deep grooves dimpled each cheek. Anna knew she stared, but never had she seen such straight, white teeth.

Quelling the impulse to crane around for another look at the woman who evoked such a response from him, she instead scanned the streets. There wasn't a single beggar. Or pauper. Or tramp. In New York, they'd lined every major thoroughfare. She wondered, briefly, how long it would have been before she'd have become one of them had she stayed at home.

Mr. Denton clicked his tongue, gently tugging on the right rein and turning them north toward Mr. Mercer's grand university at the top of the hill. They passed cottage-style homes sitting in the middle of treeless lots a block wide, white picket fences marking their sparse perimeters. For all the trees that grew in this land, the residences had nothing but flat, dirt-filled lots with few shade trees or ornamental shrubs.

Two tiny birds with rich vocal repertoires flickered by *tee-tee-teeing* in an impossibly high register, then suddenly dropped their voices to *turr-turr-turr* in a lower tone. This time she did twist around in the wagon seat.

And completely forgot about the birds as she again faced Mount Rainier. Huge, majestic, awe-inspiring. And it would be hers to look at for the rest of her days.

The wagon dipped into a sag, bumping her backside clear up off the bench. Squealing, she flailed her arms.

An iron grip clasped her leg through her skirts and hauled her back down. "Careful."

She sucked in a breath, then steadied herself. "Forgive me. I was . . ."

But he'd already removed his hand and turned his focus to something up ahead.

She smoothed her skirts and looked to see what held his attention. A little white church crowned with a pretty steeple and large wooden cross had come into view.

Her pulse began to hammer. They'd be there in a few minutes and she'd yet to raise her concerns with Mr. Denton.

Tapping the V between each gloved finger, she took a surreptitious glance at him. As anxious as he'd been to have the privacy of the wagon, he'd not initiated any conversation.

She bit her lip. Perhaps she should just wait and speak with the preacher. She'd heard things in the West were done differently, but she couldn't imagine the preacher allowing her to live alone with a single man. Surely things weren't *that* different.

On the other hand, in a territory that held a dearth of chaperones, there might not be any alternatives. She simply didn't know.

But the preacher would. So she'd wait and see.

A sweet, delicate fragrance filled the air.

"What's that smell?" she asked.

"Twinflower. It's that white wild flower creeping up the fence right there."

She scanned the fence and caught a flash of white hugging one of the posts. "Smells like honeysuckle, only more vanilla-like."

"Looks like them, too. You'll see them all over for the rest of the summer and on into the fall."

She studied the tiny blooms bedded in a patch of green until they'd completely passed them by.

A few blocks later, Mr. Denton slowed the wagon and pulled it off the road next to a burying ground with a smattering of markers. After securing the horse, he came round to her side and offered assistance.

As soon as her feet touched the ground, she turned her attention to the church. It held a number of holes in the woodwork and windows, all the size of bullets.

"You ready?" Mr. Denton asked, extending his elbow.

Shaking off her thoughts, she took his arm and headed up the steps. "What's the name of your church?"

"The White Church."

She blinked. "The White Church?"

"Yes. As opposed to the Brown Church over on Madison and Second."

"The Indians here have their own church?"

A ghost of a smile touched his face. "No. This one is painted white; that one is painted brown."

Before she had time to digest his explanation, they entered the sanctuary. A tall ceiling with exposed joists sheltered two walls of windows and several rows of oak pews split down the middle by an aisle. A hint of lemon oil tickled her nose.

"Wait here," he said. "I'll be right back."

The heels of his boots echoed off the walls as he skirted the pews and headed toward a door to the right of the pulpit.

"David?" he asked, tapping a knuckle against the wood.

A muffled sound issued forth and Mr. Denton entered the room, closing the door behind him.

Silence enveloped Anna.

Hello, God.

Removing her gloves, she glided down the aisle, absorbing the quiet, the draped cross at the front of the room, the feeling of peace.

I think I'm going to love it here.

She reached out a hand, touching the back of each pew as she passed, its smooth, varnished surface caressing her fingers.

I'd heard it rained a lot. But the last two days have been beautiful. And everything is so pretty. So green. And the mountains. Oh, Lord, they're—

The door to the preacher's office opened. Mr. Denton stood on its threshold, the light from behind him making it impossible to see his features.

"They're ready," he said, his voice loud within the quiet of the church. "If you are, that is."

She tilted her head. They? Ready for what? But she moved toward him, anxious now to meet her new preacher and to ask him for his counsel.

As she approached, Mr. Denton stepped toward her, pulling the door behind him but not quite closing it. "Anna?"

She stopped.

"I left the ring at home."

A picture of the Indian woman and her brass rings flashed through her mind. Was he supposed to trade with the Indians? And why was he telling her?

Then she realized, he'd used her Christian name. She pulled down the corners of her mouth. She'd speak to the preacher about that, too.

"I'm sorry," he said.

She nodded. "Well, you mustn't let it happen again."

He hesitated, then opened the door.

A man of medium build with kind brown eyes and a receding hairline stepped from behind a desk. He'd shaved his beard so that it ran from one ear, down under his chin, and back up the other side like a bonnet strap. "Miss Ivey? I'm Reverend Blaine and this is my wife, Rebecca."

A lovely woman with mountains of black hair and a dress that looked more suited to New York City than the Washington Territory stepped forward.

She took Anna in her embrace. *"Klahawya."* She pulled back and smiled. "That's how the natives say hello."

Anna returned her smile. "I'm afraid you'll have to settle for a simple 'How do you do' from me, Mrs. Blaine. I don't know any Indian words."

"Oh, you must call me Rebecca."

"Thank you. And, please, call me Anna."

Rebecca swept Anna with her gaze but gave no indication of her thoughts. Yet Anna felt warmth crawl into her cheeks. This past year she'd had to wash out one dress while wearing the other. Over and over and over. They weren't exactly rags yet but were perilously close to becoming so.

Fingering her skirt, she hid her hand within its folds, then lifted her chin. There was no shame in being poor. Only in doing nothing about it. But she'd answered an ad and come clear around the Horn to start a new life. A new life as a cook. Once she'd worked off her debt to Mr. Denton, fabric for a new gown would be her very first purchase.

She swallowed, hoping the bachelor status of her employer didn't jeopardize that ambition.

"She's lovely, Joe," Rebecca said, glancing at Mr. Denton.

He immediately cast his gaze to the floor, refusing to meet her eye.

Discomfited, Anna didn't know what to say. She turned to Reverend Blaine, trying to decide how best to broach the dilemma she found herself in.

Judging him to be in his forties, she noted he had the marks of a man whose wife fed him well. Before she could gather her wits, he slipped a jacket over his vest, picked up a Bible, and tucked it to his chest.

"I cannot tell you how long we have anticipated the arrival of Mercer's girls," he said.

"It's certainly been an adventure," she responded.

"I can imagine." He cleared his throat. "How, um, old are you, my dear?"

She blinked. "Nineteen."

"Perfect." Smiling, he looked at Mr. Denton. "Well, Joe. You ready?"

Mr. Denton stepped up beside her, taking her elbow.

The reverend looked at Anna. "Rebecca will act as witness."

Witness?

He opened his Bible. "Dearly beloved, we are gathered here together in the sight of God, and in the presence of this witness . . ."

Anna looked in confusion around the room. She glanced up at Mr. Denton. He was completely focused on the words being said, his expression serious.

"Wait!" She jerked her arm from his hold.

He tensed. The preacher stopped.

"What are you doing?" she asked.

Reverend Blaine looked first at Mr. Denton and then at her. "I'm performing the wedding ceremony."

"Whose wedding ceremony?"

He frowned. "Your wedding ceremony."

She took a step back. "What song in a million Sundays gave you the idea I wanted to marry Mr. Denton?"

The reverend opened, then closed his mouth. "Well, it was, it was in the contract."

"What contract?"

He looked at Mr. Denton. "Joe? Did you not discuss this with her?"

"Of course I did," he said, his face flaming.

She whirled toward him. "I beg your pardon? You most certainly did not. Exactly when did you ask me to marry you?"

"I didn't expect to have to say the actual words, Anna. It was understood in the terms of the contract."

"You do *not*, sir, have permission to use my Christian name. Furthermore, I have no idea what contract you are referring to."

His exasperation was clear. "Mercer's contract. What do you think we've been talking about all morning? All last night? What do you think we're doing at the church?"

"I thought you had an appointment with the preacher!"

"I did. I had an appointment to get married. To *you*."

She closed her eyes, prayed for patience, then opened them again. "I am aware, sir, that most wives cook for their husbands. But to assume I would agree to be your spouse simply because I said I'd cook for you goes beyond—"

"I assumed nothing," he barked, his eyes dark.

She took an involuntary step back. He really was a very large man.

"You signed a contract with Mercer, right?"

She nodded.

"Well, so did I." He removed a worn piece of parchment from his jacket, unfolded it, and handed it to her.

She began to skim it, then slowed down to read it more thoroughly.

I, A.S. Mercer, of Seattle, W.T., hereby agree to bring a suitable wife of good moral character and reputation, from the East to Seattle, on or before October, 1865, for Joseph Denton, whose signature is hereunto attached, he first paying me the sum of three hundred dollars—

She gasped.

—with which to pay the passage of said lady from the East and to compensate me for my trouble. If she is a proficient cook, a bonus of fifty dollars will be awarded to A.S. Mercer.

It was signed by both Mercer and Mr. Denton in April of 1865.

She slowly raised her eyes to his. "You paid that scoundrel three hundred dollars?"

He shook his head. "Four hundred. I had to wire him fifty because you're a cook and fifty more to get you from San Francisco to here."

A tightness seized her chest. "My contract reads much differently."

"Where is it?" he asked, his features taut.

"In my carpetbag."

He nodded. "I'll go get it."

The preacher and his wife said nothing while Mr. Denton went to fetch her bag and she carefully avoided their gazes. An old rug covered the wooden floor and had a worn path from the reverend's chair to the window and back again.

Instead of a secretary against the wall, a large gateleg table as old as time served as his desk. *Pilgrim's Progress* and *The Imitation of Christ* lay stacked in one corner. Numerous papers were strewn across its scarred, well-used surface. His quill lay carelessly atop a half-written document as if he'd been using it just prior to their arrival.

Mr. Denton returned, handing her the bag. No one said a word. She rummaged through it, dug out a folded piece of paper, then slowly handed it to him.

> *One passage on the good steamship* Continental *bound for Seattle in the Washington Territory is awarded to Miss Anna Ivey of Granby, Massachusetts.*
>
> *On the completion of the voyage, it is hereby agreed that Mr. Joseph Denton will pay the sum of fifty dollars to Mr. A.S. Mercer in consideration that Miss Ivey shall act as a cook for his lumber company until said monies have been earned back in labor.*
>
> *Signed and sealed by me this twentieth day of December one thousand eight hundred and sixty-five in the presence of Miss Anna Ivey.*

Mr. Denton gave the preacher a pointed look, then passed the document to him.

"Mercer never said anything to you about being a bride?" Denton asked.

"Once. In the middle of the voyage, he tried to extract more money from all us girls. When it was my turn to be called into his stateroom, he said he was confident I'd find a husband who'd be willing to pay whatever I agreed to."

Mr. Denton rubbed his forehead. "Please don't tell me you agreed to more."

"I did not. I also made it clear I had no intention of marrying."

He ceased his rubbing and looked at her over his hand. "What did he say to that?"

"He was rather troubled, now that I think on it. But I credited it to the fact that I wouldn't commit to more money. Not that I wouldn't commit to marriage."

"I need a wife, Miss Ivey. I *paid* for a wife."

She swallowed. "Well, I'm afraid I can't help you."

"Why not?"

"Why not?" She looked to the preacher and his wife for a show of support, but their stern visages clearly indicated they sided with Mr. Denton.

"Well," she said, "for one thing, I don't know you. Secondly, I . . . I want to make my own way."

"Make your own way? You're a suffragist?" He curled his lip. "Mercer brought me a *suffragist*?"

She narrowed her eyes. "Mr. Mercer brought you a cook. Nothing more, nothing less."

"Well, I paid for a bride."

"And I'm truly sorry about that, but as you can see, there is no mention of that in my contract."

He glanced at the preacher. "We'll be right back."

Grabbing her elbow, he pulled her out the door of the office. The slamming of it echoed in the quiet of the church. She all but ran beside him as he propelled her to the front pew. Before she could protest, he forced her to sit.

"Listen," he said, joining her. "I'm going to lose my land if I don't get married."

"Lose your land?"

"That's right. I participated in the Land Grant Act and was awarded six hundred forty acres, but my wife died before she could join me. That demoted me to bachelor status, making me eligible for only three hundred twenty acres. So if I want to keep the full six hundred forty I've already developed, I have to have a wife and I have to have her today."

She blinked, trying to follow the thread of conversation. "Today? Why today?"

"Because I was given a year to secure a bride, but it took Mercer fifteen months to get you here. So I'm out of time. If you refuse me, the judge will certainly rule in favor of the man suing me for half my land."

"Did you tell the judge your wife died?"

"I did, but the courthouse that held her death certificate burned down, destroying all its records."

"Surely the judge would take your word."

"One would think, but he did not. Most likely because the man suing me is a relation of his." Dropping to his knee, he clasped her hand. "It will be a marriage in name only. I won't press you for, for . . ." Pink touched his cheeks. "I won't press you for conjugal rights. I have a large home. You'll have your own room. I'm well off and can afford to clothe you and keep you in warmth and comfort. So," he took a deep breath, "would you please do me the honor of becoming my wife, Miss Anna Ivey?" He squeezed her hand, his eyes turning from blue to green and back to blue. "Please?"

Her heart softened at his plea, but she caught herself. This was no injured dog who needed nursing back to health. This was a huge, strapping man who wanted her to enter into a lifetime commitment with him.

Beyond his kind treatment of Mrs. Wrenne, she didn't know anything about him or his character. Nor did he know anything about her. He didn't know about her father. Her brother. Her mother. He didn't know she'd been responsible for them. He didn't know that because of her they were now all dead.

"I'm sorry, Mr. Denton," she said, gently withdrawing her hand from his. "I'm afraid I can't help you."

Chapter Seven

"But you have to marry me." Joe made a conscious effort to slow his breathing. "I have a contract. Money has changed hands." He paused. "A great deal of money, Miss Ivey."

"And I'm afraid you've been taken, sir." Her eyes showed sympathy, but no indecision.

He curled his hands into fists. He was going to kill Mercer. Tear him apart limb by limb. Unless somebody else beat him to it.

He ran his gaze over the empty church. Were the rest of the men in town discovering their brides weren't brides, or had Mercer swindled only him?

"What about the other women?" he asked. "Had they signed on as brides?"

"Not that I'm aware of, other than Mrs. Wrenne, of course."

He nodded. "The one who needs a dentist?"

"Yes."

He set his jaw. Demanding a refund from Mercer probably wouldn't do any good, but he'd insist on one anyway. Until then, he'd be jiggered if he let Miss Ivey loose. He might have been expecting a bride, but his crew was expecting a cook. He'd not disappoint them.

"Well, our papers may read differently as far as matrimony is concerned," he said, "but it doesn't change the fact that I paid your fare and you are contractually obligated to cook for my lumber company."

"I'm perfectly willing to work off my debt to you, Mr. Denton."

"All right, then. First, we'll telegraph Mercer. Then we'll visit the judge and show him our contracts."

❧

To A S Mercer STOP *Ivey refuses to marry* STOP *You owe me a bride or 400 dollars* STOP *Payable immediately or else* STOP *J Denton* STOP

❧

Anna shifted on a delicate chair in the judge's parlor. A thick wooden side door muffled the voices of Mr. Denton and the judge, though Joe's swelled several times and had a definite edge to it.

The molded ceiling, huge chandelier, and marble fireplace reminded Anna of the rooms her father had once made wallpaper for—though this one had painted walls, not papered. A rosewood sofa upholstered in maroon and gold damask had its back to a large bay window and would have easily sat four men. Its spiral ends and lion's-paw feet were intricately carved.

She studied the huge oval portraits of Judge Rountree and his young wife. Would this woman with somber eyes and serious expression become a friend?

She sighed. Probably not. The parlor exuded wealth and status. Her threadbare gown and frayed cape were completely out of place. She picked a piece of lint from her skirt, then folded her hands in her lap.

A door slammed somewhere in the house, followed by the rapid descent of footsteps on the stairs.

"Hurry it up, Two. I wanna catch him before he leaves."

A slower *clump-clump-clump* followed. "I'm comin'. I'm comin'."

"Here. Hold on to my hand."

The owner of the voice ran back up and the *clump-clump-clump* increased in pace. She kept her eyes on the entrance to the parlor and didn't have long to wait.

A brown-haired boy in short pants, hickory shirt, and bright yellow bandana rounded the corner, towing a younger, female version of himself in a cropped-off tent dress. Anna judged them to be perhaps six and four.

The boy pulled up short. "Who're you?"

"I'm Miss Ivey of Granby, Massachusetts."

He released his sister's hand and executed a formal bow. "I'm Sprout Rountree of Seattle. This here is Two."

Anna frowned. "Excuse me? I didn't quite catch your sister's name."

"Two," he repeated. "We call her Two."

The girl thrust her thumb into her mouth.

"Two? As in the number two?"

"Yep." He sauntered forward, causing a slingshot in his pocket to peek out with each step.

"I see." She paused. "And what's her real name?"

"She hasn't decided yet."

Anna blinked. "I'm sorry?"

"She hasn't decided."

"What do you mean?"

"We get to pick our own names when we're old enough. So I'm One, she's Two, my brother's Three, and the baby's Four."

Anna held back her smile, not wanting to encourage the boy in his tales. "I thought your name was Sprout."

He shrugged. "Oh, that's just what everybody calls me until I make up my mind."

"You know, Sprout," she admonished gently, "I had a brother just like you once, and I happen to know all about little boys. You'll find you can't pull the wool over my eyes quite so easily."

He scowled, wrinkling the freckles on his nose. "I'm not lying, if that's what you mean."

The connecting door opened.

"Now, now," she continued, "no loving parent would ever name his children One, Two, Three, and Four."

"Sure he would." He looked to her left. "Wouldn't he, Pa?"

Anna twisted around, then quickly rose to her feet. A diminutive man, made more so by Denton's bulk, gave her a scathing glance before turning to the boy.

"Run along, *One*. And take *Two* with you."

The boy immediately acquiesced, leaving a charged silence behind him.

"You have seven weeks to acquire a bride, Joe, and not a day more," the judge snapped.

"I understand." Denton stepped forward, grabbed Anna's elbow none too gently, and thrust her toward the door.

To J Denton STOP *Ivey obligated to work off debt* STOP *Boynton rescinded* STOP *Bertha Wrenne now yours* STOP *Contract fulfilled* STOP *A S Mercer* STOP

From the looks of it, Mrs. Wrenne was somewhere in her sixties and appeared to weigh not much more than a sack of flour. Her hand gripped Anna's arm as she descended the Occidental's staircase.

Tucking her head, she gave Joe a glimpse of pink scalp beneath sparse gray hair. The hem of her gown was several inches too short, revealing sturdy black shoes and impossibly thin ankles.

She looked almost old enough to be his grandmother. He rubbed his jaw. Did he really love his land enough to marry her?

Sighing, he knew that he did. And wasn't she exactly what he'd expected from Mercer? It was only after Anna had been dangled before him that he realized how worried he'd been.

But Mrs. Wrenne was who Mercer had now assigned to him, so Mrs. Wrenne it was. He'd be loyal, faithful, and good to her. He'd provide food, clothing, and shelter. He'd do everything a husband should—well, almost everything. He'd decided last year when he signed the contract that unless the woman was—by some miracle—suitable, their marriage would be chaste. He was sure Mrs. Wrenne would be of the same mind.

Anna whispered something to her and the older woman smiled. All gum. He looked away, taking a moment to compose himself.

"Mr. Denton," Anna said, pulling his attention back to them. "This is my friend, Mrs. Wrenne. I told her you'd asked for an introduction."

The woman nodded, careful to keep her lips together. Stepping off the last stair into the entry hall, she released Anna's arm.

He inclined his head. "How do you do, Mrs. Wrenne."

She smiled, lips tightly sealed.

He glanced at Anna, then back at Mrs. Wrenne. Perhaps he shouldn't immediately blurt out the contents of Mercer's telegram. Easing her into it might be a bit more prudent.

"May I interest you in a short stroll through town?" he asked.

Delight touched her eyes and she nodded vigorously. He held out his arm.

Anna trailed behind Mr. Denton and Mrs. Wrenne, feeling very much the fifth wheel. He'd been stiff with anger after leaving the judge's home, and she hadn't tried to engage him in conversation. She had sympathy for the predicament he found himself in, but she was also affronted that he expected her to enter into something as serious as marriage at the snap of his fingers.

They'd returned to the telegraph office to find Mercer had already sent a reply. Mr. Denton had shown no emotion while reading the missive, nor did he share its contents with her. He'd merely folded it, put it in his pocket, and said, "I need you to introduce me to Mrs. Wrenne."

They'd come straightaway to the Occidental.

He now tucked Mrs. Wrenne's hand into his elbow, bending low while speaking to her. He kept up a monologue as if sensing she was too embarrassed to reveal her toothless gums.

"Now, this is our smithy," he said, whipping a handkerchief from his pocket and offering it to Mrs. Wrenne.

She placed it against her nose and cocked an ear to better hear him.

The thunderous grinding of the sawmill several streets over underscored the clink of the blacksmith's shop. A blast of heat and the smell of acrid fumes hit Anna full force as they approached the smithy's wide, open doors. Peeking inside she could make out the silhouette of a large man holding a poker over hot coals.

"Used to be our doctor ran this shop, but he wasn't very good at it."

The blacksmith raised a hand in greeting. Denton returned the gesture.

"When young Lewis here passed by and commented on Doc Maynard's clumsiness, Maynard sold him the business on the spot for ten dollars—lot and all."

The street held very little traffic. An occasional horse stood tied to a rail, and a wagon pulled by an old mare ambled by. Anna decided most of the men must have left for the lumber camps or whatever other jobs they held.

They passed a mercantile, a boot maker, an attorney's office, and a tannery. Denton submitted an interesting tidbit about each place and took great care to center his attention on Mrs. Wrenne during the telling.

In response, she blushed, she fluttered, she patted her hair.

"Now, you must keep the tides in mind when at the end of Commercial Street," he continued. "We had a newcomer once pull up in his canoe just as the tide was going out. He was stuck on a bed of ooze for hours in the sun and rain until the tide returned to release him."

"And do you get much rain here, Mr. Denton?" Anna asked.

"Yes." He didn't turn to her when he answered, just kept walking, then bent close to Mrs. Wrenne. "Now, you may have occasion to see an Indian."

Bertha's eyes widened.

Patting her hand, he smiled. "No need to worry. They're civilized and their language is very simple to learn."

"So the relations with the Indians are friendly?" Anna asked.

"Yes." Again he kept his voice clipped and his back to her. "There's a confectionery across the street, Mrs. Wrenne. May I interest you in a sweet?"

She nodded.

"I'd heard you had a war with the Indians," Anna persisted. "Did it last long?"

"Lasted one day." After stepping into the street, he took both of Mrs. Wrenne's hands, then helped her off the boardwalk. As soon as her feet touched the packed-dirt road, he led her across the road, never once offering assistance to Anna. He didn't even glance back to see if she followed.

Sighing, she stepped down, resigning herself to silently tag along behind the couple until her *employer* was ready to leave town. Her refusal of his marriage offer had clearly stung his pride. Well, she couldn't care less. What concerned her now was his motive for parading Mrs. Wrenne through town.

The mismatched couple disappeared behind a glass door with the words *Charles C. Terry, Candies, Fruits & Nuts.*

Anna let herself in. The smell of fresh pastry, ripe berries, and ginger soothed her frayed nerves. Jars of marmalades and candied fruits lined the shelves behind a beautiful mahogany counter. The elegant platters and gallery trays decorating its surface held a variety of tempting cakes and tarts.

She judged the man behind the counter to be somewhere in his thirties. He had a head full of dark hair, wide-set eyes, and a ready smile.

"Morning, Joe." Wiping his hands on his apron, he eyed the two women. "Who do we have here?"

"This is Mrs. Wrenne and Miss Ivey. They came over with Mercer. Ladies, this is Mr. Terry."

The bell on the door jingled. The blacksmith with soot covering his face and clothes entered the establishment, bringing the smell of his shop with him. He gave a shy smile and nod.

Anna nodded back.

"What captures your fancy, Mrs. Wrenne?" Denton asked, perusing a list of confections painted on a board behind the counter. "The molasses bread pudding is always good. How does that sound?"

She nodded.

"Make that two, Charlie," Denton said as the baker lifted a lid off a warming pot.

The smell of molasses, vanilla, and cinnamon filled the small shop. Anna's mouth watered, and she tried to remember the last time she'd had bread pudding. Hoke hadn't allowed his cooks to sample the desserts. Sugar was at too much of a premium.

Taking the two bowls Mr. Terry offered, Denton turned, caught sight of Anna, and hesitated. "Oh. Would you like something, Miss Ivey?"

Refusing to give him the satisfaction, she didn't so much as glance at the bowls he held. "I'm fine, thank you. Had a rather large breakfast."

"Shall we have a seat, then?"

Guiding them to a nearby table, Mr. Denton smiled at Mrs. Wrenne and helped her into a chair. The woman might be old, but she wasn't dead. Her entire countenance glowed from the attention.

The smithy saw to Anna's chair, then quickly stumbled back to the counter.

Mr. Denton didn't seem to notice. After finishing off his dessert in three big bites, he leaned back and gave Mrs. Wrenne a devastating smile. "Do you like it?"

She touched the corner of each lip with her napkin and nodded. The pudding required no chewing—and no teeth.

After she finished, he gave a quick glance at the baker and blacksmith, then scooted forward. "I received word from Mercer that your Mr. Boynton is no longer in the market for a bride."

Mrs. Wrenne jerked her chin up.

He swallowed, his Adam's apple jumping in his throat; then he lowered his voice. "So he has assigned you to me."

Anna stiffened.

He took Mrs. Wrenne's bent hand into his large, callused ones. "Would you, ma'am, do me the honor of becoming my lawfully wedded wife?"

Mrs. Wrenne's beady eyes widened beneath the folds of skin above them. "You want to marry me?"

Mr. Terry's pastry tongs clattered to the floor. The blacksmith whipped his head around.

Anna didn't know what to do. Every instinct she had screamed at her to interfere. But she knew that her friend wanted nothing so much as a husband, and Mr. Denton certainly needed a wife.

"I would be very honored, ma'am," he said, his face warming at the sudden quiet in the room.

"Mrs. Wr—" Anna started.

"Yes! I would be happy to be your bride, Mr. Denton."

After a slight pause, his smile was full, bright, and genuine.

Straight white teeth. Deep lines of twin dimples. Hazel eyes sparkling with pleasure.

She answered his smile with a plethora of lines on each side of her mouth and a gaping hole in between.

He stood. "Shall we go find the preacher?"

"Right now?"

"Yes. Let's not wait another minute."

Her smile slowly collapsed.

He sank back into his chair. "What's the matter?"

She cleared her throat, then lowered her voice to a whisper. "Would you mind if we waited until I had some teef made?"

He hesitated. "Mrs. Wrenne, I own a logging company and must get back to it today. I've been away too long as it is."

Her eyes watered. "Please?"

He rubbed his jaw. "I really can't afford to keep coming back and forth to town. I'd rather just go to the preacher now. Today."

She pursed her lips together in a pout. "Are we habing our foist fight?"

A slow line of red began to creep up his neck.

"I don't see the harm in waiting, Mr. Denton," Anna interjected. "After all, it will only take, what, two weeks?"

"More like three," he ground out, piercing her with his gaze.

"Well, the judge said you had seven weeks. I heard him myself."

After several seconds of tense silence, he pinched the bridge of his nose with his thumb and forefinger. "Very well. We'll wait until Dr. Barnard can make . . . what is necessary." He stood. "But as soon as he's finished, Mrs. Wrenne, I must insist we have the ceremony."

She set her napkin on the table. "Tank you."

Avoiding Anna's gaze and that of the two men in the confectionery, Mr. Denton assisted Mrs. Wrenne to her feet and escorted her out the door.

Chapter Eight

The wagon rolled and swayed, jostling Anna on the seat. Mr. Denton had not said so much as a word to her since leaving the confectionery. He had simply made arrangements with a dentist to have some teeth made for Mrs. Wrenne, walked them back to the Occidental, then propelled Anna out to his wagon.

They'd been on the crude road for almost an hour and he still hadn't said anything. Perhaps they would make it all the way to his lumber camp in peace and quiet.

"Judge Rountree holds half my property in the palm of his hand." Denton's growl broke the silence. "I'd appreciate it if you didn't insult him at all, much less in his own home."

So much for peace and quiet.

"He named his children One, Two, Three, and Four," she said. "He deserves to be insulted."

"That's not the point. The point is I can't afford to alienate him and now that you are my responsibility, I can't have you offending him either."

"Well, who would have thought someone would do that to his own children? I thought the boy was lying, for heaven's sake."

"Well, he wasn't. O.B. hates his name, and rather than saddling his kids with a name they hate, he decided to let them pick their own."

"So he calls them One, Two, Three, and Four? That's his solution to giving them names they won't hate?"

"They're temporary."

"They're preposterous."

"Are you listening to me, Anna? I won't have you insulting him."

The outrage she felt on the children's behalf continued to brew inside her. "Oh dear," she said, affecting a pout. "Are we *habing* our *foist* fight?"

He yanked the horses to a stop. She'd have flown right off the seat if he hadn't grabbed her and jerked her around to face him.

"Mrs. Wrenne is the woman I'm going to marry and I won't tolerate you or anyone else making fun of her. You understand me, missy?"

She immediately felt contrite. She hadn't meant to say that, but she was just so blame mad. And it wasn't only because of the children. She narrowed her eyes. "How dare you lecture me when you're marrying her only as a means to an end?"

He gave her a shake. "I won't have you making fun of her. Do you understand?"

Wrenching herself from his hold, she straightened her backbone, refusing to be cowed by him. "Those are awfully strong words from a man who is *using* her."

"No more than she's using me." He snatched up the reins.

All the starch wilted from her. "But aren't you ashamed?"

"You're the one who ought to be ashamed. Making fun of her lisp like that."

"I am. I'm sorry I did it and I won't do again." She glared at him. "And you? Are you ashamed?"

He flicked the ribbons, causing the horse to pick up some speed. "Not one single bit."

⁂

The rain started less than an hour later. The wagon's canopy offered little protection from the moisture blowing in from the sides. It didn't take long to penetrate Anna's clothing, and try as she might, she couldn't keep her shivers at bay.

Joe shrugged off his jacket and tossed it on her lap. "Didn't it occur to you to bring a coat?"

She shoved his jacket back at him, pressing it against his side. "I don't have one."

"I thought it got cold in Massachusetts."

"It does."

He hesitated. "Well, put that one on, then."

"I don't want it."

"Put it on."

"I don't want it."

"Put. It. On."

"No."

He turned to look at her. Slowly, slowly. He really was a large man.

"Don't make me stop the wagon again."

"Will you hit me?"

His mouth fell open. "Will I *hit* you?"

"Well? Will you?"

His horrified expression was better than any answer he could have given. Still, she refused to be the first to break eye contact.

"For the love of the saints, Anna." The edge in his voice dissipated. "Put the stupid thing on."

A breeze cut straight through her wet clothing. Lifting her chin, she tucked the jacket over her shoulders. Warmth immediately encompassed her along with the now-familiar smell of cedar. He plucked off his hat and stuffed it onto her head. It fell clear to her nose.

Pushing it up she looked at him, then jerked herself straight when a rivulet of water poured off its rim and down her back.

The rain continued, saturating his shirt, his trousers, his hair, his skin. He never said a word. Never so much as wiped his face.

The farther they went, the thicker the forest became on either side of the road. Never in her life had she seen so many trees. Tall ones. Short ones. Skinny ones. Fat ones.

"The evergreens here look different than the ones at home."

He continued to stare straight ahead, moisture collecting on his lashes.

She picked up a fallen twig from the wagon floor. "They're a darker green. And the needles are different, too. Rounder. Fatter."

The horse's hooves made a suctioning noise in the mud.

"What's your horse's name?"

A gust of wind blew the hat from her head. He caught it one-handed, then slapped it back on her.

"Shakespeare."

Shakespeare? Adjusting the hat, she studied the sturdy animal of a nondescript brown and wondered what the famous playwright would think about having a horse named after him.

The strain of the last few days coupled with the rocking wagon began to pull at her. Her eyes grew heavy. She allowed herself to close them for just a minute, then jerked her head up when her chin bounced.

After the third time, Denton pulled her against his shoulder. "Here."

She stiffened.

He held her in place. "You're going to tumble right off the wagon. Just close your eyes and see if you can get some sleep. We're still a long way from home."

A long way from home? She almost scoffed, but tears stacked

up in her throat, blocking the sound. She wasn't a long way from home. She was an entire continent away from home.

Her body warmth felt good. She felt good. When was the last time he had a woman this close? Eleven years? No. More like twelve.

He'd forgotten what it was like. How good it felt. Her head lolled back. Glancing down, he allowed himself a small smile. She slept with her mouth open. Now, why didn't that surprise him?

The rain began again in earnest. He pulled his jacket more securely over her shoulders, then tucked her under his arm, shielding as much of her as he could with his body.

She sure was a pretty little thing. He looked down again. And that waspish tongue of hers would help her hold her own with the boys.

He sighed. They were sure going to rib him about his choice of bride. It was just as well he was marrying the old woman, though. Wouldn't be hard to maintain a chaste relationship with her. Wouldn't have been near so easy if he'd married this one.

He tightened his grip some. He'd have to lay down the law with the boys. Make sure they didn't bother her. She obviously had some aversion to getting married, so he'd make sure they kept their distance.

She snorted, smacked her lips, then snuggled further into his side, smashing his hat between them.

Who'd hit her? he wondered. A relation? A guardian?

From the condition of her clothing and the sparseness of her bag, she'd clearly stumbled upon hard times. To think she didn't even have a coat, just a raggedy cape that served no purpose whatsoever.

Still, she was articulate. Well-spoken. At some point or other, she'd been looked after by someone with an education.

He shook his head. Was she running from something? From someone?

Tugging his hat free, he set it on top of his head, then pulled her face against his chest and allowed himself to enjoy the chance to hold her. It'd most likely be the last time he ever would.

He smoothed the hair off her face, then took a fortifying breath. He'd make certain it was the last time.

Leon's paper soldiers faced each other across the dark wood of the kitchen table. . . .

"Hold your fire, men," he said, pushing forward a soldier he'd named after one of the town's local officers. "Wait until the enemy gets close, then aim low."

The rebel line advanced. When all were in position, Leon picked up his drum and tapped out a slow beat.

"Steady . . . steady . . . and FIRE!"

The drumsticks thundered on the snare as he sucked in his breath and blew down the entire rebel line.

"Victory!" he shouted.

Anna slammed both hands down on the table, tumbling two of the Union soldiers. "Would you please stop that infernal drumming and help me?"

"Hey! Look what you did. You knocked down Charlie Church and Marvin Onerdonk."

"I'm going to wipe out the entire regiment if you don't put that stupid drum away."

Leon rose to his full height—all four feet of it—then proceeded to march around the kitchen singing, "We'll Hang Jeff Davis on a Sour Apple Tree," keeping time with his drum.

"Mama!" Anna hollered into the parlor, where their mother sewed for hours every day. "Leon won't help me pick lint."

He pounded harder. "Picking lint is for girls."

"It's for bandaging the soldiers and it's your duty to help."

"My duty is to be a drummer for the troops and I can't do that unless I practice."

"You're never going to be a drummer, Leon. Papa has forbidden it. Now, if you don't stop your pounding and help me, I'm going to . . . I'm going to knock over your soldiers."

"You better not."

She raised her hand. "Then stop. I mean it. Stop drumming right now or else."

Leon doubled his tempo.

She swept her arm across the table, sending the soldiers in all directions.

"Nooooo!" He dropped his sticks. "That was everybody we know."

"It's not either, and you're nothing but a big baby crying over a bunch of paper nothings."

"I'm not crying!" Wrenching the drum from his shoulders, he dropped it to the floor and charged.

Anna screamed as Leon brought her to the floor, scattering her pile of lint. She kicked and shoved, but even though she was fifteen to his ten, she could not overcome the combination of wiry muscles and indignation.

Mama came from around the corner. "Anna. Leon. Stop it. Stop it at once. Both of you."

They ignored her, of course. Mama reached for Leon just as Anna swung out her fist, catching her mother on the chin. Mama staggered back, falling against the wall, then crumpled to the floor.

"Look what you did!" Leon jumped up, a look of horror on his face. "I hate you, Anna! I hate you! And I'm not staying here another minute. I'm joining the war." He grabbed his drum, then ran from the room and out the screen door.

"Leon!" she cried. Yet she didn't run after him. She couldn't. Not with Mama hurt and on the floor.

"Leon!" she cried again. "Come back!"

But all she could hear were his footsteps running . . . running . . . running.

Chapter Nine

"Anna. Wake up. You're dreaming."

She jerked awake. Rain pelted her face. The pounding of Leon's retreating footsteps continued. "Leon?"

"It's me. Joe. Joe Denton."

"What?" Darkness as thick as molasses surrounded her. "Where's Leon?"

"He's not here. No one's here. It's just you and me and Shakespeare."

"Shakespeare?"

"My horse."

She swiped the water from her eyes, trying to see through the darkness. His horse? The rhythmic pounding of Shakespeare's hooves penetrated her consciousness. Hooves. Not footsteps.

Her heart began to slow. Tears mixed with the rain on her face. "Where am I?"

"You're on a wagon in the Washington Territory."

"Yes, yes. I know. I meant *where* in the Territory am I?"

"Oh. We're about two miles from my home."

"It's dark."

"Yes."

"Isn't that dangerous? Won't we get lost?"

"No."

Anna took stock of his arms cradling her and with a jolt realized she was on his lap. She jerked upright.

Tightening his hold, he held her in place. "Are you okay?"

"Yes. I'm perfectly fine. You can let go now."

"It'd be warmer and drier if you stayed put."

"I'll be all right."

"I know. You've got the coat. I was worried about me."

"Here. You can have it back." She reached up to shrug it off and discovered her arms were in the sleeves and its front had been buttoned.

Denton stayed her hand. "I was joking. Sort of."

"I wasn't."

"I don't want it back. But I would appreciate it if you'd stay close. Two miles can last a long time when you're wet and chilled."

She gently pushed and his arms fell away. Cold immediately rushed in.

"I'll give you your coat."

"Absolutely not."

She scooted off his lap, then sucked in her breath at the puddle of water that had collected on the seat beside him. The frigid moisture soaked through the fabric with alarming speed.

He pulled his hat low, but didn't offer it to her this time.

Leaning to the right, Anna stretched. A low groan escaped before she could suppress it.

"You all right?"

"Just a little stiff." She carefully straightened her legs as best she could. "How long was I asleep?"

"You missed dinner and supper."

"You stopped to eat and didn't wake me?"

"I never stopped. Just drove right through. So we made good time. Since we're almost home, though, I'd rather eat there if you can wait?"

"Yes. That's fine." She pushed her hair off her forehead. "Has it been raining the whole time?"

"It just started up again."

She squinted, but couldn't see more than a vague outline of Shakespeare. She couldn't imagine how Mr. Denton could see.

"Who's Leon?" he asked.

She gave him a sharp glance.

"You called out his name in your sleep."

Flipping up the collar of the jacket, she burrowed into its folds. "My little brother."

"Is he still in Massachusetts?"

"He's dead."

The rain had chased away the sounds of any nocturnal creatures, leaving behind only the incessant splattering of raindrops on the trees, the puddles, and the passengers of the wagon.

"The war?" he asked.

"Yes."

"I'm sorry."

A gust of wind shook an extra dose of moisture from the leaves overhead.

"Me too," she whispered, and huddled deeper into his jacket.

By the time he pulled the wagon to a stop, Anna's fingers, toes, and ears ached from the cold, her nose was running, and she couldn't stop shaking.

"Come on," he said, lifting her from the seat. "I'll start a fire for you, then take care of Shakespeare."

Her legs buckled as soon as they met with solid ground.

He scooped her up, then took the porch steps.

She was so stunned at being suddenly airborne, she forgot to get an impression of the house from the outside. But the moment they stepped indoors, the sweet vanilla smell of what had to be twinflowers overwhelmed her.

Mr. Denton navigated his way through the dark house, passing through one room, down a corridor, and then into another room. Again, the scent of twinflowers bombarded her.

"Here, hold on to this." He guided her hand to a hard surface.

She braced herself while he set her on her feet.

"You all right?" Large hands bracketed her waist.

"Fine, fine. I'm perfectly fine."

He released her, but his hands hovered.

"You really needn't fuss," she whispered into the quiet. "I was just unsteady for that initial moment."

"Well, I have a towel on a rack right over there. Will you be okay if I step away?"

"Yes, of course. I'm fine."

He took four quick steps, then was back with a towel. She tried to free her hands, but the sleeves of the jacket were too long.

Before she could protest, he cupped her neck and tilted her chin up with his thumb, then began blotting the moisture from her face.

She stilled in surprise. This was no rough rag, but a real towel—soft, absorbent, and smelling of sunshine. He patted her forehead, her nose, her jaw, then swiped the hair away from her face.

She closed her eyes and reached for her jacket buttons, but again, the sleeves imprisoned her hands.

Denton quickly slipped the buttons free and pushed the coat from her shoulders. It slid down her arms and onto the floor.

Raindrops tapped against glass windows. Only actual glass, not greased paper, would make that particular sound. The man obviously had done well for himself. Very well.

Opening her eyes, she could just make out Denton's silhouette. He was close. Too close.

He pressed the towel against her neck. She reached up to take it from him, her hand colliding with his.

After a slight hesitation, he stepped away. A few seconds later she heard the scraping of flint and steel.

He lit several lanterns, then went to work on a pre-laid fire. They were in a kitchen. A large, well-supplied kitchen dominated by a modern stove with a ventilated oven on one side, a fire and roaster on the other, and a hot plate over all.

Scales, spice boxes, sugar, and biscuit canisters lined a set of shelves next to boilers, saucepans, and stew pans. A corner cupboard stocked with spatterware picked up the same colors as the braided rug, but it was the high level of craftsmanship that drew her attention back to the cupboard.

Never had she seen such an elaborate piece in a kitchen. Had Mr. Denton made it, or did he merely chop down the trees and leave the carpentry for someone else?

The fire crackled, its woodsy smell overtaking that of the aromatic flowers. She glanced at a cup of wilting, pinkish-white twinflowers on a table. They were bell-shaped with two blooms per stem hanging down like tassels. Each mirrored the other. She wondered if, like honeysuckle, they made good syrup or sorbet.

Crossing the room in large strides, Denton slipped through a side door, then returned with a large pot of water.

She lifted a questioning gaze to him.

"The milk room's through there," he explained, setting the pot on the stove and opening the fire chamber. He threw in some pine for a quick hot fire, then began to light it. "I have an artesian spring that runs right by the house and have piped some in to cool the room."

Her gaze returned to the door he referred to. A milk room? And a natural spring?

Turning again to face her, he rubbed his hands on his thighs. "I'm going to see to Shakespeare and the milk cows. By the time

I'm done the water should be hot. So, sit tight and I'll be as fast as I can."

He stepped to the back door, then without turning around said, "The necessary house is just out this door and around the corner."

And then he was gone.

Even though he wanted to rush, he took his time with Shakespeare, rubbing him, brushing him, and giving him an extra scoop of feed. All the while his mind was on the woman in his house.

She'd not been happy to find herself in his lap. But she'd kept sliding off his shoulder and it had been easier to keep her still in his lap. Was also easier to keep her dry. The fact that he liked having her there was beside the point.

Shakespeare paused in his eating to cast an eye back at Joe. He realized he'd stopped his brushing and immediately resumed his task.

He shouldn't have pushed his horse so hard. He was sorry he'd done it. It was one thing for him to skip his meals. Quite another to expect Shakespeare to.

Squatting down, he began to massage the horse's back leg. What was his guest doing now, he wondered. Was she wandering through the house, soothing her curiosity? What would she think of it?

He paused. What if she went into his bedroom? Would she dare? He hoped not, because if she did she'd see the twinflowers.

Shakespeare flicked his tail. Joe resumed the massage. He'd completely forgotten about the blasted flowers until he walked through the door and their smell hit him square between the eyes.

But he'd been expecting to bring home a bride. It had seemed like a good idea when he'd gathered them and set them in every available container he had throughout the house. That was before he learned he'd be bringing home a cook instead.

He shook his head. He should never have done it to begin with.

He moved to Shakespeare's front legs. *Please, God, don't let her say anything to the boys.*

Red must have seen to the animals because the cows had been milked, the oxen, pigs, and goats fed, and the stalls cleaned. More likely he'd been curious about Joe's bride and had come to have a look-see for himself, then kept busy in the barn hoping to be here when the couple arrived.

He wondered if the crew would show up expecting breakfast in the morning. He sure hoped not.

Lifting the lantern off a nail, he gave Shakespeare a pat, then let himself out of the stall. Tucking his horse in for the night was one thing. But what exactly were his responsibilities to the woman?

She wasn't his guest. She was his cook. His employee. So that should change everything.

But it didn't. Because she was a woman. A young woman. He swallowed. A pretty woman. And one that Mercer had picked out specifically for him.

He released the top button of his shirt and cast a longing gaze at one of the empty stalls. What he wouldn't give to be able to bed out here with the animals.

He didn't dare, though. It was going to be bad enough when the boys found out Anna had refused him and the only other alternative was to pledge himself to a woman in her sixties. The last thing he wanted was to add more fuel to the fire by hiding out in his own barn.

Anna's bag caught his attention. He'd dropped it by the barn door when he'd put the wagon away. Something inside had rattled. It didn't sound like coins and, for the life of him, he couldn't figure out what it might be. The tapestry-covered bag was faded, worn, and light as a feather.

He wanted to look inside. The woman was a stranger, after

all. He knew nothing about her and the contents of the bag would tell him a lot.

Lifting it again, he tested its weight, listened to the clinking, and ran his hand over the wide buckle. In the end, he couldn't bring himself to do it. That would be like her going into his bedroom and looking through his chest of drawers.

He glanced up. If she did, she'd find half of them had been emptied for her—or his bride, that is. He quickly raised the latch on the barn door, slipped out, and jogged to the house.

Chapter Ten

Several things struck Joe at once. The kitchen abounded with light and warmth. Something smelled really, really good. And Anna was wearing one of his flannel shirts with his table linen wrapped around her body in an Indianlike fashion.

She stood facing him, her back to the fire, her hands clasped in front of her. The dress she'd worn earlier along with her boots lay on the hearth drying.

He glanced at the hem of her makeshift garment. Was she barefoot?

"Where'd you get that shirt?" he asked.

She fingered the rolled-up sleeves of his flannel. "I . . . it . . ."

His jaw slackened. "Did you go through my things?"

Glancing in the direction of his room, she moistened her lips. "I was soaked to the skin and needed to rinse out my gown and my bag was still in the wagon and you were gone such a long time and I'd be of no use to you sick, so I . . ." She gave a little shrug.

"And so you went through my drawers?"

"Only two of them."

He felt his face begin to heat. There were only four drawers in all. Two were empty and two held all his belongings—including his personals.

Avoiding his gaze, she scurried to the stove, her sarong thing restricting her stride. "I found some boiled beef in the milk room and made you some bubble and squeak, without the cabbage, of course."

Bubble and squeak?

"Go ahead and wash up." Grasping the towel he'd dried her face with earlier, she lifted a frying pan off the warming plate and brought it over to the table. The flowers had been moved aside and a place set for one. One. Not two.

She shuffled around in her linen cloth, sliding some fat potato-cake sort of things onto his plate, then added fritters without sauce. She placed three pieces of toast she'd kept on the fender onto another plate, then disappeared into the milk room.

She hesitated upon her return, a glass of milk in one hand and a bowl of some concoction in the other. "Go ahead." She pointed toward the basin stand with her head. "Wash up. I've already poured the water for you."

"Lumberjacks do not eat bubble and squawk, whatever that is."

She frowned. "Squeak. And don't be ridiculous. It's all I could manage in such a short amount of time." Lifting a brow, she injected a hint of challenge into her voice. "And if you're a good boy and clean your plate, I'll make you some pancakes."

He took a second look at the bowl in her hand. "You have pancake batter in there?"

"I do. But only those who finish their bubble and squeak get some."

He tossed his hat onto a hook and strode to the basin. Reaching for his buttons, he froze. Normally he shucked his shirt and washed all over. But he couldn't do that now. Not with her in the room. By the same token, he couldn't go to the table in a sopping wet shirt that now smelled like the barnyard.

He glanced over his shoulder. She faced the stove, her back to him, her entire body swaying as she whipped up the batter.

If she was making pancakes, there'd be no reason for her to turn around. Besides, they were going to be sharing the same kitchen for several months. He wasn't about to haul water to his room every time they had a meal.

Taking one last look to ensure she was occupied, he made quick work of his buttons, peeled off his suspenders, yanked off his shirt, and tossed it by the stairs.

With a block of soap, he swished his hands in the water, then rubbed them on his arms, his chest, his armpits, and his neck. He lathered up again and scrubbed his face. Eyes closed, he splashed water everywhere he'd soaped, then reached blindly for the towel he knew was hanging on the rail of the stand.

Burying his face in the cloth, he hesitated a moment, enjoying its soft texture and the pure pleasure of being clean after the long journey home.

He sighed, finished drying, slung the towel over the rim of the bowl, and turned around.

Anna stood with mouth agape, a wooden spoon suspended in her hand. A fat drop of batter slid from the spoon onto the floor and landed with a soft *plop*. Her gaze moved from his face to his neck, to his shoulders, to his chest.

"Oh my," she whispered.

His lungs quit working, making it impossible to draw a breath.

"You're so . . . I've never . . ." She looked at him, her expression completely befuddled.

He jumped, as if he'd just heard the roaring crackle of wood fiber and the faller call "*Timber-r-r-r!*"

Crossing the room in several quick strides, he grabbed his shirt and a lantern, turned the corner, and jogged up the stairs to his bedroom. Once there, he propped his hands against the chest of drawers and hung his head, calling himself ten kinds of a fool.

I've never . . .

Never what? Seen a man wash up? Didn't she say she had a brother? A brother old enough to fight in the war? He and his older brothers had washed up in front of their sisters all the time growing up. But Anna Ivey was not his sister.

He lifted his head and looked in the mirror attached to the dresser. Same thing he saw every day reflected back at him. Same thick neck. Same blond hair dotting his chest. Same flat stomach.

But when he tried to see himself through her eyes, he realized how huge he was compared to her. His arm alone was almost as big as her tiny little waist. What had he been thinking?

Shucking out of his wet trousers, he replaced them with another pair, then pulled on a fresh shirt. His hands were shaking so badly he couldn't get the blasted buttons through the buttonholes.

He stopped and plopped down onto the edge of his bed, burying his face in his hands. He was going to have to live like a stranger in his own house. Hiding in his room when he wanted to wash up. Getting completely dressed just to visit the privy in the mornings. He'd probably even have to keep his sleeves rolled down while in her presence.

He took his time with his buttons, shoved the tail of his shirt into his trousers, then snapped his suspenders in place. All covered up again, every button buttoned. Civilized and proper—while she strolled around his kitchen wearing a tablecloth.

He took a deep breath. A whiff of pancakes reached his nose. At least he'd be eating good. But she'd best learn loggers wouldn't—couldn't—subsist on dishes called things like bubble and squeal.

He was huge. *Huge*. And he wore no undershirt. What kind of man went around without an undershirt?

Still, she could not dispel the image of him washing with such, such gusto. The byplay of muscles on his back as he scrubbed his arms was a work of art in motion. The way he chafed his chest as if it were a washboard so fascinated her, she could only stare. And the dark blond hair at the pits of his arms . . .

She bit her lip and slid a spatula under a pancake, flipping it over. She'd watched her father wash up a thousand times at least. But he was family, not an employer or a stranger. And never, ever had Papa done so without a washcloth and certainly not with such vigor.

When Denton had turned around, she could not believe the sheer breadth of him. She didn't even know men had muscles in all those places. Why, she wasn't sure she'd be able to span the width of his arm with both hands together.

And staring at him, even thinking about it, caused a weightless feeling in her stomach.

She heard his tread on the stairs and felt heat rush to her face. She'd obviously embarrassed him, but it had happened so fast. She'd been so unprepared. Should she apologize or pretend nothing had happened?

He hovered at the doorway. Even his breathing was different from Papa's. Deeper somehow. Richer.

"Go ahead and have a seat," she said, careful to keep her back to him. "These are almost ready."

A chair scraped the floor. She transferred the pancakes to a plate, took a deep breath, turned around, and froze yet again.

He sat with both arms resting on either side of his plate, his head down, his big shoulders hunched. She barely heard his "Amen" before he sat up, picked up his flatware, and began to eat with such tremendous speed, she could, once again, only stare.

He stacked the bubble and squeak, divided it in half, stuck it in his mouth, and swallowed. The fritters followed in hot pursuit. The toast in three bites or less.

She picked up his empty plate and set down the hot cakes. He spared no time for butter. Just quartered the disks and sent them on their way in a single gulp.

How in heaven's name did he have a chance to even taste his food, much less appreciate it, when he introduced the next bite so quickly?

Plate clean, he lifted his milk and poured it down his throat. Literally. Just open and pour.

She was still standing beside his chair holding the plate he'd cleaned when he swiped his sleeve against his mouth, burped, then looked up sheepishly.

"Excuse me." A single strand of his curly blond hair was caught in the corner of his mouth.

She whisked her free hand behind her back. "Did you get enough?"

"Yes. Thank you. I hadn't expected you to cook anything tonight. But it was good." He glanced at the plate in her hand. "Why do you call that bubble and squeal?"

"Bubble and *squeak*."

"Right. Squeak."

She looked at the empty plate as if it were some foreign object. "Well, it makes a lot of noise when you cook it."

"It does?"

"Yes. At least, it would if I'd had any cabbage to sauté it with."

He cleaned his teeth with his tongue. "Well, I liked it just the way you made it. No need to get fancy with your cooking—or with the names of the dishes. Just keep it simple."

"Simple." She picked up his other plate and took them to the sideboard. "I'll try to keep that in mind."

"And even though you're just the cook, you don't have to hold your meals until I've had mine."

She stiffened. Just the cook? The cook was second in command and an immediate representative of the owner. The cook was as honest, industrious, and vigilant as if she *were* the owner. Of course, Hoke wasn't exactly a model proprietor. But that hadn't affected her work code.

She rolled up the massive sleeves of the shirt she wore. Just the cook, indeed.

He pushed his chair back and stretched out his legs. They seemed to take up half the room. "It'd be faster to eat our meals together—at least when it's only the two of us. But when you're feeding the whole crew, well, you probably won't be able to eat at the same time as all of them. Not with all the running around you'll be doing."

She hesitated, then decided she may as well discover the lay of the land now. Pouring water into the basin, she began to wash the dishes. "Actually, I already ate."

A beat of silence. "Oh. Well. Sure. If you're hungry, you can go ahead without me."

She waited, but he said no more. That was it? She'd taken her meal before him and that was all he had to say?

Looking over her shoulder, she let out a slow breath. His pose was relaxed, his expression pleasant. He was going to be much easier to work for than Hoke.

"How many men are in your crew again?"

"Fifteen, counting me." He stretched his arms above his head and yawned. "You're bound to be exhausted, Anna. Why don't you just leave those until the morning?"

She turned back to her chore. "I slept the whole day away. Remember? You go on, though. I'll put everything to rights down here before I head up."

"No, no. I'll wait."

"Suit yourself." She finished the dishes, dried them, and put them away before finally turning to wipe down the table.

Eyes closed, elbow propped on the arm of his chair, head resting in his hand, Denton slept.

She smiled. He slept with his mouth open. Made him look sweet. Vulnerable.

She wiped the table and stove, hung out the cloth, put out the lanterns, and sprinkled the fire with sand. Clouds obscured the moonlight, shadows filled the room.

"Mr. Denton?" she whispered.

He didn't answer.

She felt her way to his chair, almost tripping over his legs.

"Mr. Denton?" She touched his arm.

Still no response.

She shook his shoulder. "Mr. Denton?" She shook a little harder. "Joe. Wake up."

His breath cut off. He lifted his head. "Huh? What?"

"Where's my room?"

"Anna?" His voice was drowsy with sleep.

"Yes."

He tucked his feet under him. "You all finished?"

"That's right, but I don't know where my room is."

Yawning, he stood. "Take whichever one you want, I guess."

"Here? In the house?"

"Of course."

She blinked. "Well, that's very generous. Thank you."

"My pleasure." He waved his hand. "After you."

She glanced at the back door. "Aren't you going to leave first?"

"Leave?"

"Well, yes. You just said I could have a room upstairs."

"You can."

She sighed. "If I'm upstairs, then you can't stay here, too. It wouldn't be proper."

"I live here."

"I know, but what would people think?"

"They won't think anything."

Surely he didn't believe she was that gullible. She wished she could see him better. "Mr. Denton, I'm afraid I must insist. The two of us cannot stay in the same house. It simply isn't done."

"It's done all the time."

"Not with me, it's not."

"Where is it exactly that you expect me to sleep?"

She shrugged. "With your men, I suppose."

"I can't. I'm the boss. It would make them uncomfortable."

"Well, it would make me uncomfortable if you stayed here. What about the barn? You do have a barn, don't you?"

He said nothing for a long minute. "You expect me to sleep in the barn when I have a perfectly good bed upstairs?"

She sighed. "No. No, of course not. I'll sleep in the barn."

"You will not."

"I don't mind."

"I do."

"Then we have a problem, sir."

Her eyes had adjusted enough to see him run a hand through his hair. "Fine. I'll sleep in the barn. But I'm not moving out of my own house. I'm still eating here, leaving all my clothes here, and washing up here."

She started to object but stopped herself. It was late. He was tired. And he was big.

"Thank you."

He didn't say "you're welcome." Just stood there.

"Go ahead," he said. "I'll leave after you go upstairs."

She hesitated. "You promise?"

"I do."

After a tense moment, she made her way toward the stairs, but misjudged and ran into the wall. *"Umph."*

"Here." He walked up behind her, fumbled around for her arm, then ran his fingers down until he had her hand in his. "Follow me."

Goose bumps jumped to the surface of her skin. He moved to the stairs with her in tow. She swallowed her protest, concentrating instead on keeping the dragging tablecloth in place.

Even his hands are big, she thought. And coarse to the touch. But they were gentle as he led her up the steps and to the room across from the one he ordinarily occupied.

Leaving her, he crossed her threshold and lit a lantern. He might be big. He might be handsome. No, gorgeous. But he didn't preen or sashay about like Hoke. It was as if he wasn't even aware of his appeal.

And he had complete control of his faculties. She'd refused his proposal, eaten ahead of him, gone through his personal belongings, and kicked him out of his own home. Yet he'd done no more than scowl and sputter. No, he was nothing like Hoke.

"Here you go. This will do for tonight. If you'd rather have one of the other rooms, you can switch tomorrow."

She didn't need to look at the other rooms. She'd already seen them when she was exploring earlier. This one was by far the nicest—other than his, of course. "This will be fine."

"Here are your things." He patted her carpetbag, making it clack, then set it next to the lantern. He must have grabbed it off the peg before they left the kitchen.

"Thank you."

"What's inside it making that noise?"

"Seashells."

"Seashells?"

"I collect them."

He glanced at the bag, then stepped around her and into the hall. "Don't worry about cooking breakfast in the morning. You just get some rest. We'll lay out your duties later."

"Thank you."

He ran his gaze over her hair, the shirt she'd absconded with, and the table linen shrouding her.

"Well," she said. "Good night."

"Good night."

He didn't move.

"See you tomorrow, then." She took a step back and quietly shut the door.

It was several more seconds before she heard him go down the stairs and out the door.

Chapter Eleven

Joe glanced at the angle of the sun. It'd be quitting time soon. He swung his ax a little faster. Red matched his pace.

Legs straddled and bodies hunched, they moved in harmony, their double-bitted blades striking deep. First Joe's, then Red's. They needed to fell the tree before hitting the sundown trail.

The crew had been unusually solemn all day, trying to gauge Joe's mood. Only Red had braved any direct questions.

"So? D'you get her?"

"Yes."

Two hours and three trees later, Red swiped a bandana across his freckled forehead. "You married, then?"

"No."

And that was the end of the talking. Nobody dared to say any more, knowing that Joe's land, his operation, and their livelihoods depended on his securing a wife. And if he hadn't done that, then he was sure to be short-fused.

The sun slanted lower. Their shadows lengthened. The ringing thuds of their axes quickened even more. Chips of wood flew from the deepening notch.

Joe wondered if Anna really would be able to cook for his men. There were only fourteen, but they had awfully big appetites.

He let his shoulders do the work, his arms acting as an extension of the ax handle. She'd be hard-pressed to manage it if she tried to get too fancy. Meat and beans would do for now.

Besides, beans to a logger were like oats to a horse. But they needed to have a decent flavor. He'd had many a logger walk off the job because the grub was no good.

The upper part of the notch they were cutting finally met up with the level cut they'd sawed earlier.

"She's notched," he said, sinking his ax into a neighboring tree. "Let's saw some timber."

Scraping a lock of orange hair off his face, Red moved to the side opposite the notch and bent his large frame over. In unison, the two men picked up their respective ends of a ten-foot crosscut saw. With a feathery touch acquired from years of working together, they played it to and fro, its teeth instantly biting into the bark. Crouching lower, they lengthened their strokes, each pulling the saw in turn, but never pushing.

Morning had arrived just a few short hours after Joe had retired last night. It was still dark and Anna was still abed. He'd left her a note, telling her to expect them for the evening meal. He hadn't told her what to cook. Hadn't told her to make the coffee strong. Hadn't told her the boys were partial to pies.

The saw snagged as it hit a pitch-pocket. Joe paused while Red grabbed a kerosene bottle and sloshed some on the blade; then they started up again.

He needed to tell the boys about Mrs. Wrenne, and he needed to do it before supper. No need to mention her age or her need for a dentist, though. They'd find that out soon enough.

The saw jerked and stuck again, but this time it wasn't the pitch. The weight of the tree was leaning on it. Leaving the trapped saw where it was, Joe grabbed an iron wedge and tapped it into the slot with a sledgehammer. Three blows later, the saw was free.

Leaving the wedge where it was, he and Red took up the crosscut once more. Joe concentrated on the task at hand. It wouldn't be long now.

Sweat dripped into his eyes. A spurt of sawdust flew onto his knees with each pull of the blade. A few minutes later a telltale crackle sounded a warning.

"*Timber-r-r-r!*" he shouted, leaping behind the shelter of a nearby spruce, then looking over to make sure Red had done the same.

It wasn't a large sawing tree, only a hundred feet aloft and thirty inches through the trunk. But it was big enough to kill if a fellow got in its way.

The trunk popped as the fibers between the notch and the saw-kerf split, each pop a tiny explosion. And then she was falling. Right between an old snag and a young sapling. Right where they'd aimed.

One of the branches struck a dead stub that jutted out from the snag. The stub erupted into a hundred rotten pieces. One chunk flew back, hurtling through the air and crashing to the ground with the force of a blacksmith's anvil. It landed right where Joe'd been standing during the sawing.

He and Red locked gazes. A huge grin split Joe's face; then he threw back his head and released a battle cry as loud and fierce as any warrior's. By jingo, but he loved his job.

He wanted to jog ahead. Wanted to warn her they were coming. Wanted to ask her if she needed any help. But Joe kept his pace leisurely and stayed with the men, acting as if he hadn't a care in the world.

The closer they came to the house, the quieter the fellows grew, until all fell silent. The giant lean-to attached to the back of the house came into view. Under it, his thirty-foot table had been set and stood in readiness. Smells similar to those that used to come from his mother's kitchen wafted on the breeze, overlaid with the sweet scent of warm bread.

He stopped and the men stacked up behind him. "I want everybody washing up before meals from now on. Everybody. You got that, Thirsty?"

"I heard ya."

"But I don't want you doing it in view of the house. I'll get you some soap; then I want you to head back up to the spring beyond the trees to do your washing."

Nobody moved. Nobody said a thing.

The screen door connecting to the kitchen flew open and slammed shut behind Anna as she hurried down the steps, balancing six platters on her left arm and carrying a seventh in her right hand. The woman had obviously done some serving in that restaurant she'd cooked for.

She had on the same gown she'd worn for the past two days, but it was starched and carefully ironed. A white apron covered the front of her skirt and tied in the back with a perfectly formed bow, calling attention to her tiny, tiny waist.

Her hair was neatly combed and banded at the back with a ribbon. The breeze picked up the tail of her hair and tossed it over her shoulder. She flicked it back with a shrug and at that moment saw everybody standing there as if they'd spilled a load of logs.

She came to an abrupt halt, her lips parting.

"Get," Joe said to the boys under his breath. "Red, go grab some soap."

The men scattered and Red jumped to do his bidding, making an exaggerated circle around Anna before disappearing inside the kitchen.

It hadn't rained since morning, but it had been cloudy all day. The sun hadn't made an appearance until it started descending and dropped below the clouds. Now it bathed Anna in its rays, picking out the highlights in her hair.

Red slammed back out of the kitchen, leaping over the steps altogether, then made another loop around Anna as if she had some fatal disease. Joe tracked his progress toward the section of the spring that ran through the trees, watching until he disappeared from sight.

Only then did he turn back to Anna. "Everything all right?"

She jumped forward, much like the oxen did when they heard the sound of the bullwhip.

"Yes, yes. Everything's ready." Placing the platters on the table, she glanced toward the trees. "Are they coming?"

"They're washing up."

Her gaze collided with his, one platter suspended and her cheeks filling with pink. He knew what she was thinking and she knew he knew.

Sauntering forward, he glanced at the platters. Doughnuts. Every platter on the table was heaped with doughnuts. Sweet Mackinaw. She'd have fourteen proposals before the blessing was even finished.

Why he didn't wash up at the spring with the boys, he didn't know and didn't question. He just moved past her, went directly to the stand in the corner of the kitchen, and poured water from the ewer into the basin.

He took his time, scrubbing, humming, lathering, and scrubbing some more. He knew she was looking. Could feel it. When he was all done, he toweled off, picked up his dirty shirt, and headed to his room for a fresh one, never once looking her way.

The minute he disappeared from sight, she released the gravy spoon and pressed a hand to her stomach. She hadn't wanted to look at him. Hadn't needed to, even. As soon as she'd heard the sounds, her mind filled in the rest.

Yet she'd looked anyway. Drawn to the sight as surely as

Aphrodite was to Ares. And, heaven help her, she really took her time, checking to see if her memory had served her well.

It had. Still, she noticed things she'd missed the first go-round. The way his hair kinked up at the ends when it got wet. The way his arm muscles were so big they scraped his sides. The way his waist was extremely trim compared to his shoulders. The way his trousers caught on his hips, suspenders rocking in time to his scrubbing.

She heard him come out of his room and jerked herself into motion. Grabbing the potatoes and gravy, she raced out the door—determined to be outside before he made it around the corner—snagged her heel on the bottom step, and fell. In a reflexive effort to free her hands and break her fall, she launched both bowls across the lean-to.

Clumps of creamy potatoes flung themselves from the bowl. The gravy somersaulted twice, plopping to the ground directly in front her. Its contents splattered the ground, her dress, and her face, stinging her skin with its heat. Both bowls broke, the sound loud in the awful silence.

She lay still for a second, the wind completely knocked out of her, then lifted her gaze. The entire company of men stood suspended halfway out of their chairs, some with doughnuts in their hands, all with horrified expressions.

The screen squeaked open and Joe's rapid footfalls descended. He lifted her as if she weighed no more than a mite. "Ronny, take care of this mess for her, would you?"

Then he slipped his arm around her and assisted her back into the kitchen.

Joe lowered her into a chair by the fireplace and squatted down beside her. "Are you all right? Did anything burn you?"

"I ruined the potatoes and the gravy!" She looked at him, her eyes flooding.

Oh no. Oh no. Don't cry. What am I going to do if she cries?

"Shhhh. It's all right." A blob of gravy slid down her cheek. Scooping it up with his finger, he transferred it to his mouth, then raised his brows. "Mmm. That's good. Do you mind?" He pointed to her forehead.

Frowning, she swiped her forehead, then touched the gravy on her finger with her tongue.

"So what do you think?" he asked.

"It *is* good." A tiny bit of mischief sprung into her eyes. "Is there any more?"

He chuckled. "I seem to recall a whole potful on the landing out there." He squeezed her hand. "Sit tight for a minute."

Moving to the washbasin, he grabbed the towel, poured water onto one corner, then brought it to her.

"I'm sorry, Joe," she said, cleaning her face and neck. "I know the men have put in a full day and are really hungry. I've served food for years, and never, ever have I dropped a platter or bowl before."

She wiped off her gown, scrunching up her chin in order to see if she'd missed any spots. The watch on her breast wobbled. Was she even aware she'd used his Christian name?

He didn't think so.

"It's all right," he said. "Everybody has a first time, I suppose."

"You're right, I'm sure." She sighed. "I just wish mine hadn't been before I'd had a chance to even meet your men." Squaring her shoulders, she looked him right in the eye. "Did I get it all?"

He'd probably never be invited to look his fill again, so he decided not to rush through this time. He started with her honey-colored hair, then moved over creamy skin to brown eyebrows. Their natural arch framed eyes of a much deeper and richer shade of brown. They were lined with long black lashes and shaped like sideways teardrops.

Her nose was small and dainty. Her cheeks rosy. Her lips full.

He lowered his gaze. Her long, graceful neck led to delicate shoulders and . . .

"Perfect," he whispered.

"Good." Anna placed her hands on the arms of the chair, then winced.

"Your ankle?" He glanced at the frayed hem of her gown.

"No." Flipping her hands over, she inspected scuffed-up palms.

"I'll get some salve."

"No, no." She brushed off embedded bits of gravel, then wiped her hands on her apron. "They're fine. I'm fine. You go out there now so I can finish serving supper. Otherwise your men might shrivel up and blow away."

He helped her to her feet. "Lumberjacks do not shrivel up and blow away."

"All the same, you'd best join them."

"You're sure you're all right?"

"I'm fine."

"You need any help?"

"No. I'll be careful. Now, shoo."

A dot of potatoes just beneath her ear caught his attention. He bent forward, thinking only to cut out the middleman and taste directly with his lips, when her eyes widened.

Straightening, he took a quick step back. "You, um, you missed a spot right there below your left ear."

She touched her neck, coming away with the dollop of potato. "Thank you."

"You're welcome." He continued to back up, ran into the screen, then turned and joined his men.

Chapter Twelve

Anna didn't have time for any embarrassment. Within eight minutes the men devoured the food that had taken her all afternoon to prepare. She set out platters of cold cuts, beans, salad, and vegetables, then returned to fill their cups with coffee, only to find their plates empty and ready for more.

A few of the men were young and fresh faced, but most looked to be in their thirties with weather-beaten, wind-burned faces. All were loud and rambunctious, yet perfect gentlemen.

Reaching around a stocky man with hair so blond it was almost white, she set out the last pan of spicy cinnamon rolls. The tin barely touched the table before a dozen hands emptied it of its contents.

Shaking her head, she looked up and down the long row of men. "Who's Ronny?"

A boy who'd kept his head tucked and close to his plate during the meal now lifted it. "I'm Ronny."

Her heart stopped. He looked exactly the way she imagined Leon would have if his life hadn't been cut short. Same brown eyes.

Same smile. Same brown hair with a stubborn little lock that fell just above his right eyebrow.

"Th-thank you, Ronny, for cleaning up the potatoes and gravy."

"It was no trouble, miss." He pushed up the sleeves of a shirt two sizes too big for him.

Such a simple, unconscious action, yet it evoked powerful memories that she quickly suppressed. "Where are the bowls?"

"He ate 'em."

The man who'd spoken had freckles all over, and his short, carrot-colored hair stuck out in tufts.

"The shards?" she asked. "Of the bowls?"

The men laughed.

"Wouldn't surprise me," somebody answered. "Got a cast-iron stomach, that one does."

Ronny ducked his head, turning several shades of red. "They're right over there on the chopping block, miss."

She walked to the block, expecting to find a mess of food and gravel coating the pieces of earthenware, yet other than a streak of gravy and a smidgen of potatoes, they were clean. "Where's the potatoes and gravy?"

"I told you. He ate 'em."

She turned to Ronny. "You ate them? The ones I flung all over the ground?"

Grinning sheepishly, he shrugged. "They were good. A little gritty, but good."

She smiled, then searched out Joe to see his reaction.

He'd been watching her. For how long, she didn't know. He tore a bite off his cinnamon roll, bits of sugar glaze sticking to his lips, then winked. Something deep inside her stomach tightened. Wrenching her gaze away, she returned to the kitchen for the last of the coffee.

As soon as the men left the table, they dispersed to take care of the chores. Several headed down to the barn to milk the cows, feed the pigs and chickens, muck out the stalls, and collect the eggs. All wore pants cut off at the calf.

The man with white-blond hair filled a huge caldron with water and set it to boil. Young Ronny sat on the porch churning butter. To his left a chestnut tree ripe with fruit leaned dangerously close to the house. She wondered why Joe hadn't chopped it down.

Scanning the yard, she spotted him propping a log end-up on the block. He swung his ax in a generous arc that involved arms, shoulders, back, waist, and legs. Each time he struck, the log flew off the block in two neat pieces with a loud snap. Picking up one of the pieces, he repeated the motion, splitting it into quarters.

Balancing a tin tub on her hip, Anna collected the dirty cups, plates, and flatware. The logs could have been jackstraws for as little effort as it took him. She glanced his direction again just as his ax connected with the wood.

"Water's hot," said the man with white-blond hair as he made his way to the garden.

Flushing at being caught staring, she finished collecting the dishes and moved to the caldron, keeping her attention on what she was doing. Still, she found herself scrubbing in time to the sound of Joe's chopping.

She'd just finished with the dishes when the men returned from the barn, each taking a load of the newly cut wood into the house. For the first time, she noted they all wore their shirts loose. She realized the oversized shirts gave them more freedom in their movements. But why the shortened pants?

One by one, they dropped their lunch buckets by the back door, then thanked her for their meal.

"Good night, miss. Those cinnamon rolls sure were good."

"You rest up and we'll see you in the morning."

"Hope you don't hold a grudge toward taters now. Ronny says they sure were creamy, other than the dirt, o' course."

With each parting comment, her throat filled a little more so that by the time they'd all said their good-byes, she could hardly even speak.

She'd been cooking her whole life, it seemed, but never for a more appreciative and thoughtful bunch as these overgrown lumberjacks of the Pacific Northwest.

Bit by bit the thick forest swallowed them as they walked away, a wake of laughter and easy conversation rippling behind them until only the sounds of crickets and frogs were left.

Joe planted his ax in the chopping block. "That was a fine meal, Anna. The boys will have an extra spring in their step tomorrow knowing they'll end their day with another meal like tonight's."

Darkness had fully descended, but light from the kitchen windows spilled out, providing illumination. He stood with his weight on one foot, hip cocked, hand resting on the handle of his ax.

"I'm going to need some supplies," she said. "Your storeroom's well stocked, but there's a few things missing that would really round it out."

"You make up a list for Red. He and Gibbs are driving a load of logs down the skid tomorrow. They can pick up whatever you need while they're in town."

"Thank you."

They looked at each other across the expanse of the yard.

She moistened her lips. "I hadn't expected the men to do my chores, but I'm very thankful. I wasn't sure how I was going to get all of them done and the cooking, too."

"The boys are used to it. Besides, with you here they no longer have to share cooking duty. These other chores are minor by comparison. If there's something else you need done that wasn't, well, you just let me know."

"Thank you. I will."

He walked into the kitchen, a dark stain of sweat making a *V* at the back of his shirt. She wiped down the chairs. And even though it was too dark to see very well, she swept the dirt floor of the lean-to. She wanted to give Joe plenty of time to wash up before she went inside.

⁂

Two evenings later, Red and Gibbs pulled up with the supplies Anna had requested.

"Everything go all right?" Joe asked, rubbing the noses of the oxen harnessed to the wagon.

"Yep." Red jumped down from the seat.

The rest of the men had already returned to camp for the night, so Joe, Red, and Gibbs unloaded the wagon. Anna rushed between the kitchen and the milk room showing the men where she wanted the bags of flour, crates of fruit, barrels of meat, and jars of syrup.

"I guess that does it, then," Gibbs said, following Joe out of the house and down the porch steps.

Red closed the bed of the wagon. "I'll take care of the animals."

Gibbs stopped. "You sure?"

"Yeah. You go on. If you hurry, you might just make it for a round of poker."

Changing course, Gibbs set off at a jog. "Thanks, Red. I owe you one."

Joe and Red watched him until he was out of sight.

"I thought you said everything went all right?" Joe kept his voice low so Anna wouldn't hear him through the open windows.

"Walk with me to the barn while I put the oxen to bed."

The men walked in silence. Joe knew better than to rush his friend. When Red was ready to talk, he'd talk.

Joe unlatched the barn door and swung it wide. Red was the first friend he'd made when his family moved from Georgia to Maine back in '46. Joe was nine at the time and old enough to support himself. So he got a job in a dairy milking cows for room and board. Red's family owned the dairy.

"Met the woman you pledged yourself to."

Joe stopped short for a second, then unhitched the wagon.

"Not quite what I was expecting," Red continued.

"Well, she's exactly what I was expecting."

"She was?"

Joe gave him a pointed look. "Mercer was the one conducting the affair."

His friend didn't say any more until the wagon was stored and the animals tended. Lifting a lantern off a nail, Red headed toward the back of the barn. Sighing, Joe followed.

They entered the last stall, but instead of an animal, it held a barrel, two stools, and an unmade cot. Red studied the cot, then looked at Joe. "Who's been sleeping here?"

Joe slipped his hands in his pockets. "It wouldn't be right for me to stay at the house with Anna, so I'm bedding down here."

Red stared at him for a minute before laughter rumbled up out of his chest. He didn't belabor the point, though. Just hung the lantern and picked up a worn deck of cards. They played two games of Casino before he finally loosened his tongue.

"You really planning to marry Mrs. Wrenne?"

"I want to keep my land, Red."

He shuffled the cards. *Thuuuuurump-whoosh. Thuuuuurump-whoosh.* "What's wrong with that pretty little girl you got up at the house?"

"She doesn't believe in marriage."

Red slapped the deck down for Joe to cut. "Well, I suggest you start making a believer out of her."

"Actually, I think marrying Mrs. Wrenne is really the better choice. She wants a husband, and from what I understand, any husband will do. I need a wife and any wife will do. So why not?"

"Why not? *Why not?*"

Joe raised a brow. "You going to deal?"

Red grabbed the deck. "That woman has to be sixty at least."

"Which means she'll be sensible and levelheaded. So she gets what she wants, and I get what I want."

"You want a sixty-year-old wife?"

"I want my land." He arranged his cards. "I'll be good to her. She'll be well taken care of and I'll let her have her choice of the spare rooms. No sin in that. You got any queens?"

Sighing, Red shook his head. "Go fish."

Joe drew a card, laid it on the barrel top, then pulled three out of his hand and stacked them, making a book.

"Seems to me that keeping Miss Ivey warm and dry wouldn't be too much of a chore," Red mumbled.

"I've known Anna for four days. You've only sat at her table once. How would you know if she's a chore or not? How would either of us know?"

"Anna, is it? She call you Joe?"

"Not intentionally. Only when she's distracted."

Red lifted his brows. "You got any aces?"

Stifling an oath, Joe slapped down three aces.

Red laid down his own book. "Eights?"

"Go fish."

"When are you and Mrs. Wrenne supposed to tie the knot, then?"

"The judge gave me seven weeks to find a bride and not a minute more—no matter what happens. But once Mercer assigned Mrs. Wrenne to me, I figured I better go ahead with it. She had some things she wanted to take care of first, though. I'm supposed to go back for her at the end of the month. You got any queens?"

Red handed him one. "So you have about three weeks before the big day?"

"Um-hum. Twos?"

"Go fish." Red leaned back in his chair. "You got a telegram from Mercer while I was in town today. Threes?"

Joe shook his head. "What'd Mercer want now?"

"He had some information about Mrs. Wrenne that he thought

you should know about." Red made another book. "So Harvey Kittrell at the telegraph office gave the telegram to me. I'm supposed to pass it along to you."

"Well? What'd it say?"

Reaching into his pocket, Red tossed a piece of paper on the barrel. Joe placed his cards facedown and picked up the telegram.

> *To J Denton* STOP *Urgent News* STOP *Bertha Wrenne's husband not dead* STOP *Is returned from confederate prison camp* STOP *Followed Wrenne here* STOP *Will be in Seattle in two days* STOP *A S Mercer* STOP

Joe slowly lifted his gaze to Red's. "I can't believe you sat here this whole time and never said anything. Who else knows?"

"Just you, me, and Harvey Kittrell. I told him you'd be the one to give Mrs. Wrenne the news and also told him I'd take it personally if word got out." Red smiled. "He won't be saying anything."

Joe reread the telegram.

"You think the judge will give you another extension?" Red asked.

"Not a chance."

"Then I recommend you put on your courting shoes and woo Miss Anna Ivey." Red held out his freckled, beefy hand. "Now, give me those queens you've been asking for."

Chapter Thirteen

Joe lay on his cot, the smell of animals surrounding him. He should be happy for Bertha. And he was. But that left him right back where he started.

Well, not exactly. This time, he had an unmarried, comely female living in his house. Cooking his meals. Having no interaction with anyone other than him and his crew. And she was ripe for the picking.

An owl seeking a mate let off a series of monotonous whistles. Over and over and over. Like a minstrel of old tooting the same note on his recorder, endlessly. And though the sound grated, Joe felt a touch of empathy for the frustrated male.

Hooking his hands behind his head, he sighed. He needed to tell Mrs. Wrenne. Tomorrow—before her husband showed up and found out she was betrothed to another. Thank goodness they hadn't gotten married.

He toyed with going to the judge again, but Joe'd barely gotten that last extension. If he asked for yet another, no telling what Rountree would do.

That left him with about six weeks to try to change Anna's mind. He'd like to tell her straight out what was going on. But she seemed to have something against marriage, and he still remembered her outrage on Mrs. Wrenne's behalf—claiming he was "using" her.

He kicked the blanket off, leaving the sheet. It was only "using" if the arrangement was one-sided. But marrying Anna would be just as beneficial to her as it would be to him.

She'd obviously fallen on hard times. As his wife, she'd be provided for. She'd be protected. She'd be living in one of the finest homes in the Territory. And if she wanted, he'd even be willing to make the marriage real in every sense so she could become a mother. What more could she want?

He worked his foot out from underneath the covers so it could breathe, his mind turning over the possibility of her bearing children. His children. He swallowed. Red was right on that score. It'd be no chore to take Anna to wife.

The problem was how to get around her aversion to marriage. He shook his head. A woman who didn't want to marry went against all laws of nature.

The whys of it didn't matter, though. What mattered was securing his land, and Anna was his last hope. The most expedient and logical thing to do was make her fall in love with him.

Slinging his arm across his face, he closed his eyes. Just how exactly was he supposed to do that? She'd shown a bit of interest in him those first couple of times he'd washed up, but she'd made herself scarce ever since.

Was it him personally or men in general she had an aversion to? At mealtimes, she held her own with the boys, accepting their teasing with smiles and quips of her own. She certainly wasn't shy around them, or even him, for that matter.

Yet she'd made it clear that first day she never wanted to wed. He dragged his fingers through his hair. It just didn't make any sense. But he needed to marry her, and the sooner the better. So he'd best stake a claim before one of the boys decided to.

He stilled. Had any of them caught her eye already? She seemed rather partial to Ronny, but he was just a boy. Of course, she was closer to Ronny's age than Joe's. But the attention she gave the skid greaser was more motherly than anything else. Still, he'd let the boys know she was not only off limits, but she was his.

Which brought him right back to where he started. How by all that was holy could he convince her to marry him?

Punching his pillow, he rolled to his side. Lorraine sure hadn't needed convincing. As a matter of fact, she'd done most of the pursuing.

But he'd watched his brothers court girl after girl after girl. All it took was . . . He cringed. They'd splashed tonic on their hair, picked flower bouquets, wrote sonnets, went on buggy rides, and acted like perfect idiots.

He slid his eyes closed. How was he supposed to do that way out here in the wilderness? He couldn't. He wouldn't. But he had to do something. And he had to do it quick.

⁂

The house smelled of vinegar, bacon, and bread. And no wonder. Six pies cooled on a table in the kitchen. Bacon, crisp and ready, had been set aside. Doughnuts filled a half dozen platters. *How long has she been up*? he wondered, heading straight for the coffeepot.

Facing the stove, she dumped a handful of chopped onions into a saucepan. She'd coiled up her hair and skewered it to her head with what appeared to be a larding needle. Already rebellious bits and pieces had slipped loose.

"I'm going to town."

Anna placed a pot of water on to boil. "Town?"

"Yes."

She dried her hands on her apron. "But Red and Gibbs just went."

Not wanting to tell her about Bertha's husband just yet, he merely shrugged.

She propped her hands on her waist. "Well, you sure did a lot of bellyaching about how you couldn't be away from work and how you didn't want to be going back and forth to town."

He grinned. She was already sounding like a wife.

"You going to miss me, Anna?"

Her eyes widened. "I . . . well, no, I just . . ." She whirled around and began hastily slicing up bread. The scissor motion caused her skirt to swirl and hug her hips.

She was wearing her dark blue dress today. As far as he could tell, she only owned it and the brown one. Threadbare as the wool dresses were, they still had to be hot in this kitchen. Particularly this time of year.

Maybe he'd pick her up some fabric. He couldn't bring her flowers. That would be too suspect. Especially after the twinflower debacle.

He'd wasted no time in gathering up those wild flowers and throwing them out, but it would be a while before he forgave himself for that impulse. Fabric, however, would be perfect. It would be something she'd love, yet something he could somewhat justify.

Scratching his cheek, he considered how he was going to give one girl fabric while being "betrothed" to another. "Would you like me to pick up anything while I'm there?"

She paused, cocking her head to the side and exposing the slope of that pretty neck. His gaze lingered. When they were married, that'd be his for the taking, Lord willing.

"No," she said, returning to her bread. "I think I have everything. Thank you, though."

He walked up behind her. Close behind her. She took a sudden breath, her knife snagging in the bread, then stopping altogether.

Sandwich makings lay neatly stacked on the table. Reaching

around her, he lifted several slices of ham and laid them on three separate pieces of bread. With each motion the inside of his arm grazed the outside of hers.

She didn't use any scents when she bathed, but he knew she bathed most every day. Not only because she was always so clean and fresh-looking come suppertime, but because each time he put the tub away, he'd find it back out that same evening propped against the side of the house to dry.

"I can do that for you," she whispered as he added cheese and sliced pickles to his sandwiches.

"That's all right. You go ahead with what you're doing."

She started cutting, but had taken no more than a few saws when they both froze. The motion had caused her hips to brush his legs. Joe looked down. Her chest was rising and falling in time to her quick, short breaths. The watch pin above her breast rocked.

"What do you have against marriage, Anna?"

"Nothing. I love going to weddings."

"I'm not talking about other people's weddings. I'm talking about your own." Placing a hand on her waist, he leaned far enough over to snag two boiled eggs. "Why don't you want to marry?"

She began to step out of his way, but he'd boxed her in—his hand on one side of her waist, his body leaning across the other. Setting down the knife, she laid both palms flat on the table. "I don't know. I guess I have no desire to enter into that particular state."

"Why not?"

Looking down, she said nothing.

"Were you married before? Is that it?"

Anna shook her head.

"Left at the altar?"

"No."

"You have a special someone you're pining for?"

"No. Nothing like that."

"Were your parents unhappy in their marriage?"

Her gaze flew to his, bringing her face close as she looked at him over her shoulder. "Oh no. They loved each other very much."

Looking into her earnest brown eyes, he frowned. "You don't have anything against, um, men, do you?"

His shoulders lost their tension at her look of confusion.

"There are some men I don't like, but I have nothing against the actual gender."

"Then why don't you want to get married?"

"I just don't."

"Not ever? For your whole entire life?"

"Not ever. For my whole entire life."

"Why not?"

"It's not something I talk about."

Joe hesitated, then released her to wrap his sandwiches in paper.

She quickly scurried to the table lined with vinegar pies. "Would you like some pie?"

"Sure."

She cut him a huge slice, then wrapped it.

"Thank you."

"You're welcome."

Dropping his sandwiches, the two eggs, and the pie into a lunch bucket, he decided not to press her anymore about marriage. He had a few weeks yet. He could afford to take his time. He headed toward the door.

"Are you leaving right now?" she asked.

"I am."

"Without your breakfast?"

"I wanted an early start."

"Surely you have time for some hot cakes? The batter's made. It'll only take a minute to cook some up." Whirling around, she moved a frying pan from the back of the stove to the front. "Sit down."

"Will you eat with me?"

"I eat after the men. It's easier that way." She poured several circles of batter into the large pan. While waiting for them to bubble, she peeled four boiled eggs and arranged them on a plate.

Pilfering one of the doughnuts, he tore off a bite. The sugary pastry melted in his mouth. The woman sure could cook. His crew spent the mornings talking about what they'd had for breakfast and the afternoons speculating about supper.

True to her word, Anna finished the hot cakes quickly, flipping them from the pan to a plate and garnishing them with bacon. "I haven't made the oats or potatoes yet."

"This will be fine." He stuffed the rest of his doughnut into his mouth, then broke his boiled eggs between his hot cakes and smothered all with a generous amount of butter and syrup.

She returned to slicing bread for the men's sandwiches. "When will you be back?"

"Tomorrow."

"Tomorrow?" She slowly turned.

"Yes." He made quick work of his meal, then pulled his napkin from his neck and tossed it on the table. "That was good. Thanks." Heading to the door, he snatched up his lunch bucket.

"Joe?"

He paused, his hand on the knob. She'd done it again. Used his Christian name. "Yes?"

"You'll be gone all night?"

"Yes."

"The whole, entire night?"

"Yes."

"Oh." She twisted her fingers in her apron.

"Is something wrong?"

"No, no. I just . . . wondered." She crossed, then uncrossed her arms. The watch pin begged for attention.

He ignored it. "What is it?"

"Nothing."

"It's something."

"It's nothing." She spun back to the bread.

He studied her rigid back as comprehension dawned. "You won't be scared to be all by yourself and me out of calling distance, will you?"

"No!" She took a deep breath, her shoulders slowly rising, then falling. "No. I just wondered."

He smiled. She was scared, all right. But so much the better. That would make her wish he were with her. "If we were married, I'd stay and protect you."

She stiffened. "I'll have you know I was on my own long before I came here. I didn't need a man then, and I certainly don't need one now."

She slammed a saucepan onto the stove.

He didn't even try to hide his amusement. "Anna?"

She looked at him over her shoulder.

"Sweet dreams." He gave her a wink, then let himself out.

Bertha Wrenne clutched the Occidental's staircase railing, wearing a bright purple gown with black buttons, black ruffled collar, and black braid accents on her sleeves and bodice.

"Joe," she said, extending a gloved hand. "What a pleasant surprise."

"Bertha." He removed his hat and kissed her offered hand. "So nice to see you again. Can I interest you in a stroll about town?"

"Why, I'd be delighted." Stepping outside, she opened a purple parasol—*parasol*—with a black ruffly edge, then placed it on her shoulder, twirling it as they walked.

"New dress?" he asked.

"It is. Do you like it?"

"It is very becoming." He tipped his hat to passersby, then led

Mrs. Wrenne down a less-busy side street. "We need to talk about our betrothal, Bertha."

"Oh, rest assured, Dr. Barnard is working as quickly as he can. My teef might eben be ready by next—"

"Bertha?" He stopped, turning the woman to face him and taking her hand in his. "I have some news from San Francisco."

"News?" She frowned, bringing a collection of wrinkles together at the bridge of her nose. "What news?"

"It seems your husband is not dead after all, but was a prisoner of the Confederates. He's returned and will be here in Seattle today or tomorrow."

Her face slackened. "Clement? He's alibe?"

"He is."

"And coming here?"

"Today or tomorrow."

Her breathing grew labored and her tiny little eyes filled. "Are you certain it's my Clement?"

"I received a telegram from Mr. Mercer saying it was."

She slowly pulled her hand from his and looked around as if her husband might materialize at any moment. "I . . . I can't beliebe it."

He said nothing while she took a few moments to absorb the news. A series of emotions crossed her face, before finally settling on a joy that gave him a brief glimpse of the beauty that must have first drawn Clement Wrenne to her so many years ago.

Eyes shining, she placed her hand on Joe's arm. "You are a berry kind man, Mr. Denton, but I'm afraid I can't marry you. I must go back to my precious Clement."

"I completely understand and please don't worry. I will still cover all expenses owed to Dr. Barnard, and I will pay for your room and board at the Occidental until Mr. Wrenne arrives."

"Tank you, Mr. Denton. You are a true gentleman. Before you leab, you must be sure to meet my Clement. I know he'll like you berry much."

"If I'm still in town, it would be my pleasure." He held out his arm, making a note to leave Seattle as soon as he could manage. Because if he were Clement Wrenne, he wouldn't at all care to meet his wife's former betrothed.

Chapter Fourteen

Their chores complete, the men dropped their dirty lunch buckets by the back door, each one clanging against the other.

"That sure was some good pig's fry, Miss Ivey."

"Think we could have more of that vinegar pie on Monday?"

"Is there anything you need 'fore we head to town?"

This last question was from Thirsty, a small man standing no more than five feet six. But he was strong, and she'd heard he could eat and digest hay if it was sprinkled with whiskey.

"Town?" she asked. "You're going to town?"

"It's Saturday night and Sunday's our day off. But we'll be back in time for breakfast on Monday."

She looked at the group at large. "All of you are going?"

"Well, yes, miss. If there's something you need, though, we'll be glad to take care of it before we go."

She pasted a smile on her face. "No, thank you, Thirsty. I can't think of a thing. I appreciate all the help you've given already."

"It's no trouble, miss," Ronny said, dropping his lunch bucket by the others. She noted, though, that his bucket had been scrubbed free of all dirt and grime.

She knew better than to thank him. The others would tease him mercilessly. So she simply gave him a warm smile and decided to place an extra piece of pie in his bucket on Monday. "Good night, Ronny. You behave yourself in town, now."

His cheeks turned bright pink. "Yes, miss."

She remained on the porch watching the lumber crew walk past the leaning chestnut tree, then down a path heading east until she could neither see nor hear them. Up to now, she'd loved being alone in the house.

No superior looking over her shoulder. No ceaseless gossip between kitchen workers. No Hoke harassing her at every turn. Then at night, Joe had been within calling distance and the men were only a mile away.

She swallowed. No one would be anywhere close tonight. It wasn't ferocious beasts or brutal savages that concerned her so much as her own thoughts.

The evenings used to be her favorite part of the day. Her family would settle around the fire. Papa would read out loud, the pleasant aroma of his pipe wrapping them in its arms. Leon would set up his paper soldiers on the floor preparing them for mock battle. Mama and Anna would decorate boxes or frames with seashells they'd collected over the years.

Then the war came and Papa left. The band had sailed by their house trumpeting a slightly off-key rendition of "The Girl I Left Behind." With flags flying and bayonets resting on shoulders, the townsmen, dressed in Union colors, marched toward Main Street where wagons waited to take them to the train station in Amherst.

She and Leon hung over the porch rail shouting and waving. Mr. Cheatham turned and smiled, but Papa looked straight ahead without giving them even a glance. When the regiment disappeared round the corner of Pleasant Street, she'd raced upstairs to Mama's room, anxious to talk of the parade and her father's strange behavior.

But Mama wasn't at her window. The shutters were closed and she lay on the bed, her eyes dry, wide, and unseeing. The patriotism and excitement Anna had felt dimmed. Little had she known, she'd dashed into that room a girl, but silently tiptoed out a young woman, who would, from that moment on, be forced to shoulder the responsibility for her mother's care and her little brother's well-being.

Six months later, she'd accidentally hit Mama and upset Leon so much he ran away. She'd spent hours looking for him. Only when night had fallen had she returned home.

Mama stood in the entry hall, a new letter from Papa in her hand.

Anna had closed the front door, tears clogging her throat. "I looked high and low all day, then ran in to Mrs. Evers a few moments ago. She said Leon rode out of town with Daniel August. They were heading to Amherst to sign up."

What little color Mama had in her cheeks drained. Dropping the letter, she grabbed the hall tree for support. "No."

"I'm sorry, Mama."

The anger in Mama's eyes was the most emotion she'd displayed since Papa left. "This is all your fault. I was depending on you. Your father was depending on you. And now you've gone against both our wishes and sent your brother away. You've killed him, Anna. And you've killed me, too. I'll never forgive you for this."

The chattering of the crickets and trilling of grasshoppers penetrated Anna's consciousness, bringing her back to the present. The temperature had dropped and night had fully descended. Taking a deep breath, she swiped her eyes. The best thing to do would be to keep busy. Keep her mind occupied.

Returning inside, she rolled up her sleeves and began to scrub Joe's kitchen from top to bottom.

Circumventing the house, Joe went straight to the barn. Sir Francis Bacon plodded through the pigpen and snorted a greeting, but Joe ignored him, wrestling instead with his conscience.

He was going to have to lie to Anna about Bertha. And in order to cover it up, he'd most likely have to tell even more falsehoods. Still, if she knew why he'd gone to town, and that he was once again desperate for a wife, she'd throw up barriers he didn't have time to topple.

So he'd lie by omission about his betrothal. He checked on his cows, expecting them to be miserable this late in the morning, but they'd already been milked, and a quick inspection of the hen house showed the eggs had been collected. So either Anna had done it, or Red hadn't gone into town with everybody else.

He'd told the boys before he left about Mrs. Wrenne and that he was going to marry Anna instead. None had seemed overly surprised. It was when he'd told them not to discuss it with Miss Ivey that they'd raised their eyebrows.

Still, it was none of their concern.

Tucking a package of veal he'd purchased under his arm, he headed toward the house. He wondered what Anna had made for supper last night and how she'd spent her morning off. Had she slept late? Found his shelf of books? Gone on a walk?

The chairs out back had been turned upside down and now rested on the long table. A swirl of smoke trailed from the chimney. He glanced up at the sky. The weather had been beautiful, an unbroken string of sunny days. With July now upon them, it would only get better.

Climbing the porch steps, he asked God to forgive him his subterfuge and then entered the kitchen.

Anna squealed and spun around, iron in one hand and the other pressed against her throat. More pitiful looking undergarments he'd never seen in his life. He mumbled a quick apology and immediately backed out of the room, but his mind had captured a great many details.

The tub full of still water. Anna's wet hair loose and falling about her waist. The stark corset that hugged her figure without a single bit of frippery to decorate it. Drawers so threadbare they hid absolutely nothing. Well-formed ankles extending out from those drawers. Bare feet. And her blue dress flattened against the table. Did she not have a petticoat?

He could hear her scrambling inside.

"Don't rush, Anna," he called, embarrassment for them both making him self-conscious. "I've plenty to do in the barn. I'll be back in about thirty minutes. Will that give you enough time?"

Silence.

"Anna?"

She opened the door, her face flushed. And though her dress was on, he couldn't clear the image of her in a state of dishabille. Nor how very nicely she'd filled out her corset.

He swallowed. "I'm sorry."

Her hair still hung free, curling at the ends. She touched the button at her collar. "I didn't expect you so soon."

"I didn't think to warn you. I'm sorry."

Biting her lip, she widened the door. "You can't be expected to knock on your own door."

"Yes, I can."

She glanced at the package under his arm. "What's that?"

"Some veal I picked up from the butcher."

"You can set it over there." She pointed to the table she'd been ironing on.

He glanced at her skirt, half ironed, half wrinkled, and dragging the floor. Was she still barefoot?

He cleared his throat. "Not just yet. Perhaps in about thirty minutes? Will that give you enough time?"

She blushed again, then gave a hesitant nod.

Turning, he retraced his steps, listening for the click of the door's closing, but it never came. And then he knew she'd watched him until he was safely out of sight.

⁂

This time he knocked.

The door immediately opened. "You needn't knock."

He refrained from comment. The tub was gone. Her dress was pressed. Her hair was still wet but caught up in a ribbon at the back.

Both of them blushed.

"Come in, Joe."

He surged across the threshold and tossed the meat onto the table she'd first indicated. Peeling off the brown paper, he kept his back to her.

Don't ask about Bertha. Don't ask about Bertha.

"How's Mrs. Wrenne?"

He grabbed a cleaver out of a jar and began to chop up the tender beef. "Fine."

"And her teeth? Will they be ready soon?"

Blast. "Looks like things will be delayed a bit."

"Oh my. Not too long, I hope?"

"That remains to be seen." At least that much was true.

"Well, I'm sorry. I know you're anxious to see this whole thing through."

He said nothing.

She glanced at the meat. "Did you have something particular in mind for that, because it's not going to be quite enough for the crew, I don't think."

"It's for the two of us."

"The two of us?" She crossed her arms. She wasn't wearing her watch pin. She must not have had time to put it back on. "But don't you think that's a bit too much for two people?"

He slammed the cleaver into the veal. "If I say it's for the two of us, then it's for the two of us."

Her eyes widened.

Sighing, he laid down the cleaver. "I'm sorry. I'm a bit out of sorts, I guess."

She nodded. "Understandable, all things considered."

She didn't know the half of it. "I'm going to cut this into small segments. You can salt it, cure it, smoke it, make a stew, whatever you want. But it's for you and me on Sundays only. All right?"

"Yes."

Taking a deep breath, he returned to his task. "Thank you."

Chapter Fifteen

"I'm going into camp and file the saws," Joe said, poking his head in the parlor.

Anna sat with her feet tucked up underneath her, reading *The Taming of the Shrew*. She looked up, still smiling over the last line she'd read.

He leaned against the archway. "What part are you at?"

"Everyone is pretending to be something they aren't in order to win the fair Bianca."

He cleared his throat. "Yes. Well."

"I've never seen so many books in all my life."

Glancing at the breakfront holding his collection of literature, he shrugged. "I like to read." He pulled away from the doorframe. "I need to file the saws."

"File the saws?"

"The crosscuts have to be kept sharp, straight, and clean. That means setting, swaging, filing, and hammering the kinks out."

She gave him a blank look, unable to decipher his logging vernacular.

"Would you like to come along?"

She told herself it was the idea of doing something different that appealed to her, not the thought of spending the afternoon with him. Closing the book, she set it on the table and reached for her boots. "All right. Should I make us some sandwiches?"

"Either that or we need to eat before we go."

Half an hour later, lunch bucket in hand, they headed down the path the men took every morning.

"That chestnut by the house looks as if a strong wind might knock it over," Anna said, pointing to it.

Joe glanced back at it. "It'll be all right. Besides, I like chestnuts and that's the only one in the area."

"You're sure it's safe?"

"It's been fine for over ten years. No need to start worrying now."

She wasn't so sure, but meanwhile she could make something with the chestnuts, now that she knew he favored them.

She turned her attention to the forest. At first it was similar to what they'd traveled through on their way in from Seattle. But the farther they walked, the larger the trees grew until she stopped, awestruck by the sheer size of the tall, tall evergreens. Some of the trunks were so huge, an entire horse and buggy could fit inside.

"What are these?"

"Douglas firs. The redwoods are even bigger."

She cast him a doubtful look before shielding her eyes as she once again looked up. "Surely you don't chop these down?"

"We do. Its wood is straight-grained, tough, and can withstand tremendous stress. It holds nails and screws even better than oak."

"But how? How do you chop them down?"

"We work in pairs." He continued down the path.

"But it would take months. Years."

He chuckled. "I'll admit, I could fell half a dozen white pines back in Maine in the time it takes us to conquer one of these fellows."

Picking up her skirt, she followed. "With an ax? You chop these down with an ax?"

"And crosscut saws."

"But, they would have to be more than twenty feet long."

"They are. They also need to be sharp. That's why I have to file them. Watch your step."

She skirted around a large root protruding above the ground, then hurried to catch up with him. As they walked, Joe pointed to the different trees, explaining what each was particularly suited for.

The spruce made the best ladders. The hemlock was excellent for flooring and furniture. But it was the redwoods he favored most.

"They are unsurpassed in their resistance to weathering and rot. That house we're living in?"

She nodded.

"It has redwood shingles and siding and foundation. Make no mistake, it'll still be standing a hundred years from now." His face held a fierce pride, as if he were somehow responsible for the trees' exceptional qualities.

A few minutes later they stepped into a clearing filled with gigantic stumps, two stories high. Littering the ground were trees a hundred feet long and over twenty feet in diameter at their base. The scent of fresh-cut wood still lingered in the air.

Anna gasped, partly in awe at the sheer magnitude of the trees, partly in admiration of the men's ability to fell them, and partly in distress over the hill being stripped bare. How many centuries had it taken to produce those monstrous redwoods? And how many hundreds of years would come and go before any young growth could transform into majestic full-grown trees to replace the ones lying prostrate before her?

Joe slid down a steep slope on his feet, stopping near a redwood whose undercut had been started but had yet to be felled. He picked up a long saw with huge teeth and dragged it back up the hill.

His pants were the proper length today, she noticed, not the cropped-off ones. She watched as he nailed a notched board between two small trees. He then slipped the saw into the notch and began to file each tooth with a tiny picklike tool.

"Why do you wear pants of different lengths?"

He smiled. "Because when one of these giants starts to fall, we all scatter. If our pant legs get caught on something, it could slow us down just enough to be crushed by the plunging timber." He blew some metal filings off the saw. "Since I'm not felling trees today, I don't need to wear my sagged pants."

Anna walked about the clearing, careful to stay away from the steep slope. A patch of fragrant twinflowers crawled up the base of an ash tree. Gathering several blooms, she wrapped them in her handkerchief and slipped them in her pocket. Perhaps she could dry them later and make a sachet.

Spotting some coral mushrooms, she examined them, then returned to her lunch bucket and emptied its contents into Joe's. She ran across many varieties of mushrooms, wary of most of them. She opted to harvest only the coral ones, since she knew them to be edible, and their unique twiggy shape was so easy to identify.

She had just begun to head back when she heard Joe call her name.

"I'm here." She returned to the clearing and set her bucket down.

"Berry picking?" he asked, wiping his neck with a handkerchief.

"No. Mushrooms."

He glanced into her bucket. "Are you ready to eat lunch, then?"

"I'm starved."

"I don't have a blanket to sit on."

"That's all right."

He looked around. "Hold tight for just a minute." Trundling down the slope, he gathered several boards that were all of a uniform size—about five feet long and eight inches wide—then tucked them under his arm and carried them and an ax back to the top of the slope.

"What are those?"

"Springboards."

He stopped by one of the huge stumps that stood over two stories high. Swinging his ax into the side of the trunk, he cut a narrow notch, then inserted a board into the notch so that it protruded out of the trunk like a pirate's walking plank on a ship. Climbing up onto it, he stood and made another notch, inserting yet another springboard into the new notch.

When he had assured himself the springboard was secure, he jumped atop it, then repeated the action until he'd made stairsteps of the springboards all the way to the top of the tall sawed-off tree.

Once he'd reached the flat platform of the stump, he stood like the captain of a ship looking down at her. A breeze feathered his golden curls. "Care to join me?"

Anna eyed the springboards. They were spaced much farther apart than normal stairs. "You're jesting."

He tossed down his ax and leaped to the ground. She caught her breath, but he landed with a roll and sprung back up, using a technique he'd obviously performed so many times he didn't even think about it. Joe offered her a hand.

She looked again at the makeshift stairway. "I really don't mind eating on the ground."

"But the view from here doesn't compare to the view from up there on the stump."

She stood in indecision.

"I'll go first, then help you with each step." He jumped from the first springboard to the second, then squatted down and stretched out his hand. "Come on. It's easy."

She placed her hand in his, lifted her skirt, and tested the springboard with her foot. "It's loose."

"No, it's springy. It's supposed to do that. Come on, now. Up we go." He tugged on her hand.

She stepped up onto the first board.

"Good, now come on up here with me."

"Will it hold us both?"

"Yes. But I can go up one if you'd rather. You'll have to let go of me, though."

"No!" Anna shook her head. "No. I'll come up there with you."

He stood on the end, squeezing her hand while she placed a foot next to his.

"See?" he said, pulling her up. "Simple."

They made it up several more without incident until she looked down.

"Oh!" Her eyes widened and she began to sway.

He wrapped his hand around her arm. "Easy, there."

She grabbed his shirtfront.

"Are you afraid of heights?"

"I didn't think I was."

Chuckling, Joe loosened his hold. "Well, don't look down, then, and you'll be fine."

She crinkled his shirt into her fists. "What are you doing?"

He paused. "I have to go up to the next one."

"I don't want you to go to the next one."

"You want to go up without me?"

"No."

"Then you have to let go."

"No." Her heart raced. "Please. Don't leave me."

He tilted his head to the side. "You really are scared, aren't you?"

She trembled, embarrassed at discovering this weakness in herself. One she'd not been aware of before. But then, she'd never had occasion to stand suspended twenty-five feet in the air with no railing, no brace, and no protection whatsoever—other than the man beside her.

Spreading his wide hands around her waist, he pulled her against his chest, then patted her shoulder as if she were a child. "We've only one more to go, but if you'd rather go back down, we can."

"I can't." Squeezing her eyes shut, she clung to him. "I can't go up or down."

"Then we'll just stay here awhile. There's no rush."

Murmuring soothing words to her, he stroked her back and nuzzled her hair. She slowly began to relax. And with that relaxation came realization. She was clinging in a most inappropriate manner to her employer.

And he felt absolutely wonderful. Smelled absolutely wonderful. *Was* absolutely wonderful. His massive arms enfolded her as if she were a pearl and he was the clam.

She frowned. If his hands were around her, what was he holding on to? She stiffened. He wasn't holding on to anything. Good heavens.

"I'm ready to go the rest of the way up," she whispered.

He brushed her hair back from her face and tilted her chin up. "You sure?"

There were golden flecks in his eyes. The same color as his hair. And they were surrounded by a blue that began to darken.

His thumb scraped across her lower lip. "You smell good."

Her mouth parted. The twinflowers. He was smelling the twinflowers in her pocket.

She snapped her mouth shut. She needed to squelch this burgeoning attraction. Even if he weren't betrothed—which he was—the feelings were unwelcome. Attraction led to love and love led to responsibility. A responsibility she'd failed at so miserably that everyone she'd loved was dead.

"I'd like to continue now," she said, pleased her voice sounded so steady.

He lifted his gaze from her lips to her eyes. What she saw there frightened her more than anything Hoke had ever said or done. For what she saw in him mirrored what she felt deep inside. And she wanted nothing to do with it.

"How long will it take me to pay off my debt to you?" she asked.

"A very long time." Joe's voice was low, rough, husky.

Panic rose like a living creature.

"Now I'm going to ease you up against the tree," he said. "That way you can lean against it while I go to the next springboard. All right?"

She didn't acknowledge him one way or the other. Merely followed his prompting, taking baby shuffle steps until her back connected to the solid base of the tree.

"That's a girl." He removed one hand and put it next to her on the trunk. After another moment, he did the same with his other, penning her in. He was going to kiss her. *Oh no. Oh no. Oh no.*

"I'm really all right now," she said sharply, not wanting to look at him, but not wanting to look down, either. "You can go to the next step."

He blinked, his eyes clearing. He looked around as if to get his bearings, then leapt to the next level. Sucking in her breath, Anna pressed herself firmly against the trunk.

"Here we go, now. Reach out and take my hand."

It took her a minute to release the tree and slip her hand into his. And not just because she was scared of falling.

"That's the way." He reached out with his other hand.

She accepted it, and he assisted her onto the last board.

"Keep going. We're there."

Slipping his hands around her waist, he lifted her onto the top of the tree stump. She sat down with a thud and scrambled back away from the edge.

He stayed on the springboard. "You all right?"

She nodded.

"I'm going back down to get the lunch bucket."

"Don't jump," she said.

"Don't jump?"

"Please."

A corner of his mouth lifted. "All right. Sit tight. I'll be back."

He hopped down the boards one foot at a time and was back up with the pail in no time.

Squatting down beside her, he rested one knee on the stump's surface. "Still have an appetite?"

She hadn't dared to move.

Joe smiled. "It's a pretty view, if you think you can look."

She slowly swiveled her head, then caught her breath. The valley spread out before them while snowcapped Mount Rainier dominated the far horizon. She could see streams and the skid road they dragged the logs down and . . . "What's that?"

He looked in the direction of her gaze.

"A chute. I'm building a log chute. It's almost finished. It'll go to the river; then we'll be able to float the logs to Yesler's Mill rather than hauling them down Skid Road."

She looked at it again. "Good heavens."

Settling onto the stump, he pulled out their lunch and spread it before them.

"How are we going to get back down?" she asked.

"One step at a time. But there's no rush. We can stay up here for as long as you like."

Taking a deep breath, Anna took a bite of her sandwich, wondering if he realized just how long that might be.

Chapter Sixteen

They stayed up on the stump for hours. Talking. Laughing. Sometimes doing no more than enjoying the view.

He learned she liked to make things with seashells.

She learned he'd never read *Pride and Prejudice*.

He spoke of his family with affection.

She hardly spoke of her family at all.

He told her he began to support himself at age nine.

She claimed to have earned a share of her family's living at five.

"You did not," he scoffed. He lay facing her on his side, his elbow propping him up, his head resting in his hand.

"I most certainly did." She'd long since discarded her boots and sat with her legs tucked up under her skirts, feet on the stump.

"What a young robin you are—all mouth and no tail."

"I'll have you know I supplied our home with all the wood my mother could possibly use."

He grinned. "You were a lumberjack?"

"Of course not."

He shook his head. "Then just how is it, missy, that a puny female of only five years supplied wood for her entire family?"

"We were still living in New Bedford at the time. And next door to us was a great, burly shipbuilder. Bigger than you, even."

He quirked a brow.

"Every morning he'd toss me up onto his huge shoulder and take me with him to the shipyard. Day after day, I'd imitate the workers around me with my dull but serviceable hatchet and saw."

"In your petticoats? You sawed away at wood in your petticoats?"

Looking out over the valley, Anna hugged her knees to her chest, a fond smile touching her lips. "Actually, my petticoats got in the way, so my friend had a little boy's suit made for me. Thus emancipated, I never left his side."

A picture of her this morning without her petticoat flashed into his mind. Was that why she didn't wear one even today? Because after helping her up the springboards, he knew for a fact she didn't have one on now.

"I think I require some proof of this outrageous claim," he said.

"Proof?"

Tugging her hands loose, he made a show of inspecting them. So tiny. So delicate. So incredibly soft. "All ten fingers intact. But anyone of your tender age—particularly a female—would have certainly sawed off an appendage or two."

His fingers brushed the curve of her wrist.

She pulled her hands free, then reached for her boots and put them on, all the while keeping her feet hidden beneath her skirt. "My friend made sure I didn't saw off any fingers. Though I did smash them often enough."

"And this wood you sawed, you brought it home to your family?"

"No. In exchange for the pleasure of my company—which he

never seemed to tire of—my friend carried home from the shipyard all the wood we ever needed."

"With you on his shoulder."

She smiled. "With me on his shoulder."

He was going to enjoy being married to her, Joe realized. Whatever had brought about her hard times, the war or some other catastrophe, she was well educated. And though she didn't speak of her family directly, he was able to ascertain that it had been a loving one.

He still resented being forced into marriage, but he would do what it took to keep his land, and a lifetime with Anna wasn't going to be as much of a hardship as he'd first supposed.

He'd done everything she'd asked of him, even slept in the barn. The only thing he'd refused to do was chop down Lorraine's chestnut tree. He knew he should. Not just for Anna, but because it really was dangerous. But he couldn't make himself do it.

When news of Lorraine's death had come, he'd held a private memorial for her at the base of that tree. He'd read some words, said a prayer, and laid out a bouquet of flowers. But he hadn't felt any gripping sadness or overwhelming grief. What he'd felt was guilt—for the absence of those very emotions, and for knowing that if it was his land that he'd lost, he'd grieve far more.

The tree stood in the gap for him, somehow making up for his deficiencies. To chop it down would be callous and disrespectful. And he wouldn't do it.

Pushing himself to a sitting position, he scooted forward until he bracketed her with his bent legs. The sweet vanilla scent of twinflowers aroused his senses.

She drew her knees up against her chest, her eyes widening. "What are you doing?"

"I'm going to ask you again, Anna. What do you have against marriage?"

She didn't pretend to misunderstand his motive for asking. "You are betrothed."

"I'm not wed."

"It is practically the same."

"It is not at all the same. What do you have against marriage?"

She glanced around, as if searching for a way to escape, but she couldn't get off this stump. Not without his help. And they both knew it.

"Oh my," she said. "Look how low the sun is. Shouldn't we head back?"

He gently clasped her calves through her skirt. "What do you have against marriage?"

She started. "I told you. I'm simply not interested, that's all."

"Why not?"

"Can we go now?"

"I'll have an answer."

"It's a long story."

"I have time."

A slight glistening of moisture touched her eyes. Whatever her reasons, they were deep and they were very personal.

Stroking her calf with his thumb, he gentled his voice. "You can tell me."

She wrenched her legs away and stood.

Her skirts caught on his calluses. Anna yanked harder than necessary, giving him a glimpse of ankle before her hem settled into place.

"I'd like to leave now," she said. "I will go down those springboards by myself if you make me. But I'd rather have your help."

He slowly came to his feet. "I will let you fly the coop for now, little robin. But we are not done with this. Not by a long shot."

She squared her shoulders, but wasn't able to mask the vulnerability in her eyes.

⁂

She was trying to kill him. He'd asked the woman a few personal questions and she decided to do him in. He stopped milking to spit again, but it did no good. His mouth continued to froth.

She'd fried up some of the veal with the mushrooms she'd collected and served it to him for supper. But if she were trying to poison him, why did she eat it, too? He paused. Was she frothing?

He rushed through his chore, then jogged to the house, milk sloshing over the edge of the pails he carried. It was eerily quiet inside. He laid a cloth over the pails, then hurried from the milk room to the kitchen and lit a lantern. She wasn't there.

He checked the back parlor. The book she'd been reading was exactly as she'd left it. The parlor and dining room were empty and still. He took barely a moment to register the smell of beeswax and notice the furniture shone from a recent polishing. Taking the stairs two at a time, he knocked on her bedroom door.

"Anna? Are you in there?"

"Joe." Her voice was thin, weak.

He shoved open the door. She stood bent over the washbasin, foam spilling from her mouth.

"I don't know what's wrong." She looked up, her eyes widening. "Oh no! You too?"

He spit into the basin. "Must have been the mushrooms. I know the meat is good."

"But they were coral mushrooms." Grabbing a towel, she wiped the saliva from her mouth. "Aren't they edible here? They look exactly like the ones at home."

"I don't know. I'm not a big mushroom eater."

"You don't like mushrooms?" She looked stricken.

"I can eat them. I just don't seek them out or anything." He spit.

Her breath caught. "Are we going to die?"

He took a moment to catalog the rest of his body. "I don't think so. I mean, I don't even feel sick. Do you?"

She shook her head.

"Well, then. We'll probably be fine."

Her eyes filled. "I'm so sorry."

He shrugged. "It could have been worse. You could have served them to the whole crew."

"You don't understand." She crinkled the cloth in her fists. "If you die, I'll not be able to stand it."

He pulled the towel from her grip and blotted her mouth. "Nobody's going to die, Anna."

Giving her a chance to regain her composure, he looked about her room. It offered no evidence of anyone even staying in it. No personal articles. No clothes lying about. No books being read.

As far as he could tell, other than the clothes on her back, the watch pin and seashells were the only possessions she owned.

He returned his attention to her. "Why don't you go on to bed. The boys will have had nothing but whiskey since hitting town. They'll come to the breakfast table tomorrow either weak as babes or ravenous as wolves. Either way, it's sure to be a trying morning."

Her pillow was saturated when dawn arrived, but her mouth had quit foaming. Joe didn't look any worse for the wear, either. Still, he could have just as easily been dead.

And if nothing else, her foolishness validated the concerns she held deep inside. She wasn't good enough, careful enough, or smart enough to be a man's wife or a child's mother, for everyone put into her care had come to a bad end. Her mother, her father, her brother.

After drying the last of the breakfast dishes, she returned to her room and pulled up short. On her bed lay three different lengths of cloth. A blue gingham. A yellow calico. And a maroon cotton with tiny white dots.

Confused, she fingered them, then noticed a brown package with a note scrawled across it.

The wool you wear is too hot for our summers. Please make some dresses out of this cotton. I provide my crew with the things they need. I would do no less for my cook.—JD

She opened the package with trembling fingers. How long had it been since she'd had a new dress? She swallowed. A long, long time. Thread, buttons, trim, and notions spilled from the stiff paper and onto the bed.

For many minutes she stood perfectly still, just looking. Absorbing. Digesting. When had he picked all this out? During his trip to town? And had he done it himself or had the merchant helped him?

With a tentative hand, she fingered a corner of the calico. She would not feel guilty about this. The war was over. There was nothing untoward or inappropriate about an employer seeing to the clothing of his servants. And though Anna was not a servant, exactly, she was working off a debt. And for all intents and purposes, that was close enough.

Still, she was on shaky ground as far as Joe was concerned. He'd made his interest in her very plain yesterday. She had no doubt he would cry off of any attachments he had with Mrs. Wrenne were Anna to encourage him at all.

And the more she came to know him, the more she was drawn to him. He had but to walk into a room for her senses to come alive.

She could not picture him married to Mrs. Wrenne. He needed a young woman. A vibrant woman. A woman he could grow old with. He needed her.

But even if she was willing to risk it—which she wasn't—she would not be disloyal to Mrs. Wrenne.

So she would accept Joe's note at face value and make herself some gowns. She would also do everything in her power to keep her relationship with him as impersonal as possible.

She knew he wouldn't be mentioning marriage to her if his land weren't in jeopardy. And after seeing his operation yesterday—including that chute—she had a much better appreciation of all he stood to lose.

Picking up the gingham, she held one end to her shoulder and the other in her extended hand. Were it Hoke in this predicament, he would court anything in skirts to save his land. A woman like Mrs. Wrenne. A woman like Anna. A half dozen women if need be.

She bit the insides of her cheeks. She didn't want to think that of Joe. He was as different from Hoke as the sun was from the moon.

Nevertheless, she didn't want Mrs. Wrenne to come to her new home and suspect that Joe had anything other than the most platonic feelings for his cook.

And the responsibility for that rested completely on Anna's shoulders. The female set the tone of these things. Always had. Always would.

Gathering the cloth and notions, she began a search for a pair of scissors.

Chapter Seventeen

Joe and Red spent the day arranging a long, soft bed of boughs to cushion the fall of a redwood they'd prepared. Though they displaced some playful squirrels and a few robins looking for worms, the work didn't require the power and endurance chopping did, thus allowing for quiet conversation.

"Town's all abuzz about Mrs. Wrenne's husband coming back to life," Red said.

Joe nodded. "I imagine it is."

Red tossed several branches into the middle of their layout. "Tillney's making some disparaging remarks about your relationship with her—not within my hearing, of course."

Dangling his ax at his side, Joe sighed. "You know, if he'd have put half the effort into logging as he has in trying to bring me down, I'd have never chopped his tail loose."

"You did the right thing. A lazy man is a careless one. There's no safe place in camp for a careless jack."

"Maybe so, but at some point you'd think he'd turn his

attention elsewhere. It isn't as if the stigma of being let go is going to follow him all the way to the hereafter."

"He thinks it will, and there are a lot who'd agree with him."

Joe hefted his ax and searched out more rubble.

"What was Miss Ivey's reaction to the canceling of your nuptials?" Red asked.

"She doesn't know about it." Joe cut off a stub sticking out of a snag, bringing a network of limbs to the ground with a thud.

"You didn't tell her?"

"Nope. She doesn't know about Bertha's husband, nor that I am no longer betrothed."

Red glanced up the hill, noting the boys were stopping for lunch. "Well, isn't she going to think something's amiss when you don't get married at the end of the month?"

"Nope."

"Why not?"

"I told her things had been delayed." Squinting at their bed, Joe rearranged some of their debris. "We need to angle the layout a little more to the east."

"No we don't."

"Yes we do."

After a slight hesitation, Red did as he was told. "Well? What did she have to say about the delay?"

"Said she was sorry, since she knew how anxious I was about the whole affair."

Scratching his neck, Red shook his head. "You're not going to be able to hide it from her forever. The moment she sets foot in town, she'll learn of it."

"That's why I'm seeing to it that she doesn't go to town anytime soon." Joe pointed to the branches Red had just laid. "The tree's going to fall more to the east."

Red studied their tree. "I don't think so."

"I know so."

"Want to make a wager on it?"

"You bet I do." Whisking up a skinny log, Joe began shaving one end of it into a point.

"You can't keep her hidden forever."

"All I need is a few weeks. Once I convince her to marry me, I'll have the preacher come up here to do the ceremony. After we've said the words and signed the papers, then I'll tell her." He glanced at the tree, their bed, then back at the tree. Walking to the eastern side of the layout, he began hammering his newly fashioned stake into the ground.

"You really think Miss Ivey will marry you when you're supposedly betrothed to another?"

"It'll all work out. You'll see." Stepping back, Joe nodded toward the stake. "When our giant falls, she's going to knock this stake clear into the ground."

Red stuck out his hand. "You're on."

Joe clasped it.

A commotion at the top of the hill captured their attention. "What's got Thirsty all riled up, do you suppose?"

They tried to make out the words being shouted.

"I don't know. Something about Ronny's dessert." Joe buried his ax in a nearby tree. "We better get up there before Thirsty starts talking with his hands."

The boys dug into their meat pies, rain beating the top of the lean-to and sliding off its edges. The water formed a curtain of sorts, splattering mud just inside their haven. The chestnut tree beside the porch swayed, but no one seemed concerned.

"What is this stuff, Miss Ivey?" The question came from a leathery-faced man the others called Fish. She assumed it was because of his big eyes, bald head, and sunken cheeks, but she had, of course, refrained from asking.

"Toad-in-the-hole," she replied.

Fish paused, then poked his pie with his spoon. "Toad-in-the-hole? There's toads in this?"

She smiled. "No. I don't know why it's called that. It's just rump, kidney, and onion."

Fish continued with his meal, as did the others, emptying the platters of food more quickly than usual. The steady rain not only dampened the yard, it dampened the men's spirits, keeping their customary enthusiasm and teasing at bay.

After-dinner chores were executed with quick efficiency, bringing an early conclusion to Anna's evening. The men dropped their lunch buckets by the door, said their good-byes, and set out for the night. Anna bent to retrieve the buckets, then stopped in surprise. Every single one had been thoroughly washed and cleaned.

"Ronny's extra portion of dessert didn't go unnoticed," Joe said, ascending the porch steps and dropping his clean bucket beside the rest.

"So I see." She wiped her hands on her apron. "Looks like I'll be making an impromptu batch of fritters tonight."

"You don't have to do that."

"Oh, it won't take but a minute."

Returning to the kitchen, she threw another log in the oven and set some water to boil. While she gathered up flour, eggs, and lard, Joe sat by the fireplace sharpening his ax.

He wore a blue chambray shirt she'd laundered and ironed not two days before. His rolled-up sleeves revealed muscular arms sprinkled with sun-bleached hair. The brownish blond curls across his forehead swayed with his motions. She knew the ax was heavy, but he held it with ease as he scraped it along his grinding stone.

"Joe?"

"Hmm?"

"Would you mind chopping down that chestnut tree?"

"Yes."

She blinked. "But it's leaning right over my room. I'm afraid it's going to crash down."

"You can move rooms if you want."

Frowning, she watched the careful, even strokes he took. "You aren't going to chop it down?"

"No."

"Simply because you like chestnuts?"

He continued to work, and just when she thought he wasn't going to answer, he surprised her by saying, "It's my wife's."

"What?"

"The tree. I planted it for her."

Anna glanced out the window. "Your late wife? You planted a chestnut tree for her?"

"She had one in her yard back home that she loved. I was going to surprise her with this one."

Yet Anna knew the late Mrs. Denton hadn't lived to see it. She pictured the tree in her mind. So big. He must have lost his wife many years ago if it was a sapling when he'd planted it.

She moistened her lips. A chestnut tree. A beautiful home. Twinflower blooms. The man certainly cherished what was his.

The darkness outside and throughout the rest of the house always made the kitchen a cozy haven in the evenings, but with the addition of the rain beating against the windows, the atmosphere shifted from cozy to intimate.

She wanted to ask him more questions about his wife. She wanted to ask him if he'd like his hair trimmed so it wouldn't get in his eyes. She wanted to thank him for the fabric.

But she turned her back instead and concentrated on the fritters.

Keep it impersonal, she reminded herself. Pouring a portion of the boiling water into a bowl of flour, she began to beat it into a stiff paste. It wasn't until she set it aside to cool that she realized the scraping of Joe's ax had ceased.

She glanced over her shoulder. He stared at her hips, blade and stone forgotten. She quickly spun around to face him. He raised his eyes to hers. The intensity of his gaze triggered an immediate response deep within her.

Say something. Anything.

"Why are the ax handles so long?"

Joe looked down as if just discovering what he held in his hands. "The handles? Well, I have to be able to reach the center of the redwoods from my springboard."

She frowned. "That wouldn't reach the center of a Douglas fir, much less a redwood."

He touched the edge of his blade, a tiny drop of blood springing to the surface of his finger. "No. No, it wouldn't. Not from the springboard, anyway. We actually have to stand inside the undercut to reach the heart of the trunk."

She pictured the giant wedge they'd begun to cut into the redwood she'd seen yesterday. They stood inside that wedge? Wouldn't the tree collapse and squash them?

But she didn't ask. Instead, she retrieved a frying pan, scooped a goodly portion of lard into it, and set it on the stove.

"Would you like me to read to you while you finish those?" he asked.

Anna paused in reaching for the eggs. "Read to me?"

"Yes. *The Taming of the Shrew*. Would you like me to read it to you?"

She loved being read to. Her father used to read to the family all the time. And with the rain, it was the perfect night for it, but she was afraid it would create too intimate a mood. Still, if he were reading, he'd not be able to ogle her.

"Yes, please. If you don't mind."

Placing the ax in the corner, he wiped his hands on the seat of his pants, then went to retrieve the book.

She braced herself against the pastry table and took two deep breaths. *Impersonal, Anna. You must keep things impersonal.*

At the sound of his return, she grabbed an egg and began to separate out its yolk.

"Where did you leave off?" he asked, settling into his chair.

"The beginning of Act Two. The disguised schoolmasters had just left, and Petruchio was asking Signior Baptista what Katharina's dowry was."

He thumbed through the book, then flipped back and forth between a few pages. "Here we are. Petruchio is speaking." He cleared his throat. " 'Then tell me, if I get your daughter's love, what dowry shall I have with her to wife?' "

Joe's voice was so full of expression and life that Anna soon lost herself in the story. She beat the eggs into her mixture, then dropped it a spoonful at a time into the boiling lard.

"Everyone exits but Petruchio," Joe said. " 'I will attend her here, and woo her with some spirit when she comes. Say that she rail; why then I'll tell her plain she sings as sweetly as a nightingale. Say that she frown; I'll say she looks as clear as morning roses newly wash'd with dew.' "

Anna chuckled, watching the fritters rise into balls, then flipped them when the first side turned a light brown. Katharina entered, and the sparring between her and Petruchio quickly escalated, each constructing new metaphors from the other's comments until Katharina became so furious she hit him. Hard.

" 'I swear I'll cuff you, if you strike again,' " Joe said, dropping the register of his voice.

Spooning all but two of the fritters onto a drying cloth to drain, Anna placed the ones she'd held back onto a plate, sprinkled them with sugar, and sat at Joe's feet.

Watching him read was like watching the actual play. A myriad of expressions crossed his face. Coupled with the dialogue, it pulled her deeply into the story. When Petruchio told Katharina she was mild, gentle, and affable, Anna threw back her head and laughed. And on some finite level, she realized she hadn't laughed, really laughed, in years. The realization sobered her.

As if sensing her mood, the character Petruchio also turned serious.

"'Marry, so I mean, sweet Katharine.'"

Anna took a bite of her fritter.

"'Your father hath consented that you shall be my wife; your dowry 'greed on.'" Joe lifted his gaze and looked directly at her. "'And, will you, nill you, I will marry you.'"

She couldn't swallow, her bite of fritter sticking in her throat. The rain continued to tap against the windows. The sweet smell of fried pastries filled the room.

Lowering the book, Joe removed the other half of her fritter from her hand and placed it in his mouth. Without breaking eye contact, he swallowed, stood, then slowly placed the book on the chair. "Good night, Anna. I'll see you in the morning."

Chapter Eighteen

The kitchen was empty. The fire cold. The oven untouched. Joe stood in the doorway. Usually when he first came from the barn in the morning, he'd find Anna bustling about.

He glanced at the staircase. Was she ill? Or had she merely overslept?

He crept up the steps and placed his ear to her door. Nothing. He tapped against it lightly. No response.

With great care to make no noise, he turned the knob and cracked the door open. The white-and-blue bed hangings had not been drawn but were still tied back at the posts with heavy tassels. Anna lay on her stomach in her nightdress, the cotton covers tangled in her legs, her thick honey-colored braid draped across her pillow.

He wanted to touch her to check for fever, but he didn't quite have the nerve to enter her room without permission. Squinting, he was able to determine her cheeks were neither too flushed nor too pale. Perhaps she was simply worn out.

The smell of twinflower prickled his nose. He scanned the room, spotting several of the wild flower's blooms tied to a string and hanging upside down from her mirror. She was drying them?

He looked at her again and hesitated, tempted once more to go closer while he had a chance. Was her nightdress as threadbare as the rest of her meager wardrobe? But his conscience kicked in, and he, instead, eased the door closed.

Crossing to his room, he opened a drawer and found his clothing laundered, ironed, and folded neatly inside. He'd only expected Anna to cook, but never had his home looked so fine or his clothes so fresh.

Pulling on his drawers, he smiled to himself. She couldn't possibly handle such intimate apparel without thinking of what he might look like wearing them. Even coming into his room and opening his dressing chest was an extremely personal thing to do.

But she'd certainly been skittish since he'd read to her the other night. Perhaps he'd been too direct. Too obvious.

It had barely been a week, after all. He had time to slow things down some. Give her a false sense of security.

Picking up his razor, he scraped it against a strap. He'd offered to read to her again, but she'd politely declined.

"No, thank you. I think I'll just listen to the rain."

He'd bit back his smile and decided to let her have her way. Still, he wondered if she had proceeded with the book on her own.

He'd searched out *Shrew* and found the volume tucked safely back in his breakfront. Had she put it away because she didn't wish to finish or because she'd been too busy with her stitching?

She hadn't said anything about the fabric, but she worked with it every evening, sometimes quite late. Just last night he'd left her sewing while he retired. Perhaps she'd burned the midnight oil and that was why she was still abed.

Lathering his face, he considered his next strategy. Maybe he should shave in the kitchen. Anna had either become used to his washing up or by virtue of will kept her attention diverted. Either way, it wouldn't hurt to introduce something new into the mix.

But not yet. Perhaps on Sunday, when it would be just the two of them. Until then he'd mind his p's and q's. Let her think she could drop her guard.

He finished his toilet, pulled on the rest of his clothes, and hastened downstairs.

Safely back in the kitchen, he quickly grabbed some jerky and a few lunch buckets. He wanted to catch the men before they reached the house, because once they did, Anna would wake and he didn't want her disturbed.

He set off toward the bunkhouse, remembering the profusion of raspberries close to their logging site. The boys could pick those as a supplement for their jerky. They'd be sorely disappointed about missing breakfast, but they'd manage.

Still, Joe would go back before noon and check on Anna. Once he established she was all right, he would tease her a bit, then help her put together a cold lunch and bring it to the men.

Yawning, Anna rolled onto her side, then sat up with a jolt. It was light outside! She flew from the bed, jerked back the curtains, and gasped. Not just light, but well past dawn. A robin with its jaunty *cheerily-cheery-up-cheery-o* swept from one tree to another.

How on earth had she slept through all that and why hadn't Joe woken her? Flinging off her nightdress, she dropped it on the floor and scrambled into her clothes. She took no time to wash her face, comb her hair, or straighten her room.

The kitchen was just as she'd left it the night before. Her gaze darted to the clock. Eight-thirty! Those poor men. They must be starved.

She wasted no time in lighting the oven and starting on the bread. Working feverishly, she whipped up potato pancakes, boiled eggs, crispy bacon, and dandelion dressing. She sliced up tomatoes from the garden and washed several more.

Never in her life had she slept late. Even on board the ship, she would awaken before dawn. Would Joe be angry? He may like her well enough, but she was first and foremost his cook and she had a debt to pay. Setting the bread dough aside, she ran to the barn in search of a wheelbarrow.

She flew past the chicken coop, the pigpen, and the milking cows. The wheelbarrow was way too cumbersome and smelled of animals. But in the stall where Joe slept was a barrel, two chairs, a deck of cards, and a child's wagon. Briefly wondering why Joe would need a child's wagon, she pulled it behind her, its bed jumping in protest to her rapid pace.

Once back at the house, she glanced at the mantel again. Almost ten o'clock. No time to repair her person. The men had been in the forest for hours now and needed something to eat.

Leaving the bread dough to rise, she lined the wagon with cloths and filled it with her trappings. It wouldn't all fit. Spinning in a circle, she searched for another container, gave up, then dashed to her room for a pillow sack.

Packed and ready, she forced herself to walk at a reasonable speed so as not to topple the wagon or damage the eggs and tomatoes slung in the sack across her back.

The closer she came to the logging site, the more embarrassed she felt. And all because of that silly gown.

She'd wanted so badly to see it complete. So she'd stayed up. But nothing went as it should, and the next thing she knew, it was only a couple of hours before she'd need to rise again and the gown still wasn't complete. She sighed. She'd thought to catch only a little bit of rest, not sleep all the way through breakfast.

As she topped the rise her thoughts came to a halt. The bowl-shaped area in which the men worked was rife with activity. Fish and Wardle sliced up felled trees into logs. Ronny used a long pole with a blade at the end to strip bark from the cut logs.

Gibbs, in floppy hat and galluses, poked a pair of oxen with a stick. "Hump, you, Shelley! Move, Keats!"

The giant animals towed a pair of logs to the skid road. Already a pile of them were lined up end to end waiting for their journey to the sawmill.

Young Milton—whom the boys called Bunny due to the size of his two front teeth—ceased trimming the ends of a log to help Gibbs with his load.

Thirsty worked an ax into a pine tree. A man called Pelican was overseeing construction of the chute.

In the middle of the site, Red and Joe stood high up on springboards, each opposite the other and sawing a mighty redwood with the crosscut Joe had sharpened on Sunday.

Back and forth. Back and forth. Sweat poured from both men, but it was Joe who drew her attention. His back and shoulders bulged with each pull of the saw, his knees bending in rhythm to their movements.

She wondered where the stairway of springboards was. Red had one board below him. But Joe had none. He stood on a solitary plank two dozen feet above the ground. How on earth had he gotten up there?

"Miss Ivey!" Thirsty tossed down his ax and jogged up toward her.

As a group, the men stopped what they were doing and looked her way. She glanced at Joe in time to see him leap into the wedge of the redwood, jerk his springboard free, toss it to the ground, then jump.

"You all right, Miss Ivey?" Thirsty asked, taking the wagon handle from her.

She looked again to assure herself Joe had landed safely, then turned her attention to Thirsty. "Am *I* all right? What about you? You must be practically dying of hunger. I'm so, so sorry I overslept."

"Oh, now, that's all right, miss."

Ronny sprinted up the hill. "Is that food you got in that wagon,

Miss Ivey? I surely hope it is. I'm so starved my belly thought my throat was cut!"

Thirsty rounded on him and laid him out flat with one punch.

Anna gasped. "Thirsty! What on earth?"

Before she could get to Ronny, he jumped back up like a jack-in-the-box and touched his jaw. "What was that for, Thirst?"

"You were talking when you should've been listening, so I reached you one." His tone was mild. Affectionate, even. "If you don't mind your manners, I'll finish this conversation with my hands."

Ronny said no more, just worked his jaw back and forth to be sure all was intact. A goodly portion of the crew had caught up and acted as if nothing at all had happened. They simply unpacked the wagon and pillow sack, then started passing around the food. Whiffs of their repast unfurled and blended with the smell of fresh air and wood shavings.

"Are you all right?" Joe's voice was low and very close to her ear.

She glanced up over her shoulder, then ran a hand over her braid and the mess of tendrils that had escaped it. "I overslept. I'm so sorry."

"I'm just glad you're all right."

"It won't happen again."

He hooked some hair behind her ear. "No harm done."

She didn't know if it was the touch or the tenor of his voice, but a rush of bumps skittered up her arms. "Why didn't you wake me?"

"You looked so peaceful, I didn't have the heart."

Her breath caught. *He saw me? In my bedroom?*

She bit her lower lip. "You'd better get something before it's gone."

He tapped her on the chin. "Oh, I plan to, Miss Ivey. I definitely plan to."

Clasping her hands in front of her, she pretended not to understand his implication. But she did understand. And the anticipation that sprung up within her terrified her more than his words.

He's pledged to another, she told herself. So long as he stayed that way, she should be safe.

Joe helped himself, then again took up his place behind her. He bit into a potato pancake wrapped around a boiled egg. "Mmmmm. You want some?"

She shook her head.

"Go on. I'd wager you haven't had a thing to eat yet."

Her stomach chose that moment to growl.

Grinning, he brought the rolled pancake within inches of her mouth. But he didn't offer her the end that hadn't been bitten. He offered her the end he'd eaten from. She hesitated. He waved it under her nose. Holding his hand still with hers, she took a bite. He gave her a hooded look, then popped what was left in his mouth.

The rest of the men had settled in a circle on the sawdust-covered ground. Several tawny-striped chipmunks rushed out from the brush and gathered at their feet, darting from one booted foot to another.

Anna backed up and bumped into Joe's solid mass. "Won't they bite?"

"No, those are our pet chipmunks. They come every day. They're particularly fond of Thirsty. Watch."

She looked Thirsty's way just as one of the furry creatures ran up his back, onto his arm, and helped itself to the boiled egg he held in his hand. The seasoned lumberjack lowered the critter to the ground.

Sitting back on its haunches, the chipmunk finished the egg, wiped its mouth with its tail, then licked its tail clean. Never had she seen such a tender expression on Thirsty's face.

She wondered suddenly if he had family or if he was alone in the world. Just like her.

"How did Thirsty get his nickname?" she asked.

Red threw Joe a tomato she'd not had time to slice. He caught it, then took a bite as if it were an apple. Dark red juice dribbled out of the tomato. Placing his lips against it, he caught the juices with his mouth, closed his eyes, and sucked, his cheeks inverting.

Inside, her stomach felt like a ball held long underwater that finally shot up to the surface. She placed a hand against her waist but could not suppress the buoyant commotion.

"Several winters ago," he said, wiping his mouth with his sleeve, "we ran short of grub. So I sent Gibbs and Fish to town to buy us some supplies. When they returned we were near starving."

She took a calming breath. "What does that have to do with Thirsty?"

"Well, when we went to unpack the goods, we found several cases of whiskey and only two loaves of bread. We all stared in shock until Thirsty snorted and said, 'Now what're we going to do with all that bread?' "

She blinked. "You're teasing me."

"I'm not." His eyes shone with amusement. They were dark green today, like the leaves in the forest.

"No dessert, Miss Ivey?" Ronny asked, then leapt out of Thirsty's reach.

She moved away from Joe and to the men's circle. "I'll make some extra tonight. I promise."

The men began to clean up, but she shooed them away. "I'll take care of this."

The chipmunks receded back into the forest, and all the men but Ronny returned to their work. The boy refused to leave the cleaning to her, insisting on helping her. Acquiescing, she stacked two bowls in the wagon and chanced to look up.

Joe had just stepped onto his springboard, which he'd anchored only a few feet above the ground. He drove his ax deep into the trunk above him, grabbed tightly to the ax handle with one hand,

and hung suspended from it while pulling the springboard free and inserting it into the notch above him.

The muscles in his arm bunched. Once the board was firmly in place, he put both hands on the ax handle and hauled himself up, swinging aboard the plank with ease.

He repeated the action over and over on his way up to the place he and Red had been sawing before. Arms, shoulders, back, and legs all stretched and flexed beneath his shirt.

When he reached his final position, he looked down at her, winked, then leaned a shoulder against the tree and waited for Red—who stood on one board while inserting another above him, then pulled himself up that way. Impressive, but not anywhere near as stirring as what Joe had done. And the impossible man knew it.

Ronny stepped up next to her. "He can jump farther, spit straighter, kick higher, run faster, and shout louder than anybody I ever saw." His tone held some of the awe she was feeling.

Seeing Joe out here today was much different than when it had been just the two of them on Sunday. Then, he'd been tinkering. Today he was in his element. The vastness of the forests he invaded, the forces of nature he had to combat and control, the sheer size of the trees he brought down, all helped define the man.

And if challenged, she had no doubt that he'd channel that strength and resolve with single-minded ferocity until he'd proven himself and achieved his goal. The thought gave her pause.

Red reached his position. Joe jumped into the air and did an about-face on the springboard, then sprinkled oil on the saw. The two men settled into a crouch and began to work the blade back and forth.

"Do you see that stake out there, sort of to the left?" Ronny asked, pointing.

She scanned the hill.

"Waaaaaaaaay down there," he said.

Squinting, she put her hand over her eyes. "Yes! Yes, I see it."

"Joe put it there. He bet Red that when the tree comes down, the upper end of the trunk will fall on the stake and drive it straight into the ground."

She looked at Ronny with shock. "How could he possibly know that?"

"Our lives depend on him being accurate, Miss Ivey. A tree that twists and slides backward off its stump has made many a wife into a widow." He grinned. "Still, hitting a stake that far out is gonna be tough."

She turned her attention back to Joe. They'd stopped their sawing while Red oiled the saw. Joe slipped his suspenders from his shoulders and peeled off his shirt, tossing it to the ground. He wore no undershirt. Snapping the suspenders back in place, he nodded at Red, his golden torso shining with sweat.

"Why are they so high up on the tree?" she asked. "Why don't they stay on the ground to chop it down? Wouldn't that be safer?"

"Well, for one thing, it's a whole lot thicker down at the base. That's also where all the pitch settles."

"What's pitch?"

Ronny whipped his head around, his expression horrified. "*What's pitch?*" He let out a snort. "I thought even city girls knew what pitch was."

Joe flipped his ax backwards and hammered a wedge into the cut of the tree. Wiping his forehead, he took up the saw and the men resumed their cutting.

"Pitch is the sticky stuff inside the tree that snags the saws," Ronny said.

"Sap, you mean?"

"Not exactly, but kind of like that."

Rapid popping sounds, like corks shooting out of a hundred champagne bottles, came from the unsawed part of the redwood.

"Here she goes," Ronny whispered, pulling her back.

For the first time, Anna realized the havoc the gargantuan tree could wreak if it fell anywhere other than the direction Joe was aiming for. Terror gripped her, squeezing her breath. The top of the redwood quivered and swayed.

"Joe needs to get down!" she exclaimed. "He needs to get away!"

But he and Red were already jumping.

"*Timber-r-r-r-r!*" Joe bellowed, landing on the ground with a roll and a run.

A piercing, cracking noise reverberated through the glen. The tree leaned to the east, leaned some more, and then it was falling, crashing to the ground with a roar rivaling any sound she'd ever heard. The earth shook. The bowls in her wagon rattled. She grabbed Ronny for support.

Dust and debris exploded into the air, masking the sunlight that pierced into the newly forged opening. And then all was still. The men. The animals. The very earth. As if in respect for the death of one of the forest's royalty.

A bloodcurdling shout rent the air.

Anna gasped. "Someone's hurt!"

Ronny grabbed her arm, stopping her.

She whirled around, slapping at his hand. "Let me go! Let me go! It was Joe! I know it was!"

"Miss Ivey. Miss Ivey!" Ronny bracketed her arms, giving her a gentle shake. "You can't run over there. Not unless you want everybody to know you're in love with him."

She stilled. "What?"

"If you make a big fuss, everybody will know you're in love with him."

"In love with him?"

"Well, sure. Besides, he's not hurt. He hit the stake, that's all. See?"

She glanced down the hill. Sure enough, the stake had disappeared beneath the tree's corpse. "What makes you think I'm in love with him, Ronny?"

He smiled, the action lighting up his entire face. "I got me a sister. You're just like her, too. She didn't want anyone to know about her feelings toward the fellow she liked, either. So don't worry. Your secret's safe with me."

Something well beyond her shoulder drew his attention. She turned. Joe stomped out of the brush, dirt streaking his chest. He locked eyes with Red, then held his fists in the air, threw back his head and let out another warriorlike scream.

Sinews and veins tried to burst free of his skin. A golden patch of hair curled at the pit of each arm. His massive chest jutted out above his solid, rippling waist while legs and knees locked in an unyielding stance.

Her lips parted. Cheers from the other men filled the glade and they ran to congratulate him.

"Pardon me, Miss Ivey." Ronny raced down the hill, reaching Joe and Red in time for a round of back-slapping that would have felled lesser men.

Turning her back on the scene, Anna picked up the wagon's handle and headed to the house. She knew without having to look too deep that Ronny was right. She was in love with Joe Denton.

She didn't know how it had happened, but she did know nothing could ever come of it. And he must never find out. Ronny would keep her secret. She had no doubt about that.

The question was, could *she* keep it or would she do something to inadvertently give it away? The best thing—the only thing—was to stay away from him. Not only in the evenings, but in her thoughts as well.

She determinedly tried to wipe the image of Joe's victory stance from her mind. Her efforts were doomed to failure.

Chapter Nineteen

Joe opened his eyes and smiled. Sunday. He'd have Anna all to himself for the entire day. First, he'd shave in the kitchen; then he'd take her fishing.

Leaping off the cot, he pulled on his trousers, then made his way to the house. He'd placed all his shaving equipment by the washstand after she'd gone to bed last night. As fastidious as she was, though, he was certain she'd notice it this morning.

He opened the backdoor, then stopped short.

Anna was wearing a new dress made out of the blue gingham. She was busy at the stove and hadn't heard him come in.

He could only see the back of her, but could tell the gown was all one piece. Snug at the top. Nipped in at the waist. Flared out at the skirt.

The sleeves were long and form-fitting, but not so tight she couldn't move with ease. She'd made cuffs out of the maroon fabric.

She laid some bacon in the skillet, jumping when the grease popped. Her apron's bow bounced against her back end.

Deciding to enjoy the view, he leaned on the doorframe, crossed one ankle over the other and watched. After a minute or so, she turned around.

He gave her a lazy smile. "Morning, Miss Ivey."

She faltered. She blushed. She fluttered her hands around.

The collar matched the maroon cuffs and was trimmed with the ribbon he'd bought. Tiny little buttons marched from her neck to her waist, then disappeared beneath the apron. Her watch pin held its coveted place, resting against the swell of her right breast. She'd even done something different with her hair. It was all gathered to one side and tied with a ribbon, then cascaded in curls over her left shoulder.

"You did a fine job with the fabric, Anna. You look beautiful."

The sharp sizzle of bacon filled the kitchen. She opened and closed her mouth but said nothing.

His grin deepened as he watched her fret over where to settle her gaze. He was bare from the waist up and bare from the ankles down. That left only his trousers.

Her white, creamy throat exposed by her banded hair revealed the rapid *thumpity-thump* of her heartbeat. The invitation was almost more than he could resist. But he couldn't kiss her. Couldn't even nuzzle her neck. Not as long as she thought he was betrothed to someone else.

She whirled back around to the stove.

Taking a deep breath, he closed the door, then moved to the washbasin. Picking up his razor, he pulled it back and forth across the strap several times, then tested its edge.

The clinks and clatters that usually accompanied her cooking had ceased. The bacon continued to pop and hiss. It needed turning, but he didn't say a word or glance her way. Simply whipped up his lotion and began to lather his face.

"What are you doing?" she squeaked.

"Shaving."

"Why?"

"Beards make me itch."

"No. I mean, why in here?"

He angled the mirror until he caught her reflection. "Bacon's burning."

Her gaze flew to the stove. "Good heavens."

She busied herself with breakfast, but he could feel her surreptitious looks as he held his jaw with one hand and dragged the razor up his neck with the other.

When he'd finally finished, he ran his fingers across his cheeks, chin, and neck, checking for stubble. Satisfied, he scooped water from the basin and buried his face in it.

He continued with his toilet until he'd washed and rinsed off his chest, his arms, his pits, everything he could reach. By the time he was through drying off, the flimsy little towel he'd used was sopping wet.

He hung it carefully on the rail, then turned around.

Anna leaned against a chair, one hand hovering above the table while holding a platter of fried biscuits.

He winked.

She jerked herself to attention, the platter making a *ka-plunk* on the table.

"I'm going to grab a shirt. I'll be right back."

Once in his room, he allowed himself a wide smile. She'd be his by the end of the month, maybe even by the end of the week.

The same rush of accomplishment that came with felling trees coursed through him. He refrained from giving a shout of conquest, though. There'd be time enough for that when the deed was done.

Joe hammered two boards together, making legs for the trellis supporting his log chute. Each strike of the hammer landed harder than the last. He still couldn't believe Anna refused to go fishing with him. Said she'd rather sew instead.

He shook his head. When he'd given her the fabric, it never occurred to him he'd have to compete with it for her attention. But that's exactly what was required, and not only on Sundays, but every evening after supper.

He formed a T with two boards. Maybe the sewing was just an excuse. She'd not been able to look him in the eye all during breakfast. He'd not been able to keep his eyes off of her in that dress.

Wiping the sweat from his face, he took a deep breath. Could be that if he pushed her any further, she'd think him dishonorable because of Bertha.

He picked up two nails and put one in his mouth. Maybe it was time to tell her the truth—or ease her into it. They'd be sharing some of that veal tonight. Perhaps he ought to bring up marriage again. Tell her he'd been thinking about dissolving his agreement with Bertha.

He pounded the brace into place. At least he had all night to do it, since it would be just the two of them. The men wouldn't be back until late. Of that, he was certain.

Joe had just said the blessing when Red's voice came from the yard. His spirits wilted. So much for a quiet dinner with Anna.

Pushing her chair back, Anna smoothed down her skirt, then opened the door as Red climbed onto the porch.

"Good evening, Miss Ivey."

Tamping down his frustration, Joe offered Red a smile, but Red wasn't paying him any attention. Instead, he gave a slow whistle. "Miss Ivey, you look just beautiful. Did you make a new dress?"

She lowered her gaze. "I did. Thank you."

He hooked his hat by the door, leaned back his head, and sniffed the air. "Mmmmm. Something sure does smell good."

"It's veal. Joe brought it back from town."

Red's eyes widened. "For all of us?"

"Well, actually, there's not enough for the whole crew." She glanced at the window. "Are the others here, too?"

"Nope. Just me."

"Well, there's certainly enough for three. Would you care to join us?"

"Why, thank you, Miss Ivey. I don't mind if I do."

Joe bit back a groan. "What are you doing back so early? Is everything all right?"

"Fine, fine." Red patted his chest. "Things in town were a bit slow, so I thought I'd come back early and see if you were up for a round of cards."

Joe brightened at the prospect of a game, then remembered his intent to come clean with Anna. "Well, I had actually thought to spend the evening reading."

Red snorted. "Shoot. You can read any ol' time. Besides, I came all the way back. What will I do tonight if we don't play?"

"You could try one of my books."

"No, thanks. I can't think of anything more boring than reading a book."

"What if you read out loud to us, Joe?" Anna set another place. "You should hear him, Red. He has quite a flair for it."

Red lifted his orange eyebrows. "He does? I didn't know that."

Grabbing a roll, Joe broke it apart. A puff of sweet-smelling steam ballooned up.

"We're reading *The Taming of the Shrew*," she continued.

"No foolin'? Well, I suppose I could be talked into a scene or two—especially since Joe's doing the reading and all."

Sighing, Joe cut into his veal. "Actually, I'm no longer in much of a mood for reading. Cards is fine."

"You sure?" Red asked. "I hadn't been read to since I was nothing more than a tyke. Sounds like fun."

Joe gave his friend a pointed look. "I said cards would be fine, Red."

Chuckling, his friend pulled out Anna's chair, then sat down beside her. "Whatever you say. You're the boss."

As soon as supper was over, the men headed for the barn. Anna washed and put away the dishes, but it was still too early to retire. Locating the tin she'd stored her seashells in, she scooped up a handful of shells and looked at the colorful and varied shapes she held.

She wished she knew which ones she'd found and which ones Mama had found. Collecting them was a passion they shared and they always evoked poignant memories.

But lately those memories had been overshadowed by less pleasant ones. Ronny's resemblance to her brother constantly reminded Anna of Leon. And more recently, of the blame she carried over her brother's flight and subsequent death.

She ran her finger over a smooth shell whose brown color was so rich it looked almost liquid. It was the same color as Leon's eyes. The same color as Mama's.

She wondered if at the end of his young life Leon's eyes had lost their luster, for Mama's had dulled to the same faded brown as the shirtwaist she wore. Papa had loved that shirtwaist. He'd tease her, squeezing her side and whispering in her ear until she turned all red in the face.

If he'd seen Mama then, he wouldn't have teased. The hems of her sleeves and the button placket had long since frayed. It hung in loose folds around her skinny shoulders and scraggy waist. And her face had dried up like old widow Nash's. But Mrs. Nash was a grandmother, and Mama was just, well, Mama.

The only life—real life—Mama had shown since Papa joined up was the night Anna confessed that Leon had left for good.

"It's your fault! Your fault!" her mother had screeched.

And, indeed, it had been. Tamping down her shame, Anna had slipped an arm about her mother's waist, led her to the parlor, and settled her in a high-backed chair.

Mama had picked up her needle and thread, the vacant look already back in her eyes. Never again would they shine. Her husband had left, her beloved son had left, and her daughter had betrayed her. She became as fragile and empty as the shells Anna now held in her hand.

Anna closed her fist around them, their edges sharp against her palms. With a force of will, she pushed the memories aside, moved to the floor, and began to sort the shells, concentrating instead on what she might create once she had them all organized.

She'd make something for Joe. Something special. Some little piece of herself to leave behind once her debt had been paid off.

Chapter Twenty

He didn't tell her about Bertha. Not after Red's unannounced arrival, nor on the following three Sundays. Instead, Joe continued to woo her. If Cupid had pierced her heart, though, she kept it well hidden. He, on the other hand, found himself well and truly smitten.

"He drank the entire bowl of sugar!" Anna said, her eyes filled with horror.

She wore her yellow calico, providing a bit of sunshine at the end of a rainy week. He'd spent most of the day inspecting his newly completed log chute. While he was gone, Anna had entertained her first Squamish Indian.

"He kept saying '*kabi, kabi*' and pointing to the coffeepot. But every time I warmed some for him, he filled his cup with sugar, then poured on just enough coffee to saturate the sugar."

Joe smiled. "He was only drinking the coffee for the sake of the sugar. Next time, you can sweeten it for him."

She shook her head. "He was very polite, though."

"I'm sure he was."

She turned back to an assortment of seashells spread across the floor in front of the fire. Every night after dinner, she'd pour more out and sort them by size and color and type. She was close to the bottom of her collection, and he imagined she'd finish her task before the evening was through.

He pulled off his boots and stretched out his legs. It was his custom to read while she worked, but tonight he couldn't concentrate. Closing the volume of poems by Wordsworth, he set it aside and watched her instead.

The yellow gown billowed out around her, its skirt trimmed with a design she'd made with both ribbon and fancy stitches. Her booted toes peeked from beneath her hem.

Clutching the tip of her tongue between her teeth, she turned a cylindrical brown-and-white-striped shell in her fingers, then dropped it in a bowl with other like-minded shells.

His time was running out. Only two weeks left before he lost his land. Joe needed to make his move and he needed to make it soon. He wondered again if his attempts to woo her were working. Not just because of his deadline, but because he was undeniably attracted to her.

It was several moments before she realized he wasn't reading. Glancing up, she froze. He surveyed her hair, her delicate facial features, her creamy neck, and the way her dress stretched across her shoulders and chest.

"Shouldn't you be marrying Mrs. Wrenne soon?" she whispered.

"I should have married her two weeks ago."

"Why didn't you?"

"Several reasons."

She went back to her sorting.

"Anna?"

The stiffening of her shoulders was his only indication she'd heard him.

Unfolding himself from the chair, he joined her on the floor, stretching one leg out and bending the other one. "I don't want to marry Bertha."

She stopped sorting but didn't look up. "She'll be devastated."

He rested an elbow against his upraised knee. "I don't think so."

"I know so."

"How do you know?"

"I spent many hours with her on the *Continental*. We became quite close." She raised her gaze. "You should have told her long before."

"You needn't worry. She'll be well provided for as long as needed. There's even talk of a man who's shown extreme interest in her. A man much more suited to her."

"Who?"

"You don't know him."

"That doesn't mean her distress from being left at the altar won't be humiliating." The firelight added shades of amber to her troubled brown eyes. She lowered her chin. "I just don't want to see her hurt."

"Which do you think would hurt her more? Canceling the wedding or marrying her, even though my interests are elsewhere?"

Scooping up a pile of unsorted shells, she began returning them to a tin. "It's really none of my business what you do."

He covered the tin with his hand. "Look at me."

She shook her head.

Placing his finger under her chin, Joe lifted her face. "My interest lies elsewhere, little robin. My interest lies with—"

"Perhaps you should redirect your interest."

She tried to pull away, but he captured her chin between his thumb and finger.

"Too late." He lowered his mouth.

Slapping his hand away, she scrambled back and avoided his kiss. "You're betrothed, Joe."

"Consider it broken."

"I will not. You cannot. She'll be—"

"Quit harping about Bertha. Accepting my proposal was just as calculated on her part as it was on mine. No feelings were involved for either one of us. What kind of man would I be if I married one woman when I was interested in another?" He grabbed her wrist before she could fly. "Marry me, Anna."

Her eyes filled. "I can't."

"Why?"

"It's too big a responsibility."

"What is?" he asked. "The commitment?"

"No. Not that."

"Then what?" He searched his mind for possible objections. It couldn't be homemaking. She excelled in that area. If it wasn't that or the commitment, then . . . "Children? Do you not want children?"

She started to deny it, then gave him a shattered look. "Actually, Joe, I wouldn't want children."

His mouth went slack. "Why not?"

"I'd make a terrible mother."

"That's ridiculous."

"I don't want to talk about it. My answer is no."

"Just like that? Because you don't think you'd be a good mother?"

She tugged at his hand.

"Do you have feelings for me?"

"Let me go."

"Answer me."

She pierced him with her glare, tears rushing to her eyes. "All right, then. I refuse to have feelings for a man who will marry a woman—any woman—for the sole sake of saving his acreage."

"It's not just that, Anna. It's you. I care for you."

"Really? As much as your land?"

He paused, mulling over her words. Did he? Did he care for her the way he did his land? Anna seized on his hesitation.

"You see?" she said. "You don't care for me any more than you do Mrs. Wrenne. It's the acreage you love. As a matter of fact, you care more about that one chestnut tree out there than you do about any woman."

"That's not true."

"Let me go."

"I'll never let you go, Anna." But he did and she raced from the room, skirt flouncing, ribbons flying. Seconds later, her door slammed shut.

Swiping his hand across the unsorted pile of shells, he sent them to all corners. Why couldn't he make her see they were an excellent match?

He lurched to his feet. He hadn't intended to propose. His declaration was spontaneous and clumsy. Her challenge had confused him, though. If his land were not at risk, would he have still proposed?

It was an impossible question. Because if his land hadn't been at risk, he wouldn't have bought himself a bride. He wouldn't have been in town to greet Mercer's girls and most likely he would never have even met Anna. She'd have been bought by some farmer and taken far away.

He did know one thing; he wasn't interested in finding himself some other Mercer girl—even if there were any to be had, which there weren't.

He wanted Anna. And he wanted her for a lifetime. But she'd said no. A very clear, articulate, emphatic *no*.

He grabbed the bowls of sorted shells, then slammed them onto the table, making no concession for those that jumped free. Returning to his chair, he began to pull on his boots.

Why couldn't she see he cared for her? And it wasn't just attraction. Pausing, he realized she'd carefully evaded his questions about feelings. And if he didn't miss his guess, she did care for him. Maybe even as much as he cared for her.

So why wouldn't she marry him? Was it the chestnut tree?

Swiping up his ax, he crunched across the scattered shells and slammed out the back door. If it was the tree, he could certainly dispel any doubts she had on that account.

❧

Huddled in front of the fire, Anna rested her head against drawn-up knees. It was well past time to retire, but she knew she'd be unable to sleep.

Was it possible that Joe loved her? He hadn't said those words, only that he "cared" for her. Still, he hadn't pretended to have feelings for Mrs. Wrenne.

The thought gave her pause. If all he cared about was his land, then he could simply remain betrothed to Mrs. Wrenne. Instead, he'd asked for Anna's hand.

What possible motivation could he have for that, if not feelings? Strong feelings?

She sighed. She shouldn't have accused him of loving the land to the exclusion of all else, but it was either that or tell him what happened to anyone who got too close to her.

His hurt expression played itself again in her mind. She pushed the image away. She could not afford to feel guilty. Otherwise, he might discover the truth. Something that only Ronny and herself knew: She was in love with Joe Denton.

She smoothed her nightdress over her knees. How could she not be drawn to him? With such an intriguing combination of gentleness and fierceness, loneliness and fullness, intelligence and simplicity?

She pictured him again as he shouted over the mighty redwood he'd felled. As he shaved and washed up in the mornings. As he laughed and joked with his crew. As he read by the fire. As he watched her in the evenings.

She loved him, all right. But her love would go unrequited. It must.

Scooting over to her bed, she reached underneath it and drew out her carpetbag. Its wooden frame peeked through the worn edges of the fabric. Undoing the buckle, she opened the bag and pulled away the false bottom. Her father's letters stared back at her. Smudged. Wrinkled. Dog-eared.

She drew them out and untied the leather cord binding them together. One by one she reread them, though she knew them all by heart. The first few were optimistic and full of patriotism.

Then Papa saw his first battle. And his second. And his third. And the tone of his letters changed. He became tired, weary, worried.

Fingering the last one, she closed her eyes, remembering the day it arrived as clearly as if it had just happened.

After settling her mother in the parlor, she had returned to the entry hall and picked up the letter Mama had dropped upon hearing of Leon's flight. Anna had skimmed over Papa's justification and reasons for leaving. It was a recurring theme, and even though she was older now and knew he couldn't have stayed home while the rest of the town did the fighting, she still resented it.

I know Leon wants to join up as a drummer, but you must not let him, Josephine. Tell him that when I come home I'll make him a tent he can sleep under. Then he'll see what it's like to be a soldier.

He described the countryside but never the details from the battlefields. Finally, she came to what ordinarily was her favorite part. A section at the bottom that he always addressed especially to her.

> *My dearest Anna, I received news through the Jordans that Mama is in poor health, and I worry that you and Leon are not doing as much as you should. Be sure the two of you fetch all the water, make all the fires, work in the garden, help with the wash, and take on as much as you can.*

She and Leon already did that and more. Much more. She'd

not mentioned Mama's decline in her letters, not wanting to worry her father. She wondered again if the Jordans had written him or if Ralph Jordan had caught up to him and given him the news firsthand.

> *I've also been made to understand that you have become somewhat unruly. Don't you realize that when you and Leon argue and misbehave, the rebel bullets come closer to me? But if you and Leon are good, then God will take care of me and bring me home safely.*

A slow chill had filled the pit of her stomach. The fight she'd had with Leon was, in fact, her fault. She'd been tired and irritated with him for playing when there was so much work still to be done. So she'd not only made him angry, but she'd struck Mama as well.

Had Papa been on the battlefield during all that? Had the rebel bullets gone closer to him because of her behavior? What if hitting Mama made a bullet hit Papa at the same time?

She'd squeezed her eyes shut and promised God she'd be good if He'd keep Papa safe. She hadn't known about the bullets. She hadn't known.

Three weeks later, her mother was dead. The doctor said she'd died of a broken heart. But Anna knew better. It was because Anna hadn't been the kind of daughter she should have been. She'd been impatient and surly and picked fights with Leon for the sole purpose of garnering Mama's attention.

How would she tell Papa that Leon had run off? That Mama was dead? And that both were entirely her fault? Still, she knew she must.

Penning that letter was the hardest thing she'd done in her entire life. But even worse was never hearing back from him. It wasn't until his name appeared in the local newspaper as one of the casualties of war that she discovered he'd died at the Antietam

Battle. The same day she'd picked a fight with Leon and accidentally hit her mother.

A tear fell on her nightdress. Anna looked up, recalling where she was, the letter gripped in her hand.

The rain had started again. Bit by bit, a rhythmic pounding penetrated her consciousness. Frowning, she moved to the window and pulled back its sheer covering.

She couldn't see anything but the reflection of the glowing logs from her room's fireplace. Yet she didn't need to see. She knew Joe was out there. With his ax. Chopping down a tree. *The* tree. The chestnut she'd accused him of loving more than anything else.

She leaned her forehead against the window. *Please don't do this, Joe. Not now. Not after I've hurt you. I didn't know it was her tree when I first asked you to fell it. I didn't know.*

But she'd known what it was when she'd made her nasty charge against him. Bile churned in her stomach. She hadn't changed at all. Deep down, she was that same impatient, surly girl who picked fights.

The rain's intensity increased, hammering the glass. She wondered, not for the first time, if the downpour made it hard to grip his ax or secure his footing.

He labors in the rain all the time, she thought. Only violent storms and the danger of fire could keep the lumberjacks from their work. That and darkness. But it was dark now.

Thunk. Thunk. Thunk.

She pictured his strong, agile body swinging the ax, shoulders bunched, knees bent, rain sluicing down his face and neck, finding its way beneath his shirt.

The telltale cracking of a tree ready to fall drew her attention. No shout of timber accompanied it, but then, there wouldn't be anyone in its way.

She held her breath, waiting for the impact, but heard instead a second splintering followed by two consecutive crashes. Then nothing.

The hairs on her arm rose. No scream of victory.

But, of course, Joe wouldn't consider felling that tree a triumph. Yet even as she tried to reassure herself, she forsook her boots, grabbed her wrap and a lantern, then raced down the stairs and flew out into the rain.

Chapter Twenty-one

Joe stood before Lorraine's chestnut tree, emotion clogging his throat. He should have taken it down long ago. It was just a tree.

Lifting the ax, he made his first swing. What was this one little tree compared to the three hundred twenty acres of trees he'd be losing to Tillney? Along with a portion of his skid road. And a section of his brand-new log chute. And the streams and springs coursing through that half.

And Anna. What was it compared to Anna?

It was nothing. It really was just a tree. But with each stroke, he knew the felling of it wouldn't win her hand. He was going to lose her and he was going to lose his land.

He settled into a rhythm as frustration and anger welled up inside him. He didn't want to think about Anna.

So he thought about his land. He should never have relied on Mercer. He should have gone out east himself and found his own bride. Being away all that time wouldn't have been near as bad as losing his land.

And if he was going to lose his land, why did it have to be to

Tillney? Bits of rain sprinkled through the leaves, moistening his face and hands.

The prospect of losing his land, *really* losing his land, became a serious possibility in his mind for the very first time. Before, he'd figured he could somehow work it out. But not anymore. He needed a wife and his last chance had just said no. Again. Judge Rountree wouldn't be offering any more extensions.

Joe recalled the year he'd signed up for the grant and received his acreage. He'd had nothing but an ax and six wild oxen. It had taken him three weeks to break them. Once he had, he hired a four-man logging crew, then started every day at first light.

He cooked and fed the men in one old shanty, then fed the oxen in another. He acted as foreman, bucker, bullwhacker, and faller.

It had taken years of hard work and perseverance to build what he had. And he stood to lose half. Simply because he didn't have a wife.

The rain beat down with a vengeance now, but he was almost done. Directing the chestnut to fall in the opposite direction from which it leaned was child's play. Still, he eyed the spot he was aiming for.

Between the darkness and the rain, he couldn't see a thing. No matter. He knew the lay of his land. After a couple more chops, he felt the tree start to give.

I'm sorry, Lorraine. I'm sorry for not loving you the way I should have.

The sharp splintering of the fibers gave their own cry of warning. Joe jumped out of the way, then watched as it began its descent right where he'd planned.

The sound of another tremendous crack caught him by surprise. He knew without looking up that the falling timber had struck a second tree, breaking off the top of it and redirecting the chestnut's path.

He started to run, praying the portion of the second tree—

falling who knew where—wouldn't crush him and that any ricocheting debris wouldn't impale him.

His pant leg snagged on something. *I'm not wearing my sawed-off pants.*

It was his last thought.

A cold sheet of rain hit Anna as she left the lean-to, soaking her wrapper and nightdress. By the lantern's light, she slowed as she approached the chestnut tree. Only a stump was left. The rest lay prostrate beside it. Her heart clutched; then she scanned the area.

"Joe?" Lifting the lantern, she crept closer, ignoring the rocky ground poking into her feet. "Joe?"

She picked her way along the fallen tree, but the limbs and debris made it near impossible. "Joe? Can you hear me?"

The rain swallowed any response he might have made. Something sharp jabbed into her tender sole. Yelping, she hopped back.

She would have to get her shoes. Retracing her steps, she paused to look around the clearing, squinting in an effort to see through the darkness.

The vague silhouette of a splintered log a few yards away captured her attention. Lifting the lantern, her breath caught. It wasn't a log.

"Joe!"

He lay facedown and unmoving on the ground. Dropping to her knees, she touched his shoulder. "Joe? Are you all right? Can you hear me?"

Putting the lantern down, she slid a hand under his heavy head, lifted it a little, then turned his face so it was no longer buried. She placed her fingers on his neck, then held her breath. His pulse thrummed with a strong and steady beat.

Thank you, Lord.

She ran her hands along his arms and back and legs, checking for breaks and blood. Nothing.

"Joe?"

No response.

"Joe, please. Can you hear me?" She combed his hair away from his face and pulled back quickly when she encountered something sticky.

Oh no. She tentatively reached again for the spot that had blood on it. A knot the size of a lemon grew behind his ear.

Anna's heart dropped. This was her fault. If only she hadn't been so thoughtless with her rejection of him. If only she hadn't mentioned the tree again.

"Joe?" She gently shook his shoulder, tears mingling with the rain on her face. "Wake up. Can you hear me?"

He didn't so much as moan.

She bit her lip. She was going to have to leave him and get help. Either that or sit here until he woke up. But that could be hours yet. Days, even.

She discarded that thought as quickly as it came. *Please, God. Not days.*

Surging to her feet, she ran to the lean-to and pulled a chair from the table, then dragged it out to where he lay. With great care, she positioned it over his neck and head. Rain began to puddle on the seat, but no longer hit his face underneath.

Satisfied, she ran inside to put on her boots, then gathered some blankets. When she had Joe and the chair covered as best as she could, she grabbed the lantern and ran to the men's sleeping quarters, splashing through the puddles, slipping on mud, and tripping over roots.

Anna rapped her fist against the door of the bunkhouse. "Red! Thirsty! Somebody! Wake up!"

Ronny jerked the door open. His eyes bulged. His hair stood out in discordant spikes. His faded blue union suit covered him from neck to foot.

"Where's Red?" she gasped, grabbing the ache in her side.

"Here." Red pushed the door wider, hopping on one foot as he poked the other into his trouser leg. "What's happened?"

"Joe got hurt felling a tree."

Red paused, his shoulders relaxing. "You must be having a bad dream. Joe's a seasoned lumberjack. He'd never do any chopping at night."

She turned her attention back to Ronny. "Joe got hurt felling a tree. I need help moving him inside. Will you come?"

Ronny jerked upright as if struck by a bolt of lightning, then surged forward. "Show me where."

Red grabbed him by the neck and flung him back inside. Anna hadn't realized the rest of the men had crowded behind the door until they caught Ronny as he fell. All of them were mussed. All were wearing union suits. All were staring at her as if she'd lost her mind.

"Let us get our, um, boots on first." Red turned to the men. "Well? You heard her. Get moving!"

She didn't wait but began running back home.

"At the house," she gasped when they caught up with her. "By the chestnut tree. Go on. Hurry."

"Ronny, stay with her."

The men rushed past.

Ronny grasped her elbow. "No need to run anymore, Miss Ivey. The boys will take care of him."

She didn't use up precious breath arguing. She simply alternated between running and jogging. Still, her body refused to cooperate. Several times, she had to stop until the stitch in her side eased. And once, she tripped over a root, sprawling facedown on the path.

The storm worsened, the rain pelting her face with a stinging force. By the time the two of them made it back to the house, Joe was already inside.

They had the fire roaring, the water heating, and Joe stripped of his wet clothing. Wrapped in nothing more than a blanket, he lay on the floor. The men lounged around the kitchen laughing, telling jokes, acting as if Joe's accident was nothing but a trifle.

"He woke up?" she asked.

"Not that I know of." Red glanced at Pelican. "Give him a kick, would you?"

Pelican—a great pouch of snuff swelling his lower lip and making him look like his namesake—gave Joe a little shove with his foot.

"Stop it! What are you doing?" She raced to his side and shooed the men back.

"Oh, come on now, Miss Ivey. It's not too often we get the chance to kick the boss while he's down." There was no malice in Pelican's voice, and his expression was one of amused tolerance. As if he were teasing about some child who'd scraped his knee.

The men chuckled. She could not believe they would jest at a time like this. Before she had time to say so, Fish and Milton lumbered down the stairs with a bed from the spare room.

"Be careful!"

But they paid her no heed, gouging the wall on one side and scraping the stair rail on the other. By the time they made it into the kitchen, they'd left a trail of destruction in their wake.

She quickly scooted a chair to the side.

"Hoist 'em up, boys," Red bellowed.

The men closest to Joe each grabbed a limb and swung him like a pendulum.

"No!" she screamed.

But he was already airborne. The blanket around him slipped loose, pooling at the crux of the V his body made. He landed with a thud on the mattress, his modesty barely intact. A puff of dust billowed out around him.

"Out!" Anna pointed a finger at the door. "Out before I throttle every last one of you!"

They looked first at her and then each other, clearly perplexed.

"What's the matter?" Thirsty asked.

"What's the matter? *What's the matter*? That man has a head injury and you boys are throwing him around like some log you plan to send down the chute. That's what's the matter."

Gibbs glanced at Joe. "Oh, he'll be all right. That little bump's nothing compared to the one a fellow down in Tacoma got. Why, that one was so big it killed him dead. Joe's not dead. He's just sleeping it off."

Narrowing her eyes, she advanced on Gibbs. "Well, let me assure you, Mr. Gibbs, that *bump* you saw on the Tacoma man is nothing compared to what I'll mete out to anybody who so much as touches Joe again with anything other than the most gentle attentions." She jabbed her finger in his chest. "You understand me?"

He didn't budge.

She shoved him. "Do you understand me?"

Falling back a step, he raised his hands. "Yes, miss. We'll all be very gentle from now on. Won't we, boys?"

They mumbled their agreement.

Mollified for the moment, she turned back to Joe and jerked the blanket down to cover his huge, hairy legs. It didn't stop her from noticing the sheer magnitude of them, though. Why, his thighs were twice as big as her waist.

They were also extremely white compared to the dark golden color of his chest. Grabbing the other end of the blanket, she tucked it around his torso.

"What happened exactly?" Ronny asked.

"I don't know. I was up in my room. But from the sound of it, the tree didn't fall straight to the ground. It hit something else, I think. I'm not really sure."

"What in the Sam Hill was he doing chopping that thing in the middle of the night?" Red's exasperated tone had the men nodding and grumbling their agreement.

She lowered her chin. "It's my fault."

"Your fault?" Red's voice held more than a little surprise.

"I've been pestering him to chop it down. You saw how it leaned?"

A log in the fire shifted, causing sparks to shoot out.

"That doesn't explain why he decided to take it down after dark."

She swallowed. "I made him mad."

No one said a word. The water on the stove began to bubble. A crash of thunder shook the windows.

She swiped her eyes. "Somebody needs to go for a doctor."

They looked at each other, shifting their weight.

She frowned. "What?"

Ronny cleared his throat. "Miss Ivey, I don't mean any disrespect, but we can't start out for a doctor until morning. Then it will take half a day to get to town, no telling how long to find the doc, then all those hours to get back. Joe'll be awake long before that and the doc will have come for nothing."

Anger began to simmer inside her. She took a step forward. All but Red took a collective step back.

Anna zeroed in on him. "I want a doctor, Red. And I do not plan to wait until tomorrow night to get one. This cannot be the first time you've had an emergency. What did you do the last time you needed a doctor and didn't have time to wait?"

He pulled at his collar. "Well, we waited until morning and then went and got the doctor."

"What happened to the patient after all that time?"

"He died."

The blood drained from her face.

"Not that Joe's going to die!" he assured her. "He's just got a little bump."

She opened her mouth to protest, but Red interrupted. "Listen, if you want one of us to go get the doctor, well then, I'll send somebody on Shakespeare at dawn and the doc will be here late tomorrow night."

"There has to be a quicker way."

He shook his head. "There is no other way."

"I'll go." Ronny swiped the curl off his forehead.

Anna turned and they exchanged a look. A look that reminded her Ronny knew of her love for Joe. A look that told her he understood her distress.

"You're not going." Red shook his head. "Not in this storm."

Ronny squared up. "I'm going, Red. If you want to fight me, then fight me. But after you're done, I'm getting up and going to town. Tonight."

Anna sucked in her breath, realizing the danger for the first time. "No, no, Ronny. I wasn't thinking about the storm. About the darkness. Red's right. It's much too dangerous to make the journey tonight."

His expression turned stubborn. So much like Leon's.

Panic filled her. "Ronny, please. Waiting until morning will be fine."

Red pursed his lips. "She's right, son. If the dark weren't enough, then the squall is. Best wait until daylight."

But Ronny ignored them both and strode to the door.

"No!" she cried. "Please, Ronny. Don't do this."

She started after him, but Red grabbed her arm. She struggled. Her efforts didn't even faze him.

Ronny paused at the door, his eyes locking with hers. "I'll be back. And with the doctor in tow."

"No!"

But it was too late. The door closed behind him. Just like Leon.

She whirled to face Red. "Please. Please. You have to do something."

He looked at the door, his expression contemplative. "All the time he's been on the crew, that boy's never once squared off. Not to any of us." He shook his head. "He wasn't thinking like a boy just now, Miss Ivey. He was thinking like a man. And if he's man enough to square off, then he's man enough to ride to town."

"But that's just it, Red. He's not a man at all. He is, in fact, still a boy."

Red released her. "Good night, Miss Ivey. The fellows and I will see you at breakfast."

He held the door open. The men filed out past him.

"You won't stop Ronny?"

He shook his head. "I'd have to give him a beating first, and truthfully, I think he'd go anyway. It'd be best if he had all his strength. He's going to need it." Nodding, he clicked the door shut behind him.

Anna wrapped her arms around her stomach, then doubled over and fell to her knees. *Please, God, please.*

She already had to answer to Him for her father, mother, brother, and now Joe. If something happened to Ronny because of her demands, she'd never forgive herself. Never.

The men's voices slowly faded. She lay curled in a ball praying. For Ronny. For Joe. For intervention.

Something sharp poked her. Examining the floor, she discovered seashells scattered about, some intact, some crushed. What in the world?

Her body began to shake, the chill in the room penetrating her consciousness. Pushing to her feet, she stoked the fire and added logs.

It was then she realized Anna still wore her wet, mud-coated nightdress. Good heavens. She'd stood in front of the entire crew in nothing more than a nightdress.

Pushing thoughts of Ronny to the background, she checked on Joe. The lump behind his ear wasn't any bigger, but it wasn't any smaller.

"Hang on," she whispered, smoothing the hair from his eyes. "Let me get out of these wet clothes; then I'll be back, and we'll get that nasty thing cleaned up."

She squeezed his arm, then raced upstairs to change.

Chapter Twenty-two

Joe struggled to push through the fog. If he didn't know better, he'd think he'd consumed an entire barrelful of whiskey. He tried to lift a hand to his head, but his body wouldn't obey his commands.

Something cool touched his forehead. He heard a woman's quiet murmurings but couldn't make out the words. He forced his eyes open, then immediately closed them. Too bright. And it hurt like the devil. The fog rushed in again and he let himself be pulled into its midst.

Anna dipped her pail into the cold stream running by the house. Dawn outlined the eastern horizon with a beautiful array of pinks and yellows. She wondered if the day would bring them a doctor or if Ronny and Shakespeare had ever even made it to town.

Please, Lord. Please let them have made it to town and bring them back safely.

She returned to the house, wrung out a cloth, and placed it on Joe's head. He'd been restless for most of the night. But his stirrings encouraged her. It was better than the deep sleep he'd been in those first couple of hours.

Rinsing out a second cloth, she wiped down his cheeks and jaw. His stubble snagged on the weave. At least he didn't have a fever. In fact, if she hadn't known about the injury, she'd have assumed he was merely sleeping.

She checked the lump behind his ear. Still the same.

His arms jerked, pulling the covers off his chest.

She ran the cloth across his shoulders. "Shhhhhh. It's all right, Joe. Just relax."

He immediately obeyed. It had been like that most of the night. Whenever he tossed and turned, she'd shush him, then rub his neck, chest, and arms with a cool cloth. The tension would instantly melt away.

"The men haven't come for their breakfast," she told him, glancing at the meal warming on the stove. "I'm wondering now if they'll be coming at all. Red said they would. And they need to eat. I'd hate for all this to go to waste."

A slight frown tugged at his eyebrows.

She threaded her fingers through his hair and massaged his scalp, careful to avoid his injury. "Does your head hurt? I'm sure it must. It's time to wake up, though. You need to eat. I've made your favorite. Raspberry slump. Can you smell it?"

A gold, silken curl wrapped itself around her finger. She rubbed it with her thumb. "Once you're feeling better, I'm sure they'll tell you how I made a ninny of myself, crying over you." She worried her lip. "And it's true. I did cry. I cried because . . . because I love you."

She'd tried to shut her feelings off where he was concerned. But she was living in his house, cooking his meals, darning his clothes, spending every free moment with him.

Even that would have been manageable if he hadn't been such an enigma. So kind and quick to laugh, yet so fierce. So hardheaded, yet so gentle. So beautifully packaged, yet so masculine. How could she remain unmoved under such conditions?

She couldn't. And with each passing day her resistance had fallen away like a flower shedding its petals.

She loved him. She'd known it since the day she'd watched him fell the redwood. The dilemma lay in what to do about it.

She straightened the rag on his forehead, then ran her knuckles over his prickly cheek. "My feelings don't bode well for you, I'm afraid. Everyone I love has come to a bad end. And each time it's been a direct result of something I did. And if you don't believe me, just look at yourself. If it weren't for me, you never would have chopped down that tree. And you certainly wouldn't have done it in the dark."

Her throat filled. She couldn't do this again. She couldn't be responsible for the death of another loved one.

"Wake up, Joe, please. *Please.*"

Tracing his eyebrows with her fingertip, she nudged up the cooling cloth and blinked back her tears. "If you do wake up, it would behoove you to send me packing. Though I'm not sure that will help. I managed to kill my father with my thoughtlessness while he was hundreds of miles away."

His eyes flew open.

She squeaked and jumped back.

"You killed your father?" he asked, his voice rough but laced with shock.

Relief and horror warred within her. Horror won out. "How long have you been awake?"

His eyes were clear. Completely, perfectly clear. "For hours."

She gasped. *Hours?* "I've been worried sick about you and you've been feigning sleep all this time?"

"I wasn't feigning anything. The light hurts my head. My body aches from top to bottom. I wanted to rest. So I kept my eyes closed." He frowned. "Now, what about your father?"

She slid her eyes closed. Her relief at Joe's awakening was

quickly replaced with panic over his question. She took a step back.

He grabbed her wrist. His grip was firm. Strong. "Explain."

"No."

She tried to peel his fingers off her wrist.

He grimaced but kept his grip tight. "What did you do to your father?"

Anna lifted her gaze, moisture glazing her eyes. "I killed him," she whispered.

He pulled the cloth from his head. "Why? How?"

"It's a long story."

"I'm not going anywhere."

She'd never shown anyone Papa's letter. Never confessed her sin out loud. Not even to the Lord. But God already knew, and in her heart of hearts, she acknowledged she owed Joe the truth.

She took a deep breath. "The bullets. The rebel bullets. They hit him because of me."

Joe slid his hand down, then wove his fingers with hers. "Tell me."

"I yelled at Leon. Knocked down his soldiers. And would even have struck him, except . . . except my fist caught Mama instead."

He rubbed his head. "You aren't making any sense, Anna. Slow down and start from the beginning."

Sighing, she told him everything, ending with Leon's running away, Papa's letter, and Mama's death.

"So you see?" she said, tears streaming down her cheeks. "I killed them. All of them. And I almost killed you, too."

"Come here." He tugged, trying to pull her closer, but she wouldn't budge. "You didn't do anything, Anna. None of that was your fault."

"It was. And it will happen again if I let you get too close." Wrenching free, she ran from the room and up the stairs.

⁂

The door hinges squeaked. Heavy footfalls crept to the bed. Joe opened his eyes.

Red placed a finger to his mouth, then pointed. Anna sat slumped in a chair, head tilted at an impossible angle, her mouth hanging open. Her hair looked as if a mother bird had tried to make a nest of it. Tangled and snarled, it housed leaves, twigs, and dried mud. She wore one of her old wool dresses, apron tight around her waist.

Joe smiled at first, then remembered the misplaced guilt she carried for her family. For him. He needed to convince her she wasn't responsible.

You all right? Red mouthed, capturing Joe's attention.

He nodded, then immediately regretted the movement. His head felt as if someone had taken a sledgehammer to it. Still, he should get up and get moving. The boys would expect no less.

Pushing himself to a sitting position, he swung his legs over the side of the bed. His vision blurred. The room began to spin.

Red placed a hand on his shoulder. "Easy, there," he said in a hushed tone. "No need to rush things."

Joe waited for the pain to subside, but it never did. "What happened?" he asked softly.

"Looks like the chestnut was a sidewinder and some debris caught you from behind."

Closing his eyes, Joe concentrated. "No. She was falling right where I put her. Caught the top of something else, I think, and I didn't have my sagged pants."

"You didn't have your brains, is what you didn't have. What were you doing out there like that?"

He gripped the edge of the mattress, willing his head to quiet and his stomach to still. "Long story."

Glancing at Anna, Red lowered his voice even more. "She has feelings for you."

Joe was too miserable to bask for long in the pleasure of that statement. He'd already known it, of course. He'd heard her confess it with her own lips. Still, he was surprised Red knew. "She told you that?"

"Didn't have to. She was as protective as a hound with her first batch of pups. Then started blathering about laying you low herself. Didn't make a bit of sense."

Much as he wanted to hear the rest, his stomach had other ideas. "Hand me a bowl."

His retching woke Anna.

"Out you go, missy." Red grabbed her arm and propelled her toward the stairs.

"No, he needs—"

"He needs his dignity. Now go on up and get yourself some rest. I'll stay with him."

"But I don't need any rest and the men haven't had their breakf—"

Red took her by both arms and pulled her up on her toes. "You want me to hoist you over my shoulder and bodily put you in your bed, then that's what I'll do. I don't have the time or the inclination to play nursemaid to some petticoat that makes herself sick 'cause she refuses to get her rest. Now, get."

She narrowed her eyes. "You don't scare me for one sec—"

He slung her over his shoulder.

"Put me down this minute!"

Anna's voice rose over the sound of Red's feet tromping up the steps. Then came creaking hinges. Doors opening and closing, until Red must have found the right room.

A soft thud and a furious shriek. Had he tossed her onto her bed?

"Sleep tight, Miss Ivey." Red's heavy footsteps thumped across the ceiling. "I'll see to it that the boys get their breakfast and Joe stays put. If you aren't up when the doc arrives, I'll come get you myself."

The door closed. Anna's feet bounded across the floor, and the hinges creaked one more time. "I will not—"

"Don't test me, missy. I'll put a piano in front of that door if that's what it takes to get you to rest."

"Joe doesn't have a piano."

"Don't split hairs with me."

Joe imagined them squaring off, nose to nose. His immense, freckled friend and that little wisp of a girl. After a long moment, she stomped back into her room and slammed the door closed.

Downstairs, Joe smiled and lay back down.

When Red stepped up next to him, Joe opened one eye. "If she serves you any mushrooms, don't eat them."

Chapter Twenty-Three

Anna opened her eyes, disoriented and trying to discern what she was doing in bed during daylight hours. *Red.* She lurched to a sitting position, then scrambled to the floor. How long had she slept?

Rushing down the stairs, she girded herself for battle. Red would not find her so easy to manage this time around. But the man was nowhere to be found.

She could not believe he left Joe by himself. Just wait until she got ahold of him. Joe's bed lay in front of the fireplace. He had one arm tucked beneath the covers, the other across his bare chest. His eyes were closed, his breathing even.

She knew he didn't wear anything underneath the blanket, but she didn't know quite what to do about it. Perhaps putting another blanket on top of him would be best.

After smoothing one over him, she hovered for a moment.

He opened his eyes. They were foggy with sleep.

"How do you feel?" she asked.

"Fouled and fly-blowed."

"Let me go get some fresh water and we'll see what we can do about that." She quickly replenished her bucket, then returned to swab his face. "Does that feel good?"

"Um-hum." He kept his eyes closed.

Glancing at the clock, she suppressed a groan. Almost noon. The breakfast pots and pans had been washed, dried, and put away. The lunch buckets no longer lined her shelf. Seemed Red had been busy.

"I need to get the bread started or it won't have time to rise and bake before supper."

He grasped her hand. "Can you rub my head first?"

She hesitated. It was one thing to do such a thing when she thought he was asleep, quite another to do it when he was awake. Still, if it provided him with relief . . .

"Will you keep your eyes closed?"

"Why?"

"Because those are the terms."

A brief smile touched his lips, but he complied. She bent over to begin, then jerked herself straight when her chest brushed against him. Had that happened before?

Pulling the blanket up to his chin, she tucked it in, then decided to give him a one-handed rub, one side at a time.

He frowned. "What's the matter?"

"I can't reach you."

"Yes you can. You did several times throughout the night."

"Well, I can't anymore."

He opened his eyes and she flinched at the pain she saw in them.

"Please?" he asked.

Biting her lip, she scrambled for a solution. She couldn't stand behind him. The headboard was in the way. "Would you mind if I sit on the bed?"

"Not at all." He pulled his hand free, disrupting the covers, then patted the spot beside him.

She propped her hip on the mattress. He dragged her clear

up next to him and left his hand on her hip, his elbow resting on her leg.

She swallowed, deciding this was the lesser of two evils and the sooner she finished the better. Burrowing her fingers into his hair, she watched his facial features relax, his lips part. She pulled her attention back to what she was doing.

After a bit, his grip on her loosened until his hand dangled. His breathing grew deep.

But every nerve she possessed stood at attention. The feel of his luxurious curls encasing her fingers was nothing short of delicious. The weight of his arm on her legs caused a now-familiar tugging within her stomach.

The sight of his bare chest drew her gaze time and again no matter how much she tried to ignore it. The man was solid as a redwood, but even those giants fell prey to axes and saws. Nothing was indestructible—especially where she was concerned.

When she could sit still no longer, she began to scoot off the bed. His hand found her waist. She froze.

"That felt nice," he whispered. "Thank you." He gave her a weak squeeze.

She gently removed his hand and placed it beside him, then rose and stepped away from the bed. It was a long time before her nerves settled into some semblance of order.

⁂

Joe didn't open his eyes right away, but instead took stock of his body. His head wasn't pounding, only throbbing. His leg muscles felt like springs coiled too tight. The side of him closest to the fire was burning up, the other side a bit too cool.

Much as he wanted to stretch and roll over, he had no desire to jar his head. Instead, he kept his eyes closed.

A plethora of smells gave evidence that supper was well on its way. He waited to see if his stomach would rebel against the aromas, but it gurgled in hunger. A good sign.

He listened for an indication of Anna's whereabouts. No clanging pots. No shuffling of feet. But if he concentrated, he could hear a very soft scraping.

Opening his eyes, he let them adjust to the light, then turned his head slowly toward the stove. Anna sat in a chair with a huge bowl of potatoes in her lap and peelings littering the floor at her feet.

She'd tidied her hair and changed into her maroon dress. It was his least favorite of the three she'd made, yet probably the most serviceable. No fancy trim. No contrasting collar or cuffs. No buttons running from neck to toe. Just unrelieved maroon. Still, she took his breath away.

He watched in growing admiration as she quickly worked her knife around a potato, a long coil of its brown skin trailing in the blade's wake. Not wishing to startle her while she wielded the instrument, he remained quiet.

Finishing her task, she flicked the long spiral off the knife and glanced up. "Well, there. How you feeling, Mr. Denton?"

"I'm thirsty, I'm hungry, and I want to sit up."

She raised her brows. "Sounds like somebody's doing better."

"We'll see. Last time I sat up, I lost everything in my stomach."

Standing, she set her bowl on the chair and shook peelings from her apron. "That's what you get for letting Red tend to you." Anna dipped her chin and gave him a stern look. "There will be no more of that. I'll be the one seeing to your needs from now on."

Joe dropped his gaze to her lips but banked his thoughts. He needed to build up his strength first.

"Why don't we sit you up, then see about something to eat and drink?"

"Sounds good." He began to lift himself up.

Rushing over, she gently pushed him back down. "Let's do it nice and slow this time." She circled the bed, coming around the side closest to the fire. "First, I want a look at that lump behind your ear."

He turned his head away from her. The movement intensified

the throbbing, but not too severely. Her fingers explored and pressed. He kept his features neutral, careful not to display any pain.

"I can't tell if the swelling has gone down or not. If it has, it isn't by much. Is it tender when I touch it?"

He shrugged.

"Well, the doctor will be here soon. We'll see what he says."

It took a moment for that to sink in. "Doctor? What doctor?"

But she'd left the room and gone upstairs. A few minutes later, she came back with an armful of pillows.

"What doctor?" he asked again.

"The one Ronny went to town for. He rode in the dead of night to reach him." Anna glanced at the window. "I hope he made it all right."

"You never said anything about a doctor before."

She slipped a hand under his neck and head. "Lift up a little and let me put some pillows behind you."

They spent the next several minutes propping him up against the headboard, cushioned by most every pillow in the house. The task exhausted him.

When she finally quit fussing, he closed his eyes and took several fortifying breaths. "What doctor?"

"The one from town. He should be here sometime today."

"I don't need one."

"Perhaps. It won't hurt to let him have a look, though."

"Nobody's looking at anything. He can just go back where he came from."

She lifted a brow, retrieved a broom, and began to sweep up potato peelings.

"Are you going to give me something to eat?"

"Are you going to cooperate with the doctor?"

He narrowed his eyes. "May I remind you, you work for me,

Miss Ivey. I am hungry. You are my cook. Get me something to eat. *Now.*"

She ignored him.

"Do not make me get out of this bed."

She glanced at the sheet covering his lower half, and he gave her a lazy grin. Red had helped him put on some trousers, but she had no way of knowing that.

Flouncing over to the stove, she dipped a cup into a pot, then presented it to him.

The tin cup warmed his hands. Joe tilted it this way and that. "This is nothing but broth."

"If your stomach keeps it down, then you can try some potatoes once I mash them."

He looked at the stove and pastry table. "What about all that?"

"That's for the men."

"I'll have what they're having."

"You'll have the broth and, later, perhaps some potatoes."

"I'll *have* what they're having."

"You'll *have* what I give you."

He took a sip of the broth. When he was done, if she didn't give him what he wanted, he'd get out of bed and get it himself—he didn't care how much it hurt his head. He needed to get out of bed anyway.

He was just finishing the soup when he heard the men approaching the yard.

Anna hurried to the door. "What on earth? Supper's not for two more hours."

She barely had time to open the door before they poured into the house, all talking at once.

"Ronny!" she exclaimed. "Are you all right?"

The boy's exuberant eyes connected with Joe's. "I made it to town in the rain and pitch black!"

Joe lifted his brows. "You did?"

"I did!"

Anna touched Ronny's sleeve. "Are you all right?"

He nodded. "I'm fine. And Shakespeare is, too."

"He's lucky he didn't break his neck."

Joe quickly found the owner of the amused voice. Doc Maynard. He topped most of the crew by an inch or so, though he didn't have the breadth the other men did. Joe figured it was his accomplishments that made him seem bigger than he was.

Maynard had named Seattle. He'd brought the first residents to town, established the first store, the first restaurant, first hotel, first saloon, and first whorehouse. And that last bit had endeared him to most every man in the territory.

"Hear you jumped in front of a falling tree," Doc said.

"Something like that. I'm all right now, though."

Doc nodded, then moved his gaze to Anna.

"This is our cook, Miss Anna Ivey," Joe said. "One of Mercer's girls."

"So I heard. How do you do, miss? I'm Doc Maynard."

She bobbed a curtsey. "Thank you for coming. Can I offer you some lemonade?"

"With pleasure." He shooed the other men toward the door. "You can tell Joe about your ride to town later, Ronny. For now, you and the boys leave me with my patient."

Anna slipped into the milk room.

"I don't need a doctor."

"Of course you don't. But after coming all this way, I'd at least like to sit awhile and visit." He opened the door and stood beside it, looking at the men expectantly. They filed out. Thirsty pilfered a pastry off the table before making his exit.

Joe threw off his covers and swung his legs over the bed. The room whirled. The soup threatened to come back up. He kept it where it belonged by force of will.

The doc wasn't fooled. "No need to put up a front," he said, closing the door. "Miss Ivey's out chipping ice for my drink."

Joe scowled. "You shouldn't have come."

"Where does it hurt?"

"Nowhere."

Anna came around the corner, then handed Doc a glass of lemonade. "He has a huge lump behind his left ear. The light hurts his eyes. He's tossed up the contents of his stomach and he's weak as a babe."

Joe gritted his teeth. "Would you excuse us, Miss Ivey?"

"Not just yet," the doc said. "I'd appreciate the assistance." He smiled at Anna. "That is, if you don't mind?"

"Of course not."

He raised his glass to her, drank deeply, then set it down. "How long's he been like this?"

The two discussed his accident and ailments as if he were a child.

"I can answer my own questions," Joe growled.

The doc didn't so much as acknowledge him. Scowling, Joe stood up. The sheet twisted around his legs. Whipping it away, he tossed it on the bed and moved toward the door.

The room went from normal to dark, then back to normal. Almost. Concentrating on putting one foot in front of the other, he lengthened his stride. He would *not* black out. If he could make it to a chair on the porch, no one would be the wiser.

He made it as far as the door before the room spun like a whirling dervish. Doc caught him around the waist and wedged his shoulder under Joe's. Without saying a word, he guided Joe back toward the bed, but Joe wasn't sure he'd make it that far. And once he blacked out, no telling what the blasted man would do to him.

Chapter Twenty-Four

The war had changed many things in Anna's life, not the least of which was that social conventions about ladies—particularly unmarried ladies—being present during the examination of a man had loosened. She hadn't realized the practice had reached clear out here, though.

Yet the doctor didn't hesitate to recruit her help, seemingly unaware of Joe's state of undress. She'd seen him shirtless many times, of course, and it never failed to disconcert her. But his unconsciousness and the doctor's presence made it worse somehow. Much worse.

Tan lines duplicating the exact placement of Joe's suspenders testified to how often he worked without his shirt. The pale stripes of skin contrasted sharply with the deep golden hue of the rest of him.

Maynard placed a foot-long wooden cylinder against that burly chest and listened, then moved it lower where the sun-bleached hair on Joe's body trickled down into a V. She pulled her gaze to the doctor's, but her peripheral vision didn't miss a thing, and the lower the stethoscope went, the tighter Anna's own stomach clenched.

Maynard's curly salt-and-pepper hair tumbled over a broad forehead. His china blue eyes narrowed in concentration. "Heart and lungs sound good. Stomach is very noisy."

"Is that bad?"

"No, no. He's just hungry."

She let out a sigh of relief. "He'll be all right, then?"

Straightening, Maynard unscrewed his stethoscope and placed it back in his medical bag. "It's hard to say. My examination will give me some basic information, but I might not be able to detect subtle damages that often occur."

"You mean like his dizziness?"

He lifted Joe's left eyelid, then did the same to his right. "No, I was referring more to confusion, loss of memory, an inability to concentrate, difficulty completing tasks he used to do, that kind of thing."

Anna sucked in her breath, her attention darting back to Joe. He lay still and helpless on his back.

"When will we know if he's been . . . afflicted?" she asked.

"When he wakes up, I'll be able to do a more thorough assessment, but from what you've told me, he was originally unconscious for quite some time. That never bodes well, and neither do these fainting spells."

She clasped her hands in front of her. "Will his ability to continue lumberjacking be at risk?"

Maynard turned Joe's head to the side and poked more aggressively at the lump behind his ear. "Never can tell with these things."

Her throat closed, hindering her ability to draw a normal breath.

Maynard rummaged through his bag, then removed a wooden box. It contained over fifty corked vials wedged into circular slots. "This will help with the pain," he said, removing one. He paused in the midst of handing it to her. "Are you all right? What's the matter?"

The concern in his eyes, the gentleness of his tone undid her. She didn't deserve it. Was unworthy of it, in fact. He should be condemning her, not extending sympathy.

Joe might not be dead, but if he lost his ability to lumberjack, she instinctively knew it would be a living death for him. Never to log again. Never to swing up a tree with nothing more than an ax and a springboard. Never to give voice to the sharp, arresting cry of *"Timber-r-r-r-r."*

"It's all my fault," she choked.

Maynard frowned. "What is?"

"The accident," she said, waving a hand to indicate Joe's limp body. "His injury. His predicament. Everything."

The doctor moved her to a chair, then settled down next to her. "Tell me."

He listened as she explained the events leading up to the accident, then the accident itself—though she was careful not to mention what she'd done to make Joe angry, only that she had.

Removing a handkerchief from his pocket, Maynard handed it to her. "And?"

She blotted her eyes. "So you see? If it hadn't been for me, none of this would have happened."

He leaned back in his chair. "You are God, then?"

She blinked. "I beg your pardon?"

"Well, I was under the impression God was in control of the universe. But if I am mistaken and it is you, I will have to readjust my theology."

His blue eyes held no sense of jesting, no censure, no irritation. Merely polite curiosity.

"Of course I'm not God. How could you suggest such a thing?"

"It is not me who is suggesting it. It is you. Were you the one in control of the tree when it fell?"

"He would never have chopped the chestnut down if it weren't for me."

"Ah, that's right." Doc Maynard stretched out his legs, crossing them at the ankles. "You made Joe angry."

"Yes."

"And once you made him angry, you told him to go chop down the tree?"

"Well, no. I'd asked him to do that earlier."

"Then why didn't he do it earlier?"

She hesitated, not wanting to reveal the sentimental value of the tree. "He didn't want to."

"But he did after you made him angry?"

"Yes."

"And you, somehow, orchestrated that event, along with the nature in which the tree fell?"

She sighed. If he couldn't see the obvious, she wasn't going to explain it further. It was her fault. Clear and simple.

"Tell me, Miss Ivey, where were you when God laid the foundations of the earth? Who determined its measurements? Who stretched the line upon it? To what were its foundations fastened?"

He didn't give her an opportunity to respond but continued to refer to Job 38. He asked her who shut in the sea with doors, who caused it to rain, from whose womb came the ice? Could she bind the cluster of Pleiades or loose the belt of Orion? Could she send out lightning? Did the eagle mount up at her command?

When he finally finished, a heavy silence fell upon the room. A dark-crested blue jay landed on the windowsill, announcing its presence to the occupants of the kitchen with a raucous *shack-shack-shack*.

Anna studied the bird, its feathers looking almost black until the sun touched its wings and tail, revealing a rich, velvety blue. So different from the blue jays at home, yet similar enough to identify.

And God in His infinite creativity had fashioned not only this species of bird, but this exact bird that was desperately trying to balance its big feet on her window. In that instant, the height and depth and breadth of God overwhelmed her.

She thought of the birds, the trees they perched in, the variety of leaves on those trees, the different kinds of barks, the various shapes of their trunks, the assortment of blooms they produced. It was more than her puny mind could begin to comprehend. And to think her actions had some control—*any* control—over what circumstance befell another person was not only preposterous, it was prideful.

"Are you God, Miss Ivey?" Doc Maynard whispered.

Tears spilling down her cheeks, she shook her head.

Joe opened his eyes just a sliver and kept his breathing even, hoping neither Anna nor the doc would notice he was awake while he waited for her answer. There was nothing quite so humbling as Job 38 and 39. He'd awakened while she was explaining why she thought herself responsible for his injury. Only a woman would assume something so illogical.

She clearly believed it, though. Even when he was the one who'd stormed out into the dark, angry and distracted. He was the one who knew better.

He heard Maynard rise from his chair seconds before he entered Joe's line of vision. "You're going to have to stay abed, son."

He glared at the doc.

Maynard was not intimidated. "You can't even make it from the bed to the door. You need to rest. If you don't, you're not only endangering yourself, you're endangering your men."

That was the ace up his sleeve and the doc knew it. It was one thing for a man to take risks himself. Quite another to impose those risks on his men.

"How long?" Joe asked.

"At least a week."

"Impossible."

Doc glanced over his shoulder. "He's to stay put for a week, Miss Ivey."

"I'll see to it," she answered.

Before Joe could respond, Doc asked him a series of inconsequential questions. What was the day, month, and year? Repeat in reverse order strings of digits that increased from three to six numbers.

"Repeat after me," he said. "Kite. Lantern. Foot. Bear. Quill."

"Kite. Lantern. Foot. Bear. Quill."

Joe had to recite the months of the year in reverse order, his multiplication tables, the first paragraph of the Declaration of Independence, and the Twenty-third Psalm.

"What were the list of five things I had you repeat a few moments ago?"

"Kite, lantern, foot, bear, and . . ." He searched his mind. "Quill."

"Very good." Maynard placed the wooden box of medicines back in his bag. "I think you'll be fine so long as you give yourself a chance to rest and recover. I've left some opium for the pain and to help you sleep."

"I don't need anything."

"I'll leave it just the same." He snapped his bag closed. "If you can make it to town next week, I'd like to see you then. If not, don't wait for more than two." He turned his attention to Anna. "I don't think it will be necessary, but if he worsens, send for me right away."

Joe fell asleep before she had a chance to give him the opium. She wasn't surprised, though. He'd insisted on sitting up before the men arrived and staying up even after they left. Even now, he slept in an upright position.

He'd eaten mashed potatoes, rolls, and chicken soup. She had a suspicion, though, that Red had slipped him some chicken liver when she wasn't looking.

Drying the last of the dishes, she stacked them on the shelves. Talk at dinner had been about Ronny's ride to town and the retelling of a story Doc Maynard had entertained him with.

But Anna hadn't paid much attention. Instead, she'd reflected on what Doc had pointed out earlier. She wasn't God. She was a human being. A human being who loved her family. *Faith, hope, and love. And the greatest of these is love.*

A huge weight lifted from her shoulders. There was no sin in loving someone. People all over the world loved each other. And that had nothing to do with the choices their loved ones made.

Papa had chosen to join the conflict knowing full well the risks. Leon had chosen to become a drummer regardless of what Anna did to hinder him. Mama had chosen to stop living long before Anna grew resentful of her mother's withdrawal.

And Joe had chosen to chop down the chestnut in the dark and the rain. He could have just as easily chosen to go to bed. Either way, she had no control over his actions.

Removing her apron, she hung it across the handle of the oven door. If her love did not jeopardize those upon whom she bestowed it, then she was free to love anyone she wanted. Even Joe Denton.

She turned toward him. His head lay back against the pillows. A day's worth of gold and brown whiskers covered the lower half of his face. Short, stubby lashes rested against his cheeks.

The bed linens pooled at his waist, leaving his beautiful torso exposed yet again. When she'd seen him washing, or soothed him with a cloth, or watched the doctor's exam, she'd tried to look away or, at the very least, keep herself somewhat detached.

Now, however, she looked her fill. She looked at him as a woman who admired him. Desired him. Loved him.

He'd asked her to marry him. And not because he had to, but because he wanted to. If he had to get married, and chose to enter into a loveless marriage, then he could have married Mrs. Wrenne.

But he'd said he would sever his betrothal to her. And though Anna was certain Mrs. Wrenne would be disappointed, she knew the woman didn't have feelings for Joe. She was clearly still in love with her dearly departed husband.

Anna turned down the lanterns and approached Joe's bed. The fire cast his face in patches of shadow and light. "Come, Joe," she whispered. "It's time to lie down."

His eyes opened, unfocused, confused.

"Lie down." She tugged on the pillows behind him.

He scooted down, rolled onto his side, and fell immediately back asleep.

The love she'd fought and ignored and hidden burst through its barriers, filling every corner of her being.

"If you ask me again," she whispered, tucking the covers around him, "I'll say 'yes.' "

She placed a light kiss on the top of his shoulder, then made her way up the stairs. And even though her body was tired, her soul, for the first time in years, was light.

Chapter Twenty-Five

Red poked his freckled head inside the door. "Miss Ivey said you have to stay in bed a week."

Joe looked up from his book, *The Three Musketeers*, and waved his friend inside. "Doctor's orders."

"Since when have you ever done what the doctor ordered?" Red pulled up a chair beside the bed.

"Since it suited my purposes." He glanced at the window. "Anna still pouring coffee out there?"

Red nodded and produced three pilfered doughnuts from his jacket pocket and handed them to Joe.

Joe wasted no time in taking a bite. "Well, nursing seems to agree with her, and my time is running out. So I figured if I stayed in the house for a week, I could concentrate on my efforts to woo her." He stuffed the rest of the doughnut in his mouth.

"Think it'll work?"

Swallowing, Joe nodded and ate the next one.

Red leaned forward, propping his elbows on his knees, his expression grave. "The boys have grown rather fond of her."

"You telling me I have some competition?" he asked, eating the third.

"No. I'm telling you that if you plan on compromising her somehow in order to get her to wed you, you're gonna have a bunch of fellows to answer to, and I'll be at the front of the line."

Joe lifted his brows. "I hope you're jesting, because if you really think I'd do that, we'll have to talk with our hands."

Red's shoulders relaxed. "Glad to hear it."

"You can't tell the boys why I'm staying abed, though. If Anna got wind of it, it would ruin everything."

"They're never going to believe a little bump on the head would lay you low for a whole week."

"They won't have any choice."

"They're not chuckleheads, Joe."

"Just the same, I don't want you saying anything."

Anna burst through the door, gripping three coffeepots by their handles in one hand, a fourth pot in the other, an arrangement that never failed to alarm Joe.

"You can't be through, Red," she said. "The hot cakes are coming up next."

He rose to his feet. "No, miss. I won't pass up the hot cakes. I was just checking on Joe."

"I'll see to him. You don't need to worry."

"I wasn't worried, exactly." He gave Joe a smile. "Don't overdo, now."

Joe gave him a salute, then returned to his book.

❧

He hadn't really thought about how much work Anna did each day. Already this morning she'd scrubbed pots, bowls, plates, and cups. Now she ran hot soapy water over a dishpan of silverware, then rinsed it in scalding water.

He felt guilty watching. Especially since he was perfectly fine. He'd made it to the privy without incident. Ate everything Anna had served him for breakfast as well as the doughnuts Red had sneaked him. The lump on his head had diminished quite a bit. And his headache was nothing more than a distant throb.

He desperately wanted to get out of bed. But that would be at cross purposes with his plan. So he tried to read. With Anna slamming in and out, though, he couldn't concentrate. Finally, he closed his book.

She'd drained the utensils and left them to dry on a cloth. Picking up a bucket of hot water, she headed to the door.

"Where are you going?" he asked.

"I need to wash the table, sweep the yard, and start on the potatoes."

"The potatoes? But breakfast just ended."

She smiled. "Your loggers eat a lot of potatoes. Almost a pound per man."

"Per day?"

"Per day."

He frowned. "My garden doesn't have that kind of supply."

"I give Red a list of things I need every Saturday before the boys go to town."

Joe knew she did that, of course, but he'd never paid much attention to her list. A pound per day, per man. That was a lot of potatoes to prepare.

"Is there anything I can do to help?" he asked.

The question surprised her almost as much as it did him. "Perhaps. We'll see how you feel."

Then she was out the door.

Half an hour later, the two of them had massive bowls of potatoes in their laps—him on the bed, Anna in a chair beside him. He eyed her bowl. She was on her second-to-last potato and he'd barely made a dent.

He quickened his pace. Anybody who could bring down redwoods ought to be able to peel a few potatoes faster than some puny female.

He nicked himself, sucked on his finger, then resumed his task. "What's after the potatoes?"

"I scrub the floor."

"And after that?"

"I eat breakfast."

He stilled. "You haven't eaten yet?"

"No. I don't like to eat until I have time to enjoy it."

He glanced at the stove. There was nothing on it.

"What do you eat?"

"I have a plate of cinnamon rolls and bacon set aside."

"What about eggs and doughnuts and potatoes and oats and hot cakes?"

Standing, she shook peelings from her apron. "I'm not a lumberjack, Joe. A cinnamon roll and a couple of slices of bacon is all I need." She noted his four peeled potatoes and raised a brow. "Is that all you've done this whole time?"

He scowled. "Don't you have a floor to scrub?"

Smiling, she set her potatoes on the table and swept up the peelings. He continued to work as she tossed a bucket of hot soapy water on the floor, then switched back and forth with her broom. By the time she'd rinsed the floor in the same manner, he was finishing his task, careful not to let any peelings fall from his bed to her clean floor.

"Thank you," she said, collecting the bowl.

"You're welcome." He snagged her fingers. "You smell good." He wondered if she'd made a sachet with the twinflowers she'd dried.

Blushing, she fiddled with her watch pin. She wore the blue gingham today, her hair bound in the back with a ribbon to match.

"You going to eat something, now?"

She nodded.

"Will you sit by me while you do?"

Hesitating, she glanced at his chest. "Will you put your shirt on?"

He rubbed a hand across his jaw. "I was hoping to shave first."

"I'm not sure that's such good idea. What if you get lightheaded standing up like that?"

Pretending to consider her words, he let out a long sigh. "Yes. I suppose you're right. It sure does itch, though."

She glanced at his shaving instruments. "What if I hold the mirror for you? Then you could shave right here."

He brightened. "You sure you don't mind?"

"Not at all."

"Well, eat something first. Then, we'll give it a try."

Anna tried to hold the mirror still, but she could not completely suppress the tremors besetting her. Always before, she'd taken only surreptitious peeks at him when he shaved. Now she had front-seat viewing.

The tangy smell of his shaving cream hung like a cloud around them. He angled his head to one side and painted white, frothy lotion on his cheek, jaw, and neck.

Dipping the brush back in the bowl, he glanced up at her. "Is your arm getting tired?"

"No. What about yours?"

He hesitated. "I'm all right."

But he wasn't. She could see that the entire affair was taxing his strength. She bit her lip. She should never have let him help with the potatoes. Clearly it had been too much. And now, after he'd sharpened his razor and mixed up his lotion, he could barely lift his arm.

She lowered the mirror. "Perhaps it would be best if I did that for you."

He considered her offer for a long moment, then handed her the brush and bowl.

With an air of unconcern, she whipped up the lather and began to spread it on in long, straight strokes.

He placed his hand over hers. "Circles. It's better if you swirl it on in circles."

He demonstrated, guiding her motions, then released her. The tips of his fingers brushed her arm on their way down. Bumps covered her skin and the hairs on her arm rose.

"Cold?" he asked.

"No. Yes." She swallowed. "A little."

He kept his eyes on hers. She kept her eyes on what she was doing. Finally, she set the bowl and brush down, then reached for the razor.

Frowning, he eyed the blade. "Have you ever done this before?"

"No. Never."

He pressed himself back into the pillows. "Maybe I'd better do this part."

"You can barely lift your arm, Joe."

"I'm feeling better now."

She *tsked*. "I can do it. How hard can it be?"

"It's not hard, exactly, but it does take a steady hand and a smooth touch."

"I can do it." She placed a finger on his chin and lifted.

The closer she came with the razor, the more alarmed his expression until his eyes rolled like a spooked horse. A giggle bubbled up from inside her.

He grabbed her wrist. "Stop. Your hand shakes when you do that."

Her giggle turned into a laugh. And the more she tried to stop, the more tickled she became.

He wrenched the instrument from her hand. "Hold the mirror. I'll do it myself."

"No," she gasped, clutching her side. "I'll stop. I will."

He raised a brow, sending her off into another round of laughter. When she finally settled down, he was trying to hold the mirror with one hand and shave with the other.

She grasped the mirror. “I can do it.”

“No thank you.”

She shook her head. “For a big, strapping fellow, you sure are skittish.”

“I happen to value my jugular.”

She smiled. “I value it, too.”

Heat leapt into his eyes. All humor fled from her, replaced with something just as likely to give her unsteady hands, though.

He released the mirror.

She gently took the razor from him. Touching his chin with her finger, she lifted.

“Start from the bottom and come up.” Joe's fingers closed around her wrist. “Don’t press too hard. The edge of that is extremely sharp.”

She wiggled loose from his grip. “Quit talking. Your Adam’s apple jumps around when you do that.”

Starting at the base of his neck, she pulled the blade up along the curve of his throat. A faint scraping noise accompanied its ascent. Lotion piled up along the flat side of the razor.

Keeping her finger on his chin, she swished the blade in a bowl of warm water, then repeated her action. When she came to the center of his throat, his Adam’s apple bobbed.

“Hold your breath for a minute,” Anna said, taking little scrapes around the bulge in his neck. Straightening, she released his chin and touched her neck. Nothing. She pressed along its entire length.

“What are you doing?” he asked.

“I’m looking for an Adam’s apple. Do girls not have those? Yours is gigantic.”

He touched his neck. “No it’s not.”

“Yes it is.” She shrugged. “But I’ve shaved it now. You don’t need to hold your breath any longer.”

That was a matter of opinion. He’d thought only to find an

excuse to get her near. Never occurred to him that she hadn't done this before. But of course she hadn't. How could she have?

She held her tongue clamped between her teeth as she finished his neck. Twisting around to swish the blade clean, she gave him an unrestricted view of her silhouette. The blue-and-white fabric strained against her chest. He flattened his hands on the sheet.

Grasping his chin, she turned his face to the side.

"Wait," he said. "Why don't you sit down for this part. It'll be easier to reach that way."

He scooted over. She settled down next to him, then leaned close. Very close. Contorting her face, she flattened her cheek against her jawbone, mimicking what she needed him to do. He mirrored her actions. She shaved his cheek.

When she got to the part between his nose and lip, she stretched her lips down over her teeth. Joe did the same, wondering if she even realized what she was doing.

He inhaled, trying to see if he could catch another whiff of the twinflower, but all he smelled was the minty aroma of his shaving cream.

When Anna finally finished, she turned his face this way and that, inspecting her handiwork. "Not so much as a nick." Smiling, she picked up the shaving instruments. "Hold on and I'll get a warm cloth."

She returned, both of her hands covered with a steaming rag. He sucked in his breath as she laid it on his face, then began to relax as the heat dissipated. Cupping the cloth—and his face—with one hand, she used the opposite corner of it to blot up remnants of the shaving cream.

He could have easily taken over the task, but did not. Her gaze followed her ministrations. Down his sideburns, over his jaw, round his chin, across his lips.

She lifted her gaze and stilled, the rag in her hand forgotten.

Without breaking eye contact, he took the rag, then dropped it on the chair beside the bed. Sliding his hand to the back of her neck, he slowly, slowly drew her to him, giving her plenty of time to withdraw. Her eyes fluttered shut.

The kiss was soft, hesitant, and gentle. Then she moaned and all cognizant thought deserted him. Pulling her against him, he deepened the kiss. Her hands slid up his arms, onto his shoulders, and into his hair. He ripped his mouth from hers, kissing her eyes, nipping at her ears, nuzzling her neck.

She squirmed against him.

Recapturing her lips, he pulled her onto his lap and fell back against the pillows, twisting her around so she lay half on the bed, half on him.

If you plan on compromising her somehow in order to get her to wed you, you're going to have a bunch of fellows to answer to.

He stilled, then gently pulled back. Pillows cushioned her head. She stared at him, wonder and desire fogging her eyes. Bits of honey-colored hair curled along the white of her neck.

She blinked. Once. Twice. Then her eyes cleared.

Gasping, she shoved him back and scrambled off the bed. "Good heavens!"

Her cheeks filled with color. Whirling, she ran from the room and up the stairs.

Chapter Twenty-six

Anna fell onto her bed, burying her face into her pillow. Was that what people referred to as sins of the flesh? She rolled onto her back and touched her lips.

No wonder mothers were so adamant in their warnings. If Joe hadn't stopped, no telling what would have happened. He certainly was gaining his strength back in a hurry, though.

She flung an arm over her eyes. How could she ever go down those stairs and face him again? What must he think after she'd sprawled herself clear across him and his bed?

Shame and embarrassment washed through her. She might have decided she'd marry him if he asked again—and if that kiss was any indication, she felt sure he would—but that was no excuse for putting the cart before the horse. And it was up to her to see that things remained circumspect until after the vows had been said.

She glanced out the window. In another hour or so, she needed to serve him his lunch. Yet she couldn't simply hide in her room the whole time.

Pushing herself up, she went to her washstand and poured a

bit of water into the bowl. It had been a while since she'd given the upstairs a thorough cleaning. Maybe she'd do that now.

She cooled herself with a rag and water, then headed to one of the vacant upstairs rooms. She worked her way through the entire floor and all too soon stood at the threshold of Joe's room. Pushing on the door, it slowly swung open.

A massive family bed—a symbol of strength and stability—dominated the far wall. She'd been in his room many times before and it always disconcerted her. This time it was worse. Worse because she'd given herself permission to accept his marriage proposal. Worse because the remnants of their kiss still lingered. Worse because she realized much more than kisses would take place in here once they wed. *If* they wed.

The walnut headboard consisted of three levels of carved finials that triangulated to a narrow peak near the ceiling. A nightstand and matching bureau topped by a huge mirror completed the bedroom set. Stepping into the room, she opened the curtains, illuminating the exquisite Rococo Rose wallpaper.

It never ceased to surprise her. It simply wasn't what she imagined a lumberjack would choose. Of course, he'd prepared this room for his bride. The one who didn't live long enough to see it.

She smoothed his bed covers, which featured an English countryside printed in red against a white background, then wiped down the oil lamp on his nightstand. *The Taming of the Shrew* lay on top of a small writing box.

Had he continued to read it? He must have. Why else would it be here? She quickly dusted it and the writing slope. A piece of paper protruded from a corner of the box. Lifting the lid, she tried to tuck the correspondence back inside, but it was snagged on the pages above it. She pulled it from the stack, meaning only to lay it on top of the pile, when Bertha's name leapt from the page.

> *. . . Bertha Wrenne's husband not dead* STOP *Is returned from confederate prison camp* STOP . . .

Sinking onto the edge of the bed, Anna read the telegram in its entirety. Not dead? Mrs. Wrenne's husband was alive? Her friend must have been thrilled at the news.

Anna looked at the date. July thirteenth. The telegram had been sent four days after their arrival in Seattle. One day before Joe had returned to town to see Mrs. Wrenne.

A knot formed in Anna's chest as pleasure for her friend was quickly overridden by an impending sense of betrayal. He'd known about Mrs. Wrenne all this time? Before he'd shared the picnic with Anna on the redwood stump? Before he'd purchased the fabric on her behalf? Before the quiet evenings in which he'd read to her?

She glanced at the volume of Shakespeare. *Will you, nill you, I will marry you.*

Her breath came in short, erratic spurts. He'd known. He'd known about Mrs. Wrenne's husband. Yet he'd pursued her, wooed her, then culminated with a marriage proposal. All under false pretenses.

A pain similar to the mourning she'd felt after her family members died seized her. What a fool she was to think he loved her. And she'd responded completely. But clearly, he was only manipulating her. Using her to save his land.

She felt hot. Light-headed. Nauseated. Shoving the telegram in her pocket, she clutched her stomach, bent over, and hung her head between her knees in an effort to regain her equilibrium. She recalled the staunch arguments she'd foolishly given him on Mrs. Wrenne's behalf.

I just don't want to see her hurt.

Which do you think would hurt her more? Canceling the marriage or marrying her even though my interests are elsewhere?

His interests were elsewhere, all right. They were in his land and himself. Her stomach tightened. Seemed he was a bit like Hoke after all.

Tremors took hold of her body, starting on the inside and spreading to the outside. She tried to relax but couldn't. She tried to take a deep breath but couldn't. Moisture collected on her face, neck, and hands. No longer able to stay balanced on the side of the bed, she moved to the floor and pulled her knees up to her chest, curling into a ball. She waited for the pain to go away. But it never did.

Joe glanced up from his book when Anna entered. One look at her face and he knew he had some apologizing to do. At least he'd had the presence of mind to put his shirt on before she returned.

"Anna?"

She stepped next to the table and uncovered a plate that held the same lunch she'd packed for the men earlier. "What would you like to drink?"

He threw off the covers and moved to the table where she stood. He wanted to touch her but thought better of it.

"You're supposed to stay in bed," she said.

"I'm sorry, Anna," he whispered.

Her eyes filled.

Taking the plate from her hands, he set it back on the table. "Please don't cry. I took advantage and I had no right. I'm sorry."

She moistened her lips. "Can you be more specific in what you mean when you say you took advantage?"

He frowned. "This morning. I'd only planned to . . . well, it was supposed to be a simple kiss. I got carried away. I'm sorry."

"You *planned* it?"

"I've been planning to kiss you for quite some time now."

"I see." She glanced at his plate, her tone flat. "Would you like some milk with your lunch?"

He studied her face. Something wasn't right. He could understand her being upset, but she looked awful. Ill, almost. Still, he knew she'd enjoyed the kiss as much as he had. Slipping his hand into hers, he gave her a gentle squeeze. "What is it, Anna?"

"I was wondering when I would be released from my debt to you?"

He stilled. "Actually, I was hoping you would reconsider your answer from the other evening and would consent to marry me."

"What about Mrs. Wrenne?"

"The agreement between Mrs. Wrenne and me is no longer."

"Oh? Why not?"

"Does it matter?"

"Yes." Anna looked him square in the eye. "It matters a great deal."

He needed to tell her. If he didn't, someone else would the next time she went to town, and then where would he be?

Bracing himself, he intertwined his fingers with hers. "It turns out Bertha's husband is still alive and came to Seattle to collect her."

Surprise briefly touched her eyes, but other than that she gave no outward reaction to the news. "Well, that must have come as something of a shock. When did you discover this?"

Does it matter? But he didn't voice the question again, because he already knew the answer.

She pulled her hand from his. "When will I be released from my debt to you?"

"I haven't worked out the exact date yet."

"Don't you think you should?"

Swallowing, Joe took a deep breath. "It will take a while. Your passage ended up being four hundred dollars."

"I knew nothing about all that. I only agreed to fifty dollars."

He stood his ground. "And my offer of marriage?"

"I'm sorry. I won't reconsider."

"Why not?"

She pulled a crumpled piece of paper from her pocket and handed it to him.

His breath hitched when he recognized it. "You looked through my things?"

"Not on purpose. It was sticking out of your writing slope when I was dusting. Now, if you'll excuse me, I believe I'll go collect some eggs."

He tried to catch her wrist, but she swerved out of reach.

"Anna, please."

She stopped with her hand on the doorknob, her face pale and void of expression. "How much longer do you have before losing your land?"

"Twelve days."

She nodded. "I am sorry, Joe. I really am. And I will stay until my debt is paid off, but then I'll be leaving."

No. "To go where? To do what?"

"Does it matter?"

She threw his words back at him, then didn't wait for his answer as she slipped out the door. And it was just as well. There was nothing he could say. The game was up. He'd taken an all-or-nothing gamble and gone bust.

He was going to lose his land. In twelve days' time, Tillney would walk onto half of his land and harvest the wood Joe had staked his future on. He could divert the stream. He could build a house. He could set the whole thing on fire and Joe could do nothing.

So why was the loss of Anna grieving him even more than the loss of his land?

By the time she returned with the eggs, her calm had been restored and her stomach had settled. Joe was nowhere in sight. His bed by the fire was made. His shaving utensils were cleaned and put away. His book was gone.

Was he in the necessary? Had he gone to his room to lie down? She tiptoed upstairs. His door stood open. His bed, untouched.

Returning to the kitchen, she kept an ear cocked for any noise from outside. What if he'd fainted again? She slipped out the door and slowly approached the privy.

"Joe?"

Nothing.

She knocked. "Joe? Are you in there?"

Shielding her eyes so that she'd only see his boots if he were inside, she opened the door. It was empty.

Where was he? Should she go to the logging site? If she did, supper would be late.

In the end, she did nothing. She was Joe's cook. Not his nanny. Not his nurse. And certainly not his family.

When the men finally approached the yard, she stood on the porch waiting, coffeepots in hand. Joe was with them. She let out a sigh of relief.

Yet the carousing and revelry that normally accompanied their arrival were blatantly absent. Had he told them she'd refused his offer? Even though the men didn't know the full truth of the situation, the thought still gave her pause. Her rejection of Joe's offer and the resulting loss of his land would greatly impact his crew. Would he have to let them go? And if he did, what would they do? What would Joe do?

A thread of guilt infiltrated her resolve. She'd grown terribly fond of these men, and she actually loved Joe. His actions might have been subterfuge, but hers were the genuine article. That part hadn't changed.

And standing on the porch watching their approach, Anna realized she had no real ambitions. No planned future. She'd simply come out west to escape and hadn't thought beyond that.

But Joe had come out west with huge aspirations. Huge plans. And all would be ruined now through no real fault of his own.

She swallowed. He should have been honest with her. But she could certainly see why he hesitated. Especially when considering her resounding refusal of him when she'd first arrived.

She glanced at him. He looked horrible. His skin was a pasty color. His dimples were completely absent. And his eyes held such bleakness, she had to look away.

The men mumbled a greeting, then gathered round the table. Joe said nothing. Did his artifice mean he was untrustworthy in every area?

Not necessarily.

And what if he wasn't? What if he was simply acting in desperation in order to save his land?

She shook her head. It was one thing to be desperate. It was something else entirely to entice her into marriage on false pretenses.

Joe said the blessing. She began to pour the coffee. The men thanked her, but no one teased or joked. Not with her. Not with each other.

They concluded their meal in swift order and started on their chores. She frowned when Joe picked up his ax. Surely he wasn't going to chop wood. She looked at Red, but he wasn't paying any attention to Joe. He was staring at her, his expression accusatory.

Spinning around, he headed to the barn, making no effort to interfere with Joe's chopping.

She cleared the table as quickly as she could, then finished the cleanup inside. At long last, the men left. She hung her rag on the oven-door handle, removed her apron, then hesitated. She was unsure if she should retreat to her room, stay and sort shells, or make sure Joe didn't need any opium.

Before she could decide, he entered and went straight to the stairs. She heard him climb the steps, then cross the hall. His drawers opened and closed. Moments later, he reappeared with arms full. He walked out without so much as acknowledging her.

He was moving to the barn.

She stood for a long while before finally placing her tin of shells on the table. She knew the decision she'd made was the right one. The best one. But that didn't make it hurt any less.

Smoothing her skirt beneath her, she began to sort her shells. One thin spiraled shell in pink and brown, one white clam shell, one sand dollar. She ran her thumb over the exquisitely formed star in the middle of the chalky treasure she'd found on the South American coast.

Pressing a little too hard, she accidentally broke it. She stared, bereft, at the broken pieces. How quickly something so beautiful, so perfect, could be shattered.

Chapter Twenty-seven

The next morning, Anna heard Joe enter through the door. Should she turn from the stove to greet him or wait until he greeted her? Should she ask if he needed a packed lunch, or would he be staying here? Should she offer him a cup of coffee or let him get his own?

She waited for him to make the first move, but he simply collected his shaving instruments and left again. No greeting. No coffee. No nothing.

She moved the oats to the back of the stove and began to assemble the men's lunches. The longer Joe stayed away, the tenser she became until she thought she'd break apart as surely as the sand dollar had.

Breakfast was cooked and the men had arrived before he finally came back. Still, he said nothing and the men took their cue from him. During the entire meal, she found herself hiding in the kitchen, coming out only for refills and subsequent courses.

When breakfast was finally over, the men filed past the porch, picking up their lunch buckets. Red said nothing. Pelican, with a wad of snuff already tucked into his lip, nodded. Fish mumbled a thank-you without making eye contact. Wardle, Milton, Gibbs, Thirsty, and the rest took their turn, and with each one, the confusion and hurt she felt at their reticence built until she wasn't sure how much longer she'd be able to stay on the porch and still keep her emotions in check.

One more and she'd be done.

Ronny extended his hand. She handed him his bucket.

"Thank you, Miss Ivey," he said, looking like a puppy who'd been kicked but was willing to come back on the off chance that this time, his master would offer love instead of cruelty. "The chestnut dressing sure was good."

She bit her cheeks, not trusting herself to speak. He searched her face for a long moment. Walking up, Joe nudged him. The look of hostility Ronny shot back at him caused her to suck in her breath. But the boy obeyed and hurried to catch up with the others.

Joe glanced at the empty porch. His color wasn't perfect, but it was better than yesterday. She wondered if he'd liked the dressing, too, and if he knew she'd made it especially for him.

"Where's my bucket?" he asked.

She sighed. "I wasn't sure if you were going or not."

"I'm going."

How's your bump? Did you sleep all right? Are you still suffering from headaches? What about the dizzy spells?

"The doctor said you were to stay in bed for a week."

"I'll manage."

"But I told him I'd make sure you did as he instructed."

"I said, I'll manage."

"I see. Well. Your lunch is made, of course, but I'll need to transfer it from the plate to a bucket. It'll only take me a minute."

He didn't follow her inside. Her hands shook as she wrapped his sandwiches and the rest of his lunch, then packed it into his bucket.

When she returned to the porch, he stood in the middle of the yard, head bowed, hands in his pockets.

"Joe?"

He looked up. "I've figured out how much longer it will take for you to work off your debt."

Her heart began to clamor.

He moved to the bottom step. "It will take until Saturday. Then you'll be released from any obligation."

The tears dammed at her throat broke loose and rushed to her eyes. With tremendous effort, she managed to keep them from falling. "Five and a half weeks of work doesn't even begin to cover a debt of fifty dollars."

He took the steps and stopped on the last, placing them at eye level. "I know, little robin. But seeing you day in and day out and never touching you would be . . ." He looked at her lips, then averted his gaze to the wooden slats running along the floor of the porch. "I just think it'd be best if you went ahead and left."

She crinkled her apron with her free hand. "And the fifty dollars?"

He looked up. "You were brought here under false pretenses. You owe me nothing."

That wasn't true and they both knew it. Mercer was the one who'd brought her here under false pretenses.

He reached out, snagging the bucket from her hand and grazing her fingers at the same time. "I'm sorry, Anna. I should have told you the truth sooner. Much sooner." He swallowed. "Because it's not what it looks like. I really do care for you. I do."

Turning, he left the yard. He walked by the chestnut still laying prostrate on the ground, but didn't give it a glance. After another curve in the path, he was out of sight and earshot.

She didn't dare believe him. He'd received that telegram only days after she'd arrived. Hardly long enough to develop feelings of any kind, much less deep, lasting ones.

Sinking onto the steps, she covered her face with her apron and sobbed.

❧

"We'll be leaving after breakfast on Saturday," Joe said.

The boys had removed the bed from the kitchen and returned it to its proper place upstairs, then retreated for the evening. She'd hoped Joe would stay and keep her company, but he stood at the backdoor poised to retire.

"You don't have to run off to the barn, Joe."

"Yes I do." His voice was low. Intimate.

She swallowed. "It's your house. Your kitchen. If I make you uncomfortable, then I need to be the one to sleep in the barn, not you."

"You have no idea how you make me feel, Anna. And believe me, I'd rather not be up there imagining you in that cot I've been keeping warm these last many weeks."

Blood rushed to her cheeks.

He opened the door.

"Are you going to see the doctor while you're in town?" she asked.

"I'm going to find a cook." He closed the door.

A click of the latch. A creak on the porch steps. A padding of footsteps on the path. The farther he went, the heavier the weight in her chest.

He was going to look for a cook. But the person he found wouldn't know that Milton liked his meat burnt, while Thirsty liked his still mooing. That Ronny didn't care for vegetables but had an insatiable sweet tooth. That Fish would eat pork seven days a week and that Joe would eat anything at all—except mushrooms.

But a cook was the least of Joe's worries. In a little over a week, he'd lose his land and most likely his men. She'd be kidding herself to pretend she didn't care. To pretend she didn't know that if she married him on Saturday, he'd have it free and clear. And the crew she'd come to care for would have secured their jobs.

Should she marry him, then, for the sake of his land and for the sake of his loggers? Could she? How far, exactly, was she willing to go for Joseph Denton?

She didn't know. She simply didn't know.

Looking at the shelf holding the shells, Anna considered the time and effort she'd spent separating them. Yet she hadn't even begun to make anything. All at once, finishing at least one keepsake before she left became of utmost importance.

Placing the assorted jars on the table, she decided she had time for a small frame. With paper and pen she sketched a rough design. Tomorrow, she'd try to find a wood plank to use as a base, and she'd cook up some hide glue. And at some point, she needed to think about where she'd go from here.

The gray Saturday morning matched everyone's mood. Joe headed to the barn to hitch up the wagon, the rain rapping against his hat and jacket. His loggers filed by her, taking the last lunch bucket she'd ever prepare for them. Their feet dragged. Their expressions were somber.

"You be careful in town, Miss Ivey."

"If you need anything, you know who to call."

"I'll sure miss your vinegar pies." Milton jumped when Thirsty elbowed him. "Oh. And you too, Miss Ivey. I'll miss you, too."

One by one they left until only Ronny stood before her. Water slid off the roof, screening in the lean-to.

"You're really going?" His bucket dangled from one hand.

Her throat thickened. "I'm afraid so."

"But why?" His face showed confusion, hurt.

"Because my obligation to Joe has been fulfilled."

"No, I mean, why won't you marry him?"

She fingered her watch pin. "It's complicated."

"I don't see how. You love him. He loves you."

She reached out and took his free hand. "He doesn't love me, Ronny. He loves his land."

"He loves both."

"I don't think so."

"I know so."

She gave him a sad smile. "Don't worry. I'm sure the new cook will take good care of you."

He worked his jaw back and forth.

Oh no. Don't cry.

"What will you do?" he asked. "Where will you go?"

"I hope to find another job in town."

His Adam's apple bobbed. "Why can't you stay and work here?"

Anna strengthened her resolve. "I just can't."

"Yes you can. You just don't want to." His tone was sharp. Defensive.

"Ronny, I—"

"It's okay. I understand." He backed out of the lean-to and into the rain. "Good-bye, Miss Ivey."

She pressed a hand to her throat. "Good-bye, Ronny."

He turned, and she realized that the moisture she'd seen on his cheeks hadn't been solely from the rain.

Joe had attached the black isinglass curtains to the wagon's canopy. Still, it didn't keep the rain from angling onto them. Anna shivered. Snatching a blanket from behind the seat, he settled it over her shoulders.

"Thank you." She draped it over her hair, then wrapped it round and round her body in mummylike fashion until only her eyes showed.

The ride to town had been torturous so far. Not so much because of the weather, but because of the tension between the two of them. He'd not been fit company all week and had therefore steered clear of her. To now sit side by side in strained silence for half a day was making him a candidate for Bedlam.

Still, he didn't feel like talking. Not when he was about to lose her and his land all in one fell swoop.

They'd reach Seattle within the hour, though, and he'd take her straight to the Occidental. He'd get her a room, then leave her to her own devices while he headed to the dining area. Maybe their cook, Owen Nausley, would have some idea who Joe could hire to replace her. Because there'd be no going back to the simple fare he and the boys had survived on for the last eleven years. Even if the boys could stomach it, he couldn't.

All of Mercer's women were long gone, of course, so it would have to be a man. A couple of months ago, that wouldn't have bothered Joe in the least. But now, it would be quite an adjustment.

No man would keep the place as clean as Anna. No man would cause the boys to wash up before supper. No man would brighten the house with calico dresses. No man would smell like twinflowers.

Of course, the house had smelled like glue for the past two days. He'd caught glimpses of her shell collage drying on the table but hadn't lingered long enough to study it. He'd wanted to, though. But if he'd stayed too long in the kitchen, her artwork wouldn't be the only thing he'd study.

So he'd quarantined himself to the barn. If he thought that had been lonely, he knew the house would be unbearable once the new cook started. No need for a male cook to sleep in the main house. He'd bunk up with everyone else.

The rain turned to mist, and Anna pushed the blanket back from her head.

"You cold?" he asked.

"No. I'm fine, thank you."

The wagon hit a rut, flinging them together before settling back into a rhythm. Even through all the layers that separated them, the single point of contact sent longing shooting through him. What would she do if he yanked the horse to a stop, wrapped her in his arms, and kissed her like he had the other day?

Would she think he was making a last-ditch effort to manipulate her into marriage? Or would she respond? Respond the way she had last time?

Just thinking about it made his heart hammer. And what did he have to lose? The worst he could get was a slap in the face. The most he could get was . . . he swallowed. The most he could get wasn't anywhere close to what he wanted. Not unless they were wed. And what he wanted had more and more to do with Anna and less and less to do with his land.

He slowed the horse. His hands began to sweat. It was now or never.

Shakespeare shook his head, then came to a stop.

Anna looked around. "What's wrong? Why are we stopping?"

Joe said nothing. Just stared straight ahead, wrestling with his conscience. His desires. His feelings for this woman.

"Joe?"

He wrapped the reins around the dash rail.

"Is something wrong?"

Then he turned and looked at her, holding none of his thoughts back. Her eyes widened. Her lips parted.

He wiped his hands on his thighs, then reached out, cradling her face. "I'd like a kiss good-bye."

"What?"

He leaned down and brushed his lips against hers.

"Joe, I—"

Digging his fingers into her hair, he pressed his mouth more firmly to hers, increasing the intensity of the kiss. He'd barely gotten started when she began to struggle. Disappointment assailed him at her protest, but he pulled back.

"The blanket," she gasped, wrestling with it. "My hands, I can't, they're . . ."

He quickly freed her from the blanket's confines and she launched herself into his arms. He dragged her across his lap and kissed her as if there were no tomorrow, because in fact, there would be no tomorrow for him.

Every part of them was involved in the kiss. On and on it went until he thought he'd scatter like debris after the felling of a tree.

He wrenched back and held her head tight between his hands. "Marry me."

Her chest heaved in an effort to capture her breath. And with each upward motion, she pressed herself more closely against him.

He gave her a quick, hard kiss. "Marry me."

"Oh, Joe." Her eyes searched his.

He kissed her again. "All you have to do is say 'yes.' We'll do it today. Now. As soon as we get to town."

Something changed then. She calmed. She slowed her breathing. She collected herself. "Do you love me, Joe?"

"I . . ."

Did he love her? Well, he certainly felt more for her than he had for Lorraine.

"If we waited until next week," she continued, "would you still want to marry me?"

He frowned. "Next week? Why would we wait until next week when we're practically in town already?"

"No." Anna brushed a lock of hair from his forehead. "I mean, if we waited until you lost your land. Would you still want to marry me?"

He reared back. "Why would I do that? If we're going to get married, it is of utmost importance that we do it before I lose the land, not after. You're not making any sense."

Sighing, she stroked his lips with her fingers.

He nipped her little finger with his teeth.

She extracted herself from his embrace, then moved back to her side of the seat. "Well, it doesn't matter anyway. The whole thing is hypothetical."

"What do you mean it's hypothetical?"

"The question."

"There was absolutely nothing hypothetical about my proposal."

She pulled the blanket up over her shoulders. "No. I don't suppose there was."

"Then what the blazes are you talking about? Are you going to marry me or not?"

"Not." She flipped the blanket over her knees. "I'm afraid I'm not."

He closed his eyes, trying to figure out exactly what had happened. "How can you kiss me like that, then tell me no?"

"I didn't mean to give you the wrong impression. I'm sorry."

"Give me the wrong impression? *Give me the wrong impression?* If you'd kissed me any more thoroughly, I'd have gone up in smoke. Just what impression was I supposed to have gotten?"

Her entire face flushed. "I'm sorry. It won't happen again, I assure you."

He flung up his hands in a gesture of disbelief. "And that's supposed to make me feel better? Just what was that, then?"

"A good-bye kiss, I believe, is how you described it."

He stared at her. Shocked. Confused. Angry. And frustrated as the devil. Jerking the reins from the dash rail, he slapped Shakespeare with a bit more intensity than he should have. The horse jumped, then trotted, making the wagon jostle so much Anna flew clear up off the seat.

But he didn't slow their pace, nor did he help her stay anchored. She could fall off the stupid wagon for all he cared. And when she did, he'd be hanged before he even looked back.

Chapter Twenty-Eight

Hound Dog, Anna's private nickname for the clerk at the Occidental, handed Anna a missive and a purse of coins. "Mr. Denton said this was yours."

"Thank you, Mr. Collins."

The pouch's weight and jingling indicated it held quite a bit of money. Frowning, she looked around. "Is Mr. Denton here?"

"No, miss. He's headed back to his place."

She blinked. "But we just arrived an hour ago."

Hound Dog shrugged. "He went over to Yesler's Cookhouse and hired Ollie Rendorff right out from under Mr. Yesler. They left not fifteen minutes ago."

She glanced at her watch pin. "Why didn't you come and get me?"

"He said not to bother you."

But he'd not even said good-bye, she thought. Well, unless she counted that kiss, but that had only been an act of desperation on his part.

"Did he leave my carpetbag with you?"

"No, miss. Only that pouch and the missive I just gave you."

"I see. Well, thank you."

Moving to the porch, she broke open the letter.

Anna,

I forgot to put your bag in the wagon. It is still in the house. Please accept my apologies. I will bring it to town next week when I come for other business.

I have told the Occidental to forward your bills to me until you have found a new job or made other arrangements. I have enclosed a modest remittance to help you launch whatever pursuits you decide to follow.

Sincerely yours,
Joe

She looked inside the pouch. He'd left her enough money to live on for several months, longer if she was careful. And if she didn't have her bag, she'd have to wear the clothes on her back for another week and finger-comb her hair.

Leaning back in the chair, she watched the rain pummel the ground in an unrelenting gush. Lightning seared the sky with a flash of light so bright it took her a moment before she could see again. The crash of thunder followed several seconds later.

Joe was driving home in this mess. Just like the last time he'd taken a new cook to his place. Sighing, she pulled the drawstrings of the money bag closed.

She'd keep the coins. She had no delusions about what it meant to be destitute. Once she secured a job, though, she would return the balance and pay back any she'd used. The sooner the better. She probably ought to repay the fifty-dollar fare she'd agreed to, also.

Anna read the note again. His "other business" must be the transfer of his land to Mr. Tillney. Joe's twelve days would be up a week from tomorrow.

Propping her elbow on the arm of the chair, she buried her face in her hand. When he brought her belongings next week, it would be her last opportunity. If she didn't marry him then, the land would be lost and so would her chances of marrying him.

People married for convenience all the time. She already loved Joe and he certainly wasn't immune to her. But did she really want to live in a loveless marriage until Jesus took her home?

No. She did not. But that didn't make her feelings for him lessen. Nor did it make her guilt go away, for her decision would affect Red, Ronny, Fish, Thirsty . . . all of them. But especially Joe.

Gathering up the money purse, she stood, then returned to her room. The room Joseph Denton was paying for.

Joe was dog-tired, yet he couldn't sleep. It was the first time he'd been in his own bed for six weeks and the house was quiet. Empty. Lonely. Giving up, he flung the covers back, then walked across the hall.

Her room was dark. A hint of twinflower still tinged the air. After lighting a lantern, he wandered about opening drawers, touching the washstand, smoothing the bedsheets. The carpetbag he'd forgotten to load caught his eye.

It sat by the doorway where she'd left it for him to carry to the wagon. The temptation to open it tugged at him. She'd been in his bureau. She'd scrubbed, washed, ironed, and folded his clothing and even his drawers more times than he could count. What was good for the goose was surely good for the gander.

He picked up the bag. Its sides bulged; its threadbare seams strained. It hadn't weighed more than a feather when she'd first arrived, but with the new dresses she'd sewn, it was much too small to hold everything. What she needed was a trunk.

Straightening, he dropped the bag, then hurried to one of the spare rooms. Finding an extra trunk, he carried it back to her room.

He'd give it to her as a going-away gift, of sorts. And as a courtesy, he'd pack it for her. Squatting down, he unbuckled the carpetbag, wondering how many times she'd performed that very action.

Squelching the voice in his ear that warned him of wrongdoing, he opened it. The yellow calico lay on top, the green buttons he'd longed to touch divided the bodice in half.

He fingered them now, one after the other before smoothing his hands over the fabric that had once touched her. Unfurling the gown, he brought it to his nose and breathed deeply of the twin-flower scent woven into it.

One by one he removed the items from her bag and laid them in the trunk until he uncovered a set of underclothes. He sat back on his heels without touching. She must have two sets, just like she'd had two dresses at the beginning, because she'd have surely worn some undergarments to town.

He'd only had a quick glimpse of her in them that long-ago day. Pushing the sides of the bag wider, he tucked his hands inside and drew her shift out. It was in worse shape than he'd first imagined. He slipped a hand beneath the hem and spread his fingers. The cloth was as transparent as a cobweb and almost as fragile.

He'd never once seen them on his clothesline. She must have hung them out only while he and the boys were away at the logging camp.

He wanted to draw it to his nose but didn't dare. Only a flimsy pair of drawers remained in the bag. No corset. No petticoat.

Lifting them out, he accidentally pulled loose a false bottom. Setting the garment aside, he examined the bag and uncovered a bundle of worn, wrinkled letters. The top one was addressed to Josephine Ivey.

Settling onto the floor, he held the bundle for a long while before finally untying them.

He read every single one. The themes were the same: Her father felt honor-bound to enlist. He expected Anna to all but run the household and Leon to take his place. By doing so, they would be just as patriotic as if they were soldiers in the field.

It was the last one, though, that made Joe downright angry.

> *Don't you realize that when you and Leon argue and misbehave, the rebel bullets come closer to me? But if you and Leon are good, then God will take care of me and bring me home safely.*

What a great bunch of tripe. And what kind of price had Anna paid for those thoughtless words? She was no more responsible for her father's death than Joe was.

He remembered her discussion with Maynard. Hopefully, Anna realized the truth of the matter now. Either way, it was all Joe could do to keep from crinkling up the letter and throwing it in the fireplace—dead though the fire was.

Instead, he refolded it, slipped it back into the envelope, and tied it up with the rest of them. Once he'd secured them in the false bottom, he flattened the bag, laid it on top of the clothes in the trunk, and carefully closed the lid.

Anna stared at Doc Maynard, then slowly set her teacup on the table. After nearly a week of looking for employment, she could scarcely believe her ears. "You'd like me to what?"

"I'd like you to be my nurse." The doc cut into his breakfast steak, then stuck a bite in his mouth.

The dining room of the Occidental was almost deserted at this late hour of the morning. Which was fine with Anna. The less crowded, the less conspicuous she felt.

She blinked. "Why?"

"I'd heard you were in the market for a job." The doc wiped his mouth with his napkin and leaned back. "What do you say?"

"Well, goodness. I . . . I'd be happy to assist you, I suppose. If you think I could be of help, that is."

"I think you'd be a great help."

"I have no formal training."

"Does the sight of blood upset you?"

"It never has before."

"Then I'll teach you what you need to know."

She stared at the food on her plate. Yesler would have hired her on the spot, but she'd wanted to try something different. She'd hoped to find a position as a nanny, but there weren't many children in the Territory. And the families who had children also had mothers at home to care for them.

Domestics weren't in much demand either, unless she wanted to work for an unmarried man again. And she definitely didn't want to do that. She'd resigned herself to going to Mr. Yesler today. But now she wouldn't have to.

Maynard took a sip of coffee. "Well, what do you say?"

"I say 'yes.' "

He smiled. "Good. Can you start today? Right now?"

"Right now?"

"Unless you already have plans?"

"No. No plans at all. Just, um, let me freshen up and I'll be right with you."

"Very good. I'll wait for you out front."

She made her way to her room, her feelings bittersweet. Her situation was improving on the cusp of Joe's situation deteriorating. For tomorrow was Day Twelve.

Guilt over his loss slowed her steps. It wasn't too late. She could tell the doctor she'd changed her mind, then find Joe and marry him. She knew he was in town. The men had made sure to tell her last night at dinner.

She'd watched for him all evening, lingering over dinner, rocking on the porch, taking a stroll through town. But she never saw him, and if she had, what would she have said? That she was sorry about his land? A rather paltry statement, all things considered.

He wouldn't believe her anyway. Not when she had it within her power to rectify the situation. Still, her refusal to marry him didn't mean she wouldn't mourn for his loss. Wouldn't harbor guilt over it. She would. And she'd do so for a long, long time.

Slipping into her room, she poured water into the basin. At least with this new job she'd be able to start paying him back for her accommodations. And the sooner she released him from any sense of obligation he might feel, the better for both of them.

❧

Joe stood in the Central Store staring at the document in his hands. He'd stopped by Hind's to give him a list of supplies when the grocer had handed him his mail.

"How long has this been here?" Joe asked, unable to keep the disbelief from his voice.

Hind shrugged his bony shoulders. "About a month."

"A *month*? Why didn't you give it to Red?"

"Wasn't addressed to Red."

"What does that have to do with anything?"

Hind rubbed the lens of his spectacles with his apron. "Denny doesn't like it when we give mail out to anyone but the person it's addressed to. Denny was Postmaster long before me, you know."

Joe tamped down his exasperation. If only he had stopped at the store when he'd brought Anna to town last week. "From now on, you can give my mail to Red. And if Arthur Denny doesn't like it, you have him come speak to me."

Stepping out onto the boardwalk, Joe glanced up at the sky. All this time. A copy of Lorraine's death certificate had been sitting in the Central Store this whole entire month.

It hadn't burnt in the courthouse fire because his aunt had it. Heard he needed it and mailed it to him.

He fingered the document. Lorraine Cowden Denton had been written across the middle in elaborate Edwardian script by some unknown clerk. Some clerk who filled out a dozen of these a day. Who had no idea of the beautiful girl whose life had been snuffed out before her time. The girl who'd married one Joseph Roy Denton when the daisies were in bloom.

What a puppy he'd been back then. Full of enthusiasm and optimism and adventure. He'd packed a lot into the intervening years. How would all those years have been different if he'd had a woman by his side?

But it wasn't Lorraine he was picturing. It was Anna. Anna tripping down the steps and sending potatoes to every corner of the yard. Being caught in her underclothes while ironing her dress. Sorting seashells with her tongue trapped between her teeth. Cleaning his house until it shone. Washing his clothes, then secreting them away in his drawers. Kissing him until his entire world narrowed down to nothing but her. Only her.

Taking a deep breath, he turned north and headed to Judge Rountree's place. It was of no consequence now. The important thing was that nobody could ever threaten to take his land from him again. Not Tillney, not the judge, not anybody.

Immense satisfaction washed over him. The spring in his step lessened, however, when the what-ifs began to run through his head. What if his aunt hadn't gotten word? What if he'd not stopped by the Central Store? What if he'd married Bertha? What if he'd married Anna?

The thought brought him up short. What if he *had* married Anna? Would he have been sorry?

No. Not even close.

And in the middle of that glorious Seattle morning, with wagons kicking up dust and merchants sweeping their landings and horses dozing at the rails, Joe realized what he'd only suspected before. He was in love with Anna Ivey of Granby, Massachusetts. That without her, his land was not near the prize he thought it was.

He played their kiss back in his mind for the thousandth time. What he'd missed before was now glaringly obvious. When she'd asked him if he loved her, he'd never given her an answer. Because he hadn't known. Not for certain. Not with his land hanging in the balance.

But he knew the answer now. And he needed to convey it to Anna. Telling her wouldn't be enough, though. Not anymore.

"Watch out!"

A ball of brown yarn sailed toward him. Instinctively, he caught it.

One of Sprygley's sons broke away from the group of boys playing shinny in an empty lot.

"Sorry, Mr. Denton! Ernie hit the thing a little too hard."

Joe tossed him the yarn. "It's all right. Who's winning?"

"We are!" Waving, the boy raced back to the center of the lot, placed the ball at his base, and struck it with a shaved tree branch. The game ensued, each boy trying to move the ball toward the opposing team's goal with their shinny-sticks.

Joe took a moment to watch, wondering for the first time what it would be like to have a son of his own. Would he look like Anna or himself or a mix of the two?

His thoughts veered toward the creating of those sons and again he pictured Anna in her threadbare underclothes. He straightened. That was it. He'd buy her some fabric for a new petticoat, corset, shift, and drawers. A man's intentions would be pretty clear were he to give a woman a present like that.

He hesitated. His intentions could also be completely misconstrued. Perhaps he should include cloth for a bridal gown along with the cotton. No mistaking that. But first he needed to see Judge Rountree. As soon as all was settled concerning his land, he'd return to Hind's store and make his purchases.

Doc Maynard pulled up the buggy next to a white picket fence surrounding a well-kept lawn and a gable-roofed house.

The attractive home was shaded by maple trees, set back from the street and had a wide porch lined with spice pinks and lavender. They had no more come to a stop when the most beautiful woman Anna had ever seen burst through the front door.

"One fell off the barn loft and broke his leg," she cried. "You need to get over to the Rountrees' right away."

Doc waved, turned the horse around, and whipped the reins. Anna glanced back at the woman. Was that Doc Maynard's wife? She was so young. So beautiful. So . . . unexpected.

She looked again at the doctor. He wasn't homely, of course, but neither was he handsome in the classical sense. Oh, he had fine shoulders, but not as big and broad as Joe's. His salt-and-pepper hair had a bit of a wave to it, but nothing like Joe's blond curls. His blue eyes were nice, but nothing like—

She closed her eyes and forced Joe from her mind. It was over. Done. He didn't love her. He loved his land. And as soon as he'd realized she wouldn't help him gain it back, he'd cut her loose.

The horse's hooves clipped at a rapid pace, jingling its harness and making the buggy sway. Way up in the distance, she could make out a team of oxen pulling a huge load of logs down Skid Road.

Joe's oxen wouldn't have to do that anymore. Not with his log chute.

Gritting her teeth at the direction of her thoughts, Anna turned to the doc. "Who's broken a leg?"

"One. Judge Rountree's oldest."

Ah, yes. One, Two, Three, and Four. How could she have forgotten? She had to think a moment before the boy's nickname came to her, then along with Sprout's name came memories of his smile and freckles and scuffed knees.

She furrowed her brows, praying the break wasn't a bad one. She'd seen many breaks, especially during the war, that left the unfortunate victim with a limp or worse.

Though the sun was out, the road was still muddy from rains earlier in the week. Doc said little as they drove past a smattering of houses and toward the center of town. A scruffy dog ran out into the street, barking and yipping at their wheels before abandoning his chase.

A few minutes later, Doc stopped the buggy in front of the ornate home Joe had brought her to that first day after her arrival. The Rountrees' lot covered almost an entire block. Long windows with inside wooden blinds flanked the sides of the house. The front paneled door had tiny panes of glass on either side. And a bell for visitors to ring dangled from a post on the porch.

Doc jumped from the seat, grabbed his bag, and turned to offer her a hand.

"Go, go," Anna said, shooing him. "I'll secure the horse and meet you in the barn."

He didn't argue but ran off, his coattails flapping. She checked the brake, wrapped the reins on the dash rail, and hung on to the wing as her booted toe felt blindly for a foothold.

A few minutes later she hurried behind the house. The cries and whimpers coming from within the barn had her lifting her skirts and running the rest of the way with no regard for the puddles of mud on the path.

As she slipped inside, the smell of manure hit her like a wave from the ocean. Flies buzzed about her face, her ears, her hair. Just below a loft in the back, a half dozen people holding lanterns huddled around what she assumed was the boy.

But it was the tallest man that caught her attention. He'd looked up as soon as she entered. And the spurt of joy she felt at seeing Joe was quickly overshadowed by the concern on his face.

Chapter Twenty-nine

She was here. He wanted to tell her. About his mail. About his land. About his love. But now wasn't the time or place. Besides, he hadn't had a chance to buy the fabric. He and the judge had just concluded their business when Two had burst into the room with news of Sprout's accident.

Joe hoped the boy's break wasn't compound, not just for Sprout's sake, but for Anna's. He wasn't sure what she was doing here, nor if she had the constitution for this sort of thing.

He wondered if she had somehow heard and come to assist. She might have been an excellent nurse for Joe, but that was quite a bit different than dealing with emergencies like this.

As it was, she showed no visible reaction to her initial sight of Sprout or the smells around her as she settled next to Maynard. The boy's head lay cradled in his mother's lap while she smoothed his brown hair and softly sang nursery rhymes Joe hadn't heard in years. Anna gave the woman's arm a comforting squeeze.

Mrs. Bretchtel, a well-padded woman from down the street, bustled in with a batch of clean towels. Her fourteen-year-old son, who'd yet to shed his baby fat, followed behind with a pot of hot water.

"Here's the water, Doc," he said. "The judge is pulling nails out of a one-by-four plank. Said he'd be right in."

"Thank you, son." Doc finished cutting Sprout's pants up the seams and across the top of the leg, then peeled the soiled fabric off.

Sprout cried out. His shin had swollen to twice its normal size. Blood trickled from a jagged cut imbedded with bits of dirt and trouser.

Joe let out a sigh of relief. The break wasn't compound—no bone protruded from the boy's leg.

Doc withdrew a block of soap from his bag. "Come, Miss Ivey. We need to wash up."

Joe had never seen a doctor with such a penchant for cleanliness, but everyone humored him. If the man wanted to wash every other minute, so be it. But why had he asked Anna to wash, as well?

She rose, and when Maynard began rolling up his sleeves, she did the same.

"You'll find a small flask of chloroform in my bag," he said, giving his hands and arms a vigorous scrub. "Pour a few drops onto a towel and hold it a couple of inches from One's nose."

Nodding, she washed and dried her hands, but left her sleeves up. Joe honed in on the bit of skin she'd exposed. White. Delicate. And, he'd be willing to bet, soft.

"Keep the chloroform off his face, though. He doesn't need to be put out."

Anna did as instructed, and the boy began to relax until Maynard felt along the injury.

"No!" Sprout jerked, causing more pain from his movement than from the exam.

"Shhhhh." Mrs. Rountree shooed a fly from Sprout's face, then continued to stroke him, tears slipping from her eyes.

"It huuuuurts!"

"I know, but you must try and hold still, darling."

"Keep count of his pulse, Miss Ivey," Maynard said. "It shouldn't be abnormally fast, slow, or faint."

Anna touched her fingers to his wrist.

Doc finished his examination, then glanced at the judge, who'd come in with a small wooden plank. "It's not a severe break. It should heal in a few weeks. I'll splint it, then you can move him inside, where he'll be more comfortable." He glanced about the circle of men, stopping when he got to Joe. "Do you think you can hold the chloroform for Miss Ivey?"

Nodding, Joe handed his lantern to the judge and squatted beside Anna. Unobtrusively, he squeezed her fingertips in the exchanging of the cloth. She glanced up, then immediately returned her attention to the boy.

Doc pulled a roll of bandage material and a shiny silver dish from his bag and handed them to Anna. "Pour some of that hot water in this bowl, add several ounces of laudanum, and soak the bandage in the mixture."

Anna moved to do as instructed while Maynard began to clean the wound with some peroxide of hydrogen. Joe kept the chloroform close to Sprout's nose. The fumes were strong and unpleasant.

The boy's glazed eyes focused on him. "Wuz your name?"

Joe tried not to show any alarm at the question. Had the boy broken more than his leg in the fall?

"It's Joe. You remember me now, don't you?"

"I mean your real name."

Frowning, Joe glanced up at Mrs. Rountree.

"I believe he means your full name," she said.

"Joseph Roy Denton."

The boy searched the sea of faces above him until he found his father's. "That's what I wanna be called. Joseph Roy."

Joe's breath left him as if he'd taken a swift blow to the stomach.

The boy was choosing a name? Right now? And he was choosing *Joe's*?

Anna held the splint against Sprout's leg while Maynard wrapped it in the laudanum-soaked bandage. Tears spilled from the boy's eyes, but he held back his cries.

"Well, I'm very pleased to meet you, Joseph Roy Rountree." The judge's voice sounded as if it had been through a meat grinder.

Joe couldn't tell if it was because of the pain Sprout was in or because of the name his son had chosen. After a moment, the boy began to relax once again.

"I'm gonna go by Roy," he said, his eyes heavy. "So's we don't get confused."

Rountree nodded. "I think that's a fine idea."

Sprout turned his attention back to Joe. "I'm gonna be a lumberjack. Just like you."

Joe smiled. "You'll make a fine one, son. I'm sure of it."

Sprout closed his eyes and Joe counted his pulse. Good and steady.

"That's what I was doin'," Sprout said, eyes still shut.

"Doing?" Joe asked, trying to keep the boy's mind occupied.

"When I jumped off the loft."

"Jumped? You didn't fall?"

" 'Course not. I was practicin'."

Joe was having trouble following the conversation. "Practicing what?"

"Jumping off my springboard. Like you."

Joe swallowed. The loft was a good fifteen feet from the ground.

Flies buzzed around the adhesive plaster Maynard had begun to mix.

"Well, Sprou—" Joe cleared his throat. "Roy, landing is just as important as the actual jump. It has to be learned. And nobody starts from the top. You have to practice a little closer to the ground first. A *lot* closer to the ground."

Sprout opened his eyes. "Will you show me?"

He glanced at the boy's mother. Though her expression was pained, she gave a slight nod.

He returned his attention to Sprout. "I sure will. When you get well, maybe you can come up and spend a few days with me."

The boy's pulse took a quick leap. "Can I, Mama?"

She gave a slight hesitation. "If Doc Maynard says you're fit enough. And only if you don't do any more jumping until Mr. Denton shows you how."

His pulse settled back to normal. "Yes, Mama."

Doc wiped his hands with a cloth, then began to pack his bag. "He should be much more comfortable now. Here's some paregoric solution for the pain."

Mrs. Rountree accepted the corked vial.

"A teaspoon every hour if he's awake and needs it. If he gets a fever, send word to either me or Miss Ivey right away." Maynard assisted Anna to her feet.

Miss Ivey? Why send word to Anna? Before Joe had an opportunity to ask or to even have a word with her, the doc escorted her to the door, the judge right behind them. She never once looked back.

Joe judged the height of the sun. He'd been waiting for Anna on the porch of the Occidental for much of the afternoon and she still wasn't back. It hadn't taken long for word to get out that she was Doc's new nurse.

So he'd checked at the doc's place. But Mrs. Maynard said she hadn't seen the two of them since that morning and didn't know where they'd gone after tending to Sprout—*Roy*—nor when to expect them back.

So he'd parked himself on this porch. He wanted to tell her that he didn't lose his land. That he loved her. That he wanted her to marry him.

The wait had given him too much time to think, though. What if she said no?

He could make her return to his house and work off her debt, but he didn't want to go back on his word. He could act like he was sick and needed a nurse, but he was through with plotting and scheming.

The safest course of action was to court her. Yet he'd only be able to get to town on Saturday nights and Sunday mornings. Which meant his competition would have her the rest of the week.

And he didn't kid himself into thinking there'd be no competition. She was like fresh meat in a dog pound. The entire male population would be all over her.

Joe didn't think she'd rush into anything, though. Especially if the doc kept her too busy for socializing. Still, the other men had a slight advantage.

He looked at the sun one last time and rose to his feet. Already he wouldn't make it home until well after dark, but he couldn't wait around any longer. He needed to go, and he needed to go now.

Should he leave her a note? But no, he wanted to be the one to tell her he hadn't lost his land. He also wanted to ask for permission to court her. A man didn't do a thing like that with a note.

Moving to the street, he stepped up next to his wagon bed and pulled a trunk toward him. He wished he could ask her to court him before she opened the trunk. But there was nothing for it. He had to go.

Hefting it on his shoulder, he carried it inside and left it with the clerk. Joe would be back, though. And this time, there'd be no hidden motives. This time, his intentions would be honorable and perfectly clear.

❧

He'd packed her clothes in twinflowers. And not just any clothes. But her *underclothes*. Conflicting emotions jumbled together inside her. Surprise. Shock. Embarrassment. And something undeniably improper.

Running the tips of her fingers along the soft pink buds peeking out from the neckline of her shift and the waist of her drawers, Anna pictured his big, masculine hands handling the delicate unmentionables. Goose bumps shot up her arm.

The trunk had been such a surprise. But when she opened it, she'd expected to find her carpetbag inside, still packed. Never did she dream he'd take everything from it and transfer it to the case.

She brought her fingers to her nose, inhaling the fragile scent of the flower. Without dislodging the blooms, she lifted the white personals and placed them on the bed.

Turning back, she sucked in her breath. Yards of folded, gauzy cotton voile lay next to an equal amount of the finest white satin brocade she'd ever seen. Even completely alone in her hotel room, she could not stop the blush from creeping up her neck and face.

What on earth had he been thinking to buy such things for her? What had he told the proprietor? If anyone found out about this, her reputation would be in shreds.

But things were different here. She'd stayed in the home of an unmarried man for weeks and no one thought a thing about it. But, surely, buying an unmarried woman cloth for her underclothes was beyond the pale. Surely.

She lifted the brocade and brought it to her cheek. So silky. So rich. It was way too much fabric for a simple corset. Why, there was enough to make a whole gown. But she knew she never would. It'd look too much like a wedding gown.

She stilled. Had he known that? Had he given her the fabric with that in mind? No. Surely not.

Looking down, she saw something wrapped in brown paper peeking out from beneath the cotton voile. She let the brocade slither to her lap and reached for the package, then turned it over in her hands. He'd not written a note on this one.

Inside it held ribbon and lace and ties and thread and boning and cords and tiny, tiny pearl buttons. All white. All of the very best quality. All completely and totally inappropriate.

She sat on her heels staring. How could so many parts of her body respond to a man miles and miles away as if he'd just this very moment touched her?

Anna tried to picture him in the mercantile picking these items out. Had he simply told the proprietor he needed notions for a woman's undergarments, or had he looked at the choice of ribbons, lace, and buttons himself, picking the ones he liked the best?

Either way, his actions were nothing short of scandalous. She would not, could not, accept these. But how on earth would she give them back? What would she say? She couldn't stand in the lobby of the hotel and hand them over to him. Someone would see. She shook her head. The whole situation was impossible.

He'd dismissed her, replaced her, and deserted her, yet she knew he hadn't purchased the fabric and notions until after he'd returned her to town. She'd cleaned every corner of his house. She'd have known if these items had been in it.

So that raised the question: Why would Joe buy her these items *after* he'd secured his land? For she'd heard of his good fortune the moment she'd returned to the hotel. A rush of joy on his behalf had whisked through her. She knew he must be ecstatic. She also knew he no longer had any reason to angle for a wife.

Her first reaction had been to offer up a prayer of thanksgiving—for him and for her, thanking the Lord that they hadn't wed. What would Joe have thought if he'd married her, only to then discover all was for naught?

Now, she wasn't so sure. Could it be he was trying to state in his own roundabout way that the feelings he'd professed earlier were not, in fact, linked to his land? Or was she grasping at straws simply because she wished it were so?

Anna fingered the cotton. No question it was for the making

of undergarments. This message was clear: He cared for her as a woman.

She fingered the brocade. This message was not so clear. Yet she couldn't determine what possible use she'd have for so much white satin if not for a wedding gown. And if that were the case, then Joe didn't care for her just as a woman, but also as a bride.

The more she thought about it, the more hopeful she became. The land was Joe's and was a part of what made him who he was. Strong. Tough. Resilient. He cherished it just as he would cherish whatever woman he chose to spend his life with.

She nibbled on her lip. She couldn't make a wedding gown. Not without confirmation of some kind. That would be too presumptuous by half. But she could make a petticoat, a shift, new drawers, and a corset. Still, she wouldn't wear them. Not until she'd ascertained his intentions.

Smiling, she shook out the cotton. Either way, they'd be the prettiest undergarments a girl could ever own.

Chapter Thirty

Ollie, the new cook, didn't have the repertoire Anna had. He left the kitchen a mess of crusted food and splattered sauces. And his bad mood had no end.

By the close of each evening, Joe could hardly wait to have him out of the house. But when Ollie and the crew left, the hours before bedtime crawled interminably. Hours of silence and solitude and memories.

Settling into a chair by the fire, Joe picked up the frame Anna had made with her seashells and rubbed his thumb across a tiny white clamshell. Inside, the frame held a Scripture. He'd never seen her handwriting before. Her *l*'s and *e*'s were widely looped, as if they were lassos.

Where your treasure is, there will your heart be also.
Matthew 6:21

He grinned. Not very subtle, the little minx.

He looked at the fire. Tomorrow was Saturday. If he worked

the whole day, then headed out, he wouldn't arrive in Seattle until the wee hours of the morning.

That might suit the boys, since the places they frequented stayed busy the whole night. But he wanted to see Anna. Talk to Anna. Court Anna.

She'd be long asleep by the time he reached town. Then Sunday morning would be taken up with church, and that gave them precious few hours before he'd have to return home.

That was no way to conduct a proper courtship. He needed to be in town early enough on Saturdays to escort her to dinner or go for a ride. To do that, though, he'd have to leave after breakfast.

The men were thrilled the land and their jobs were secure, but every single one of them missed Anna. They wouldn't begrudge him the time it would take to woo her back. Even if it meant they stayed to work while he went on ahead to town.

He set the frame back down. No, they wouldn't mind—especially if it meant she might whip up a batch of doughnuts now and then.

For the first time since leaving her behind, Joe felt a weight lift from his shoulders. He wondered what her reaction to the cloth and notions had been. And the twinflowers. And the packing of her new trunk.

He'd have his answer soon enough. If a petticoat belled her dress out when he saw her next, then he'd know his feelings were reciprocated.

Leaning back in his chair, he closed his eyes and proceeded to imagine just what that petticoat—among other things—would look like.

Anna had never in her life been inside a saloon. But when a young man tottering from drink intercepted them, jabbering about a stabbing at McDonald's Saloon, the doc immediately followed, never indicating she should return to his office.

As they drew closer, a breeze brought with it the excited voices of McDonald's patrons. Doc and Anna picked up their pace, then hurried through the swinging doors. The oppressive smell of whiskey and cigar smoke assailed her. Before she could look around, a man with a stained apron banding his large girth shouted out to them.

"Over here, Doc!"

As Anna's eyes adjusted to the smoke, she saw a middle-aged man with a handlebar mustache lying on two tables shoved together, blood seeping from his neck.

Shooing the owner back, Maynard yanked open his bag and handed Anna a cloth. "Apply pressure to the wound. Quickly."

The acrid smell of blood made her stomach churn. She didn't ask why they weren't going to wash their hands. She already knew. There wasn't time.

Blood immediately saturated the cloth, seeping through her fingers and onto the table's scarred surface. The man's dark eyes were wide and frightened. She swallowed, then offered him an encouraging smile.

The doc threaded a needle. "Keep the pressure steady."

"Should I get the chloroform?" she asked.

"He probably has enough whiskey in him to do the trick, but I suppose it wouldn't hurt." Tying a knot at the end of the thread, he took her place and peeked beneath the cloth. His shoulders relaxed. "Well, it's not as deep as I first thought, Rufus. You're going to be all right."

Anna found the chloroform cloth and poured more anesthetic onto it. Her stomach jerked. The etherlike odor reminded her of men in the War Hospital she'd volunteered at back home. Though she'd never tended to actual patients, she'd seen them. Heard them. Felt for them.

Lately, the constant smell began to trigger a bit of nausea—particularly when mingled with the odor of blood. The whiskey and cigar smoke infiltrating her every breath intensified her dilemma. To compensate, she breathed through her mouth.

The man cried out when Doc poked the needle through his skin. Anna cringed. Two men grabbed the patient's arms and legs, holding him down—one still had a cigar clamped between his teeth with ashes threatening to fall at the slightest provocation. She placed the cloth beneath the man's nose, wondering if the fumes would make it past his overgrown mustache.

She couldn't take his pulse with the other patrons restraining him, nor could she bear to watch the procedure. So she took in her surroundings. Rickety tables, spindly chairs, a billiard table, and walls papered with years of smoke and residue. The bar behind her was out of her range of vision.

After several long, excruciating minutes, Doc tied off his stitching.

Anna removed the chloroform and retrieved a bandage from the medical bag. She supported the man's head as Maynard dressed the wound. The man's hair was greasy and clumped together with blood.

Please don't let him have lice, Lord.

"Find a table or some planks to carry him home on," Doc said to the men who'd been holding the patient down. "And be gentle about it. I'll check on him in the morning."

Anna wiped the dregs of filth from her hands, but blood had seeped into her cuticles, staining them. Her nausea increased.

Maynard grabbed a bottle of whiskey from a nearby table. "Hold out your hands."

She hesitated, then did as she was told. He poured the foul liquid all over them. The fumes burned her eyes, but it served its purpose. The dirt and bloodstains disappeared.

She followed the doc out, surprised to see darkness had descended while they were operating. An occasional street lantern threw small pools of light onto the muddy avenue, making a trail up the hill like oversized breadcrumbs.

"Shouldn't we alert the law about the stabbing?" she asked, gulping in fresh air.

Maynard shook his head. "The men will do that if Tillney survives, which I'm sure he will. Now, I don't know about you, but I'm starving. Would you like to come to the house for supper?"

She pulled up short. "Tillney? *That* was Mr. Tillney? The Mr. Tillney who sued Joe?"

Doc stopped. "It was."

She looked back toward the saloon. "What happened? How did he come to be in such dire circumstances?"

"I don't know. Not my business to know. I simply do the doctoring."

Good heavens.

"Do you regret ministering to him?" he asked.

She looked at him in surprise. "Of course not."

"Good."

They started back along on the boardwalk. At the intersection of Washington and First, Doc hesitated. "Would you mind if I stopped by Kellogg's Drug Store?"

"Not at all. I think I'm going to continue on to the Occidental, though."

He glanced up the street, clearly torn about leaving her to walk the last block alone.

"Go on," she said. "I'll be fine."

"Well, what about supper?"

"Not tonight, Doc. I'm going to retire early, if it's all right."

"You're sure?"

"I'm sure."

"What about tomorrow, then?" he asked. "Have you found a church?"

"I visited the Brown Church last week."

"Would you like to join Catherine and me this week? We attend the White Church."

She'd purposely avoided that one last Sunday. The only other time she'd been in it was when Joe had been expecting to marry her.

Still, she'd liked the preacher and she adored the Maynards. "I'd love to. I'll meet you there."

"Excellent. We'll see you then. And thank you for all your help."

"Anytime. Good night, Doc."

The walk up the steep hill required all her effort. In the last week she'd helped deliver a baby, extract a tooth, lance an infection, set a bone, soothe a colicky baby, treat a burn, and stitch up more cuts and abrasions than she'd seen in a lifetime.

Placing one foot in front of the other, Anna gauged the distance to the Occidental. The last several yards were always the most daunting. Her legs ached at the exertion it took to traverse them.

Horses lined the hitching posts surrounding the hotel, and gas sconces on the front porch silhouetted a bevy of men. She groaned. The men had made a habit of lingering until she returned at night, all jumping to attendance when she arrived. She'd done everything she could to discourage them, but to no avail.

Just seeing them drained the last of her energy and patience. One by one, they straightened, like dogs with ears perked at their master's return. Before she even made it across the street, several rushed out to escort her to the door.

"Let me assist you, Miss Ivey."

"How was your day, miss?"

"May I treat you to supper?"

Politely refusing, she kept her eyes downcast, but she didn't have the wherewithal to protest when they took her elbows. She'd almost made it through the gauntlet and to the door when a voice stopped her.

"Anna?"

She ground to a halt, jerking her head up. "Joe? Joe! What are you doing here?"

She drank in the sight of him. He stood a head above the rest, his hair curling up tight in the evening air. The top two buttons of his plaid shirt had slipped open as if they couldn't quite contain the width of his neck. His denim trousers outlined those muscular hips and thighs.

He gave the men on her arms a penetrating look, but they didn't relinquish their hold. If anything, their grips tightened. He took a step forward, his chest expanding. They straightened, holding their ground.

Good heavens. Gently disengaging herself from the men, she took a step toward Joe. He reached for her hand, touching it to his lips, then frowned.

The sweetness of his kiss turned to horror when she realized he smelled whiskey. He didn't say anything, of course. Not in front of the men. Nor could she explain without sounding ridiculous.

"You look terrible," he said.

She choked. The man on her left growled.

"I'm tired," she replied.

"Where have you been?"

"With the doc."

He tightened his lips. "He has no business keeping you out this late. Have you had your supper?"

"Not yet."

"Well, go clean yourself up and I'll have Nausley stoke the stove."

She arched a brow. Every man on this porch had been pestering her to share supper with them and that was the best Joe could do? *You look terrible* and *go clean yourself up*?

He must have had an inkling of her thoughts, for his cheeks filled with color. But he didn't rephrase his invitation nor relax his stance.

"I'm tired, Joe," she sighed.

He narrowed his eyes. "I left the house directly after breakfast, missed an entire day of work, and have been cooling my heels on this porch for hours. If you're too tired to freshen up before the meal, then you can go as you are."

He couldn't have established his territory more clearly had he crowed like a rooster. Before she took exception, though, his words began to sink in. He skipped work? And had been waiting on her? For hours?

"Now see here, Denton," the man on her right said, "if the lady doesn't—"

"Just give me a few minutes, Joe," she interjected, hoping to keep the men from coming to blows.

Lumberjacks loved nothing so much as a scuffle. It wouldn't matter to Joe that the other men weren't jacks. He was clearly itching for a fight, and she wasn't about to do any more doctoring today.

"You don't have to let him bully you, Miss Ivey," the man on her right said.

She smiled at him. "Thank you, sir. I don't mind having supper with him."

"Don't *mind*?" Joe said, the bite in his voice unmistakable.

Suppressing a smile, she gave him a deep curtsey. "I'd love to share my evening meal with you, Mr. Denton. If you would excuse me, though, I'd like to *clean up* first."

Relaxing, he gave her a nod. With as much dignity as she could muster, she went inside. It wasn't until she was safely tucked into her room that she allowed her smile to bloom.

Joe was here. And he'd been waiting for her. And if she wasn't mistaken, it had nothing to do with his land and everything to do with her. Racing to the washbasin, she poured water into it, stripped off her dress, and began to scrub the day's smells from her person.

Chapter Thirty-one

Joe had always known that maidens were an anomaly to the boys in town, but he'd never paid much attention to it before. Probably because there usually weren't any unmarried women around to bring out this particular phenomenon.

He was paying attention to it now, though. The men had simply moved from the porch to the dining room to do their gawking, making private conversation impossible.

Anna had changed into her maroon dress and straightened up her hair. She no longer smelled like whiskey, but she still looked terrible. Circles under her eyes. An unhealthy pallor to her skin. No appetite.

It was all he could do to keep from gawking himself—but for entirely different reasons. He took a breath, planning to question her about her health, and about why she reeked of alcohol when she'd first arrived, then stopped himself. Every ear in the place was attuned to the exchanges they made. So he took a bite of food instead, not even tasting it.

She pushed hers around on her plate.

Finally, he couldn't stand it any longer. "Is something wrong?" he asked quietly.

"No, no. I'm just . . ." She put down her fork. "My head hurts, actually."

Joe tugged his napkin from his neck and tossed it on the table. "Come on. Let's go get some fresh air."

She laid her hand on his arm, stalling him. "I think what I really need is to get some sleep."

He swallowed his disappointment. He knew she was right, but they'd barely said three sentences to each other.

Standing, he helped her to her feet. The men around them rose. He gave them a look that promised retribution if they so much as thought about following.

He wove Anna through the tapestry of men, the faintest hint of twinflower touching his nose. He smiled. She still packed her things in the blooms he'd placed in her trunk.

He looked at her dress more closely. It didn't appear as if she'd made herself a petticoat. But had she made herself anything else?

As soon as they cleared the door, the men reluctantly settled back into their seats.

"I'm sorry, Joe," she whispered.

"It's all right."

At the stairs leading up to the rooms, Joe still couldn't say what he wanted to. Not with Collins behind the counter watching and listening with rapt attention.

"Congratulations on your land," she said. "I'm so, so glad you didn't lose it."

"Thank you. Me too."

She made to leave, but he snagged her elbow. "Do you think you'll be well enough to go to church tomorrow?"

"I'm not sick, Joe. Just tired. And yes. I of course plan to attend church."

"Will you let me escort you?"

Struggling to keep her eyes open, she stifled a yawn. "Yes."

"I'll see you in the morning, then." He gave her arm a gentle squeeze. "Sleep tight."

"I will. You too."

She trudged up the stairs. Just watching her made him angry. He couldn't wait to get ahold of Maynard. The man must have dragged her all over the Territory and back again. Well, Joe would put a stop to that. And he'd do it before church tomorrow.

"She's dead on her feet, I'm telling you." Joe stood in Doc's surgery room watching him pack his medical bag for the day.

"She was fine when I left her last night," Maynard said. "Did she complain of anything?"

"She didn't have to complain. Anybody with eyes could see she wasn't well."

"Then why did you drag her to supper instead of letting her go to bed and rest?"

"She needed to eat."

The doc moved to a pot of hot water his wife had brought in earlier. "What are you doing here, Joe?"

Sighing, he moderated his tone. "I'm worried you're overworking her. It was well after dark when she returned to the hotel and on a Saturday, no less."

"I see. She didn't cook for your crew on Saturdays?"

"That was different."

"Oh. At your place she finished serving, cleaning, and preparing for the next day all before dark?"

Joe hesitated. "It's not the same. I know you. You go from one patient to the next without ever taking a break."

"Really?" Maynard swished an instrument in the water, then scrubbed it with a soapy rag. "Interesting."

"Don't patronize me, Doc. Anna isn't well. You need to remember she's female and must make concessions because of it."

Maynard laughed. "Anna is no fragile flower, as I'm sure you're aware."

Joe stiffened. "Neither is she a work horse with an unending source of strength."

The humor slowly fell from Maynard as he studied Joe. "You in love with her?"

He didn't even hesitate. "Yes."

"Then why haven't you married her?"

"I'm working on it."

He lifted his brows. "And what would she think about your coming here on her behalf?"

"She'd be furious. I trust you can keep it to yourself."

Maynard smiled and turned back to his washing. "I can keep it to myself. And I'll watch her, Joe. You needn't worry about that."

❧

Anna made it halfway down the steps when she caught sight of Joe, then came to a complete halt. He was wearing a suit. She'd never seen him in anything other than his lumberjack garb. Not even on their wedding day. Or what he'd thought was their wedding day.

He looked up, his eyes zeroing in on her, and walked to the bottom of the stairs. She continued her descent, taking in the thin black tie knotted around a crisp white collar, the swirling pattern of his green, single-breasted waistcoat, the lines of his dark jacket framing massive shoulders, then tapering down to a trim waist. His trousers held a newly pressed crease.

Tucking his derby beneath his arm, he held out a hand and assisted her with the last two steps. "Good morning."

"You look beautiful." It was out before she had a chance to recall it.

Flashing both dimples, he leaned in close. "You needn't sound so surprised."

She again gave him a once-over, this one much briefer than the last. "Where did you get all this? I don't remember seeing it in your wardrobe."

Joe took a quick glance about the lobby, offering no reply. She blushed, realizing how her comment might be misconstrued if it had been overheard. But with most of the men sleeping off their Saturday night revels, the entryway was, for once, lacking in spectators.

They stepped outside, but instead of heading down the boardwalk, Joe escorted her to a waiting coal-box buggy harnessed to Shakespeare.

"What's this?" she asked.

Placing his hands at her waist, he lifted her up. "I believe they call it a buggy."

"But church is within walking distance."

Anna slid over, making room for him to mount. The buggy dipped beneath his weight, causing the fringe around the top to ripple and swirl.

"I was hoping to talk you into a Sunday ride after church," he said.

Clicking his tongue at Shakespeare, he gave the reins a shake. She twisted around to get a better look at the vehicle. Coal-box buggies had been extremely fashionable in New York. She didn't even know they had them in the Territory. This one sported a black carriage with broad stripes of dark blue and cloth trimming to match.

"Will you?" he asked.

She returned her attention to him. The derby hat he wore seemed so out of character she lost her train of thought. "Will I what?"

"Go for a ride with me after church?"

"Oh!" She couldn't imagine what the wagon shop must have charged him for the buggy and could certainly understand that he wanted to get his money's worth. "Well, all right."

"Only 'all right'?" he teased.

She folded her hands in her lap. "I'd like to very much."

Smiling, he sat a little straighter.

For the first time, Anna realized the sun was out. Not because Mount Rainier postured in all its glory on the horizon, but because the sun and Joe's green waistcoat had turned his eyes to an emerald-like quality.

"Are you feeling better this morning?" he asked.

"Much."

"Your headache is gone?"

"It is." That wasn't exactly true—it still rumbled along the edges—but she was so struck with him she couldn't quite get her bearings.

"I've missed you." He wasn't making any attempt to watch the road but centered his attention entirely on her.

A shimmer of anticipation rushed through her. Anticipation of something she was sure she shouldn't be contemplating on her way to church.

Drawing in a raspy breath, she tried to lighten the mood. "You missed me or my cooking?"

"You." His tone was low, intimate, not at all acknowledging her attempt at humor. "Definitely you."

She faced forward. Time to move the conversation in a safer direction. "Wasn't that our turn back there?"

He looked around, then gave a small huff of amusement. "I believe it was."

Even with the detour, they arrived at church much too soon to suit her.

Jumping from the buggy, he held his hands up to her. "Why are you frowning?"

"I was just thinking the day was entirely too beautiful to be indoors."

She rested her hands on his shoulders, but instead of grasping her elbows, he clasped her waist, then lifted her from the carriage.

"For shame, Miss Ivey," he whispered, holding her even though her feet now touched the ground. "What will God think about your reluctance to enter His house?"

He smelled of the mint from his shaving lotion. "I think He'd understand," she said. "After all, He made the day and asked us to rejoice in it."

Stepping back, he released her waist only to then capture her hands. "Well, we'll do both. First, we'll praise Him in His house, then we'll praise Him out-of-doors." He brought her knuckles to his lips. "In any event, I'm sure He'll be glad to see you've rid yourself of your vices before entering church."

"Vices?"

His eyes took on a gleam. "Well, it was clear to me yesterday that you've developed a thirst for whiskey since you left me."

She gasped. The quick intake of breath caused her to cough. She knew he was teasing, but she still wanted to explain. Instead of giving her an opportunity, though, he handed her his handkerchief, then whisked her inside.

Chapter Thirty-two

Joe regretted his decision to leave the top up on the coal-box. If ever there was a day for riding in an open buggy, this was it. Seattle might enjoy more than its fair share of rain, but all it took was one day like this to obliterate from memory a month's worth of gray ones.

He glanced at Anna. She'd worn her blue gingham dress, as he'd hoped she would. The temperatures were beginning to cool, though, and she'd need something more suitable before too long.

He couldn't keep buying her fabric, though. Not until they were married or at least betrothed. He wondered again if she'd made use of his most recent offering, but refrained from asking.

She looked more rested than she had last night, but he could tell she wasn't completely herself. Another subject he wished to broach, but one which wouldn't exactly further his cause.

He bit back his impatience with the entire courting flubdub. It wasn't as if they were animals whose only way of communicating was through elaborate rituals. He and Anna both spoke English.

Why couldn't he simply state what he wanted and then go see the preacher?

They hit a rut in the road, thrusting Anna against him momentarily. He was tempted to hit every furrow they came across just for the brief contact it would afford him.

It wouldn't be hard. The road out to Lake Washington was hilly, bumpy, and gravelly. Dense forest and brush rose on either side as if the road were a river carving out a canyon.

Anna coughed.

"You cold?" he asked.

She shook her head, but he slipped off his jacket and hooked it on her shoulders.

"Thank you."

He searched for an appropriate topic of conversation, couldn't think of one, then finally gave in to temptation. "Doc seems to keep you busy."

"I can't imagine how he's done it by himself all this time. People think nothing of calling on him all hours of the day and night."

"He gets you up in the middle of the night!"

"No, no. But one morning I arrived at his home only to find he'd never even gone to bed. Can you imagine?"

"Guess I never thought about it much."

She sighed. "Neither had I."

A dove high in a tree crooned to its mate. When she didn't respond in kind, he tried again, his *coo-oo-oo* a sad, mournful sound. Joe scanned the maples, pines, and oaks, but the bird's tan color made it impossible to spot.

His thoughts drifted back to Anna's nursing. "Do you like it?"

"Like what? Helping Doc Maynard?" She cocked her head to the side, pondering his question. "I can't really say I enjoy it, exactly. How can I when most everyone we see is in some degree of pain? Yet I can see why the doc finds it rewarding."

"But you don't?"

"Oh, I do. I guess."

They started up an incline.

He placed his arm on the seat back, giving her extra support. "You don't have to work for him, you know."

"I know. But what would I do then?"

Marry me. But he couldn't say that. Not yet, anyway. *Come back to us*. But he didn't want to offer that either. The next time she set foot in his home, he wanted her to be Mrs. Joseph Roy Denton, not his cook.

"I don't know," he said. "I just don't like how he keeps you out until all hours."

"He doesn't." Her surprise was genuine.

"He did yesterday. Can you honestly say that was an exception?"

She overlapped the lapels of his jacket, cocooning herself inside. "I've only worked for him for one week. It's a bit early to have established a pattern, don't you think?"

"Maybe. But last night you were almost sick you were so tired. And don't try to deny it."

They crested the hill.

"It was just a headache. Hardly anything to be alarmed over."

He refrained from commenting. Doc said he'd be more diligent, so hopefully it was a moot point. After a bend in the road, the lake came into view. Several ducks paddled through the water. The males' iridescent green heads and fawn-colored breasts were much more showy than the females' drab, mottled plumages.

Just the opposite of people, Joe thought. *With us, it's the females who are resplendent.*

Anna straightened. "Oh, Joe. Look how beautiful it is."

Removing his arm from the seat back, he took the reins in both hands and picked up the pace, guiding Shakespeare to a break in the trees that gave way to a sloping shore.

Dark evergreens lining the distant side of the glistening lake looked like upside-down feathers against a backdrop of mountains far on the horizon.

"Whoa, boy." Joe jumped to the ground, then lifted Anna from the buggy, resisting the temptation to pull her close.

They spread out a blanket he'd confiscated from his room at the Sires Hotel, anchoring it with a basket of food Owen Nausley had packed for them.

The serenity of the surroundings calmed him, and by the time they'd finished lunch, the old familiarity had returned.

She asked about his men.

He asked about her patients.

She wanted to know about his new cook.

He wanted to know how long she'd had her cough.

She asked about the securing of his land.

He asked if she liked the fabrics he'd bought her.

Averting her eyes, she pulled on a tendril of hair. "Very much."

"Have you made anything with them?"

She tossed a piece of crust to one of the ducks waddling along the shoreline. "What exactly was it you wanted me to make?"

A wedding gown. But he couldn't say that. Too late, he realized a declaration of that sort might scare her off. He loved her and he suspected she loved him, but it was their first Sunday drive. A little patience was in order.

"I figured you could use a new petticoat, I guess. Among other things."

"It was terribly improper," she whispered. "Giving me fabric for those kinds of things. We shouldn't even be discussing it."

He suppressed a smile, though her whispering amused him. The only thing close enough to overhear was the duck, and their conversation wouldn't upset its sensibilities.

"You're probably right," he said. "But will you make something just the same?"

She raised her gaze to his. "Yes."

The look in her eyes took his breath away and he could no more stop himself than he could stop the sun from setting. Slipping his arm around her waist, he pulled her up against him and lowered his mouth to hers.

She offered no resistance, accepting him as if it were the most natural thing in the world. And it was.

The kiss began softly, slowly, then built. He splayed his hands along her back in an effort to touch as much of her as he could. But it wasn't enough. Wasn't near enough.

She encircled his neck with her arms. He skated his palms to her sides, sliding them from the curve of her waist up to her raised elbows, then down again.

A tiny moan from the back of her throat tripled his craving. He pulled his mouth from hers, kissing her jaw, her eyes, her ears, her neck.

Tightening her hold, she pressed herself against him so hard he felt sure the buttons marching down her dress would leave imprints on his chest.

Marry me. When could he ask her? How much longer must he wait?

He wrapped his arms completely around her, holding her. Hugging her. Rocking her.

When she began to have difficulty breathing, he reluctantly loosened his hold. Still, she couldn't catch her breath.

He frowned. "Are you all right?"

She tapped her chest. "It hurts."

He leaned his forehead against hers. "Mine too."

"No," she gasped. "I mean it *hurts*."

He reared back. "Anna?"

Her face filled with panic. She sucked for air, but only made thin, rasping sounds.

"Anna?" His heart began to pound. "What is it? What's happening?"

Her chest heaved as it struggled for breath. He had no idea

what to do. Jumping to his feet, he pulled her up. Maybe standing would make it easier.

She squeezed her eyes shut. He placed her hands on his shoulders for support and she gripped him like a vise.

"Breathe," he whispered, bracketing her waist with his hands. "Come on, love. Breathe."

Her knees weakened. She wasn't turning blue, but he could see she was struggling. A few moments later, her grip loosened, her shoulders relaxed, her breathing grew deeper.

He found his own breath keeping time with hers. When all was normal, he smoothed the hair from her face. "What happened?"

"I don't know. All of a sudden, I couldn't breathe."

He blew out a puff of air. "Well, I've heard of a kiss taking a person's breath away, but I thought it was just a saying."

Her chuckle turned into a cough.

He pulled her against him, careful to keep his embrace loose. "Anna, something isn't right. Has that ever happened to you before?"

"Never."

He tipped her head up with his hand. "Well, you're going to have to find out what it is, because if that's what's going to happen every time I kiss you, then we have a problem."

Smiling, she slid her eyes closed. "I'm sure it's nothing. I must be coming down with something is all."

Joe wasn't so sure, but he decided not to press her. He'd find the doc before he left town and ask him.

Scooping her into his arms, he headed toward the buggy. "Well, it's time to go anyway. You rest while I get our things."

"I can help, Joe. I'm fine now."

"No. You took ten years off my life. You're going to sit in that carriage and rest."

She outlined his ear with her finger, causing him to miss a step.

"At least I didn't wrestle with a tree and lose," she murmured.

He scowled. "I didn't lose. If I'd lost, I'd be dead." He deposited her into the seat of the buggy. "Stay put. This will only take me a minute."

Scrunching up the blanket, his concern escalated. He'd already lost one wife. He wasn't about to lose Anna, too.

Chapter Thirty-three

"She was coughing throughout the day, then all of a sudden she couldn't breathe." Joe strode up First Avenue, the doc by his side. Between its being Sunday and the supper hour, the streets were all but deserted.

"Every time she tried, she gasped and hiccupped."

Maynard frowned. "Do you know if it happens to her often?"

"Never. She said it had never happened before. It gave her quite a scare, too."

"How long did it last?"

"Seemed like forever, but I think it was actually only about a minute, no more than two."

"Perhaps something brought it on. What was she doing just before it started?"

Joe groped for an answer. "Um, nothing. She wasn't doing anything."

Doc gave him a sharp look. "Nothing? Nothing at all?"

Joe swallowed. Maynard stopped, grabbing Joe's arm. The

doctor wouldn't stand a chance in any physical confrontation between the two of them, but he garnered a great deal of respect in the community and in Joe's sight as well. So Joe allowed the rough handling.

"What was she doing?" Maynard repeated.

"Nothing that should have brought that on."

The men studied each other. Music and a burst of raucous laughter from McDonald's Saloon two blocks down reached their ears. The longer they stood in silence, the more strained it became.

Maynard's expression hardened. "Was she struggling?"

Had it been anyone else, Joe would have flattened him. "I cannot believe you have to ask."

"It's my job to ask."

Debatable, but Joe let it pass. "She was not."

"How far had it gone?"

The anger percolating just below the surface came perilously close to spilling over. Fisting his hands, Joe kept his voice low and even. "It went nowhere at all. We are through with this topic."

Whirling around, Joe strode up the street. He'd told the doc about Anna's ailment. That's all the man needed to know.

September turned into October, bringing with it nature's display of oranges, reds, and yellows on an evergreen backdrop. Descending the steps of the Occidental, Anna headed toward Doc Maynard's home.

A gust of wind lifted yellow maple leaves from the ground and swirled them at her feet. Tightening the cape across her shoulders, she skirted a puddle, though moisture from the morning rains still dampened the toes of her boots and the hem of her skirt. But nothing could dampen her spirits.

Joe was going to propose to her tonight. She was certain of it. He'd courted her steadily each and every weekend for the past six weeks. In the entire time, he never failed to come to town, and as a result, the local men had ceased to shadow her every move.

Then last week, after a particularly potent kiss, he had told her to take extra care with her toilette for tonight's supper, but wouldn't say any more. She wished she could wear a brand-new dress for whatever it was he had planned, but she simply didn't have enough coin.

With the money she'd earned, she'd tried to pay him back. He wouldn't hear of it. Became downright angry over it.

So she'd backed down and instead purchased wool for two outfits, wearing them alternately. Her cape, meanwhile, needed to be read its last rites. It offered little to no protection from the encroaching cold.

At least she was no longer making house calls. After that first week as an assistant, the doc decided he no longer wanted her to accompany him on the road. Instead, Anna stayed in his surgery room. Cleaning, organizing, and taking his messages when he wasn't there, assisting with his surgeries when he was.

Though she missed the spontaneity of going from house to house, she didn't miss traveling about in wet weather. Especially not with her cough and headaches.

As she turned onto Cherry Street, a light mist began to fall. She draped the cape up over her head, tossing one end over her shoulder. Today was Saturday, which meant she only worked in the morning, and Joe would be in town by the afternoon. Her excitement over his impending proposal resurfaced. She couldn't wait for him to ask her and couldn't wait to tell him yes.

Opening the gate in front of the Maynards' home, she walked through, then headed toward the side entrance. Raindrops had just begun to fall when she slipped inside.

Hanging her cape on a hall tree, she knocked on the surgery room door.

"Come in."

The smell of soap, chloroform, and carbolic acid overpowered

Anna. Her headache pounded. "Good morning. I didn't expect to see you yet."

"No?" The doc sat with his back to her at a large oak desk, flipping through a giant volume whose title was obscured. "And why is that?"

"Because you're hardly ever here on Saturday mornings."

"I wanted to talk with you." Arriving at the page he was looking for, he skimmed it with his finger, then took a few moments to read.

Anna washed her hands, then opened his medical bag and began to take inventory of its contents. He was low on bandages, arnica, and mutton tallow. She turned to retrieve replacements from a cupboard, then paused. Doc had swiveled his wooden chair around and leaned back to watch her.

"What is it?" she asked.

"I need to talk to you."

She frowned. Had he gone on a call last night? Had someone had a terrible accident? Or worse, died?

Taking advantage of the chair's rollers, he propelled himself to a corner, snatched up a stool, then brought it back. "Please. Have a seat."

She sunk down. "What's happened?"

"Nothing's happened."

She took a deep breath of relief, triggering a faint rattling noise in her chest. "You scared me."

"I'm sorry." Pursing his lips, he propped his elbows on the arms of the chair and threaded his fingers across his stomach. "I want to talk about your cough."

"Again? But you just gave me another exam a few days ago. I thought everything was fine."

"I never said that. As a matter of fact, I didn't say anything at all because I didn't want to alarm you."

She blinked. "Alarm me?"

He nodded. "It's been going on too long, Anna."

"I'm sure it's nothing. Just a—"

"I don't think so."

Folding her hands in her lap, she squelched her protests. It was nothing, but she would do him the courtesy of listening. "Go ahead."

"For the six weeks you've been with me, you've had a cough, difficulty breathing, headaches, poor appetite, and weight loss—all getting increasingly worse instead of better."

She moistened her lips. "I haven't really lost that much. And I'm sure it's due to the fact I haven't been eating like I should. I'll make a concerted effort to do better. I promise."

"That's good, but it doesn't explain the cough, the raspy sound in your lungs, the headaches, and the breathing episodes."

"Maybe if I retire a little earlier, I'd be—"

"Have you had any fever?"

"No. You asked me that before. I haven't had any."

"You never feel overly warm at night?"

She'd been having trouble sleeping but not because she was hot. More because of her cough. "Not that I can remember."

He tapped his thumbs together. A frisson of panic zipped through her. She'd seen this expression on his face before but only when he had bad news. Very bad news.

"Tell me," she whispered.

Leaning forward, he propped his elbows on his knees. "I think you might have tuberculosis."

She gasped, triggering her cough.

"Have you coughed up any blood at all?"

Shaking her head, she whipped a handkerchief from her pocket and pressed it to her mouth. It hurt to cough. Way deep down in her chest. Could it be true? Did she have tuberculosis?

She'd had a neighbor in Granby who'd died of consumption. It was slow and painful. The woman eventually drowned in her own lungs. Tears rushed to Anna's eyes.

Taking her hand in his, Doc patted it. "Since the symptoms

have come on since your arrival in the Territory, I imagine it's our climate that's the problem." He took a deep breath. "I think it would be best if you moved to a place with dry weather."

"Moved?" The idea so startled her, she could hardly comprehend it. "Back to Granby?"

He shook his head. "Down toward Texas, where it's drier."

"Texas!" Her coughing started again. A deep, hacking cough that doubled her over. *But southerners live in Texas,* Anna wanted to scream. Yet she could do nothing until her coughing subsided.

Maynard stood and made a mixture of onion juice and honey, but before he could give it to her, her neck and chest muscles tightened.

Oh no.

In order to breathe, she had to take quick, rapid intakes of air. The wheezing grew more severe. The pain in her chest increased.

Doc rubbed her shoulders. "Sit up straight, Anna. Try to relax. Take slow breaths."

But she couldn't. She couldn't do anything but wait until the episode passed. And when it did, she acknowledged to herself that they were, in fact, getting worse instead of better.

Exhausted, she dabbed the sweat beading across her nose and cheeks. She would have collapsed if Maynard hadn't braced her and guided her to his examination table.

"Lie down for minute until you regain your strength."

Stretching out on the table, she covered her eyes with her arm. "I don't want to go to Texas. I don't want to go anywhere. I love Seattle."

I love Joe, she thought. A fresh bout of tears filled her eyes. She had loved him for some time now, had even told him so back when he was hurt and she thought he was asleep. But he'd never acknowledged it, never asked her about it, so she wasn't sure if he'd actually heard her or not. Tonight, though, he'd be wide awake, and when he proposed to her, she intended to tell him again.

"If you don't go, Anna, I'm afraid you won't survive."

Moaning, she curled up into a ball. This couldn't be happening. She could count on one hand the number of times she'd been sick. Until recently. Until she'd arrived in Seattle.

"I was fine when I was up at Joe's," she cried.

"Sometimes it takes a while for the moisture to have its effect."

Anger ripped through her. Why her? Why now? Hadn't she suffered enough? Pushing herself to a sitting position, she swiped her eyes. "I want to go home."

"I don't think that's a good idea. I'm really concerned about Granby being dry enough. You need to head south. If you don't want to go to Texas, Kansas would probably be all right."

"No. I meant *home*. The Occidental." She slipped off the table.

Maynard cupped her elbow. "Of course. Let me drive you."

She jerked away from his clasp. "No, thank you. I'd prefer to walk."

She knew she was behaving poorly, but she needed to get away. To be alone. Hurrying from the room, she grabbed her cape and ran outside.

A sheet of rain hit her face, mingling with her tears. She made no attempt to protect herself from it. What difference would it make? If she stayed or if she left, one thing was certain: She was going to lose Joe.

Crushed, she could hardly stay upright. But she plodded ahead. Through the puddles, the rain, the remorse.

Bitterly she cried out to the Lord. *I can't bear to leave him. I can't.*

Nor could she ask him to go with her. The land was a part of him. Leaving it behind would kill him. Not right away, maybe, but eventually. And as much as she wanted to marry him, she knew what she had to do.

Give me strength, Lord.

Chapter Thirty-four

Anna studied her reflection in the cheval mirror. The cotton voile shift next to her skin might have been velvet, it was so soft and supple. She'd spent entirely too much time on the trimmings. Along the neckline, ribbon wove in and out of the fabric with delicate forget-me-knots bordering it on both sides. She'd added scalloped crocheted edging to both that and the sleeves.

Her drawers matched her shift and the whiteness of her brocade corset captivated her. She hadn't wanted to make a wedding dress until he'd actually proposed, but she couldn't resist sewing up the undergarments—though this was her first time to wear them.

Stepping into the new petticoat, she pulled it up over her hips, luxuriating in the freedom the hooped boning provided. Glancing over her shoulder, she checked her reflection one more time, admiring the undergarment's pintucks and its elliptical shape—which would provide extra fullness to the back of her dress.

Even though the night with Joe was certain to be bittersweet, she wanted to look her best. She'd chosen to wear her navy wool with its tiny white leaf pattern. More than once he had mentioned his appreciation of that particular gown.

Its boned darts and tucked back displayed her figure in a positive light, while the cartridge pleating of the skirt's train would be shown off by her new petticoat. Before buttoning the bodice, she removed a jar of scented oil she'd made from the twinflowers he'd packed in her trunk.

The perfume was her own recipe of water, oil, crushed twinflower, and her secret ingredient—a drop of vodka. She wasn't able to make it often, for obtaining vodka was always a challenge. But Doc had been more than willing to share his once she explained what it was for.

Dipping a finger into the jar, she touched behind each ear, each wrist and the shadow between her breasts. She quickly finished buttoning herself up, then attached white collar and cuffs. She didn't want to be late.

When she made it downstairs, Joe was waiting in his Sunday best. It was the first time she'd seen him in it for anything other than church. He smiled, a series of dimples pleating his face like a parted curtain.

He slid his gaze from her head to her toe, lingering on her skirt. Did he notice the new fullness to her dress? Did he realize she was wearing a petticoat made from the fabric he'd given her?

His eyes met hers, pleasure and heat emanating from his. "You look lovely." He tucked her hand into his elbow, his voice low, husky. "Something's different and I like it. I like it very much."

He knew. Heat flashed through her as he led her outside to the coal-box buggy. His leg brushed her skirt, each step causing the boning in her petticoat to kick out to the side.

Clasping her waist with his huge hands, he paused, giving her the briefest of caresses with his thumbs. "I want to kiss you right now."

He'd whispered it, then lifted her off the ground and into the carriage. Flustered, she frantically pressed her skirt to keep it from bowing out like a bell.

They rode toward the bay, the buggy top down. Puddles had collected in the deeper potholes, offering the only evidence of earlier rains. Stars covered the now clear night sky as if God had thrown a handful of sparkling jacks while the moon, like a ball, waited to be bounced.

Ordinarily Joe and Anna began talking the moment they saw each other and didn't stop until he brought her home. But tonight, neither said a word, his whispered declaration echoing in both their minds.

He usually took her to supper at Our House, an expensive hotel run by the Widow Hill, but instead of turning right on Jackson, he continued toward the wharf. Anna didn't ask any questions. She didn't really care where they ate, so long as they were together.

The smell of Elliott Bay and the sound of gentle waves bumping against a pier soothed her frazzled nerves. She loved the water. Any kind of water. Lake, river, bay, sea. How could something so beautiful and calming be the cause of her cough?

As they approached the shore, a canoe decorated with Chinese lanterns bobbed next to the dock. The water reflected its lights, making it look as if a pixie had left sparkling dust all about the vessel. An Indian arrayed in citizen's garb—complete with white shirt and standing collar reaching halfway up to his ears—stood inside the boat.

Before she could comment on it, Joe pulled Shakespeare to a stop. Another Indian, also dressed in *itkahs*, white man's clothes, rushed forward and took the horse's reins.

Anna's confusion lasted only a moment before realization struck. Joe had decorated a canoe and planned to take her on a moonlit ride. Her mind grappled with the image of him doing such a frivolous thing while her heart felt Cupid's arrow strike with loving precision.

Help me tell him, Lord. Help me be strong.

Jumping from the buggy, he reached up for her. Instead of assisting her to her feet, however, he swooped her legs out from under her and carried her to the dock.

"What are you doing?" she asked, pressing her petticoat down.

"I didn't want you to soil the hem of your dress." But even when they reached the pier, he didn't release her.

Stopping next to the canoe, he lowered her into it. "*Iskêm.*"

The Indian took hold of her, guiding her to a plank where she sat down. She noticed his feet were bare beneath his trousers and smiled to herself. The natives went only so far in their adoption of civilized clothing.

Joe loosened the moorings, then dropped into the boat, causing it to sway before he settled across from her. "Anna, this is Clat Scoot. He'll be piloting the canoe for us tonight."

She nodded. "Hello, Mr. Scoot."

"*Klahawya.*"

The Squamish were a marine-oriented society. More than once she'd admired their finely crafted dugouts as they paddled up and down the coast, trading with the *tkup*, or white man. But Anna had never been in one.

Scoot maneuvered the canoe around and in seconds they were cutting through the bay, the rhythmic *blup, blup* of his paddle filling the silence.

Joe slipped his large booted foot beneath her skirt and toed her hem. The boning in her petticoat lifted.

"What's this?" he asked.

The lanterns provided enough light for her to see him, but not enough to see the nuances in his expression. She had no trouble recognizing the intimate tenor of his voice, however.

When she didn't respond, he tapped her skirt again. "Are you, by chance, wearing something new?"

She glanced at Scoot.

"He doesn't speak English," Joe said. "That's why I arranged for him to do the piloting."

Still, she didn't answer, trying to decide if she was pleased or mortified that he'd noticed her undergarments.

The forward motion of the canoe brought with it a breeze. The length of hair she'd gathered with a ribbon and draped over her shoulder fluttered. Joe tapped her petticoat in time with the canoe paddle.

She slapped her hands against her shins. "Stop that," she whispered.

"Answer me."

"You already know the answer."

"What else besides the petticoat?"

"Joe."

"What else?"

"All of it."

The tapping ceased. "Petticoat, shift, corset, and drawers?"

She gasped, triggering her cough.

Joe offered her his handkerchief. "Did Doc give you something new for that last week? He told me he would."

When the coughing stopped, she took slow, careful breaths. The breeze seemed to help, despite the moisture it picked up from the bay.

Still, she didn't rush herself. The last thing she wanted was to have a breathing episode. Joe had only observed that first one when they were at Lake Washington. She had no desire to have him witness another.

"Have you been taking your elecampane and licorice?"

Anna nodded.

"And it hasn't helped?"

"Not too much." Her voice came out scratchy and rough.

She should tell him. Now. Before the evening progressed. But before she could, the canoe veered toward the shore. She looked over her shoulder.

In a clearing not far from the water, a half dozen torches surrounded a temporary house like those the Indians summered in. All her good intentions disappeared. He'd clearly gone to a great deal of trouble on her behalf. She wasn't about to spoil it. Not yet, at least.

Pushing thoughts of her illness to the back of her mind, she committed to simply enjoying the evening. Two squatty youths ran out, splashing into the water to help pull the boat on shore.

Once they reached the sand, Joe stepped out, scooped her up, and carried her toward the house made of woven cattail mats. The smell of food made her mouth water. She hadn't realized how hungry she was.

Inside, Joe set her on her feet. Indian women in the adopted skirt and shirtwaist of the Americans bustled around a wide trench that held the cooking fire. All were barefoot.

Smoke from the fire spiraled up through an opening in the roof. A modern table complete with two armchairs, a cloth covering, two place settings, and a small candelabra graced a corner of the hut, looking completely out of place amid the handmade baskets and stools scattered about the dirt floor.

The thing that snagged Anna's attention and held it, however, was the Indian woman with brass rings on every finger, including her thumbs, brass rings in her ears, and a string of ten-cent pieces hanging about her neck.

It was the same woman Joe had waved and winked at back when Anna had first arrived. She was the only one who wore the traditional Indian wraparound garment of woven cedar bark. She wasn't undersized like the rest of her tribe, but tall and striking, her dark brown hair falling about her shoulders in long, satiny freedom.

Joe placed his hand at Anna's waist. "*Ukuk nayka kluchmên.*" He gave her a gentle squeeze. "Anna, this is my friend and our host, Kitlu."

Anna curtsied. The unfamiliar words and guttural sounds rolling from Joe's tongue fascinated her. "What did you say?"

"That you were my woman."

She gave him a sharp glance.

He escorted her to the table and pulled out her chair. "Please, have a seat."

Looking at the other women in the hut, Kitlu brought her fists to her sides and then pushed them out. Activity amongst them increased threefold.

One girl dropped red-hot stones from the fire into a watertight basket holding soup of some kind. Another peeled back a mat, uncovering a steaming pit.

"Anna? Are you listening?"

She jerked her attention back to Joe. "I'm sorry. I was watching the women. What are they making? It smells wonderful."

He tucked his napkin into his collar. "Venison."

Her gaze wandered back to the fire pit, taking stock of all he'd done to prepare for the evening. It had taken no small amount of time, effort, and planning.

"The boat ride was wonderful, Joe. The lanterns were beautiful. And all this." She waved her hand to encompass the elaborately set table and the food being prepared. "I'm completely charmed."

Before he could respond, Kitlu served them each a bowl of soup in small handwoven baskets.

"*Mersi,*" Joe said, then waited politely for Anna to take the first bite.

"What is it?" Dipping her spoon into the concoction, she tried it.

"Squirrel."

The liquid trickled down her throat, but the meat stayed in her mouth. Squirrel? Anna looked at the soup. She was eating a rodent?

Trying not to picture the varmint with its beady eyes and bushy tail, she chewed and swallowed.

In true lumberjack form, Joe had already eaten almost half of his. "Do you like it?"

He was trying so hard, she didn't have the heart to tell him the truth. "I've never had squirrel before."

"Never?" His expression registered shock.

"No."

"Well, what do you think?"

She shrugged. "I've only had one bite so far."

"You better eat up, then. The clams are almost done."

Sure enough, one of the women was scooping clams from a pit.

"I thought we were having venison."

"That's the main course."

Nodding, she took another bite, doing what her mother had taught her whenever she was eating something unpleasant.

Just put it in your mouth and say, "Mmm, mmm, mmm." That way you'll trick yourself into thinking it's good.

"How's Sprout?" he asked.

Mmm. Mmm. "You mean, Roy? He's coming along quite well. Doc said his young body is still making bone, so his leg will not only heal, but will in all likelihood be stronger than his other one."

"No limp?"

"No, thank goodness." *Mmm. Mmm.*

Joe scraped the edges of his bowl. "I need to talk with Doc and find out when I can bring the boy up to camp like I promised."

"What on earth would he be able to do?" *Mmm. Mmm.*

"I have a little wagon in the barn. When the fellows and I chop an undercut with our axes, Spr—Roy can fill his wagon with the chips that come flying out and take them to Ollie for the stove. Just the walk to and from the house will keep Roy busy for most of the day."

"Feels strange calling him Roy, doesn't it?" she asked.

"I still can't get over him picking my name. Bet that knocked Rountree's raker out of line." Chuckling, he nodded at her soup. "You going to finish that?"

"I'm afraid I'll fill up on it and not be able to enjoy the rest of the meal."

He extended his hand and she tried not to look too relieved

as she passed her basket-bowl to him. They caught up with each other's news during the subsequent courses.

Finally, the venison was served. It had been rolled in leaves and baked in a pit covered with hot stones.

"Good heavens," she said, taking her first bite. "This tastes nothing like beef."

"Do you like it?"

She closed her eyes in concentration. "Yes. It's different, but very good."

He asked her to finish telling him about her week. She regaled him with stories from the various surgeries Doc had performed, ending with Henry Yesler's. He'd almost sawed a finger off at his mill.

"I'd heard that. Is he all right?"

"Yes, but I must say he could stand to read a few books from your library."

"Why's that?"

"He has a rather limited vocabulary and uses the same words over and over, even when he's swearing." She clucked her tongue. "I'm telling you, the man's language is a fire hazard."

Joe threw back his head and laughed. The action involved his entire body—head, neck, shoulders, chest. Land sakes, but he was handsome.

Kitlu took their empty plates and replaced Anna's with a small box tied in white ribbon. The amusement slowly left his face. He looked from the box to her.

Her stomach tightened. "What's this?"

"Dessert."

The evening had been wonderful. She didn't want it to end. She definitely didn't want it to end on a poor note. But what could she say? That she was full and wanted to skip dessert?

"Go ahead," he said, his voice low. "Open it."

Taking the ends of the bow, she unraveled it and opened the box. "A wonder turner!"

She hadn't seen a child's thaumatrope in years. Leon used to have one with a picture of a drum on one side of the cardboard and a boy holding drumsticks on the other. When Leon twisted the strings attached to each end of the cardboard, the pictures spun, merging the images into a drummer playing his drum.

The cardboard in her box was about the size of a silver dollar and had a silhouette of a woman looking up. The opposite side held an image of a lumberjack looking down.

Grasping the strings on each side of the turner, she rapidly twisted them. The figures merged into one of a couple passionately embracing.

"Will you marry me?" he whispered.

She continued to spin the thaumatrope. Faster, faster, until it blurred. Not because of the speed in which the cardboard rotated, but because of the tears filling her eyes.

A man did not go to the extent in which Joe had unless he was confident of the answer to his question. And she'd given him every reason to assume she'd answer affirmatively.

She quit twirling the toy. It slowly came to a stop. The couple was one no more.

Carefully tucking it back into the box, she closed the lid and retied the ribbon. "I'd very much like to marry you."

The only sound in the hut was that of their breathing. Kitlu and her women had all vacated the house.

"Then why are you crying?"

Every muscle in his body was coiled like a bear trap. What would happen when she triggered the spring?

She slid her hand across the table, palm up. He grasped it. Closing her eyes, she took a moment to relish the feel of his large hand, hard and knotty from hours of wielding an ax. Finally, she could put it off no longer.

"The doc says I have tuberculosis and if I don't move someplace dry like Kansas or Texas, I'll not survive." She squeezed his hand. "So, I'm afraid, love, that I'm not going to have the pleasure of marrying you, after all."

Chapter Thirty-Five

Too many thoughts came at once, so Joe zeroed in on the one that scared him the most. "You have tuberculosis?"

"Evidently." Anna kept her chin up, though it quivered.

He slowly pulled the napkin from his collar. "I thought it was just a cough."

"So did I."

"What is the exact prognosis?"

"It's in the very early stages. I should live a long and healthy life, so long as I am someplace dry."

His relief was short-lived. She would be safe, but only if she left the Territory.

He shot to his feet, then paced. "I don't understand. This isn't making any sense. You were fine the whole time you were up at home with me."

"I know." A tear slipped down her cheek.

He grabbed the back of his chair. "When did you find out?"

"This morning."

"You've barely coughed all night."

"It's not just the cough."

"What else? Blood? Fever?" Skirting round the table, he placed his palm against her forehead.

"No. It's my breathing. Remember what happened at the lake?"

"Yes."

"That same thing happens twice, sometimes three times a week."

He ran his thumb under her eye, capturing the moisture there. "What are we going to do?"

"You're going to go home and I'm going to go to Kansas." Her words were matter-of-fact, but her face crumpled.

He pulled her up against his chest. *No!*

But he knew she couldn't stay. Not if it would put her in danger. He also knew he couldn't let her go.

Which left him with only one option. He would have to leave, too. His chest seized up. What about his land? His crew? Red?

He knew they'd understand. Men started over all the time and for much more trivial reasons than his. But could he simply walk away?

Eleven years he'd invested in his land. Two of which he'd spent fighting to retain ownership. He had practically kissed the forest floor every day since the judge had ruled in his favor. And now he'd have to voluntarily walk away or lose Anna?

She slipped her hands inside his jacket, then buried her face against his shirt, suppressing a cough. He rested his chin on her head.

Why, Lord? You already took one wife. Do you have to have Anna, too?

But He wasn't taking Anna. He was relocating her. To Kansas. But men didn't log in Kansas. They farmed.

Joe swallowed. He hated farming. He would not, could not, reconcile himself to such a fate.

So that left Texas. And cattle ranching. He could probably do that.

The reality of leaving, though, of starting all over, began to register. He'd never log again, never see the Territory, the redwoods, his friends, his land, the new log chute, the house he'd begun to think of as Anna's. Did Texas even have trees?

She gently pulled away. "I'm so sorry."

He swallowed the tears stacking up in his own throat. He wanted to say it would be all right. That he'd go with her. But he didn't. No words came out. He let his hands fall to his sides.

Turning around, she picked up the box with the wonder turner inside. "Would you mind if I kept this?"

"Dash it all, Anna." Putting his hands on her shoulders, he made her face him again, then hauled her into his arms and kissed her. Not a kiss of passion or hope, but of anxiety. Of sorrow. Of frustration.

He clung to her, frantic to get as close as he could. But no matter how fully he kissed her, nothing soothed the desperation inside him.

He slowly withdrew. "Do you love me?"

Biting her lower lip, she nodded.

"Then marry me."

"I can't. I have to leave."

"Then we'll both leave, because I'll never let you go, Anna." And he realized it was true. He loved his land, but it would be nothing without her.

"No, Joe. The land is as much a part of you as the heart that beats inside here." She splayed her hand over his chest. "I won't be responsible for tearing your heart out."

"If you leave me, that's exactly what you'll do." He hooked a tendril of hair behind her ear. "Marry me."

Tears spilled from her eyes. "You're sure?"

"I'm sure."

She catapulted herself against him. "Yes!" She fisted her hands in his hair and pulled his lips to hers. "Yes!"

Her tears salted their kiss.

Finally, he pulled back and rested his lips against the top of her head. "How soon do we need to leave?"

She laid her cheek on his chest. "Right away. Otherwise, we'll get caught crossing the plains in the winter."

"It's already too late to go by land. We'll have to go by boat."

She pulled back, her eyes were red, swollen. "You can't get to Kansas by boat."

He hesitated. "I guess I was thinking Texas."

She wrinkled her nose. "Southerners live in Texas."

"Cowboys live in Texas."

"Close enough."

Sighing, he kissed the tears from her eyes. "We can worry about that later. Come on. We need to give Kitlu her home back."

Anna glanced about the summer house. "It is beautiful, Joe. I'll remember tonight for the rest of my life. I'm sorry I ruined it for you."

He slipped off his jacket and draped it over her shoulders. "The only way you could have ruined it is if you'd said no. Now, let's get you home. I'm sure the cool night air isn't good for you."

Joe was having second thoughts. When he was with Anna, he felt like he could walk away from it all. It wasn't until he'd left town and passed tree after tree, acre after acre, that he began to doubt his resolve.

A week. They were supposed to leave in a week. How could he leave so soon? If only he had more time.

He slammed his ax into a cypress. It was only about twenty inches in diameter, so he could easily fell it himself. And it was a good thing, because he hadn't felt like partnering with anyone today. So he'd left the boys back at camp, then ventured out to a far section of property that hadn't ever seen the sharp side of an ax.

Virgins. That's what these trees were. And if he didn't leave with Anna, they were likely to be the only virgins he'd ever have. He took another swing, chips flying from the undercut.

Eleven years he'd been without a woman. He'd been happy. Content. Lonely now and then, but nothing that didn't pass. Would he be able to recapture that?

He tried to remember how he'd felt after receiving news of Lorraine's death. He'd been shocked, saddened, but he hadn't experienced this suffocating grief that had a hold of him now.

Of course, he'd only been eighteen at the time. Barely out of short pants. Three months after he'd married her, he'd left for the Territory. It was another six months when news of her death arrived. By then, the land had seeped into his veins. Any feelings he'd had for Lorraine had mellowed to the point of near-nonexistence. He'd had his whole life ahead of him, after all.

It could be the same with Anna. He'd only known her for three months, too. All he needed was a little time. Joe eyed the angle of his cut, then began working on the crosscut and wondered how long a man could lie to himself.

He imagined some did it for a lifetime, but he knew he couldn't. He knew that deep down Anna was more important than a bunch of trees. And that's, basically, what his land was. But it wouldn't make leaving it any easier.

I want both, Lord. Anna and my land. Is that so much to ask?

Flipping his suspenders off his shoulders, he pulled his shirt from his trousers and used it to wipe his face. He took a moment to rest.

Fir, cedar, pines, oaks, and maples densely timbered this section. But it was the redwoods that never failed to fill him with awe. Their feathery-looking needles and reddish bark. The way they stretched up to incredible heights and the sheer magnitude of their circumferences. How long ago had God planted their seeds? Hundreds of years? Thousands?

As he stood amongst those mighty giants, he realized the land wasn't his at all. It was God's. God had formed and planted the seeds. He'd tended the soil and caused it to rain. He'd needed no man. Least of all Joe.

Yet over and over Joe had thought of this as his own. My land. My logging camp. My house. My woman. My everything.

Picking up his ax, he returned to his work. But in his mind, he reviewed a list of men in the Bible who'd left everything they held dear for parts unknown. Abraham. Jacob. Joseph. Moses. Even a woman. Esther.

In every case, their circumstances were much more severe than his. God hadn't commanded Joe to leave his land, though he'd prayed for guidance. Fasted. Read his Bible. But God had remained silent.

Joe simply assumed God was letting him choose. But no matter what he chose, none of it was really his. It was all God's. And God was sharing it with him.

So which did he want? Both. Like a spoiled child, he definitely wanted both. But if he could only have one, wouldn't he still be a man blessed?

Yes. And he'd praise God and thank Him. But that didn't immediately make the grief shrivel up and blow away.

Eyeing where he wanted the tree to fall, he adjusted his stance.

I want Anna, Lord. I choose Anna.

Yet as long as he lived, he'd always miss this land. He'd miss the Territory. He'd miss the logging. He'd miss his friends.

The cypress began to pop and splinter. Jumping away, he braced his feet, threw back his head, and shouted with everything he had.

"Timber-r-r-r-r-r-r-r-r-r-r-r!"

The tree wavered, then crashed to the forest floor. Noise resounded through the copse. The ground shook. Debris flew.

Before any of it settled, Joe fell to his knees, doubled over, and sobbed.

⁂

Red threw down his cards. "I don't believe you."

Joe slid the newspaper across the barrel.

> FOR SALE. Valuable Lumbering Business on 640 acres of well-timbered land one-half day north of Seattle. Inquiries at office of Judge O.B. Rountree, Jackson Street, Seattle, W.T.
>
> JOSEPH DENTON

Red's face turned as bright as his hair. "Just like that? You're giving it up just like that?"

"She has tuberculosis. What am I supposed to do?"

Red swiped the cards from the barrel, scattering the newspaper and their game of Casino. Ollie and the rest of the crew had headed for the bunkhouse as soon as the chores were done. But not Red.

No, Joe's best friend had taken one look at him and said, "After dinner, we're having us a game of cards."

Joe hadn't argued. He needed to tell Red before he saw it in the papers for himself.

"You want to know what you're supposed to do?" Red shouted. "I'll tell you what you're supposed to do. You let her go to Kansas or Texas or straight to the devil for all I care. But you do *not* go with her."

"I love her."

Red jumped to his feet. "You've known her for three months. Three. That isn't long enough to do more than work up a powerful case of lust."

Joe made himself stay seated, but he tensed. "Careful, Red. Be very careful."

"Or what? You want to talk by hand?" Red slammed his fists against his chest. "Well, come on, you slab-sided blighter. I'll take you. I could fight the devil himself for a cup of cold water and give him the first three bites."

Tempting. Very tempting. But if he was going to get married this week, he didn't want to do it with a broken jaw and his eyes swollen shut.

"My mind's made up."

"What about all this?" Red swiped his arm in an all-encompassing gesture. "Don't you care about any of it?"

"I care about every tree, every blade of grass, every speck of dirt. But none of it means as much to me as she does."

With a bloodcurdling scream, Red whirled around and kicked a hole in the side of the barn. The oxen, cows, goats, pigs, and horses squealed and whinnied. Cool air whistled in from outside, vibrating the broken siding and sending the cards airborne.

Joe ignored the destruction. "I'd like you to come with us."

Red looked ready to brawl. "I'm a jack. I'm not about to go someplace where the owls cross with the chickens."

"You went from Maine to the Washington Territory. That's about as far away as two places can be. I don't see much difference in going from here to Texas."

"There's a world of difference. We were logging in Maine and we're logging here. Those misbegotten gaycats in Texas prance around in their fancy boots and flashy buckles riding on nothing but a bunch of hayburners. That what you plan on doing, Joe?"

Joe took a deep breath. "That's what I plan on doing."

Red paced the stall. The string of profanity spewing from his mouth would do any lumberjack proud. Made Henry Yesler sound tame. Joe waited until it had run its course.

Finally Red stood still, his fingers pinching the bridge of his nose. Joe was going to miss him. They'd been friends since they'd both been about Sprout's age.

They made a good pair. Joe was always willing to save and invest and take the risks. Red was happy to do the labor. All he wanted was his weekly earnings so he could blow them within twenty-four hours, then start all over again.

"I depend on you, Joe. I depended on you when we were kids. I depended on you when we moved out west. And I'm depending on you now."

"You don't need me, Red. You can jack anywhere. Here. Oregon. Maine. Anywhere."

"It won't be the same."

Joe sighed. "No, I don't suppose it will. And I'm sorry." He hesitated. "I'll sell it to you for a song, if you want it."

"Sell what?"

"The place. I don't know why I didn't think about it before." He sat up straighter. "You want it, Red?"

Red looked up. "You'd do that? You'd sell it to me? For next to nothing?"

"Faster than you could blink. I'd much rather you have it than sell it to some stranger."

"But I haven't put a dime into this place."

"You've put in your sweat and more hours than I can count."

The animals weren't squawking anymore, but they were restless, though the tension between the men had all but vanished.

"I love this place, Joe, but the thought of being boss makes me want to bolt like a jackrabbit in tall grass. And you know it. That's why you put the ad in the paper. That's why you didn't think of it until just now."

"Come on, Red. Why not give it a try?"

Red shook his head. "Your tongue's just getting plain frolicsome. Besides, you need the money you'll get from selling the place at full price."

"I've plenty of money."

"Maybe so. But you can never have too much. Not when you're starting all over in a foreign land with a woman and, most likely, little ones before you know it. You need to sell."

"I did it with nothing last time. I surely can do it again with full pockets."

"Not with a woman, you can't. Even back then, you knew better than to bring your woman with you."

"I'm not leaving you empty-handed."

"And I'm not buying so much as one blade." Red stooped down and gathered up the cards. "Now, come on. Let's finish our game."

Chapter Thirty-six

"You have to go get him," Anna said, standing in the lobby of the Sires Hotel, where Joe was staying.

Leslie Pike, the youth behind the counter, shook his head. "It's bad luck to be seeing the groom before the ceremony, Miss Ivey. Everybody knows that."

"Oh, that's nothing but a bunch of fiddle-faddle. Now, go get him, Leslie. It's crucial that I talk to him."

Sighing, the boy left his post. Moments later, Joe hurried into the lobby, his face half shaved, bits of white lather dotting his chin. "What's happened? Are you not feeling well?"

She wrung her hands. "I'm fine. I just . . . I needed to ask you something."

"What is it?"

She glanced at Leslie. The boy made no effort to disguise his interest in their conversation.

Taking her elbow, Joe led her out the door, down the walkway, around the corner and into the alley. "What's wrong?"

The shadows of the narrow alley shrouded them with privacy.

Beyond their haven, horses slept at the rails, a couple of men discussed politics, and beneath the boardwalk, a mama cat bathed her mewing kittens.

"I'm worried, is all," she said.

He reared back. "You're having second thoughts?"

"No, no. Not me. I was thinking of you."

"You think I'm having second thoughts?"

"No," she said, fiddling with her watch pin. "I'm thinking perhaps you ought to be. I mean, are you sure you want to do this, Joe? Are you sure you won't regret putting your land up for sale?"

The tension immediately left him. "I'm sure."

"But how do you know? What if years from now when we're old and gray you think back on all this and wish you'd stayed?"

He studied her for a long time, a look of pained amusement on his face. "Don't move. I need to go get something."

"What?"

"Stay right here. Okay?"

"All right."

He raced around the corner. One of the kittens darted into the alley, its back legs bouncing in unison. Squatting down, Anna held out her hand. The yellow, fuzzy bundle crept closer and closer until it finally touched its wet nose to Anna's proffered hand.

Scooping the critter up, she brought it to her face. "I don't know what to do, kitty. I want him so bad, I can't hardly stand it. But I'd hate it if he came to regret his decision."

The kitten purred and rubbed against Anna's neck. Its breath held a hint of mother's milk and some indefinable odor unique to baby kittens. A few minutes later, Joe returned with a small package in his hand.

"What's that?" Anna asked, rising.

"Your wedding present."

Her eyes widened. "You're not supposed to give me that until after the wedding."

"And you're not supposed to accost the groom before the ceremony."

"I didn't accost you." Still, she handed him the kitten with one hand while taking the brown package with the other.

The look of consternation on his face at finding a kitten in his arms caused her to giggle.

"Don't worry," she whispered. "I won't tell anyone you were cuddling a kitten."

"I am not cuddling it." Leaning over, Joe let it jump from his hands. "Now, open your package."

Untying the string, Anna folded back the edges of the paper only to find the frame she'd made out of shells. But it didn't have the Scripture she'd written about a person's heart being where their treasure was. Instead, it had Matthew 13:45–46 scrawled across a piece of parchment in thick, bold strokes.

> *The kingdom of heaven is like a merchant seeking fine pearls, and upon finding one pearl of great value, he went and sold all that he had and bought it.*

Parting her lips, she lifted her gaze to his.

"I have no regrets, Anna. How could I, when I have you?"

Joy, relief, and happiness created a whirlwind within her. Launching herself into his arms, she gave him a quick, hard kiss. "I love you."

"I love you, too. More than you know." He backed her against the side of the hotel and gave her a kiss that built an insatiable desire inside the very core of her being.

"Mmm . . ." she murmured, tightening her hold.

"Mr. Denton! The women are looking for Miss Ivey."

Joe lifted his head. Leslie Pike stood just inside the alley, forming a blinder with his hand so as to give the couple privacy.

Sighing, Joe put some space between him and Anna. "It's okay, Leslie. You can look now."

The boy peeked over his hand with one eye, his face flushing red, then looked frantically between Joe and the street. "They're coming. You go round back and I'll head them off while Miss Ivey slips by. Now hurry."

Stepping out onto the boardwalk, Leslie greeted a group of women approaching the hotel.

"We're looking for Miss Ivey, young sir," they heard Mrs. Rountree say. "Have you seen her?"

"Why, yes, I have. Saw her just a minute ago leaving Mr. McAleer's Tinware. If you hurry, you just might catch her."

"Well, for heaven's sake. The ceremony is in just over an hour and she's visiting Stoves & Tinware? Come on, ladies."

Joe swiped a dollop of shaving cream from Anna's face. "You'd best make your escape, Miss Ivey, before you're found out."

She relaxed against the wooden siding. "It just might be worth the risk."

Lifting a brow, he peeled her from the wall and pointed her in the direction of the street. "Go on. Before I take you up on it."

Tossing her hair over her shoulder, she poked her head around the corner. "All clear."

He shooed her with his hands.

She waggled two fingers at him, then hurried up the hill to the Occidental.

SEATTLE INTELLIGENCER
OCTOBER 14, 1866

Though there was no stringed orchestra and tall calla lilies and picture-hatted bridesmaids, what a happy wedding it was! Joseph Roy Denton and Anna Louise Ivey were married in the Occidental Hotel, and that evening all the young people in town came down to the hotel and made merry to the strains of the Seattle Band. The Indians lined up outside the door and looked curiously in, wondering at all the strange white people who made so much ado about a mere squaw.

⁂

The hotel room Anna had lived in for the last two months was not a large room, but never had it felt so small as when Joe stepped in and closed the door behind him. She'd become so accustomed to him, she'd forgotten how really large he was.

His suit had been freshly laundered and pressed, a sprig of twinflower pinned to his lapel. Though his blond curls had been combed down and slicked back for the ceremony, the night air had done its magic and loosened those beautiful locks. Locks she could now touch whenever it suited her. She swallowed.

"You cold?" he asked.

She shook her head.

"Hot?"

She shook her head.

A corner of his mouth tilted up. "Nervous?"

She didn't answer.

Surveying the room, he wandered through it, pausing to open the wardrobe and peek inside, to poke the fire with an iron, to adjust the towel by the water pitcher, to look out the window at the view, to reposition the shell-framed Scripture he'd given her, to pick up her brush and run his fingers over the bristles.

She wasn't sure how to proceed. She hadn't had a mother to tell her of such things. Was he waiting for her to . . . to what? Undress? While he circled the room?

Her legs lost their ability to hold her up. She needed to sit down. But the only place to sit was the bed. She reached out and braced a hand against the wall.

He looked up, his interest in the brush forgotten. With slow, deliberate intent, his gaze traveled over every inch of her from the twinflowers in her hair to her gown's V-neckline to the watch pin on her chest to the buttons running from her bodice clear down to the etching on the hem of her skirt.

The trembling in her legs spread to every place his gaze touched.

"You are beautiful."

The heat in his eyes caused her to take a step back. Her petticoat touched the wall and bowed out.

"Your wedding gown is exquisite. I wasn't expecting anything so . . . elaborate."

"Several of the women helped me. They were all quite taken with the fabric. I never thanked you for it. It's magnificent."

Joe smiled. "My pleasure."

The brush slipped from his fingers, clattering onto the dresser. He moved toward her, engrossed. Captivated. Absorbed. With the watch pin on her gown.

She thought of the thaumatrope and how the lumberjack practically swallowed up the woman. She backed completely against the wall.

He didn't stop until his trousers touched the hem of her skirt. Still he looked at the watch pin.

Breathing grew difficult. Not like when she had an episode, but like when he kissed her. Really kissed her.

Finally, he raised his gaze. "Have I ever told you I love the way you smell?"

It was a compliment. She knew it was. But his choice of wording made her choke back a nervous laugh, which came out as a snort.

He didn't notice. Instead, he freed the twinflower from her hair, held the bloom to his nose, and inhaled. She was glad she had the support of the wall behind her.

He tossed the flower onto the bed. She tracked its flight as it landed on the quilted cover.

Threading his fingers through her hair, he tilted her face up and gave her one of those kisses. The kind that made breathing difficult and standing near impossible. Still, she didn't touch him. No matter how badly she wanted to. She didn't dare.

Ending the kiss, he kept his forehead against hers, but his fingers trailed from her face to her neck to her shoulders to . . . her watch pin. He enfolded it with his fingers, his knuckles brushing her.

Her lips parted.

"It's cool to the touch," he said, his voice husky. "I expected it to be warm. Very warm."

"It was my mother's. I've gone without many a meal rather than sell it. It was all I had."

"You have me now."

Anna smiled. "Yes. Yes I do."

Unpinning the watch, he laid it on the nightstand, then moved his fingers to her buttons.

She sucked in her breath.

"This gown is lovely, little robin, but there are some items of clothing I have wondered about and wanted to see for a long, long time."

Joe slipped the first button free. Then the second. The third. On and on until the gown was held up only by her back and the wall. He encircled her waist, drew her to him, and kissed her again.

The gown fell to the floor.

Ending the kiss, he took her shoulders and placed her at arm's length. She blushed, knowing he'd see how much time she'd spent embroidering her new underclothes. But every forget-me-knot, pintuck, ribbon, and scalloped frill had made her feel connected to him somehow.

His Adam's apple bobbed. He fingered the crocheted edging on the neckline of her shift. "You did a beautiful job, Anna." He looked at her. "But there are some other items I have wondered about and wanted to see for a long, long time."

Her eyes widened. Scooping her into his arms, he lowered his mouth to hers and carried her to bed.

Chapter Thirty-seven

San Francisco
October 15, 1866

Anna had just begun to brush off the weariness of their steamer ride when their carriage pulled to a stop in front of a huge building four stories high. She straightened.

"I thought since we started our wedding trip at the Occidental," Joe said, stepping out of the carriage and offering her a hand, "we'd continue it at San Francisco's version."

She could only gape. She'd been to the city for a short time with Mr. Mercer, but never to this part of town. Still, San Francisco's Occidental Hotel was something she'd have expected to see in New York City, not the West. The Italianate stucco façade loomed over its neighbors. "It's so tall."

He tucked her hand into his elbow. "It's said to have a magnificent view of the city and bay."

She'd never stayed anyplace so grand. Inside, a plush rug cushioned her feet. The woodwork was solid mahogany. The doorknobs, silver plate.

Joe headed to the desk, leaving her to wonder at the windows, which were as wide as a man and almost two stories high. The red coloring of the massive rosettes decorating the ceiling brought life to the otherwise white surroundings.

Joe returned to her side. "Ready?"

"It's magnificent," she whispered. "But shouldn't we wait until your land sells before staying in such an extravagant place?"

Shrugging, he gave the lobby a cursory glance. "We'll be fine. Besides, I thought to pamper my bride before we take a very long boat ride around the Horn."

She smiled. "Thank you."

A smartly dressed porter indicated they should follow.

"As soon as we're settled," Joe said, his hand riding the back of her waist, "we'll find us a place to eat. The clerk said there was an establishment in the Plaza called The Cottage Café that is extremely popular and offers some of the best food in town."

After a thrilling ride in the lift, the porter escorted them to a corner room and threw open the door. "Mr. and Mrs. Denton, your bridal suite."

Anna gasped. Joe had arranged for the bridal suite? She entered the sumptuous parlor decorated in whites and golds with a breathtaking view looking down on the city and bay. The parlor opened onto a lavish bedroom with a very large, roomy bedstead. Thick brocade curtains pulled back by large gold tassels framed the massive structure.

But it was the bathroom that thrilled her the most. It had a real toilet, a tub, and pipes that brought the water in and took the water out.

She heard a murmuring of voices, the door click shut, and Joe's footsteps as he followed her to the lavatory.

"Oh, Joe," she said, still staring at the tub and toilet. "I've never seen anything so glorious in my life."

He slipped his arms about her waist and nuzzled her neck. "Hungry?"

"Yes."

"How hungry?"

She glanced up over her shoulder, then felt her insides respond to the heat in his gaze. "I'm not in any great hurry. Are you?"

"No hurry at all." Turning her around, he pulled her against him and lowered his mouth to hers.

The Cottage Café was no small cottage, but a large restaurant with rows and rows of long tables and benches filled with patrons. A barlike counter ran the length of one wall. Lining the mirrored shelves behind it were jars and jars of candy and confections.

Manning the counter was what had to be a father-and-son duo, the former a handsome man with a touch of gray at his temples. He wasn't as broad as Joe, of course, but he was a good deal bigger than most. His son looked to be following in his footsteps—heightwise, at least. He'd yet to fill out, though.

The restaurant held none of the luxury of the hotel, but instead offered a relaxed, homey feel. Anna loved it at once. Sliding in next to a group of men at one of the long tables, she smiled as Joe greeted those around them.

Most were professional-looking men in fancy suits, though a few were rather rough and rowdy. She eyed them, assuming they were gold diggers.

Young women in matching black dresses with crisp white aprons poured from the kitchen and served the meal family-style, much the way she'd served her lumberjacks.

Her lumberjacks. A pang of sorrow intruded on the moment as she watched the women laugh and tease with the men.

Joe's crew had all attended the wedding, of course. All danced with her. Still, she missed them already.

She glanced at Joe. He must miss them even more, though he'd not said so.

A woman with startling blond hair and a ready smile plunked massive platters of beef, potatoes, and bread on the table in front of them. "Eat up, fellows. Today's dessert is almond pudding, but only for boys who clean their plates."

The waitress waggled her finger at them as they exchanged badinage. So much like the jacks at home. Anna sighed. When had she begun thinking of Seattle as home instead of Granby?

The food smelled savory and appetizing. The men were careful to see that she partook first, and she quickly learned to take only what she thought she'd eat because these Californians ate almost as heartily as her lumberjacks.

Dessert was winding down when a woman of the same generation as Anna's mother came from the kitchen and moved down each row of tables greeting customers. She was attractive and hearty, and she lit up when she smiled.

Anna couldn't help but notice the difference between her and Mama. She'd been so emaciated those last few years. Was that what Anna had in store for her with the tuberculosis? Or would the southern states that had killed her father and brother be the very thing that would save her life?

She'd not had one breathing episode all week. Her cough had subsided a bit more each day—particularly after she'd stood on the deck of the steamer enjoying the fresh air and breeze. And her headache had settled into nothing more than a slight irritant.

This upward swing had begun before she'd even left Seattle. Was it that she hadn't had time to notice her ailments because of all the excitement? But, no. If anything, she'd have thought the excitement would cause her symptoms to escalate, not dissipate.

The woman now stood across from Anna. "Hello. I'm Rachel Parker. Are you new to town?"

Joe began to rise.

"No, no. Sit. Please."

Settling back down, he nodded to the woman. "Actually, we're visiting. I'm Joe Denton and this is my wife, Anna."

The man who'd been behind the counter joined Mrs. Parker, slipped his hand about her waist, and pulled her against his hip.

She glanced up at him and smiled. "Johnnie, this is Mr. and Mrs. Denton. They're visiting from . . . ?"

"Seattle," Joe said, rising to shake the man's hand.

"Joe. Johnnie Parker. Welcome." He smiled at Anna. "Mrs. Denton."

"How do you do?"

The man may have been old, she thought, but he was still quite attractive. Especially when he smiled.

Mrs. Parker smoothed her hand under her skirt and sat sideways on the bench across from them. "I'm sorry to hear you're only visiting. Women are always a welcome sight around here. How long will you be in town?"

Anna looked at Joe, then Mrs. Parker. "We're not sure, exactly."

And over the course of the next half hour, Anna found herself telling the woman of their wish to go south and why. By the time she was done, the restaurant was empty and the Parkers both sat across from them, sipping coffee the girls had brought out.

"But you don't sound sick at all," Mrs. Parker said.

"I know." Anna sighed. "It's the strangest thing. I've felt almost like myself for a week now, yet we just arrived in San Francisco this morning."

Mrs. Parker looked at her husband. "Are you thinking what I'm thinking?"

He raised his brows. "Woman, I have yet to keep up with what goes on in your mind. What is it you're thinking?"

"That doctor." She laid her hand on his arm. "You know. The one from Kentucky who worked with that other doctor in a cave?"

Mr. Parker nodded as comprehension dawned. "Dr. Shepard."

"Yes! Dr. Shepard." She turned to Anna. "He and another doctor ran a clinic of sorts in a huge cave for people with tuberculosis.

It was somewhere around Louisville, I think. In any event, they thought the constant temperature and purity of the air there would help cure their patients."

"Did it work?" Joe asked.

"I'm afraid it didn't, but Dr. Shepard studied the disease thoroughly and is considered an expert. Perhaps you could see him while you're here."

Joe slipped his hand into Anna's. "Perhaps we will."

⁂

Anna straightened her clothing, left the exam room, and joined Joe and Dr. Shepard in his library. Both men rose.

The room reminded her of Doc Maynard's place. The smell of chemicals wafted about her. Shelves lined the wall with books of all sizes and shapes. Rolls of papers protruded from pigeonholes above his desk, while the surface of it was covered with more papers, an open medical dictionary, a jar of eye wash, another of glycerin powder, and a pair of spectacles.

"Mrs. Denton, please have a seat." The doctor was much older than Doc Maynard. He had kind blue eyes, a bulbous nose, a gray goatee, and a severely receding hairline.

Joe held the chair while she settled. Instead of sitting in the adjoining one, he stood behind her and rested his hands on her shoulders. She lifted her hands to his and squeezed his fingers.

Drawing a fresh piece of paper from the bottom of a pile, Dr. Shepard put on his glasses, dipped his pen in an inkwell, and began to write. "I'd like to ask you a few questions, Mrs. Denton, if you don't mind."

"Of course."

"Do you remember exactly when the symptoms began?"

She looked up at Joe. "I don't remember having any while I was at your house. Do you?"

He shook his head.

"No, I'm sure of it. I didn't start feeling ill until I returned to town. That would have been mid-August."

The doctor scribbled on the page, his pen making scratching noises in the quiet. "And your complaints included headaches, coughing, and what you call 'breathing episodes.' "

"That's right."

"How often do they occur?"

"They were rather infrequent at first, but have steadily worsened over time."

"Do you ever sweat at night while you sleep?"

"No."

"Ever experience any fever?"

"No."

"Any blood when you cough?"

"No."

He continued to write, never once looking up. "And did the symptoms you mentioned earlier ever lapse?"

She cocked her head. "Not until last week, no."

His scribbling stopped. "What happened last week?"

Joe proposed to me. But she knew that wasn't what he was asking. "The breathing episodes stopped altogether, and the coughing and headaches practically went away. At least until a few moments ago."

He looked at her over his glasses. "A few moments ago?"

"Yes. Almost as soon as I entered the exam room, my head began to pound and I experienced shortness of breath."

Returning his pen to its holder, he leaned back. "How did you occupy your time while you were in Seattle?"

"I was an assistant to the local doctor there."

He raised his brows. "You're a nurse?"

She shook her head. "No, no. I just cleaned his utensils, soothed patients, administered the chloroform. That kind of thing."

"You went on his calls with him?"

"Only at the very beginning, and then only for about a week. After that, I helped with his scheduled surgeries."

"In his exam room."

"Yes."

"Like mine?"

"One very much like yours."

"How often?"

"Whenever he had a surgery scheduled." Anna shrugged. "Several days throughout each week, I guess."

"And you administered chloroform during most of those?"

"During all of them."

"And when did you quit working for this doctor?"

"A week ago."

"And during that week, your symptoms steadily decreased?"

"They did."

Removing his glasses, he tapped them against his lips. "I think I can say with complete confidence, Mrs. Denton, that you do not have tuberculosis."

Her lips parted. Surely he was mistaken. A clock on the mantel chimed three times.

Joe slid into the chair beside her. "How can that be? I've heard her coughs. Witnessed her breathing difficulties."

"I've seen tuberculosis in every stage of the illness and in patients of all ages and sizes. Many times over. Your wife doesn't have it."

"But Doc Maynard is very good. Well respected."

"Many doctors employ the 'better safe than sorry' philosophy. Tuberculosis is dangerous, and the earlier it's caught, the better the chances the patient has. I think he did the right thing by recommending you take Mrs. Denton to drier climes."

"But not anymore?"

"No. Drier climes won't help cure your wife."

"What will?"

"Staying away from chloroform."

Joe frowned. "What?"

"For whatever reason, your wife's body has a strong aversion to it."

Anna shook her head in confusion. "What are you saying, Dr. Shepard?"

"Think back, Mrs. Denton. Were your symptoms worse while you administered the chloroform, or perhaps right after?"

She searched her mind, then turned to Joe in wonder. "Why, yes. They were."

"And they began to improve that week you quit assisting with surgeries, correct?"

"Yes."

"At least, they did until you entered my exam room, where I performed a surgery requiring chloroform not thirty minutes before you arrived."

Hope began to wiggle inside her. Joe reached for her hand.

She looked at him and smiled. "That's right."

Dr. Shepard tossed his glasses on the desk. "Well, Mrs. Denton, I'm afraid you will have to give up any aspirations you have of becoming a doctor's assistant. But as for your illness, so long as you stay away from chloroform, I think you will find your coughs, headaches, and breathing difficulties will all but disappear."

Moisture rushed to her eyes. "You're sure?"

He smiled. "Quite sure."

Joe squeezed her hand so hard her fingers overlapped each other. The relief and joy he felt was apparent in his eyes.

"My illness has nothing to do with the climate in Seattle?" she asked the doctor.

"Not a single thing."

"We . . . we can go back?" she whispered.

"You most certainly can."

Unable to hold her euphoria at bay, she turned to Joe, then sucked in her breath.

Silent tears trickled down his face. "You're going to be all right." Taking a wobbly breath, he tugged her toward him. "You're going to be all right."

Smiling, she moved to his lap and let him hold her, right there in front of Dr. Shepard.

Chapter Thirty-Eight

Seattle, W.T.
One week later

Red met them at the dock, assisting Anna onto the pier. "Welcome back, Miss Iv—Mrs. Denton."

"It's wonderful to be home, Red." She smiled. "And please, call me Anna."

"Thank you. I'll do that." He turned and clasped Joe's hand for a hearty shake. "The boys and I sure were glad to get your telegram."

"They were able to come back to work, then?"

"Every one of them. And I canceled that newspaper ad."

They grinned at each other, then pitched together in a brief and ebullient bear hug.

The three of them traversed Occidental Avenue, Joe helping Anna dodge the logs and drift from Yesler's Mill. She noted that Mount Rainier had come out from behind the clouds to welcome her home. She gave it a private greeting, thrilled that she would have the pleasure of being its neighbor for the rest of her life.

"I didn't hire back Ollie," Red continued. "Wasn't sure what you wanted to do about the cooking."

"Oh, I'd like to cook." She looked up at Joe. "Can I? Do you mind?"

"That's a lot of work, Anna. I'm not sure I want you doing all that."

"Oh, please, Joe. I love it."

He hesitated, then slipped his arm about her waist. "For now, then. But when the little ones start coming, we're making other arrangements."

Blushing, she glanced at Red, but the men were already on to other topics. It was a bit early to be thinking about little ones. For now, having the house in the woods to themselves sounded like a slice of heaven.

"Asa Mercer's back," Red said. "He's reopened the university and everything."

Joe pulled up short, causing Anna to stop, too.

"He's back? He had the nerve to show himself around here?"

Red shrugged. "Everybody's married up to their Mercer girls, so I guess he figured all's well that ends well."

"What about all the men who paid for brides and didn't receive them?"

Red scratched his chin. "That money's long gone, but the boys will have a reckoning, I'm sure."

Anna gasped. "They won't hang him or anything, will they?"

Red shook his head. "We aren't in California, Miss—Anna. Things are a bit more civilized here in the Territory."

For Mr. Mercer's sake, she certainly hoped so.

"What about you?" Red asked, eyeing Joe. "You plan on saying something to him?"

"You're dead right I do. The blighter owes me four hundred dollars."

Red looked from Joe to Anna and back to Joe. "I think you

might have a hard time collecting. I mean, after all, you married the gal he brought you."

Joe scowled. "That has nothing to do with it."

"It has everything to do with it. Besides, there isn't a person in town who doesn't know you'd put up all you had in the world for her, 'cause you already did."

After a slight hesitation, Joe shook his head. "Well, there's no arguing with that, I suppose."

"You leave Mercer to the others who never got anything for their troubles. They'll take care of him." Red slapped him on the back. "Now, go on before you run out of daylight. I've got Shakespeare all harnessed up and ready."

The rain started less than an hour after they'd left Seattle. The wagon's canopy offered little protection from the moisture blowing in from the sides. It didn't take long to penetrate Anna's clothing, and try as she might, she couldn't keep her shivers at bay.

Joe glanced at her. "Don't you think you should put on your coat?"

She huddled inside her new wool cape. "I don't have one."

"I thought I gave you fabric for one."

She nodded. "You did, but I haven't had time to sew it up yet."

He shrugged off his jacket and laid it on her lap. "Well, put mine on, then."

"No, no. I'll be fine."

"Put it on."

"But then you won't have anything."

"Put. It. On."

"But, Joe . . ."

He turned to look at her. Slowly, slowly. "Don't make me stop the wagon." His voice held a mixture of teasing and seriousness.

She tilted her head. "And just what exactly do you think you'd do then, Mr. Denton?"

He gave her an exasperated look. "For the love of the saints, Anna. Put the stupid thing on."

A breeze cut straight through her clothing. Smiling, she tucked the jacket over her shoulders. Warmth immediately encompassed her along with the now-familiar smell of cedar, which still lingered after a week away.

The farther they went, the thicker the forest grew. Many trees had long since lost their leaves, but the conifers were still verdant. Shakespeare's hooves made a suctioning noise in the mud, lulling her with its repetitive rhythm.

Her eyes grew heavy. She allowed herself to close them for just a minute, then jerked her head up when her chin bounced.

After the third time, Joe pulled her onto his lap. "Here, little robin."

She grabbed his shoulders to steady herself.

"You're going to tumble right off the wagon. Just close your eyes and see if you can get some sleep. We're still a long way from home."

A long way from home? Wrapping her arms around his waist, she snuggled close. She wasn't a long way from home. She was already home. And there was no place she'd rather be.

Author's Note

The premise for this book is based on fact. Asa Mercer was a real man who did, in fact, collect three hundred dollars from the bachelors of the Washington Territory in exchange for eastern brides. I managed to find copies of a couple of contracts that Mercer used, and the contracts for the women differed considerably from the contracts for the men!

His scheme garnered quite a bit of media attention. The newspaper clippings I used were real ones, though I confess to condensing and combining a few of them in order to make them more manageable (they were *really* wordy back then). And in the case of the wedding announcement toward the end of the book, I exchanged Joe and Anna's names for a real couple's.

As often as I can, I try to include real anecdotes in my novels. Though Bertha Wrenne was a creation of my imagination, there was an actual account of a woman on the *Continental* who "lost" her teeth during a bout of seasickness, and the other women on the boat nicknamed her "Toothless." There was also a woman onboard who was in active pursuit of a husband and was described in a journal as being "as old as the Flood."

As hard as it may be to believe, the letter of warning that Anna received from her father was based on an actual letter written by a Civil War soldier to his daughter. The man was, in fact, killed and some sweet girl back in 1866 really did feel responsible for her father's death. So tragic!

Doc Maynard was an actual person and instrumental in Seattle's birth and growth. If you visit the city today, you'll see his influence everywhere. I'm pretty sure he wasn't doctoring anymore by 1866, but he was such an intriguing character that I couldn't help but include him. I hope I did him justice.

When I started this book the only thing I knew about lumberjacks was that they were big, burly men who chopped down trees. You would not believe some of the stories I uncovered. I could never have used them in fiction—they were too unbelievable! So if you read something and thought I was exaggerating, I wasn't.

I found accounts of men who climbed trees the way Joe did—with no more than an ax and a springboard. They also thought nothing of jumping from ridiculous heights to get down from their work or to escape a falling tree.

One thing I left conspicuously out was the spiked (caulked) boots that lumberjacks are famous for wearing. I looked and looked but could never find reference as to when spiked boots were first used. In all the research I did, they were never mentioned in any of the early records I found. So I left them out. If I am in error, please accept my heartfelt apologies.

I couldn't convince my sister that they really did have redwoods in Washington. They weren't like the ones in California or Oregon, but they definitely had them. So I promised I'd put a disclaimer in for the rest of the doubting Thomases out there.

One of the things I found peculiar was the complete lack of information about what happened between Mercer and the fellows who paid three hundred dollars for brides that never showed. Nothing is recorded—at least not that I could find. So I guess we'll just have to use our imaginations.

Last, I had to bend the timeline a little to suit my story. The real Mercer girls started arriving in Seattle in May 1866. But if I'd done that, then Joe and Anna would've had to go to town for a Fourth of July celebration and I just did a Fourth of July thing in my last two books. I didn't want to do another one. Nor could I afford to have Anna go to town and find out about Bertha.

So I made Anna's boat land in Seattle on July 8. Not at all accurate, but necessary for my story. The rest of the Mercer-girl timeline was as close as I could get to being accurate.

All in all, I fell in love with Seattle. If you ever have a chance to go, please do. The bluest skies and greenest hills you'll ever see really are in Seattle.

Blessings, Deeanne

Don't Miss These Other Delightful Reads From
Deeanne Gist!

Do You Believe in Love at First Fight?
When Drew O'Connor wins the headstrong Lady Constance Morrow as his bride, he soon finds this marriage of convenience has become a most inconvenient thing indeed.

A Bride Most Begrudging

What Is The Measure of a Lady?
Shocked at the unrefined way of life in Gold Rush San Francisco, prim-and-proper Rachel van Buren is about to learn an eloquent but humorous lesson on what *truly* makes a lady.

The Measure of a Lady

She Has One Mission: Find a Husband
After deciding the Lord has left her to find a husband on her own, Essie Spreckelmeyer writes down the names of all the bachelors in town, closes her eyes and picks one. But convincing the lucky "husband-to-be" is going to be a *bit* more of a problem.

Courting Trouble

A Texas-Sized Tale of Unexpected Love
She's a headstrong woman. He's out to prove himself to the world. When their worlds collide, is it love or are they deep in the heart of trouble?

Deep in the Heart of Trouble